DON'T
LOOK
TWICE

DON'T LOOK TWICE

ANDREW GROSS

WILLIAM MORROW
An Imprint of HarperCollins*Publishers*

HarperCollins books may be purchased for educational, business, or sales promotional use. For information please write: Special Markets Department, HarperCollins Publishers, 10 East 53rd Street, New York, NY 10022.

FIRST EDITION

Designed by Renato Stanisic

Library of Congress Cataloging-in-Publication Data

Gross, Andrew.
    Don't look twice : a novel / Andrew Gross. — 1st ed.
        p. cm.
    ISBN 978-0-06-114344-1
    I. Title.
    PS3607.R654D66 2009
    813'.6–dc22   2008044643

09 10 11 12 13   WBC/RRD   10 9 8 7 6 5 4 3 2 1

To my brothers,
Michael and Rick

PART ONE

CHAPTER ONE

*M*ango Meltdown or Berry Blast?"

Ty Hauck scanned the shelves of the Exxon station's refrigerated cooler.

"*Whatever . . .*" his thirteen-year-old daughter, Jessie, responded with a shrug, her eyes alighting on something more appealing. "*What about this?*"

Powie Zowie.

Hauck reached inside and read the brightly colored label. Megajolt of caffeine. Highest bang for the buck.

"Your mother lets you drink this stuff?" he asked skeptically.

Jessie looked back at him. "Mom's not exactly here, is she?"

"No." Hauck nodded, meeting her gaze. "I guess she's not."

In just the past year, forbidding new curves had sprung up on his daughter's once-childlike body. Bra straps peeking out from under her tank top. Jeans clinging to the hips in an "unnatural" way. *Gangly* suddenly morphing into something a bit more in the range of *troubling*. Not to mention the newly mastered repertoire of eye rolls, shrugs, and exaggerated sighs. Hauck wondered if the request for an ankle tattoo or a belly piercing could be far behind. "You don't get to win," a friend who had teenage daughters once warned him. "You only *delay*."

Jesus, he recalled, *it was just a year ago that she liked to get shoulder rides from me.*

"Toss it in the basket," he said, acquiescing. *"One."*

Jessie shrugged without even the slightest smile, failing to grasp the significance of his offering. "Okay."

At the end of the aisle, a man in a green down vest and tortoiseshell glasses reached into the cooler and met Hauck's gaze. His amused, empathetic smile seemed to say, *Know exactly what you're going through, man!*

Hauck grinned back.

A year had passed since the Grand Central bombing. A year since the events set in motion by the hit-and-run accident down on Putnam Avenue had thrust Hauck out of his long slumber and into the public eye. In that year, Hauck had been on the morning news shows and MSNBC and Greta Van Susteren, the case rocking not just the tall iron gates of the Loire-styled mansions out on North Avenue, but the financial circles in New York as well. It had turned Hauck into a bit of a reluctant celebrity—the object of friendly ribbing from his staff and the local merchants along the avenue. Even his old hockey buddies, who used to tip their mugs to him because of how he once tore up the football league at Greenwich High, now joked about whether he knew Paris or Nicole, or could get them past the bouncers into some fancy new club in the city on a Saturday night. Finally Hauck just had to step back, get his life in order.

And keep things on a steady keel with Karen, whose husband's death had been at the heart of the case.

And with whom he had fallen in love.

At first, it had been hard to bridge all the differences between them. She was rich. Hauck was the head of detectives on the local force. Their families, lifestyles, didn't exactly merge.

Not to mention all the attention the case had generated. That in solving the mystery of her husband's death Hauck had unleashed something buried and now restless inside her. In the past year, her father, Mel, had taken ill with Parkinson's. Her mother wasn't handling it well. Karen had gone down to Atlanta to help take care of him, with her daughter away at Tufts and her son, Alex, now sixteen, recruited to play lacrosse at an upstate prep school.

It had been a year in which Hauck had finally learned to put much of the pain of his own past behind him. To learn to feel attached again. To fight for someone he wanted. He knew Karen loved him deeply for what he had done for her. Still, a lot of things stood in the way. Not just the money thing or their different families and backgrounds. Lately, Hauck had detected something in her. A restlessness. Maybe a sense of wanting to finally be free after being tied to a man her whole adult life, one who had so painfully deceived her. It was always a roll of the dice, they both knew, how things might work out between them. The jury was still out.

"C'mon," he said to Jess, "grab some M&M's; the boat's waiting."

The autumn chill was late in coming that October Saturday morning, and they were heading out for a final jaunt on his skiff, the *Merrily*, over to Captain's Island before taking it out of the water for the winter. Maybe kick the soccer ball around a bit—not a mean feat these days for Hauck (whose leg had still not fully healed from the .45 he had taken to the thigh). Grill a few dogs. Who knew how many more of these Saturdays he'd have with Jess. Just getting her up before ten was already becoming a hard sell. They'd just stopped off on the way to fill up the Explorer and pick up a few snacks.

Sunil, who ran the Exxon station next to the car wash on

Putnam, was always a friend to the guys on the force. Hauck always made it his habit to fill up here.

As they reached the counter, a woman was at the register ahead of them. The man in the green down vest stepped up, his arms wrapped around two six-packs of soda.

"You guys go ahead." He waved them ahead and smiled good-naturedly.

"Thanks." Hauck nodded back and nudged Jessie.

"Thanks," she turned back and said.

While they waited, Hauck said, "You know, I really hope you'll come up for Thanksgiving this year. Karen'll be back."

She shrugged. "I don't know, Dad."

"You should. She likes you, Jess. You know that. It would make me feel good."

"It's not that . . ." She twisted her mouth. "It's just that it's different. They're, you know . . . *rich*. Samantha and Alex, I mean, they're nice, but . . ."

Hauck knew the adjustment had been toughest with her. His daughter felt like a fish out of water with them. Sam and Alex had grown up on rented boats in the Caribbean and on spring breaks flew out to Beaver Creek to ski. She went up to Massachusetts to visit her cousins and once they'd all flown down to Orlando to do the theme park thing. He squeezed her on the shoulder, careful not to draw any attention to it. "Yeah, but that doesn't make them from Saturn, Jess."

"It's Mars, Dad," she corrected him.

He shrugged. "Or Mars."

The woman at the register finally finished up. Hauck stepped up to the counter.

Sunil greeted him with his usual smile. "*Lieutenant!* So, how is the big star these days? I don't see you on the TV so much any-more."

"That gig's over, Sunil. They don't pay me enough."

The Pakistani laughed at Jessie. "Pretty soon, we're gonna see your father on *Dancing with the Stars* . . . Doing the tango with some fancy celebrity. I bet you are very proud of your famous father, young lady . . ."

"Sure." Jessie shrugged.

Hauck put his arm around her. "She thinks I'm famous in my own mind . . ." He brought up the basket. "So, Sunil, we have a couple of sandwiches and sodas, and we also took a—"

It was the screech that Hauck heard first.

Grating. Terrifying. The red truck jerking to a stop right in front of their eyes. The heavily tinted passenger window slowly rolling down.

Then the man in the red bandana leaning out—*not a man,* Hauck recalled later, *barely more than a boy*—extending the short black cylinder as Hauck, unable to believe what he was seeing, stared at the protruding barrel.

A second before the body-blow of dread set in. Before he realized in horror what was about to take place.

He grabbed Jessie.

"Everyone get down!"

CHAPTER TWO

*T*he barrel erupted, spitting orange flashes of death and terror all around. The station's storefront shattered.

"*Jess!*"

Hauck pulled his daughter to the floor, the earsplitting *zip, zip, zip* of twenty rounds per second exploding glass, toppling counters of candy and shredding magazines all over them. He heard Jessie's high-pitched shrieks from under him. "*Daddy! Daddy!*"

Above, the window sign promoting discount tune-ups crashed in.

All Hauck could do was press himself into her as tightly as he could, shouting back above the deafening rain of glass and noise something he wasn't sure of, something he didn't know was true: "It's okay, Jess, it's okay! It's going to be okay . . ."

But it wasn't okay.

Bullets tore through the walls all around them, the store shaking like an earthquake was happening. Hauck had seen the muzzle pointed at his face. He felt sure the attack was aimed at him. Covering his daughter, an even more terrifying fear rippled through him:

What if the gunman tried to come in?

Suddenly, the barrage came to a stop. Just as quickly as it had begun. Hauck held there and prayed for the sound of the truck's engine revving up. He didn't hear it—only a heart-stopping double-clicking noise, which terrified him even more.

The shooter was shoving in a second clip.

He knew he had to do something. And do it now. From outside, he heard frightened wails and screaming. He had no idea if anyone might have already been hit. He slid off Jessie, fumbling at his waist for his gun—and, in panic, found only the empty space where it normally would have been, realized it was back in the Explorer. *In the fucking glove compartment!*

He was unarmed.

The second wave of gunfire started in.

"Stay down!" Hauck screamed above the noise directly in Jessie's ear, rounds zinging through the remaining jagged shards of glass that still clung to the front facade.

Jessie reached for him. *"Daddy, no . . . !"*

Hauck cupped her face in his hands. "Jessie, please, just stay down!"

He pulled out of her grasp, his heart colliding back and forth against his ribs, and scrambled over to the door. He grabbed the largest object he could find, a two-gallon drum of motor coolant, and, using it as cover, crawled outside.

The red truck loomed directly above him. The muzzle jutted from the passenger window, jerking wildly from the recoil. Hauck realized his only option was to wrestle the gun from the shooter's grip. He slid cautiously along the pavement, ducking under the gunman's view. Suddenly the truck's engine revved.

He got ready to lunge.

As if in answer to his prayers, the shooting suddenly stopped.

Above him, he heard the deafening roar of the truck's massive V-8, the gunman shouting something he couldn't make out over the noise.

Then the sparkle of silver rims zooming by, the cab careening off a stanchion as it shot past him, veering into the street.

Hauck scrambled after it, focusing on the make and plates. A Ford F250, *ADJ . . . 9,* dealer plates. The rest he couldn't make out. It jerked a sharp left, bouncing wildly over the curb at the corner, and took off south, toward the Connecticut–New York border.

A plume of dark gray smoke crept out from the scene.

One by one, stunned bystanders began to crawl out from behind their cars.

Hauck looked around. *"Is everyone alright?"*

One man got up from behind a fuel pump, nodding uncertainly. Next to him a woman was still curled up on the asphalt, sobbing, shell-shocked.

"I'm a policeman!" he called again. *"Is everyone alright?"*

Amazingly, he didn't see anyone who appeared to have been hit. He turned back to the shop, the stench of smoke and cordite biting his nostrils. The caved-in storefront looked as if a missile had slammed into it. He had to call it in! Frantically, he dug through his jeans for his cell phone, his fingers fumbling on the keys, 431, the emergency code to the Greenwich station's front desk.

His gaze drifted back inside.

"Jess . . . ?"

Hauck's heart slammed to a stop, his eyes falling on his daughter. She was on the floor. Curled up. Inert. Not replying. The phone fell from his ear.

There was blood all over her.

CHAPTER THREE

J_{ess!"}

It may have only been an instant—the same terrifying instant in which he begged his lifeless legs to move.

But in the freeze-frame of that moment, Hauck was hurtled back.

To Jessie—only six. In a Teletubby T-shirt, cross-legged on the grass outside their two-family home in Woodside, Queens. Curled up there, she looked as clear to him then as she did now.

All they heard was her shriek. *"Mommy! Daddy!"*

He and Beth, rushing to the kitchen window. Knowing immediately that something was wrong, seeing only their white van as it bounced silently down the embankment and came to a stop in the quiet street.

Jess—too scared to even point or move. Just frozen there. His and Beth's eyes falling on the tiny yellow tugboat that their younger daughter, Norah, had been playing with only moments before. The truth taking hold of them. Petrifying them. Beth's eyes already filled with terror and fleeing hope.

Oh, Ty, please, they said, *don't let this be happening. Please . . .*

Now Hauck fixed on Jessie and ran over to her across the glass-strewn floor.

His daughter lay motionless, crimson matted on her sweat-shirt. He lifted her by the shoulders. Blood spatter was all over her cheeks and chest. Frantically, Hauck searched her limp body for a wound.

Oh, Jesus, Jessie, no. He peeled back his daughter's matted brown hair. *This can't be happening again!*

Like an answer to his prayers, he felt her stir.

Just the slightest murmur. She blinked and slit open her dazed brown eyes.

"Daddy?"

"Yes, baby, yes . . . !" Hauck's chest exploded in a spasm of joyful relief. "Oh yes, honey. Jessie, it's me."

Fright flared up in her. "Are they gone?"

"Yes, honey, they're gone! It's over. It's going to be okay." Hauck shut his eyes and felt tears stinging. Every bone in his body seemed to rattle in a joyful exhale. He drew his daughter up to him, squeezing her. He brushed the specks of blood off her cheek. "They're gone."

Behind him, Sunil slowly rose from behind the counter.

Hauck looked up at him. "Are you okay?"

The manager nodded, his dark brown skin blanched almost pale. "I think so." Sweat glistened on his forehead.

"Call 911. Tell them there's been a shooting. Tell them I'm here and we need immediate medical support."

"Yes, Lieutenant, okay." With eyes as white as moons, he scanned around the store. "Gracious God in heaven . . ."

Hauck lowered Jessie back down. "You just lay there, honey . . . let me look. Where are you hurt?" He carefully checked over her clothing but couldn't find any wound. No signs of fresh blood seeping out.

"I don't know, Daddy."

"It doesn't matter. You just stay there. Help will be here soon."

He flipped open his cell phone and punched in the 431 line to the station that signaled *Emergency.*

The duty officer answered.

"This is Lieutenant Hauck. I'm at the Exxon station on Putnam and Holden. There's been a shooting. The manager here just called in a 911. We have wounded. We need immediate medical response. Cars on the scene, EMTs, everything . . ."

"This is Reyes, sir. We're already on it. We should have cars there any second . . ."

"Listen to me, Sergeant, I want you to put out an interagency APB on a red F250 pickup, Connecticut plates, ADJ . . . 9 . . . That's all I could make out. Raised chassis, chrome rims. Shooter may be Hispanic and may be wearing a red bandana. When it left here it was headed south on Putnam. You get that out immediately, Sergeant, you hear?"

"I'm all on it, sir."

Hauck hung up. He yanked off his fleece pullover and bunched it like a pillow underneath Jessie's head. "You just sit tight, baby. Help'll be here soon."

She nodded hazily. "Okay . . ."

He checked her again. Miraculously, he couldn't locate any direct wounds. *Where the hell was all the blood coming from?* Slowly, he felt his heart crawl back into his chest.

As a droplet of blood fell onto her sweatshirt.

Scared, Jessie looked up. "Daddy, you're bleeding!"

Hauck felt for his neck, which was suddenly throbbing. A sticky red ooze came off in his hand. He felt his stomach turn.

"Daddy, you're hurt!" Jessie said, lifting onto her elbows.

"Don't worry," Hauck said. But suddenly he wasn't sure. *"Sunil . . ."*

The manager, who was now on the phone with his family, ran around the counter. "Yes, Lieutenant?"

"Go and see if anyone needs medical assistance out there . . . Tell them ambulances should be here in a second . . ."

"Yes, sir." Sunil was about to run out, making a last broad sweep around the store. Suddenly he stopped. *"Merciful God . . . ,"* he muttered, gazing over Hauck's shoulder.

Hauck stood up, following the manager's crestfallen gaze. *"Oh no . . ."*

Suddenly it became clear where all the blood on Jessie had originated from. The man in the green down vest—who had smiled at them by the cooler and stepped up behind them in line . . .

He was on the floor, covered by toppled racks of magazines and candy, eyes like glass, his tortoiseshell frames thrown to the side.

In the center of his chest, dotting his brown Shetland sweater, were two dark red holes.

CHAPTER FOUR

*I*t took just minutes—frantic minutes—for Freddy Munoz and two other detectives from Hauck's Violent Crimes Unit to make it to the scene.

A phalanx of local blue-and-whites had blocked off lower Putnam from Weaver all the way down to the car dealerships, lights flashing and sirens wailing like a war zone. An EMT van had already arrived from Greenwich Hospital and was tending to Jessie, as well as to a couple of the other bystanders.

A med tech kneeled over the guy in the green vest, confirming what Hauck already knew.

Freddy Munoz hopped out of his car, took in a long, disbelieving sweep of the shot-up storefront, the dozens of holes in its facade. "Jesus, Lieutenant, are you alright?"

Freddy had been one of Hauck's first hires on the Violent Crimes team when Hauck had taken the position heading up the staff in Greenwich. Hauck was fond of the young detective, grooming him, in the back of his mind, for his own job one day. Looking over the scene, Hauck suddenly realized just how close that promotion had almost come.

"Yeah." Hauck rubbed the gash on his neck. "I'm okay."

"*Jessie?*" Munoz pressed with concern. "I heard she was here."

"She'll be alright." Hauck pointed toward the EMT van. "Just a little shock . . ." As he looked at her there, reliving those initial moments, a queasiness rose back up in Hauck's gut. "At first I just saw her there, all covered in blood. Not moving . . ."

Munoz squinted. "*Whose* blood, Lieutenant?"

Hauck turned his gaze back inside. "The guy over there . . . We were heading out to the boat, stopped to pick up a few things. He was right behind us in line."

Spotting the body through the open storefront, the detective issued a short, grim whistle of disgust. "Oh, man . . . Anyone else hit, LT?"

"No." Hauck placed a hand up to his neck.

"You better get that checked out, okay? You get a chance to ID the vic?"

"Not yet. I've been with Jess."

"Where you ought to be, Lieutenant. You just let us handle it, okay? Go be with your daughter. I'm glad she's okay . . . And get them to take a look at that gash. Damn, LT, you know how lucky you are?"

A sobering exhale accompanied Hauck's nod. "The son-ovabitch shot right at me, Freddy . . . I just stood there, the window rolling down. Stared right at him. Froze."

"Don't beat yourself up, Lieutenant. Anyone would freeze."

Hauck nodded, eyes fixed on the body, unconvinced. "That could be Jessie."

"Yeah, it could be, Lieutenant, but it's not. You said you caught a glimpse of the shooter?"

Hauck nodded. "Twenties. Hispanic. Wearing a red bandana across his head. I put an APB out on a red Ford pickup,

CT plates. ADJ9 or something . . . Couldn't get more of a read. Listen, Freddy, I want you to get an ID on the guy inside. Have Stevie and Ed start in with the witnesses."

"Will do."

"And, listen, Freddy . . ."

"Yeah, Lieutenant?"

"I'm okay, got that? It's business as usual here."

"You bet your ass you're okay, sir." Munoz tapped Hauck on the shoulder, grinning. "Like my mother would say, LT, you had an angel riding on your shoulder today."

"Yeah." Hauck looked at the caved-in storefront, the man in the green vest's legs visible through the shattered door. "Been meaning to talk to you about your mom's take on angels, Freddy."

CHAPTER FIVE

Hauck got the gash on his neck looked after, while Ed Sweeney and Steve Chrisafoulis started to interview the by-standers and Munoz went to check out the body.

Maybe he and Jessie did have an angel watching over them. There were at least eighty to a hundred bullet holes where rounds had slammed into the station, and only three people had been hit, including a woman outside, struck in the arm from a ricochet.

Eighty to a hundred shots—and only that one poor bastard killed.

Vern Fitzpatrick, Greenwich's police chief and Hauck's boss, was on his way down from Darien, where he had been at a golf outing. News vans were starting to line up across the street, camera crews pushing for witnesses. Patrolmen were keeping the pressing reporters at bay.

Hauck could only imagine the headlines. "Posh NY Suburb Ripped by Deadly Gunfire." "Bystander Killed in Drive-By At-tack."

Greenwich had Saks and Ralph Lauren and Laura Ashley. *This kind of thing just didn't happen here.*

While they bandaged his neck, Hauck flipped out his phone

and called Jessie's mom. "Beth, something happened . . . ," he said at the sound of her voice, then stopped, the freeze-frame of his daughter there and all that blood rushing back to him. He moistened his lips. "Listen, Beth," he said, "Jess is alright. She's fine, but . . ." He took her through what had happened, his ex-wife gasping, *"Jesus, Ty, oh, my God . . ."*

"Beth, listen, please . . ." They had spent ten years together. He had been a New York City cop then. A young detective in the 122nd in Queens, fast-tracked to the department's Office of Information, who acted as a liaison officer during 9/11 with the FBI. That was before the accident with Norah. Before the blame and their marriage fell apart. "She's alright," he said, "just a bit scared. They're going to take her to Greenwich Hospital—just to look over her a bit. You should come. Now. There are people dead here. I'm gonna have to go . . ."

"Oh, Jesus, Ty, tell Jess I'm on my way."

"I'll see you there." He hung up. The med tech finished taping his neck. Hauck went over and sat beside Jessie in the van. They were running an IV. Hauck put his arm around her and pressed her head to his shoulder, trying to smile away the scared, confused tears welling in her young eyes.

"You okay?"

She nodded, donning the brave veneer. "I think so, Dad."

"Mom's on the way. They're going to take you to the hospital here. They may give you something—just for shock, honey."

"I'm alright," she insisted. "You're the one who's been shot."

Hauck winked at her and grinned. "You okay with putting off that boat ride for the rest of the day? I know you weren't so keen on it." That made her smile. "Listen, honey, you know I have to go to work now. You know they need me here . . ."

"I know, Daddy . . ." Her baby-blue sweatshirt was still

damp and matted with someone else's blood. "How's that guy?"

Hauck shrugged. "I don't know, baby doll."

"He's dead, isn't he? I saw him, Dad."

Hauck bunched his lips and nodded. "Yeah, he's dead." He pressed her face into his chest and squeezed. "You know I love you, Jess. I'll check in on you at the hospital. Mom will be there soon."

Patrolmen were setting up barriers, cordoning off the scene. Hauck knew this was one you were going to hear about. No avoiding that. This was Greenwich. The people with the big rap sheets here were hedge fund managers and CEOs. Investor fraud and Sarbanes-Oxley violations were the typical crimes of passion.

Drive-bys just didn't happen here.

Hauck had looked squarely into the shooter's eyes as he squeezed. He tried to think: *Who might want to take this kind of revenge?*

Three months ago, he and his team had shut down a meth ring operating out of a bodega in nearby Byron. Word was it was connected to the Vine Street gangs up in Hartford. They were bad people.

He had busted the son of a local real estate magnate for coke; the kid had been bounced out of Brunswick Academy in his senior year. The dad had threatened to ruin Hauck.

But this? Right in front of everybody's eyes? That would bring the whole goddamn system of justice down on top of their heads. That would be suicide.

It didn't make a goddamn shred of sense.

Inside, Ed Sweeney was taking a statement from Sunil, who still looked like a ghost, dabbing at his brow.

Freddy Munoz kneeled over the body. The dude had seemed

friendly, nice. They'd shared a smile; he was sympathetic to what was going on with Jessie. He probably had a daughter himself.

As Hauck came up to him, Munoz whistled and rolled his eyes. "This ain't so good, Lieutenant."

"What?"

The victim looked about forty. Sandy hair, flecks of gray in it, tortoiseshell frames. Two rounds had caught him squarely in the chest, knocked him back into the magazine rack—probably why no one had seen him at first. He'd never had a chance. Must've been killed by the opening barrage. A foot or two either way, that could've been Jessie or him.

"*This*, LT." Munoz handed Hauck the dead man's wallet.

Hauck's stomach fell.

This wasn't just any victim, a bystander who had happened into the line of fire.

They were staring at a Department of Justice ID.

CHAPTER SIX

The victim was a federal prosecutor working out of the Hartford, Connecticut, office. David Sanger. His driver's license indicated he was forty-one years old. The address on it was on Pine Ridge Road off Stanwich, just five minutes out of town.

The headline had just changed.

Once more, Hauck thought back through the chain of events. The red truck screeching to a stop. The darkened window rolling down. The muzzle of the gun extending.

At him.

Sanger had been standing only a few feet away, right behind Jess in line. The bullet pattern seemed to go from right to left. It seemed likely he had been hit in the initial barrage.

"Any chance you're thinking he was the target?" Munoz questioned. The victim's ID made anything possible.

Hauck thought back. The attack had continued for a full minute after Sanger would have been struck. The shooter had even reloaded. Bullet marks were everywhere. Glass shattered on the refrigerated unit in back. The type of weapon used, a Tec-9 or a Mac-10, wasn't exactly the kind of pinpoint weapon one might choose if they were trying to target someone.

"No." Hauck shook his head. "Just the wrong place at the wrong time, Freddy."

Still, a federal prosecutor gunned down this way would bring a lot of attention to this. Every media outlet across the country would be on their backs. Not to mention the Feds. They'd have to take a look at everything. What Sanger was doing here. Any personal vendettas against him. What cases he was working on.

"You know what this means, LT?" Munoz said, standing up.

"Yeah, I know what it means . . ." He slid out a small photo from David Sanger's wallet. His wife—pretty, blond, her hair in a ponytail. Smiling. Two kids. Just a few minutes ago that had been his world.

He handed Munoz back the wallet. "It means you can forget about that angel, Freddy."

The shells were nine-millimeter. Dozens were lodged all over the walls. Judging from what Hauck recalled—the amount of bullets, casings, the fast reload—the gun was probably a Tec-9.

Not the kind of weapon one could expect to make a precision shot with.

A canvas of the witnesses mostly confirmed Hauck's own recollection of events. No one had been able to get a clear description of the assailants. The truck's windows were tinted. The shooter faced away from the crowd. Only Hauck had caught a glimpse. Everyone else had ducked or panicked as soon as the initial shots rang out. It had all happened so fast.

Except several people recalled the shooter shouting something prior to driving away.

The woman who had been in front of Hauck at the counter just before it happened said it sounded something like "*Tarantino*, asshole . . ."

"Like the director?" Hauck asked.

"That's what she heard," Steve Chrisafoulis said. "The guy filling up his Prius on pump two heard it different. More like 'Porsafina.'"

"Porsafina?"

"Just telling you what they heard, LT."

It was going to be difficult, if not impossible, Hauck realized, to get any agreement. The sudden shock and panic. Twenty people were going to have twenty different recollections of what had taken place.

Munoz turned to Hauck. "You said the shooter was Hispanic, right?"

Ed Sweeney offered, "No one seemed to get much of a view, Lieutenant."

Hauck said, "I think so. Why?"

"'Cause what if it was more like, For Sephina, maybe? Por Sephina? That mean anything to you, LT?"

"No." If he had somehow been the target of this, he didn't see the connection.

He went back inside the store. Sunil still had a medical tech attending to him. "You doin' okay?"

The Pakistani had a cut on his arm from flying glass. He blew out his cheeks. "I suppose so, Lieutenant."

"Lemme ask you, Sunil, any reason someone would want to do something like this to you? Any enemies we should know about? Any money you owe out there?"

"Enemies?" The gas station manager rounded his eyes wide. "No, I'm a good guy, Lieutenant. I don't have enemies . . ."

"People heard the gunman shouting something like 'Tarantino' as they pulled away."

Sunil furrowed his brow. "You mean like that Hollywood guy, Lieutenant?"

"I don't know what I mean, Sunil. 'Tarantino.' Or maybe 'Por Sephina.' Spanish. Anything like what I'm saying meaning anything to you, Sunil?"

The Pakistani looked perplexed. He dabbed a hand through his thinning dark hair. "You know me, Lieutenant. I don't make problems for anyone."

He wasn't lying. Hauck patted him on the shoulder. "I know. You get that nick looked after, Sunil."

The ME van had arrived, lights flashing, from the state facility up in Farmington.

So had Chief Fitzpatrick. In golf attire. He wove his Saab through the maze of news vans and police lines right into the station. Hauck saw him chat for a second with a patrolman, then jog his way.

"Jesus, Ty, I just heard . . . How's Jessie doing?"

"She's okay, Vern. Just a little shock. Thanks."

"What about *you* . . . ?" Fitz's eyes shot to the bandage on Hauck's neck.

"Just some flying glass. From the window . . ."

The chief of police looked at him skeptically and snorted back a smile. "Flying glass, my ass, Ty. You're a lucky dude."

Hauck smiled wistfully at him, scratched the back of his head. "We got issues, Vern. The dead guy's a federal prosecutor from up in Hartford. Best I can say, he just stepped into it. Random. I don't know who this goddamn thing was aimed at—*me,* Sunil here—you can see they tore the place up pretty good. But there's going to be a lot of eyeballs on our backs. Freddy will brief you, if that's okay. I'd appreciate it if you could run some interference on the press for me on this."

"Don't even think about that, Ty. You should stay with Jessie . . ."

"Jess is fine. Her mom's on the way."

A sharp beeping tone rang from inside. It took a moment for everyone to realize just where it came from. The victim's cell phone. Still on him.

"*Christ.*" Hauck bent down and found it inside David Sanger's vest.

The digital display read HOME. Everyone stood around and just listened as it continued to ring, four, five times, looking at one another silently before it finally went into voice mail.

"No." Hauck exhaled at Vern. "There's something else I have to do."

He jotted down the address they had found in the victim's wallet, 475 Pine Ridge Road. Only a mile or two from there. This was one of the jobs nobody vied for, the unenviable responsibility of rank. He grabbed a local patrolman he knew and asked him to follow in his car. This sort of thing was always done better in twos.

Outside, by the fuel pumps, Hauck grabbed hold of Munoz.

Freddy asked, "You want me to come with you, LT?"

"No. I want you to stay and brief the crime scene guys. And listen, Freddy—I got that APB out within a minute or two; no way they could've gotten very far. If we haven't heard anything back, you know what I'm thinking . . ."

Munoz nodded. "That the truck's still somewhere around here. That they dumped it somewhere."

Hauck backed away to where his Explorer was and pointed at Freddy. "You find that truck."

CHAPTER SEVEN

Wendy Sanger had the bags packed and dragged downstairs. Haley was in the midst of her usual early morning tortured-teenager routine, whining on about why they had to drag her up to Vermont when Ariel had a party planned for Saturday night and it was "just leaves up there, Mom, not even goddamn snow!" Wendy shouted back at her up the stairs, stuffing the case with Ethan's medicine. "Don't you give me a hard time this morning, Haley! Just get your butt down!"

They were heading up to the ski house at Stratton, lugging the ski stuff up with all their clothes for the season. Easier than packing it all up and transporting it to New Britain, near Hartford, where the family was moving before Christmas. It was a stressful time for all of them. Maybe the most for Haley—leaving her friends smack in the middle of the school year.

But it was hard on all of them. And Wendy knew her daughter would probably spend the whole weekend on the couch yapping on the phone anyway, so what the hell did it even matter where she was?

"C'mon, Hale, I mean it, get moving! Daddy'll be back soon."

"Who the hell took my goddamn iPod, Mom?"

Ugh. Wendy put down the medicine case in frustration. "I don't know, hon!"

David had gone into town to wash the car, like he did every Saturday morning. His compulsive little ritual. Vacuum it out like it was the queen's bedroom, polish down the chrome.

She checked the clock. That was over an hour ago. *Where the hell is David?* she wondered.

She had tried him on the cell, twice, and left a message: "Just wondering what it is you're *doing*, David . . . You remember, we have this little trip planned today. *We're sitting here ready* . . ." But he wasn't answering, which struck Wendy as odd. David always picked up unless he was in trial. That was starting to worry her a bit.

Maybe he'd stopped at the station for a cup of coffee. That would be just like him, Wendy knew. Getting everyone up at dawn, pushing them to get moving, promising, "Greenburgers at Dot's in Manchester by one!"—while he chatted someone up at the car wash about some new bond initiative in town, dawdling over the morning editorials as he filled up the car, and all the while she was running around like a chicken without a head, getting everything together, dressing and making breakfast for Ethan. And then he'd finally come home with an innocent look on his face and clap. *"So, hey, what's everyone been doing, guys? We gotta go!"*

That would be just like him.

Ethan was eating cereal in the kitchen, watching *Teletubbies.* He was six, the love of their lives, though not everything was right with him. Asperger's syndrome. Not full-out autism, they hoped, but still, a little impaired. And now with the move they had to change schools from Eagle Hill, and maybe doctors too, though they had found a fabulous program up near Hartford with people who seemed to really care.

"Aargh!" Wendy heard Ethan shout something, followed by the sound of something hitting the floor.

"Ethan, no!"

She went over to the wall and picked it up. "Haley!" she called upstairs. "I think Ethan found your iPod . . . !"

She'd miss this place, Wendy realized. It was an old, refurbished colonial. Her folks had helped them buy it when David took a job with the government after law school. The kitchen was small, they had never quite gotten around to giving the bathrooms a do-over, but there was that terrific yard in back, which faced a nature preserve no one could ever build on. And some of the elms on their property were over a hundred feet tall. And they'd made friends.

Still, David's Monday-to-Friday commute was growing exhausting. Some nights he wouldn't get home until after nine, when Ethan was already asleep. Some weeks he didn't make it home at all. The new promotion at Justice was what David had dreamed of. Why he left private practice in the first place and sacrificed all the money. A chance to really do something and make a difference. Before law school, he'd taught English in Guatemala. A chance to serve.

Speaking of which . . . Wendy glanced at the kitchen clock again—it was already after ten! He had wanted to be on the road by nine thirty. She tried David's cell one more time. Again, his voice mail came on.

What the hell is going on, David?

She started to get worried. She knew she sometimes tended to overstress a bit. She'd lost her dad at eighteen to a sudden heart attack. And David had this mild arrhythmia himself, though the doctors convinced her it was nothing to really worry about. Even at forty-one. Still, she always carried around this tiny fear . . . That one day she would be alone, just like her mom had been left alone. That she would have to bring up Ethan by herself. Stupid, she knew, maybe even a little selfish. *But where the hell was he, anyway?*

That's when she spotted the two cars pulling up in the drive outside the kitchen window.

One was a black SUV, just like theirs. Except it had lights on top. *Flashing lights!* The other was a regular blue and white Greenwich police car.

The wave of worry in her chest had now grown into full-out panic. *What are they doing here?*

She told herself that there were a million things it could be. It could be the car had broken down, or that he'd had a little accident. *But then David would've called!* Or that he'd been taken to the hospital. It could be he'd just taken sick. It could be anything.

"Ethan, you stay right here, honey . . . Mommy's just going outside." Wendy put down her phone and ran to the front door.

But as she opened it, heart starting to race, and stared quizzically into the face of the man coming up her walk—saw how he stopped, solemnly met her eyes, and how there was just something in them—*she knew*.

She knew it was the worst. What she'd always feared.

"David!" she yelled, though there was just this man, staring at her.

She always knew.

CHAPTER EIGHT

Wendy Sanger sat numbly on the couch, her daughter's raw face pressed into her shoulder, eyes bleary from tears. A neighbor had come over to take care of her son, who seemed a bit handicapped, in a TV room.

Hauck sat across from them in the pleasantly decorated living room.

"I just can't believe it." She shook her head. "He just went into town to wash the car. He did that every Saturday. That was David's thing. How he relaxed. You know . . . David's a prosecutor with the U.S. Justice office—in Hartford. We're supposed to be moving up there before Christmas. We were just . . ."

She caught herself, tears rushing into her eyes, her face a blank. Hauck noticed the packed suitcases at the door. "You were all headed somewhere?"

"We were just going to pack up the car. We were heading up to our place in Vermont. Stratton."

Wendy Sanger cupped her face in her hands and shook her head, trying to keep from crying. Her daughter sniffed back tears.

"I know how hard this is for you, Ms. Sanger . . ." Five years ago, Hauck had had to pick up his own four-year-old daughter in his arms. He looked at Haley and tried to give her a supportive smile. "But if you can manage it now, there are some questions I need to ask . . ."

She didn't say yes or no, just shrugged, her head shaking like a door off its hinge. "Why would anybody want to kill David, Lieutenant?"

"I don't think anyone intended to shoot him, Mrs. Sanger. A truck pulled up and someone sprayed dozens of bullets all around the station."

"Like a drive-by?"

Hauck nodded. "I was there myself. With my daughter. Your husband was standing just behind us in line. He was just in the wrong place at the wrong time."

"*Wrong place at the wrong time* . . . This is fucking Greenwich, Lieutenant, not Newark. He just went out to wash the goddamn car!"

"We're not sure yet, but we're pretty sure this was aimed at something else. But I have to ask—you say there was no one who would want to hurt your husband? Were there any cases he may have tried where someone might have threatened him? Anybody he ever spoke of who he felt was out to get him? Maybe gang-related . . ."

"*Gang-related?*" Wendy Sanger looked back, incredulous. "My husband tried mostly bankruptcy cases. CEO malfeasance. He didn't try gang-related cases."

"And none of these people ever made threats toward him? Sent him letters, calls at the house? Maybe he wouldn't even have told you?"

"No." Wendy shook her head. "He would've told me. David and I didn't hide things from each other. No one was threatening him. They were grooming him for bigger cases. That's why we had to move up there."

"Daddy said they were going to put him in charge of this big department," his daughter said. She wiped a Kleenex across her nose. "That we had to move up there. I made it so tough on him, Mom. I—"

"It's okay, baby, it's okay." Wendy Sanger squeezed her tightly. Hauck swallowed hard.

"My son, he's got Asperger's syndrome, Lieutenant. He needs a lot of attention. David commuted up to Hartford for two years. Left before dawn and came back at ten sometimes. He didn't want Ethan's situation to have to change. *That's* the kind of man he was. He pushed off this promotion for over a year. Didn't want to upset the kids' life. Haley's just finishing up at the middle school. Ethan's in a special program . . ."

"I understand," Hauck said, giving her a little time. "Listen, I know this is a long shot, Ms. Sanger, but does the name 'Tarantino' have any special meaning to you?"

Wendy Sanger looked confused. "Like the director?"

"I don't know. Maybe."

She shook her head. "No."

"What about '*Por Sephina*'? In Spanish. I know how tough this is. I know this is out of the blue."

"This is crazy, Lieutenant. I can't do this! No one wanted to kill my husband! No one had any ax to grind with him."

"*Why did this have to happen, Mom?*" Haley dug her fists into her mother's sweater and cried.

Wendy stroked her hair. "I know, baby, I know . . ."

Hauck looked into Wendy Sanger's swollen eyes. Her straight blond hair falling over her Fair Isle sweater and turtleneck. Her sharp chin and high cheekbones. There were pictures on the walls. The four of them together. Skiing. At Disneyland. Posing with Goofy. He knew there was no reason to press. He could check with Sanger's office in Hartford about his cases.

"Do you have anyone that we can call? Give you some help in getting someone here?"

Numbly, she shook her head. "My sister lives in New Hampshire. I don't know how she's going to take this news . . . You never know how this feels, do you, until it happens to you."

"No." Hauck shrugged. "I'm going to leave an officer outside for the time being. You just let him know if there's anything he can do."

Wendy nodded vacantly. "Thanks."

Hauck stood up. "We're gonna find the people who did this, Ms. Sanger. I give you my word. I'll let you know as soon as we know something."

"Thank you again, Lieutenant." Her daughter's face was pressed to her lap.

Outside, Hauck paused on the steps. A carved jack-o'-lantern was already sitting on the slate landing.

You never know how this feels until it happens to you . . .

Yes, I do.

All over again, he saw the window rolling down, the man wearing the red bandana extending the gun—his face light-skinned, chiseled, a thin mustache. David Sanger, in his down vest, stepping up behind them. *You guys, go* ahead *. . .* He smiled.

Was it me . . . ?

Was it him they were aiming at? Was it because of something he had done, some stray act of vengeance, that this family's life had to be upended too?

They had been packing up for a weekend in Vermont. The guy had just gone to gas up the car. Only an hour before he'd had a life like Hauck's, a daughter not much older than Jessie.

I know what you're going through, man . . .

A fist dug in Hauck's gut. If someone somehow wanted him dead, they could have gotten him any day of the week. At home in Stamford. On a jog. With no one around, and not in the middle of the day. *In front of the whole fucking world!*

No, it would be suicide to go at it this way.

His cell phone rang. Munoz. "Yeah, Freddy?" He snapped it open, heading toward his car.

"Looks like that angel of yours is still on duty, Lieutenant."

"What angel are we talking about, Freddy?"

"We found the truck!"

CHAPTER NINE

*T*he vehicle's a file one, LT." Munoz took Hauck around the red truck's side. "*Stolen*. From a Ford dealership up in Wallingford yesterday afternoon. The plates are registered to a Monica Kassel out of Waterbury."

ADJ-977, the number Hauck had been unable to make out at the station.

"Dollar to a dime they've been stolen too."

The vehicle had been abandoned on the curb of a hilly street just off the Post Road, a little over a mile from where the shooting had occurred. A roving patrol car, alerted to the APB, had spotted it. There was a nail salon and a framing store on the corner, a row of modest middle-class homes rising up the block where the street wound up the hill past St. Roch's church, where Hauck's family had belonged as a boy. From there, they could have easily blended into traffic along Railroad Ave. and hooked onto the thruway.

It was definitely the same vehicle. Hauck ran his hand along the dented rear fender. The same spanking-new rims he had seen from the station's floor. Scratch marks on the rear driver's-side panel where it had careened off the stanchion. Scrape marks on the rear chrome.

"They clearly had another vehicle waiting. Any chance they left anything inside?"

Munoz shook his head. "They left it pretty clean, Lieutenant."

Wearing plastic gloves, Freddy opened the front passenger door, careful not to disturb anything. It looked like the damned thing had been driven fresh off the lot.

Hauck looked up the hill. "You check those homes up there? Someone might've noticed the second car while it was waiting, or when they switched it. This mother would've barreled in here pretty fast."

"Val and Tim are up there now," Munoz said, referring to two of Hauck's detectives who were supposed to be off duty today but were called in, both of them helping out.

"What about the dealership? Maybe there's a security camera there? Or any of those businesses up on Church Street?"

Munoz looked at him. "I called you as soon as we got here, LT."

The stress of all he had been through was starting to show. "It's just that this has to be buttoned up, Freddy—tight! There's gonna be a lot of eyes all over this."

"I know." Munoz nodded. He tapped Hauck on the arm. "We all know, Lieutenant. How's Jess?"

Hauck had checked in with the ER on the ride down and was planning to head up there after this. "I think she's doing fine, Freddy. Thanks."

What wasn't fine was that they now had no idea in the world what kind of car they were looking for or what the shooter had yelled out as he sped away. And that someone had been shot dead right in his own town—right in the goddamn light of day—and that the victim was guaranteed to bring the nightly news right down their throats, not to mention the FBI.

Other than that, it was just like Freddy said: *angels*.

As Hauck nodded for Freddy to shut the truck's door, something caught his eye.

A piece of paper wedged under the driver's seat. Maybe a dealership sticker.

"What's that there?"

It was barely visible, caught in the seat adjuster track.

"You do the honors," Hauck said.

Munoz bent down and carefully pulled it free by the edges.

It was a page from a newspaper. Folded in half. Torn slightly.

Munoz held it up and chuckled. "What do we have here?"

It was from the *Bridgeport Sun*. Hauck noticed the date, July 11. Almost three months before. On the top of the page was an article about some well-known Connecticut businessman, Richard Scaynes, caught up in an Iraq War corruption scandal. PROSECUTION SETS A DATE FOR SCAYNES'S CORRUPTION TRIAL.

But it was the headline below the fold that got their attention.

TEEN GIRL DIES IN POOL ACCIDENT.

Hauck raised his eyes toward Freddy. "Live and learn."

The detective read out loud, "Bridgeport's East End is mourning the tragic loss tonight of a promising high school sophomore who drowned Saturday in a suspicious pool accident . . ."

Then he stopped. It seemed as if Hauck's and Freddy's eyes hit on the same thing all at once.

The victim's name.

Suddenly it became clear just what the shooter had been shouting.

Her name made a lot of things clear.

It was Josephina. Josephina Ruiz.

CHAPTER TEN

You have any connection to this case, Lieutenant?" Freddy looked toward Hauck, trying to connect the dots.

Hauck shook his head. "No." In a strange way that made him feel relieved.

They read through the rest of the article, which recounted how the victim, a high school honors student, and a group of her friends had sneaked into the fenced-in community pool at night. They'd been drinking a little, which led to them horsing around in the pool. Apparently, the victim's bathing suit got entangled on an underwater filter duct that had been left open and she couldn't tear it free. The rest of the kids scattered, panicked. The body ended up being found by a night security guard. Then one by one, the next day, they started to come forward, identified by the school and local police.

No charges were ever filed.

Por Josephina. Hauck was sure now that this was what the shooter had been shouting. That was what this thing was about. Revenge. The East End was a tough section of Bridgeport. Lots of local gang turf up there. But why here? In Greenwich. At an Exxon station, in the middle of the day?

But it didn't have to do with him, Hauck realized now,

recalling the window rolling down and the barrel pointed in his eyes.

Nor did it connect to David Sanger. That now seemed clear. Simply in the wrong place at the wrong time. The poor guy had no idea what was behind the attack that killed him.

But one person might.

Hauck folded the paper by the edges and dropped it in a plastic evidence bag. "Let's find out from Sunil if he does."

CHAPTER ELEVEN

Greenwich Hospital was on the way back to the station. Hauck gave his name to the attendant at the ER desk and she took him down the hall to a small, curtained-off room where Jessie was being treated.

"She's doing fine," the attendant said to him. "Just a bit unnerved. We gave her a little Valium through her IV to take the edge off, so she's resting. Your wife's there with her now."

"Thanks," Hauck said, choosing not to correct her, following her through the ward.

"*Hey . . . !*" He brightened as he drew open the curtain to the room.

Jess was on a gurney in a light blue hospital gown. Beth was sitting next to her, gently stroking his daughter's hair.

"Hey, Daddy." Jessie perked up a bit, blinking, and lifted her hand.

"Beth, thanks," Hauck said to her, placing a hand on her shoulder. He bent down and gave his daughter a kiss and squeezed her hand, taking care not to jostle the IV. "How're you feeling, honey?"

"She's doing okay," Beth said. "Just a little woozy. They gave her something. They're just waiting an hour or so before releasing her."

Jessie tried to push herself up on her elbows. "How are *you* doing, Dad?"

"Just a flesh wound." He grinned, recalling the skit from Monty Python's *Spamalot,* which they had seen last Christmas.

"Are you okay, Ty?" Beth asked. She was in a rust-colored velour outfit; her brown hair was back in a short ponytail. Hauck saw the concern in her eyes.

Hauck nodded and put his thumb and forefinger about an inch apart. "That's about how much, Beth," he said, indicating how close they both had come. He and Beth had already lost one child together. Blame was something that had knifed back and forth between them for a long while.

It had cost them everything. His ability to face his job. Their marriage. Years of their lives.

Beth nodded, seeming to understand. "She's been asking for you, Ty. She was wondering where you were." He detected the edge in her voice.

"I know, Beth, I know. I had to go. Someone died."

"Did you see his family?" Jessie asked groggily.

"Yes, I did see them, sweetie. I had to." He stroked his daughter's hair. "He had a daughter, not much older than you. And a son. They took it pretty hard . . ."

"God." Jessie closed her eyes and shook her head. "It was so awful, Daddy."

Beth said, "*Ty . . .*"

"I know, baby, I know." He squeezed her again. "But it's gonna be okay now. I promise . . ."

"*Ty.*" Beth placed her hand on his arm. "Can I talk to you outside . . . ?"

"Sure. I'll be back in a minute, hon . . ."

They stepped down the hall. Beth's face had lines of worry in it. She asked him again, "You alright?"

"I suppose." He let out a long breath, finally shaking his head. "No. When I saw her lying there, all that blood, and at first she wasn't moving . . ."

She nodded. "I know. I guess that's what I want to talk to you about."

Hauck leaned against the hospital wall. "What?"

"Maybe it's not such a good idea if she comes up here again so soon. I know you were expecting Thanksgiving—"

"*Beth* . . ."

"She saw someone killed, Ty. She's seen that before. She came within an inch of it being her."

"This could have happened anywhere, Beth. This wasn't because of me."

"No, it couldn't have happened anywhere, Ty . . ." Her eyes shone, both sympathetic and judging. "It just couldn't."

Hauck pressed his back into the ER ward's wall. He lifted his cap and ran a hand through his short, sweaty hair. "I want her to be with Karen and her family, Beth. I need a family. This doesn't have anything to do with that."

Beth looked up at him. "She doesn't want to, Ty. She doesn't want to hurt you, but . . ."

A doctor and a nurse went by. Jessie was the one thing in his life he could cling to.

Beth placed her hand on his arm. "You're a good dad, Ty. You really arc. I know that I've made you feel otherwise at times . . . But please, hear what I'm saying. Just for a while . . ."

Hauck swallowed back a final rebuttal and blew the air out of his cheeks. He nodded.

"Thank you. The doctors have given the okay. We're going

to be heading back to Brooklyn soon. I'm going to go check her out."

"Right."

The intensity of what had happened started to rise in him again. The sting in the back of his eyes, of seeing Jessie there like that . . . The feeling it was happening all over again and that he could do nothing about it.

"Listen, Beth . . ."

"Ty, maybe you ought to call someone." She squeezed his arm. "Angela . . . Or Warren?"

His sister lived outside of Boston. She had two young kids, worked full-time, and had a husband she was divorcing. His brother, Warren—two years older—had a law office up near New Haven and was tight with a lot of the politicos up there. He was doing pretty well. They hadn't been so close since high school. Basically, they just checked in with each other once or twice a year. This didn't seem to fit the occasion.

Hauck nodded. "I'll just go in and say good-bye."

CHAPTER TWELVE

When Hauck got back to the station, Sunil and Munoz were sitting in interview room one.

"I think Sunil's got something to tell you, Lieutenant."

The manager of the Exxon station nodded sheepishly as Hauck stepped in. "Lieutenant . . ." He drew in a fitful breath, his dark, round face showing barely more life than when he'd come up from behind the counter a couple of hours ago.

"I didn't have any idea that this was what this was about, Lieutenant. I thought this was all over . . ."

Hauck sat on the edge of the table. "Thought *what* was over, Sunil?"

The Pakistani swallowed.

Munoz leaned against the wall. "Tell him, Sunil."

"Okay . . ." Sunil ran a hand through his dark, thinning hair. "I've been here thirty years, Lieutenant. I operate this business. I've never been in trouble with the law . . ."

"I know that, Sunil."

He nodded. "This young girl, the one who died. The one in the newspaper you found. This *Josephina* . . . My son, Azzi, he knew her. He was in school with her."

Hauck suddenly realized where the man was heading. "He was there with her that night? At the pool?"

Sunil slowly nodded. "Look, he's a good boy, Lieutenant. He's no trouble, you understand? He does well in school. He's already taken his SATs. They were just kids. Messing around."

"What do you mean by 'messing around,' Sunil?"

"I mean, it's not like he was doing drugs or tried to hurt someone. There was a whole group of them who were there. Six. When he came home that night I could see in his face that something was terribly wrong. During the night he came into my room. He told me what had happened. How everyone had run. We called the police. We told him he had to take responsibility. We told him he could not hide behind his friends. Azzi was the only one who came forward. He didn't mean to run away that night. He was just scared. It was a boy's reaction. You understand this, Lieutenant. Sometimes boys do stupid things . . ."

"No one's judging what he did, Sunil."

"Yes, I know that, Lieutenant. You're fair. You've always been fair. But not everyone is. Where we live, *we* are the outsiders. He was afraid. Not just for him. For *me*. Afraid it would hurt me. What I'd worked for. We said we would help make restitution. *Did anyone else?* We never consulted a lawyer." Sunil's face was caught between remorse and anger. "He was all the way on the other side of the pool, Lieutenant. That poor girl, they were just horsing around." He shook his head. "Why would they do this to us? Why . . . ?"

Hauck felt the pieces starting to fit. Sunil's face was like a sheet of wax. He took a sip of water.

"Was anyone threatening you over this, Sunil?"

"*Threatening?*" His eyes were round and startlingly white against the dark color of his skin. "Where we live, it's not the most settled neighborhood, Lieutenant. There are clashes. They have gangs. There were accusations. Many of them. The girl's family, they were upset. Who can blame them? She was by all accounts a good person too. Her brother, he might have said some things . . ."

Hauck leaned forward. "Name those kinds of things, Sunil."

The Pakistani looked up, a little scared. "I don't want any more trouble, Lieutenant. Enough is enough. I just didn't think . . ." The manager was still in the blue Exxon work uniform, his name emblazoned on his chest. "When I saw your daughter lying there, I was so scared. Then that poor man . . ." He ran two hands over his hair and sank back in his chair. "Yes, there were threats. They called us names. Pakis . . . *Pakis,* Lieutenant! I've been living in this country for thirty years! The girl's brother . . . people told us he was in some kind of gang. They are commonplace up there now. My son stood up, Lieutenant. He came forward. We offered to make restitution. The others . . ." Sunil shook his head. "Why would they want to take this horrible thing out on us?"

"I'll talk to someone on the force up there, Sunil. I'll make sure they station someone outside your house."

"It was an accident." The manager somberly shook his head. His eyes were round and sad. "Now look what it's done."

Outside, Munoz asked Hauck, "You still want us to take a look into Sanger's case files?"

"Not any longer." Hauck shook his head. "But grab your jacket; we're going to take a ride."

CHAPTER THIRTEEN

*B*ridgeport was just twenty minutes up the thruway from Greenwich, but it might as well have been in a different century.

The last fifty years had not been kind to Bridgeport. Once home to factories for companies like Underwood Typewriters, Singer Sewing Company, and Bassock Tool and Dye, it was always a blue-collar town, home to blacks and Hispanics and Portuguese. By the 1980s, its downtown had decayed and its factories had been abandoned. It had a lagging school system with clashing minorities living in throwback 1960s projects.

Artie Ewell was the head of the Gangs and Street Crime Unit. Hauck had worked with him several times on cases and at Fairfield County youth conferences where their interests overlapped.

Ewell was already familiar with Josephina Ruiz. An imposing black man, he had been a lane-clearing forward at UConn before it became a national power, and his office was covered with photographs of the charter school basketball program he ran each summer. He had interviewed the Ruiz family after the tragedy and decided not to pursue any charges.

"Good family," Ewell said, motioning to Hauck and Munoz

to take a seat in his small office at the central police headquarters on Congress Street. "What could I do? The father's back in Guatemala somewhere and the mother held down two jobs. There's an older sister studying to be a nurse, I think, or something. Another brother somewhere. They live up in the Tombs . . ." Ewell sighed. "We looked it over two ways to Sunday, but we couldn't find anything other than some awfully bad decision-making on the part of the kids involved. The DA decided not to charge. I heard about what happened down there today, Ty. You think this is connected?"

"The brother," Hauck said, still in his jeans and pullover, "someone said he was in a gang?"

"*Gang?*" The burly detective linked his thick hands together, leaned back, and crossed his ankles. "The Ruizs live in the Tombs, Ty, a housing complex over on Pembroke. You're familiar with that part of town, are you not, Detective Munoz?"

"I'm familiar." Munoz, who was from neighboring Fairfield, nodded.

"If we brought in everyone who was part of some gang"—Artie Ewell laughed—"we'd have more kids in jail than in school. Everyone connects to the gangs up here. Every neighborhood has its own colors. The Cobras, they're over on Grove; 9-Tre, they're over on Sherman. Even the Crips and the Bloods have set up chapters now. You know what they say . . . Bridgeport's a third black, a third Hispanic, and the rest just plain poor."

Hauck knew he was right. The high school graduation rate was something like 70 percent. There were twenty murders committed last year. The crime index was twice the national average, ten times that of Greenwich. Like a sore on the perfect complexion of Fairfield County, Bridgeport was the town all the hedge funds and market booms forgot. The place you passed on the thruway, where the people who washed your linens and mowed your lawns went home every night.

"Any of them decked out in red bandanas?" Hauck asked him.

"Red bandanas . . . ?" Ewell pursed his thick lips. "DR-17, maybe. Why?"

"Because that's what the shooter was wearing, Artie."

The heavy-set detective let out a cynical breath and rocked back in his chair. "Someone sees a black dude or a guy in a bandana in Greenwich and they immediately finger it for us . . . Must be something else you're holding, Ty."

Hauck glanced at Munoz, who took out the newspaper article, still in the evidence bag. "We found this in the getaway vehicle. Which was dumped about a mile away."

The Bridgeport detective read the bold headline through the plastic.

"The manager of the Exxon station where this occurred was Sunil Gupta, whose son was one of the kids involved. The girl had a brother, Artie, who's reputed to be in a gang. The shooter yelled out the victim's name as they drove away."

"So you're thinking it was revenge?"

"I happened to have been there, Art. My daughter was with me. When it occurred. I guess I don't know what I'm thinking, other than we're lucky to be alive."

Art Ewell shook his head with a disgusted air. "Yeah, I understand." He pushed his large frame out of the chair, reached into his desk drawer, and took out his gun. "C'mon, let's find that kid," he said. "Just remember, keep your eyes open, Dorothy . . . You're not in Kansas anymore."

CHAPTER FOURTEEN

*T*he place known as the Tombs was actually the Harry Larson housing project on Pembroke in Bridgeport's East End, two tall gray towers built in the sixties amid a neighborhood of run-down single-family homes.

Just stepping into the decrepit, paint-chipped lobby, the smell of disinfectant and island cooking, the sense that he was stepping into hostile territory, took Hauck back to when he used to work for the NYPD or to *Gangland* documentaries on TV. He felt safer since Artie had brought along two uniformed patrolmen.

They took the jerky, urine-smelling elevator up to Anna Maria Ruiz's apartment on the fourth floor. Outside, Ewell motioned to them to check their weapons. He rapped his knuckles against the door.

"Mrs. Ruiz? Please open up. It's Detective Ewell of the Bridgeport police."

There was no reply.

Ewell knocked again, louder. "*Mrs. Ruiz . . .* ? This is the Bridgeport police."

Finally a woman's voice came back. "One *meenit,* please . . ."

A lock opened and the door came ajar slightly. Through the

chain, a face peeked out. It was Ruiz's older daughter. Rosa. The one in nursing school, Hauck recalled.

"Do you remember me?" Ewell said. "I'm Sergeant Ewell. We're looking for Victor, Rosa."

She shook her head. "*Veector's* not around."

"You mind if we come in? Is your mother at home? It will only take a second."

"*Mamá, es la policía,*" Hauck heard the daughter say. She opened the door.

It was a small two-bedroom apartment with chipped plaster walls and a large crucifix on the wall over the small wooden table in the dining area. It was clean and well kept, with a wear-worn patterned couch and plants in the corner near an outmoded console TV. Hauck noticed an arrangement of photos on the wall. A young boy in his confirmation suit who he took to be Victor. On a console was a larger, framed photograph: a pretty, dark-haired girl in a pink gown at what looked like her middle school graduation.

The TV was turned to the local news channel.

Anna Maria Ruiz was a tiny, small-boned woman with fearful dark eyes. She spoke Spanish, punctuated with a little broken English. She explained she was only home because she had been recently laid off and was about to head to her night job as a housekeeper at the Hyatt in Stamford. Rosa translated.

"My mom wants you to know that my sister was a good girl. She wasn't into trouble. She was preparing to go to college. She hoped to be an accountant."

"Tell your mother we're all very sorry for her loss," Ewell said, "and for having to be here today . . ." He introduced Hauck and Munoz. Mrs. Ruiz's eyes drifted to the stains on Hauck's blood-speckled jeans.

"You can tell her I've lost a daughter too," Hauck said. "I understand what she may be feeling . . ."

He waited while Rosa translated. The mother's small, slightly wary eyes showed life in them. "May God shine his love on you . . . ," she said softly, in Spanish.

Hauck put up his hand. "Tell your mother I understand."

"*Él comprende, Mamá* . . ." Anna Maria Ruiz forced a tight smile.

"But something bad happened today that might be related to your daughter." Hauck went through the events as Rosa translated. The red truck at the station, the guy in the red bandana leaning out, shouting. The guy in the green vest.

Anna Maria Ruiz shook her head.

"He was a very important man," Hauck said to her. "There will be a lot of attention on this . . ."

"We need to talk to Victor, Mrs. Ruiz," Artie Ewell interjected.

"Victor *no está aquí.*"

"You think my brother would ever try to kill a federal attorney?" Rosa said, her dark eyes lit with both anger and outrage.

"No," Hauck said. "I don't think that's what he was trying to do at all."

Munoz took out the newspaper article they had found in the abandoned pickup. Rosa read, and the mother took one look at it and her eyes stiffened in fear. She shook her head.

"Victor would no do something like this."

"The person who did do it shouted out your daughter's name," Hauck said. "I was there, Mrs. Ruiz. With my own daughter."

"*Su niña?*" the woman said, wide-eyed.

"Where is Victor?" Artie Ewell pushed.

The mother looked at Rosa and shook her head again. "Victor *no está aquí*."

"He made statements to some of the other families after the accident," Hauck said. "Some of them interpreted them as threats . . ."

"*No, no threats,*" the mother said in English, seeming to comprehend. "I always feel bad, for those children. I never hold it against them, never, what happened. They were foolish. Foolish children. They were my daughter's friends."

"Maybe Victor didn't do it," Art Ewell said. "Maybe someone he knows did. We just want to talk with him. We know he's involved in a gang."

"No. *No gang* . . ." The woman shook her head; this time fear shone in her eyes. "I tell you, we have nothing against that family. I no know them, but I know their son is good, like Josephina. He came to her Mass. This is not a thing we would ever wish on them . . ."

"Where is he, Mrs. Ruiz?" Artie Ewell asked again.

Hauck's gaze fell on something underneath the couch. The tip of a white high-top sneaker peeking out from under the upholstered flap. Munoz noticed it too, then Artie. They looked in the direction of the bedrooms.

Anna Maria Ruiz saw it as well, her features suddenly twisted in alarm.

Munoz took out his gun and kept it by his side. "*Victor Ruiz!*" he called out. "If you're in here, I want you to identify yourself and come out with your hands in the air."

"He wouldn't do such a thing," Rosa pleaded. She clutched her mother's arm. "It wasn't him, please . . ."

Drawing his own gun, Hauck headed toward the bedrooms. He slowly opened one of the doors as Rosa shouted behind them, "Mama, tell them, please . . . !"

It was a teenage girl's room. Posters on the wall. Marc Anthony. Beyoncé. A baby-blue bedspread. Books on a makeshift desk. Like it hadn't been disturbed for months.

"Victor Ruiz!"

No answer.

Hauck made his way inside the larger bedroom. The mother's room. A white work uniform was neatly draped over a chair next to an ironing board. On the dresser, there was a statuette of the Virgin Mary.

"Victor?"

He kicked a pair of slippers out from under the bed and glanced underneath. He looked, brushing clothing aside, inside the closet.

Nothing.

Slowly, Hauck pushed open the bathroom door. The room was plain, undecorated. A few toiletries crowded around the sink. A pink plastic shower curtain was drawn across the tub.

Hauck edged off the safety from his gun. *"Victor?"*

He heard a click.

Hauck raised his Sig. "You open that curtain slowly," he said, "and I want to see your hands out first, you understand?"

There was silence at first, then the rustle of someone shifting on his feet.

Hauck took a step back. "Son, if you're there," he said, "please don't make me do something both of us will always regret."

There was no answer and Hauck's grip tightened on the gun. From back outside, there came a cry. *"Don't shoot him! Don't shoot him! Victor, please!"*

Hauck drew back the bolt.

A voice rang out from behind the curtain. "Okay, okay . . . *Don't shoot!* I'm not carrying, please . . ."

There was a rustle from behind the bath curtain. Two hands poked through. One had something in it. "It's just a cell phone, man."

"*Put it down!*" Hauck said. "On the floor. And slowly step out of there! *Now.*"

The curtain pulled aside, and the person climbed out from the tub. He was just a kid. Sixteen, seventeen. In an oversize gray hoodie, baggy jeans, a red Yankees cap, a thin, teenager's mustache.

"Okay, okay, easy, man . . ." He put his arms in the air. "*Just don't shoot!*"

The good news was he was staring at Victor Ruiz.

The bad news was that he didn't look a thing like the person Hauck had seen leaning out of the red truck.

CHAPTER FIFTEEN

*F*reddy Munoz flipped a cassette into the recorder in interview room one. "So listen, Victor, we're gonna ask you a few questions . . ."

Victor Ruiz nodded, biting his lower lip. "Okay."

"I'm just gonna turn the tape recorder on," Munoz explained, "so there are no misunderstandings . . . And I would think on how you answer very carefully, if I were you, 'cause how you do is gonna help determine how we can help you get through this, bro. You understand . . . ?"

Victor nodded. Hauck, leaning against the wall, noticed the kid's legs bobbing like crazy.

"So where were you this morning, Victor?" Munoz began. "Around ten o'clock."

"I was home."

"No, you weren't home, Victor. Your mother and sister don't back that up. They told us you didn't sleep at home last night."

"Well, they're wrong. They didn't see me. I was home."

"You remember what I said?" Munoz said. "Please don't crap me, Victor. That doesn't help things, you understand? You have any clue what you're in here for?"

"I don't know what I'm in here for." Victor tilted back his chair. "I was home."

Munoz nodded. He gave the kid a smirk that made it clear he didn't believe him. "Lemme see your arm."

"*My arm?*"

"Your arm, Victor. Your left arm. Whatsamatter, I don't speak clearly enough for you, hombre?"

Nervously, Victor yanked up the sleeve of his sweatshirt. Munoz twisted it over. On his forearm, there was some kind of tattoo. Like a pitchfork. In black and red.

"What's that about, Victor? That the new fashion color scheme for fall?"

"It's about nothing, man. It's just—"

"*Man?*" Munoz's eyes widened and he glanced toward Hauck. "You see a *man* anywhere in this room, Victor? I'm a police detective who's trying to save your ass from this bucket of shit you're about to step into. You understand? You want to know about a *man?* There's a man dead who was shot at a gas station in Greenwich this morning, and guess who's number one for it on our list. So you got any brains left in that little head of yours, Victor, take another look around and tell me if you see anyone named *man* in here, 'cause Lieutenant Hauck and me, we're the only ones between you and spending the rest of your life in jail."

"No." Victor wet his lips and rubbed his scalp underneath his cap. "I don't see no one named *man* in here, Detective."

"Good. Let's start over again. What's that on your arm?"

"Colors." Victor Ruiz shrugged. "El Diablos."

"Diablos? Not *Diablos,* Victor. Didn't someone see you wearing a red bandana this morning, bro?"

"*Red bandana?* No way, man, that's DR-17. Ask that cop from Bridgeport, Diablos and 17s don't mix."

"I didn't ask you if they mixed, Victor. I asked if you wore a red bandana sometimes. Like maybe this morning . . . ?"

"You must be kidding, ma—" Victor caught himself. "*Detective.* You got it dead wrong. That's a sure way to get me killed."

"I know another way, Victor, and that's by not telling us the truth. You heist a truck yesterday?"

"No way. I never stole no car. I swear."

"We got the people who did it on camera. Security video, Victor. How's it going to look if you're in here lying to me and then I show you that mug of yours up there on the screen winning a fucking Oscar?"

"It's not gonna look any way, Detective, 'cause I never stole no truck. I swear . . ."

"So let's get back . . ." Munoz turned a page. "What's a big, brave boy like you, in some macho gang, hiding like some scared poodle in the shower for, anyway?"

"I saw the news. About those guys that lit up that place. When I heard you coming, I got scared."

"What do you have to be scared for, Victor? Because you made some threats? Because you were heard making threats against the family of the man who runs the place that got hit? I bet you weren't so scared when you were running around saying how you were going to even things up. What you were going to do to those kids who took off and left your sister to die. You did say those things, didn't you, Victor?"

Victor swallowed drily. "You got some water in here?"

"Sure." Munoz shrugged toward Hauck. "We got some water, don't we, Lieutenant? You want pizza? We can send out for that too. Maybe you'd like to order in some fajitas, some guac . . ." Munoz leaned back over the table. "You did say those things, Victor, didn't you?"

"Yeah, I said them." Victor nodded. He brought his hands

across his scalp. "But that was months ago. How would you feel, Detective? They left my little sister for dead. But I never meant them no harm."

"But you understand, don't you, Victor, given those things you said, how if you were us you might be looking your way too? You tight with any hombres that might want to make this thing right for you? Maybe DR-17 . . . ?"

"You crazy, Detective. I told you, that'd get me killed."

"So then where the hell were you, boy? We're gonna keep going back to that, Victor, and don't keep telling me you were at home, not with me trying so hard to be your friend."

Victor stared back at Munoz. Worry had started to build up in the kid's eyes. He dropped back his head, slowly shaking it from side to side. "I just can't tell you, Detective."

"Can't tell us *what*, Victor? Can't tell us something that might save your life? You know at all just what you're looking at here? You know who that was who you shot?"

"I didn't shoot anyone. I swear."

"Then help us see that, Victor. We can square this up, just like that. 'Cause that was a federal attorney killed there today. Someone very important, Victor, and the lieutenant and I . . . we're all there is from turning your ass over to the FBI and making this a federal crime. And that means the death penalty, Victor. You're seventeen. Once that happens"—Munoz shrugged—"nothing we can do."

Victor rubbed his hands across his face.

Munoz glanced at Hauck. "Look, we know you didn't mean to hurt that person, Victor. We know it was just an accident, that you were just trying to settle some scores about your sister. Anyone who calls himself a man might do that. And it just got out of control. That's manslaughter, Victor. That's something entirely different. That's something we can work with, if that's what you want. So I'm gonna ask you one more time and you're gonna tell us, Victor, if you have any sense left in that head of yours—where were you this morning?"

"I didn't shoot anyone!" Victor said again. He stood up. His cap fell off his head. He brushed his wiry hair back with two hands and leaned against the wall, palms flat, shaking his head. Tears glistened in his eyes.

Hauck stepped over to him. He placed his hand on the frightened teenager's shoulder. "Victor, listen to me. You're not being smart today, son. And I know you're smart. I know you're in school and that you do well and I promised your mother I'd watch out for you here, and that's what I'm trying to do. I swear.

"But Detective Munoz here is right . . . There's gonna be a witch hunt for whoever killed that man, Victor, and right now we're the only thing in between you and being handed over to the Feds. And if that happens, son, there's no one who can watch out for you then. Wherever you were, whatever it is you're protecting, you have to tell us now, 'cause there ain't nothing, *nothing* you could possibly be protecting in this world that's more important. Your mother's already been through hell, Victor. You don't want to put her through all that pain all over again . . ."

Victor turned around. He was on the edge of sobbing.

Hauck pulled the boy against him. He let the kid cry. When he was done, Victor pulled away, wiped his nose, and took a breath that made his whole body shudder. "I didn't shoot anyone, I swear. Whatever I may have said back then—that wasn't me. I tell you where I was, you have to involve anyone else in it? You can keep someone out?"

"We're trying to solve a murder here, son." Hauck looked the boy in the face. "Nothing else."

"Okay . . ." Victor nodded, drew in a deep breath. "I was with someone. All night. A girl. Her folks were away. She's only fifteen. Her father finds out, she's dead as that lawyer at the station you're talking about . . ."

Munoz glanced at Hauck. "You can prove this, Victor?"

"Yeah, I can prove it. People saw me. People knew I was there."

Munoz pushed a pad of paper across the table. "Start writing, hombre."

CHAPTER SIXTEEN

*I*t was after ten when Hauck finally made it home to the two-level renovated cape he rented near Hope Cove in Stamford.

The raucous press conference set up on the station's front steps had been a mob scene. Reporters shouting about the "person of interest" being held in their cell. Hauck urging them not to jump to any conclusions. Everyone demanding to know if this was indeed some kind of twisted act of revenge.

As Hauck climbed up the outside stairs and put the key in the lock, he realized he was still wearing the same blood-soiled clothes from the shooting twelve hours before.

Tobey, Karen's Westie, whom he'd been taking care of while she was in Atlanta, scratched at the door when he heard Hauck's footsteps on the landing. Hauck opened and knelt down as the excited dog jumped against his chest. "Hey, bud . . ."

It seemed like days ago that he and Jessie were supposed to pick him up before heading onto the boat. But it was only hours. "You must be starved, guy."

He went into the bedroom, pulled off the soiled fleece pullover, and flung it into the hamper. He took a long look at himself in the mirror.

His short, dark hair was matted from sweat, his clear blue eyes dulled and drawn from the day. Hauck's body, still fit and athletic at forty-three, ached like it did after he'd been pounded by two-hundred-and-fifty-pound linemen back in college. He was exhausted. The bandaged gash on his neck had begun to throb. He couldn't remember his last meal.

He trudged back to the kitchen and opened a can of dog food and a Yuengling beer. He clicked on the TV, still standing there bare-chested in his jeans.

"Brazen gunfire erupts in one of the area's poshest suburbs . . . ," the newscaster announced, *"and a rising young attorney is dead."*

Hauck listened as the pretty reporter recounted the details of the drive-by shooting, set up in front of the darkened, blocked-off Exxon station on Putnam. She went through the details of how David Sanger was killed, the suspicion that he had stepped into a hail of gunfire intended for someone else. "A tragic act of revenge gone wrong," she called it. He saw a shot of himself on the screen, a quick sound bite of him trying to urge calm and not sounding very effective.

His cell phone rang.

Hauck reached for it, pleased to see Karen's name on the caller ID.

"So, how the hell was *your* day?" He exhaled, throwing himself on the couch in front of the TV.

"Ty . . ." Karen exclaimed. "I just heard. I can't believe what I just saw on the news down here . . ."

"See what happens," he sniffed, "when you bail out on me."

"Ty, don't joke about this, please. I just saw you being interviewed. *You were there?"*

"Jess and I were getting ready to take the boat out one last time. We were waiting in line to pay."

"Jessie was with you?"

"Don't worry, Karen, she's okay. They took her to Greenwich Hospital, just for precautions. She's back in Brooklyn with Beth now."

"My God, Ty, that must have been awful! What about you? Are you okay?"

For a moment he thought about telling her. His horror as he turned at the register and saw the red pickup's window roll down. The feeling of hugging his daughter with everything he had, flashes of orange death all around. Seeing her body lying there, covered with blood.

Instead, he just took in a breath and shut his eyes. "Yeah, I'm doing okay, Karen."

"I saw that someone was killed," Karen said. "A lawyer."

"Not just a lawyer, a United States attorney. Based in Hartford. He lived here in town. We were all just sort of standing at the cooler a minute before picking out drinks."

"They're saying revenge?"

"Not on him. Just the wrong place at the wrong time."

"Oh, God, that's so horrible, Ty."

"Yeah. The guy's cell phone started to ring. The body's just lying there on the floor, eyes wide, whatever he'd been carrying, cans of soda, off to the side . . . And his phone starts chiming. His wife calling in. It goes into his voice mail. What the hell do you do then, Karen?"

"I don't know, Ty. I don't know what you do."

Hauck paused, lowering the volume on the TV. "You just let it ring; what the hell else is there? You just stand there and suddenly you realize—she's just wondering where he is, why's he taking so long. He just went to fill up the fucking car. Like any day . . . Except her whole world is about to implode on the other end of that line. It's *already* imploded—she just doesn't know it yet."

"I do know what that feels like, Ty. Having someone walk out the door and never come back."

"Yeah." He caught himself. "I know you do, Karen."

For a moment, they didn't say anything. Then Karen asked, "Ty, are you alright?"

"Am I alright?" He gritted his teeth and shook his head. "I don't know if I'm alright. I tried to go after the truck, to get a read on the plates, and when I looked back around I—" He chugged a swallow of beer, cooling the dryness in his throat. "I saw Jess. Curled on the floor, this little mound, not moving, blood . . ."

"*Blood?* Whose blood, Ty?"

"*His* blood. The guy who was killed. He stood right behind her in line. For a second, I just looked at her and I thought . . ."

"I know what you thought . . ."

"I was just so relieved and happy when she came to. That the blood wasn't hers. That it belonged to someone else. That she was okay. You know what I mean?"

"Of course I know what you mean. It's alright to feel that way."

"Yeah." He let his head drop back. "I know it's alright."

Tobey jumped up on the couch. Hauck drew the dog to him, bringing his face up to the phone. "I've got your little pooch here. He wants to say hello."

"*Hey there, baby . . . ,*" Karen called, her voice both cheery and forlorn. "Mommy misses you."

"He's wondering when you're coming back. I think he needs

to shit on his own lawn. He says he's looking forward to Thanksgiving . . ."

There was a pause, which Hauck expected would be followed by *Yeah, honey, I am too* . . . But instead he heard only a long, stretched-out silence.

Finally, Karen said, "Listen, we're gonna have to talk about that, Ty . . ."

"Talk about *what*?"

"Not now. It can wait. You've got other things . . ."

"We're gonna have to talk about *what*, Karen?" He sat up and brought in his legs off the table.

"About Thanksgiving. I was going to tell you, Ty, just not today . . ." She cleared her throat. "Listen, I'm not going to be coming back up there. At least not for a while."

CHAPTER SEVENTEEN

*I*t hit him like a fist to the solar plexus. Air rushing out of him. The feeling, from out of left field, that his heart had just been kicked.

"I just can't now," Karen said. "Do you understand? Mel's not well. He's not getting better. I asked the kids to come down here on their school breaks. I was gonna have Samantha bring Tobey down for a while . . ."

"Jesus, Karen . . ." Hauck took the phone out of the crook in his neck.

He had felt her pulling away, just a bit. Her dad was in the latter stages of Parkinson's. And deteriorating. That's why she had gone back home. To be with him and help her mother through. That and maybe to find out who she was after picking up with Hauck so quickly. But the couple of weeks had turned into a month. Now a month had become . . . *At least not for a while.*

"You could come down here," she said. "I just need to be here right now, Ty. You can understand that. They need me. I was with my husband for twenty years, then when everything happened last year with Charlie, and you . . . I love you,

Ty—you know that. I owe my life to you . . ." She cleared her throat. "But this is where I need to be, honey, until whatever happens does. Not just for them, but for *me,* too. Don't be angry with me. I didn't know it was going to be this way. I told you from the start there were things I couldn't promise . . ."

"I'm not angry, Karen. I'm hoping the best for Mel."

There was a lull, both of them stumbling over what they could say. Karen ultimately broke the silence. "Well, I guess this caps off one helluva day . . ."

"Did I mention that I was shot, also?"

"Shot?"

"More like a graze on my neck. I've done worse shaving. It does, however, make it onto the list."

"Jesus, baby," Karen said, "won't you stop at anything to get yourself on TV?"

Hauck laughed. Karen did too. There was another pause until she asked, "So, what do you think?"

"What do I think about what?"

"What do you think about *what*? About the state of the goddamn economy, Ty . . . What do you think about you coming down here?"

"I don't know . . ." He brought his knees up on the table. "I've got Jess. We've got Thanksgiving this year." He winced at the lie, not sure why he said it. "Anyway, it's probably better to just keep it a Friedman thing down there, don't you think?"

"In that case, Ty, how do you feel about giving me back the dog?"

He laughed again. "I don't know. You'll have to ask him. I've been feeding him pretty good . . ."

"Ty . . ." Karen said, sniffling, "I do love you, baby . . . You know that. You're one of the best men I've ever met. I just

hope you can somehow understand. I've been gone since I was eighteen. And now they need me. I don't know how long. I can't say no. I always told you I wasn't a perfect bet."

Hauck took a sharp breath. He guessed he'd seen it coming. "I always thought you were a damn good bet, Karen."

"You keep yourself safe, Ty Hauck," she said, "you hear? I'd make you promise me that, but we already know just how little that means . . ."

"I'll do my best."

They hung up, the click of the phone carrying a kind of finality that made Hauck pause. He rubbed his head and drained the last of his beer.

Tobey sat up, his ears perked.

He could call someone, like Beth had suggested. His sister, Angela. In Massachusetts. Or Warren.

Talk.

Instead, he looked straight at the dog, who seemed primed for something. "C'mon—before you bail out on me too."

He threw on a sweatshirt and went out on the landing, climbed the stairs leading up to the flat, tarred roof. Tobey followed. It was a clear, starry night, warm for late October. He stared out at the dark expanse of the sound, the lights of Long Island twinkling in the distance, six miles away.

He kept an old set of golf clubs up here, along with a trove of beat-up range balls he had scrounged. Hauck looked out at the sound and then back at Tobey, who sat watching him.

"Whaddya think, guy, go with the eight or a friendly seven?"

The terrier cocked his head.

Hauck took out his eight.

He dropped a ball on the worn carpet remnant he used for a tee mat, swung through a couple of practice swings, then launched a crisp, high-arcing fade over the lot next to his neighbors, Richard and Justine, and deep into the darkness of the sound.

I do love you, Ty . . .

He hit another.

Karen had brought him back from the long slumber he'd been trapped in, in the years after Norah died. From the vise of guilt he felt. From hiding out up here . . .

He sent another ball deep into the darkness.

She taught him how to smile again. To fight for someone again. How to love. He thought of the freckles on her cheeks and the laughter in her drawl and the time they'd spent together. He couldn't help but smile. *You're a damned good bet, Karen . . .*

His mind flashed to David Sanger. His daughter, not much older than Jess, in tears. *"Why did this have to happen, Mom?"*

I'll find out, he'd promised.

Hauck blasted six more balls into the darkness. The last was a high-arcing beauty, soaring with the perfect right-to-left draw, plopping to a stop on some green deep in the void, six feet from an imaginary pin.

He looked at Tobey. The dog jumped up. Hauck threw the eight iron back in the golf bag.

"C'mon"—he winked—*"we're puttin', dude!"*

CHAPTER EIGHTEEN

*I*t was the end of a long, crazy Saturday night, and Annie Fletcher was beat.

They had served over forty tables, a hundred and twenty plates. For the first time in the restaurant's life, they'd gotten a three-time turn.

Since Annie's Backstreet had opened, just over a year ago, they'd been trying to get the place off the ground. She'd been at it since seven that morning, starting with the fish market and the farmer's market in Weston, picking out squash and heirlooms, and the local bakery she used for fresh-baked sourdough and olive bread. They had stuffed twenty veal chops, hand-rolled two hundred *agnolotti* stuffed with chicken and feta, made twenty off-the-charts chocolate crespelles. Her hair smelled of spattered grease. Her nails were caked with allspice and Madras curry.

They call it sweat equity, right?

Annie looked over the rows of empty tables, finally sitting down to pick at an iceberg wedge salad and sip a glass of wine. *This exhausted never felt so good.*

It had been a slow, building process. They didn't have the "glamour" opening. They weren't in the hot location. They were situated in Stamford on the other side of I-95, amid the antique warehouses and next to a tiling factory. OTMO, they called it, tongue in cheek. *Other Side of the Metro-North*. Not exactly Tribeca. They didn't get throngs of young people lining up on the sidewalk drinking beers or families pouring out of the movie theaters. But it was her place. In her style. Crossbeams on the high ceiling. Linen-colored, stuccoed walls. An open kitchen with copper pots hanging from the racks. "Comfort food with a point of view."

After the debacle at her last place in the California wine country, with her partner (and husband) siphoning off the register (and the checking account!), it closed literally overnight. She had put everything she had into that place. Her dreams, every penny in the world, her trust.

It had almost cost Annie her son.

She'd gone from someone who had everything going for her to a person who had no place to go the next day. To someone who had liens. Nothing. Jared, who was eight and needed a special school. She'd tapped into money from her parents, and she hadn't done that since she had left home.

Then Sam, whom she had gone to the Culinary Institute with, called out of the blue and offered her this chance to do a new place. Start a new life.

So she left. Healdsburg. San Francisco. Where she had a history and a name. To come east, start over.

Everything rode on this.

It was eleven. The staff was finishing wiping the place down. Annie was leafing through the receipts over a glass of wine. Some of them were heading to Café Mirage, where a lot of restaurant people got together after-hours to let off steam.

She knew she should go. She could meet up with everyone there. Hell, she was thirty-five and had been working in kitchens for ten years. Pretty, funny, now divorced. She'd made a clean break. Now it all just seemed about two people who ended up headed in different ways.

Jose, the dishwasher, was tying up the garbage, hanging the last of the pots and pans.

"Go on home," she told him. Jose had a wife and kids and went to church early in the morning.

"I finish, ma'am," he said, picking up the broom.

"Nah," Annie said, getting up. "I'll close. Here . . ." She handed him the tray of the last of the crespelles. "*Para los niños.* Go on."

Jose took the tray and smiled. "*Gracias,* Miss Annie."

He left through the back door. Annie heard the rattling sound of Jose's Nissan as it clunked away. Still in her whites, she got up and hung a few last pots, made a note about the specials for Monday, and picked up the last two bags of trash.

One hundred and twenty meals.

It still felt as if she was carrying most of them!

She pushed open the back door and headed out to the Dumpster. The cool night air hit her face and felt good. A single light illuminated the back. In this part of town, at night, even on a Saturday, there were no cars, no one on the streets. Just closed-up warehouses and the sound of the thruway overhead.

Something Annie saw made her stop.

A car was idling next to the Dumpster. The passenger door was open. She heard voices. In Spanish. A kid in a hooded sweatshirt and a red bandana lobbed a large black trash bag over the rim.

She stepped back into the shadows.

The kid turned to get back into the car; then his eyes fell on her.

A chill ran down her spine. There was something cold, almost spooky in the way he looked at her—not even startled to see her standing there. The driver revved the engine. A rust-colored Jetta. Some kind of marking on the trunk.

Don't let him see you. Get the hell out of here, the tremor said.

With an indifferent nod, the kid in the bandana stared at her for what seemed forever. Then he jumped back in the car.

With a jolt, it took off onto the street and sped onto Atlantic, which led into the ramp and onto the highway. Annie saw the kid turn one last time and give her a long look through the car's rear window. It was a look she had seen only in films—dull, fixed, implacable. Like in *Blood Diamond* or *Hotel Rwanda*. The smirk of someone capable of hacking bodies apart or shooting up people, yet no more than a boy.

Like he was saying, *Lady, I know where to find you. I know who you are.*

Annie let what seemed a full minute pass to make sure the Jetta wasn't coming back. Then she went over to the Dumpster.

She knew she shouldn't do it. *Just toss in the bags. Don't get involved.* Monday morning, the cartage company would come. Whatever was in it, no one would ever know.

You have a son. Everything's just starting to turn for you. Go home. Go to Café Mirage. Get drunk. Write Jared.

Instead, she reached over the side and pulled out the heavy, bound bag. She undid the tape. It was crammed full with newspapers and cartons. Used food containers. Slop.

Then she felt the black metallic shape at the bottom of the bag.

Put it back, a voice said. She knew she had just stepped into something.

She was staring at an automatic gun.

CHAPTER NINETEEN

You don't have to do this, she said to herself. *Things are just starting to turn for you. For Jared.*

You don't have to get involved . . .

It was later, in the small one-bedroom apartment Annie rented on the point neighboring Cos Cob, with a glimpse of the sound. A few French liquor posters hung on the walls. Her favorite majolica pitchers were arranged on the kitchen shelves. Basically all the possessions she had brought east with her.

Two glasses of wine hadn't made much more sense of it for her.

Annie sat in her flannel pj's writing a good-night e-mail to Jared. He always checked in before going to sleep.

Hey, dude, how'd your day go today? I had a great one. Our best night yet . . .

She took her fingers off the keyboard and paused.

She had seen the TV news reports. They all had. It was on at the restaurant all afternoon as they prepped for dinner. That horrible drive-by shooting in Greenwich.

Only five miles down the road.

When they first heard it, everyone stopped working and fixed on the screen. Manuel, her sous-chef. Tim, preparing the desserts. Claudia, from the waitstaff. The rumor was that it was some kind of crazy revenge attack. Involving gangs. Eighty shots. And this poor federal prosecutor had been caught in the line of fire. Just filling up his tank. Anyone could have stumbled into it.

"Jesus." Claudia turned pale. "I fill up there all the time. It's near where I work out."

Manuel, always the conspiracy buff, weighed in. "You wait, there's something deeper. This is all about drugs. Wait and see."

"It's not about drugs," Tim shot back. "Didn't you hear? It's about some girl who drowned."

Manuel spread out a flour mixture on the counter. "I know these people. You don't want to mix with them—you just stay clear. What do you think, boss?"

"I think you better get those tamales filled," Annie yelled over, "or you'll be in *my* line of fire."

They all laughed. Gradually they went back to work.

But now she was involved.

She had found the gun. She knew it. She had seen the police lieutenant on TV. Heard how they'd found the shooter's truck. How they had a "person of interest" in custody. The red bandana. How they knew what kind of gun it was.

A Tec-9.

Annie knew exactly what she'd found.

The only question was, what was she going to do about it? Things were going well. Starting to turn around. This was a place she could bring Jared. There were good programs here.

This was a life she could build for herself.

Now all she could think of was the warning in that guy's eyes.

Stay out, his stare had said bluntly. *I know where to find you. I know who you are.* If they had done that horrible thing at the Exxon station, what would they do to her?

Everything rode on this. *Everything, Annie. It's not your business. Don't get involved.* But yes, it was her business. They had made it her business. She took a sip from her glass of wine.

The poor man, he had kids, a family. Just like Jared.

And now he was dead.

She knew exactly what she'd found.

CHAPTER TWENTY

*T*y . . ." Vern Fitzpatrick's voice crackled over the office inter-com around nine the next morning. "Can I get you to come on up here?"

Hauck was at his desk by seven. During the night, the crime scene team had scoured the truck. They picked up a set of sneaker imprints on the driver's-side floor mat, which they tried to match to Victor's. They also found a partial print on the newspaper article. Both weren't panning out.

Worse, Victor's alibi checked out—*completely.* Artie Ewell had located the girl he claimed to have spent the night with. She confirmed his story that Victor had been with her until almost ten that morning, about the time the shooting had taken place. On top of that, two people from her building recalled seeing him heading out around that time as well.

"I'll be right up," Hauck said to Vern, reaching for his jacket. He was just processing the paperwork now to let the kid go.

His cell phone rang. A number he didn't recognize.

"Ty . . ."

Hauck was surprised to hear his brother's voice. *"Warren . . ."*

"Christ, Ty, I called as soon as I heard. Ginny called me. I'm up in Hartford. Jesus, are you alright?"

Warren was two years older. He'd built a tidy law practice for himself up near Hartford, gotten cozy with a bunch of the movers and shakers up there. Built the big house for himself and Ginny. Kids in some fancy school. He never seemed to have much time for anyone, even getting the cousins together. It had been that way for years. Hauck couldn't even remember what had drawn them apart.

"Yeah, Warren, I'm alright."

"What about Jessie?" Warren asked. "I heard she was there too."

"She's okay as well. Just a little shocked. She's back in Brooklyn with her mom."

"Can't exactly blame her, can you? This is fucking crazy, Ty! Right there in town . . . What kind of riffraff are you letting through there these days, anyway? The TV's saying it's revenge?"

"I don't know," Hauck said. "Maybe."

"That you got someone in the pen?"

"I can't exactly talk about that right now. You looking for a gig, Warren?"

His brother chuckled. "Not exactly my clientele, little brother."

Hauck's thoughts went to the hundreds of times he'd wondered why they were no longer close. Growing up, they had shared a room until Hauck was ten. Fought over who rode "shotgun" in the family car, dibs on the bathroom. Like a lot of brothers, they were always challenging each other. On the court. For friends. Always rivals.

"*When I heard* . . ." Warren said tightly, seemingly unable to finish. "You know I rely on you, Ty. Anyway, where the hell else am I gonna turn to get my clients' kids out of those traffic tickets, right?"

"Yeah, I figure you owe at least the kitchen in that house of yours to me," Hauck said, laughing.

"*At least.*" His brother paused. "You know, we ought to get together, Ty. It's been way too long. What are your plans for Thanksgiving? You could come up."

"That might work," Hauck said, taken by surprise. "Lemme see."

"You could bring Jessie. The cousins could get together. We haven't done that in a while."

"No, we haven't. Sounds good, Warren. But maybe just me."

"Whatever. Sounds like a plan."

There was a knock on the glass. Brenda, tapping her watch, pointing upstairs. "Listen, Warren, I gotta scoot . . ."

"Go ahead. I just wanted to hear your voice. Let you know I was thinking of you. You nail these bastards, huh, bro? And hey—Thanksgiving, right?"

"Thanksgiving," Hauck agreed. "And, Warren . . ." He wished he could think of something more meaningful to say. "Thanks for the call, guy."

CHAPTER TWENTY-ONE

*H*auck knocked on the door of the chief's office, at the end of a long hall lined with portraits of past chiefs, overlooking Mason Street.

What he found wasn't a surprise.

"Come on in, Ty . . ."

Fitzpatrick rose, dressed in a V-neck sweater and a plaid shirt. Seated across from him were two men, one balding, ruddy complexioned, in a navy sport jacket and open shirt. The other was black, stocky, in uniform: tan suit, crisp dress shirt, club tie. Even on Sunday.

"Ty, I want you to meet Jim Sculley . . ." The balding man stood up and put out his hand. "And Stan Taylor. They're from—"

"I'm pretty sure I know where special agents Sculley and Taylor are from," Hauck replied. For a year after 9/11, he had been an NYPD liaison officer to the FBI.

"Right." Vern exhaled, motioning to Hauck to sit down. "They're out of the Hartford office."

"Sorry you all have to come all the way down here on a Sunday morning . . ." Hauck reached across and shook hands.

Sculley, the agent in charge, shrugged. "You know the job. I saw how you handled that Grand Central bombing," he said admiringly. "Great work. How's that neck doing?"

"Holding up." Hauck shrugged. He touched it, feigning surprise. "Still attached."

Vern sat back down and looked at Hauck. "I was just bringing everyone up-to-date."

"This person of interest," Taylor, the preppy black one, chimed in, "we understand he didn't pan out?"

"His alibi completely checks," Hauck said. "He's got no priors. There's nothing to tie him to it other than a few random threats that he made three months ago after his sister's death. And he's not the person I saw with the gun."

"Still," Taylor questioned, "you're pretty sure this adds up to a gang-related shooting?"

"I'm pretty sure it adds up to a *revenge*-related shooting. You got a better idea?"

"Only that when a federal prosecutor is gunned down, it might at least seem prudent to knock over every possible angle. The personal backgrounds of everyone involved. Their contacts, case loads . . ."

"Then you might as well start with *me*." Hauck looked back at him. "*I* was there too."

"What Special Agent Taylor is suggesting," Sculley said, a hand on his colleague's arm, "is totally customary in the case of a federal investigator who's been killed. I'm sure you'd do no less here. We're only down here to offer our support . . ."

Hauck knew that when the FBI offered their "support," it generally meant that his case files were being requested as they spoke and that a room full of eager recruits down in Washington would soon be pouring over them. And that things continued to remain an entirely *local* matter as long as nothing was happening that might advance anyone's career, but as soon as a possible suspect was in custody, everything quickly became *joint,* with someone with a federal seal on the podium leading the press conferences.

"I think you realize better than anyone, Lieutenant," AC Sculley said, rubbing a small Band-Aid on his temple, "that there are a lot of important interests at play in a town like this who would have a keen desire to see this incident managed in the quickest and most thorough way—"

"If by *interests,*" Hauck said, nodding, "you mean a wife whose husband was murdered going out to fill up his tank, or two young kids who've just lost their father, I'm with you one hundred percent. The rest—" He shrugged, rubbing the back of his head. "Why don't we just see how they play out as we go along?"

Hauck looked at Vern, sensing what was going on. A brazen act of violence. A rising star in the Justice Department killed. The press all over it. This was Greenwich. Behind those high stone gates and redbrick office complexes, the cogs of influence were turning. The governor himself had probably already called in.

"All we're suggesting, Lieutenant," Agent Sculley said, "is that we have a Gang Violence Task Force, C-12, a phone call away. Our lab guys could be all over that pickup within the day . . ."

"So far, what we have is a homicide," Hauck said, his tone declining.

"In which the victim was a government prosecutor," Stan Taylor chimed in.

"No worries, Lieutenant." AC Sculley smiled at him, rubbing his sore. "It's your case."

"This thing has everyone pretty well riled up, Ty," Fitzpatrick said. "All I promised was that you were the type of guy who would do whatever he could to see this solved."

"We can probably use all the help we can get," Hauck said, meeting their eyes.

There was a rap against the door. Freddy Munoz stuck in his head.

"Sorry to interrupt, Chief . . . Lieutenant . . ." His gaze fell on Hauck. "When you're done there's someone you need to speak with downstairs. Something's come up."

"We were just finishing," Hauck said. He stood up, said to Taylor, "You'll let me know whatever you need. I'm sure we'll be in touch."

"I'll be sure to do that, Lieutenant."

In the hallway, he patted Munoz on the back. "Thanks for bailing me out. I owe you one, Freddy."

"Hey, I wasn't kidding, Lieutenant," his detective said. "There's someone down there you need to talk to now."

CHAPTER TWENTY-TWO

She was sitting on the bench outside the squad room, a gray cowl-neck sweater underneath a short leather jacket over jeans, her hands cupping a mug of coffee.

"This is Lieutenant Hauck," Munoz said. "This is Ms. Fletcher. I want you to tell him just what you told me."

"Annie . . ." She nodded, standing up. Hauck shook her hand. She was pretty, maybe around five-four, with dark, round eyes. Her black hair was clipped up in a barrette, loose strands curling along the sides.

Hauck led her back into his office. "Why don't we talk in here?"

He cleared a spot on his long Formica desk, which was piled with papers, a photo of Jessie and Norah, and his yawl. A large glass window partitioned them off from the busy squad room.

Hauck pulled out a chair. "You want some more coffee?"

She shook her head. "I'm fine. I've never been inside an important police detective's office before."

Hauck smiled. "Neither have I."

Munoz leaned against the glass. "Just tell the lieutenant what you told me . . ."

"I have a restaurant." Annie Fletcher hesitated slightly. She pushed the hair out of her eyes. "In Stamford. Just off I-95, near exit eight. Annie's Backstreet. We've been open about a year . . ."

"Tell the lieutenant about last night," Munoz redirected her.

"Sorry . . ." Annie smiled, contrite. "Don't ever ask me to tell a joke. I never get to the punch line . . ."

Hauck smiled too.

"It was a little after eleven. We'd just finished up. I let my dishwasher go home and I was just taking out the last of the trash. I think I saw them, Lieutenant . . ."

"Saw who?"

"The ones who did that awful thing yesterday. Who shot up that place . . . I saw the piece on what happened. Everyone did. I saw you on the news. I know you're looking for whoever did this . . ."

Hauck pulled a chair around and sat across from her. "What exactly did you see?"

"A car pulled up in back of my place where the Dumpster's located when I went to take out the trash . . ."

"Go on . . ."

"I saw these two guys. Heard them talking. One was behind the wheel and the other was outside and had tossed something into the Dumpster—a black plastic trash bag . . ."

"Did you get a look at them?"

Annie Fletcher nodded. "Hispanic, sort of young, maybe early twenties . . . The one who tossed something in the Dumpster might even have been in his teens. It was dark. But not so dark that I didn't see just how he looked at me, Lieutenant. Sent chills up my spine. He wore something around his head. Saw the news. That's what made me think at first. A red bandana . . ."

Hauck gave Munoz a look, a surge of optimism jolting through him. "You said you overheard them talking?"

"Sort of. The guy driving just said to the kid, 'Let's get out of here, now . . .' The car was a tricked-out old Jetta or something. Sort of rust colored. My ex-husband was deep into cars. It was parked directly in the light. I wished I could've picked up the plates—I mean, I wasn't really looking at them. It was dark; I was a little scared. I was pissed off at myself that I had let everyone else go home. I didn't put it all together right then . . ."

"I understand," Hauck said.

"But there was something about the car I do recall. Some kind of marking on the trunk in back. A kind of cross . . ."

"Cross?"

"Not a religious cross. Sort of blue and red slashes . . ." She held her hands apart. "Maybe six inches . . ."

"That's DR-17, Lieutenant." Munoz met Hauck's eyes. "Dominican colors."

"DR-17?"

"It's nothing." Hauck tried to put her at ease. "Just something that fits into the case . . ."

"It's some kind of street gang, isn't it?" Annie Fletcher looked up anxiously. "The news said this was a revenge attack. That you've been bringing in people from a gang."

"We're looking at a lot of possibilities, Ms. Fletcher . . . ," Hauck said.

"So what am I supposed to do, just go back about my business? Pretend that it's not?" There was a troubled look in her eyes.

Hauck shrugged and leaned a little closer. "Yes, it's a gang, Ms. Fletcher. Out of Bridgeport, but—"

"*Jesus* . . ." Annie Fletcher shook her head and blew out a breath from her cheeks. "You know, I asked myself whether I should even come here . . . I was just minding my own god-damn business. You hear stories of people who come forward. I'm not a coward, Lieutenant. I wanted to do the right thing. I saw the picture of that poor man who got killed. I just don't exactly need this kind of thing right now . . ."

"No one actually plans these things, Ms. Fletcher . . ."

"No, but this person I saw . . . I mean, I'm the one who saw the sonovabitch's face. He wasn't even hiding it. He just sort glared at me with this smug, self-assured smile. It was like, 'Just stay out and mind your own business, lady . . .' Nothing more. Like he knew I wouldn't do anything. So what happens now? What happens to me if this goes anywhere, Lieutenant? I have to come forward. I have to testify . . ."

"Why don't we take one thing at a time, Ms. Fletcher? You said you believe these were the people who did this. What makes you so sure?"

She stared back, her eyes tremulous, glistening. "Because I saw the news, Lieutenant. I saw you on it—talking about the type of gun . . ."

Hauck glanced toward Munoz. "*Gun . . . ?*"

Annie turned away, pressed her lips, then came back with "I have a business to run. So how are you gonna protect me, Lieu-tenant? Not just me, people who work for me. I saw how he looked at me. I know what these people do."

"I promise, I'll make sure it doesn't come out." Hauck leaned forward and looked in her eyes. "Until we figure out how to handle it."

"Everyone makes promises, Lieutenant . . ." Harried, Annie ran a hand through her dark hair. "What are you going to do, take up a post outside the door every night?"

Hauck shrugged. "Whatever it takes."

Annie Fletcher closed her eyes and shook her head. "In that case, I defintely hope you like curry, Lieutenant . . ."

"I love curry, Ms. Fletcher. Just tell me what is it you found."

There was something in his deep-set eyes Annie Fletcher trusted.

"On the news you said you were still searching for the gun. What did you call it, a Tec-9?"

Hauck nodded.

"The guy in the bandana, he tossed something into the Dumpster."

Hauck shot a glance toward Munoz, who had already sprung into motion. "Tell me again where your place is, Ms. Fletcher. I'm going to send someone out there right now—"

"No need . . ." Annie Fletcher shrugged resignedly. "I brought it with me. I have it in my car."

CHAPTER TWENTY-THREE

*I*t was the gun.

Bundled in newspaper, taken apart. The registration filed down, wiped clean.

The muzzle indicated it had been recently fired. They ran a trace through the National Tracing Center. Hauck wasn't exactly optimistic.

The results took a couple of days.

The Tec-9 had been purchased at a gun show in Virginia, then reported stolen from a dealer in Pennsylvania six months later. Part of the thousands of weapons that drop through the system every month and end up on the street.

Hauck was a little more hopeful they could locate the car.

That came the next day. There was another case Hauck had been working, trying to track down this bond trader who had closed three multimillion-dollar mortgages on the same property here in town and now was nowhere to be found.

Freddy Munoz ran into his office. "We got it!"

"We got what?"

"The Jetta. Ewell got a beat on it through one of his con-tacts. They know where it is."

Hauck jumped up, strapping on his Glock. "Tell him we'll be up there in twenty minutes."

"Not Bridgeport, LT. Hartford."

CHAPTER TWENTY-FOUR

The Jetta was left in a vacant lot in a run-down area off Vine Street in central Hartford. It had the rusted color and the same blue and red marking on the trunk that Annie Fletcher had described.

Art Ewell had traced it to a street figure named Hector Morales. Morales had been living in this country for only two years, but his rap sheet already read like a lifetime offender's. Assault. Possession of cocaine. Possession of a stolen weapon. Burglary. Attempted murder. Fleeing the scene of a crime. Resisting arrest.

Morales had come here from the Dominican Republic when he was nineteen. Since then, he'd been making his way in the world in the only way he knew how. He basically lived on the streets, cracking heads, shooting people, doing jobs for people. Tough jobs. Whatever needed to be done. In street terms Morales was known as a "recruit." Someone from back home who came here and did things. Climbing the rungs of the one organization that understood his roots. Where he came from.

And he was gone.

The people where he lived said Morales had left a few days before. Paid the rent. Said he wouldn't be back.

"We missed him, Artie." Hauck had already looked through the guy's file and recognized the carved jaw, the light complexion, the thin mustache, the same cold, dark eyes. Definitely the guy he had seen rolling down the window of the red pickup. "He's gone. Maybe out of the country. Took his passport."

The Bridgeport detective replied with an audible groan. "Probably back in the DR. We can try to track him. But you know as well as I do that's a whole different ball game, Ty."

A completely different game. Bringing in the Feds. Sculley, Taylor. Putting pressure on the Dominican government. Getting the local police involved. It also meant getting caught up in whatever issues happened to be going back and forth between the two countries. Not to mention trying to extradite the guy.

If they even located him.

Something started to pound in Hauck's brain. "Why the hell would DR-17 do this, Artie? We've found nothing between them and Josephina Ruiz. No link to the girl's brother either. The shooter yelled out her name. They left behind the truck, that newspaper article. They bring in this dude from back home to do the job and now he's history. You think we're being played?"

"*Played?*"

"This didn't just happen, Artie. Someone authorized it. Someone gave the okay. Who's running this show, Art? Who's calling the shots?"

"*DR-17?* The guy's name is Vega, Ty. Nelson Vega. His street name's L'il Nell. I rounded him up once or twice. Nothing ever stuck. They wouldn't be making a move like this without him pulling the strings."

"So how do we get a face-to-face, Artie? I think it's time we find out what the hell's going on."

"Your buddies at the FBI ought to be able to help you on that one."

"Run that by me again?"

"Vega's awaiting trial on drug trafficking and attempted murder charges," Ewell said. "He's a guest of the federal government these days. Stowed away at some facility in upstate New York. I think it's called Otisville, Ty."

CHAPTER TWENTY-FIVE

*A*nnie was rushing.

They had a full house tonight and there was still tons to do. Sauces to finish, the menu of specials to print out.

She pulled her Prius into the lot behind the restaurant.

She tucked a bag of farm-stand veggies under her arm and three bottles of Barolo she'd had to run for to complete a sauce. Though it was still before five it was already dark.

She balanced the two bags in her arms, kicked the car door shut, and headed into the restaurant through the kitchen door.

She never saw a thing.

Just felt the heavy, blunt weight force her up against the wall. Before she even realized what was happening, her face was pressed against the cold, rough siding.

A voice whispered close to her ear. *"How you doin', Annie Fletcher?"*

Annie's heart went wild. She heard the crack of the wine bottles shattering on the concrete, her eyes fixed on the puddle of dark red spreading around her feet.

She knew immediately who they were. What they were there for.

Her blood came to a stop. *"Don't hurt me, please . . ."*

"Why would we want to hurt you, Annie Fletcher, of 2262 Soundview Cove. Apartment 2B. In Cos Cob . . ."

They knew her name. Where she lived.

That terrified her even more. "What do you want?"

"What do we want . . . ?" The man chuckled. The accent was unmistakable. His breath crawled over her like a snake on the back of her neck. She felt his thick hand slide down her side to her jeans.

She cringed. *"Don't . . ."*

"Don't *what*, pretty lady? Don't stick your little nose into where it doesn't belong? Don't see things you weren't meant to see?"

"I didn't . . . ," Annie said, shutting her eyes against the fear. She didn't know if she should scream. Manuel's car was in the lot. She knew if he came out, they would kill them both for sure.

"Didn't what, Annie?"

Her voice was shaking deep in her throat. "See anything."

"So that's good." The hand released her side. " 'Cause the news, it's saying something completely different. It's saying you found things that were none of your business, Annie Fletcher, and turned them over to the wrong people. People who aren't really your friends, yo . . ."

"I'm sorry."

"Sorry?" He pressed her face back against the wall and laughed. "You don't get sorry, lady. You get dead, you understand?"

Suddenly, Annie felt something cold and hard brush against her cheek, and her heart started to almost jump out of her rib cage as a bolt of horror rippled down her spine.

She nodded against the rough concrete. "Yes, I understand."

"That's good. You know . . . 'Cause you see how easy this is—Annie. You see why you gotta be careful these days. When you see something . . ."

All of a sudden she felt a cold, hard shape pressed into the back of her skull. Tears flooded her eyes. *"No, don't . . ."*

The next sound was a click.

Annie froze. The man pushed the muzzle up against her. She sensed there was more than one attacker. "So you see now? You see who your friends really are? 'Cause we're the only ones keeping you alive. Not them—*us*. You see?" He tapped her skull with the gun. "You see how you have to *think* about what to do? Whoever you might talk to? What you think you may have seen?"

"I see," Annie said. Every cell in her body was shaking. "I see."

"You bet your sweet ass you see, lady. 'Cause you make me say it again, I'll shoot you in the head."

Annie cringed against the concrete. Nodded. Let out a grateful breath.

"You're a lucky lady, Annie. Most people don't get no second chance. You cook with beets? You make me come back here again, they'll be wiping you off the floor here. Like beet soup. So help me God. You understand?"

"Yes." She closed her eyes and whimpered. "I understand."

"Good." The man eased the forearm from her back. Annie sank against the wall, her legs like weights. "That's all I came to tell you, Annie. Be seeing you then, Annie. Be watching how things go."

She heard footsteps hurrying toward the street. She gulped air deep in her lungs, the night chill suddenly sweet and cool on her sweaty cheeks. She didn't move a muscle until she heard the car door slam and the sound of the vehicle speeding away.

CHAPTER TWENTY-SIX

Annie was sitting on a stool at the bar when Hauck ran in. She looked drained, in a gray Napa Valley T-shirt under her kitchen whites, her hair in a short ponytail, while a couple of local detectives finished up.

She seemed relieved to see him.

"I came as soon as I heard. Are you okay?"

"Yeah." She nodded, ashen. She took off her glasses and ran a hand through her hair. "I knew this was going to happen."

"And *I* knew I should've assigned someone to look after you. I'm sorry." He sat next to her. "I know you've probably already been through it more than once, but I need to hear what happened . . ."

"*What happened?* Someone slammed me up against the wall and put a gun to my head and basically said to forget about whatever I may have seen or next time I wouldn't have the option. You promised me it wouldn't get out. That I'd be protected."

"I know." Hauck grimaced guiltily and shook his head. "I wish to hell I could've controlled what happened. But listen, this is important: was this the same person you saw the other night?"

"I didn't see him. I was pressed up against the wall. He cocked a gun to my head. He . . ." Her voice was shaky and her eyes filled up. Hauck squeezed her hand. "They knew my name. They knew where I lived. What am I, some kind of target now? I was just taking out the fucking trash . . ."

"*Listen* . . ." Hauck turned her around to face him. "I know how you must feel, but you're not a target. They came here to scare you, Annie, not hurt you. Otherwise they would have. They wanted to show you how easy it was. You gave the detectives here a description as best you could? For the complaint."

"You don't get it, do you?" Her eyes shone at him. "Look, you seem like a good guy, Lieutenant, and I know you're just trying to do right by me, but I don't *want* to file a complaint. I want to go back to my life. I want this over. I'm sorry about that man who was killed. I'm sorry about what happened. I hope to God you get these guys . . .

"But these people want to give me a message . . . I'm not exactly dense, Lieutenant. I'm out! This is your case, not mine. I wouldn't have even goddamned called in the police if Manuel didn't come out and find me there. I just want to go back to running my stupid restaurant."

"That's all I want for you too," Hauck said. "I promise."

"So what are you going to do—relocate me to somewhere in Arizona? Help me open up a little taco joint out there? I have a son. I've got my life in this place. How's it going to play once the press gets hold of it? 'Local Eating Place Target of Gang Intimidation.' 'Half off on any entree if you come in wearing a red do-rag.'"

Hauck wished he could answer. Then Annie shut her eyes, shook her head in frustration, and came back with almost a smile. "Might just give me a bit of a lift with the Bridgeport market . . ."

Hauck smiled back.

"He cocked a gun against my head, Lieutenant. He said next time he'd shoot me."

"I promise, this won't happen again," Hauck said.

"*How?* Are you going to come in here and keep watch at the door every night?"

"I don't know. That depends . . ."

"*Depends* . . . That depends on what, Lieutenant?"

Hauck shrugged. "The food, mostly."

Annie Fletcher stared at him. She brushed a wisp of dark hair out of her eyes, then smiled. "It's good. I promise. Before I became a witness intimidation target, I ran a pretty tight little kitchen here."

"Let me drive you home."

"Yeah, right . . ." Annie sniffed. "You must be kidding. We have a full house tonight."

"Your crew can handle it."

She tapped her fists on the bar, lightly at first, then with more force, something brewing up in her between anger and tears. "I wanted to do the right thing, do you understand? For that man. And his family. I wanted to fight them back. Say 'You can't do this to people' . . ."

Her eyes started to flood. "When he put his hands on me, I wanted to turn and say 'No, you can't . . . You can't hurt me.' But you know what? They can. *They can totally hurt me.* And you know how that makes me feel?"

"I know exactly how it makes you feel . . . ," Hauck said. He put an arm around her and she sank against him, squeezing the lapel of his jacket tightly in her fist.

"All I could think about was seeing Jared again. That I just had to get through it. Whatever they wanted. You know what I mean?"

Hauck stood there with her leaning against him and nodded back against her head. "I know exactly what you mean."

CHAPTER TWENTY-SEVEN

The federal prison in Otisville, New York, was in the foothills of the Catskills, about ninety minutes from Greenwich. It housed mostly midlevel felons, drug dealers, and prisoners shuttling to trial in Manhattan. Not exactly Florence, Colorado, or Pelican Bay.

But someone had gone to a lot of trouble to keep Nelson Vega away from the old neighborhood.

Hauck and Munoz stowed their guns at the entrance in the administrative building, and the assistant warden, Rick Terwilliger, met them and took them through a network of checkpoints to the facility's Secure Housing Units, SHUs, the maximum-security detention pod.

"Don't let the street punk act fool you, Lieutenant. If you read Vega's file, you already know he had a couple of years of college. A stint in the army. He tests high. He's been very active in his own defense."

Hauck asked, "What kind of contact is he allowed with the outside world?"

"He's permitted unmonitored phone calls and outside visitors three times a week. Mr. Vega is merely in a holding status here. To this point he has not been convicted of any crime."

Which, Hauck knew, didn't mean Vega wouldn't be the first crime figure who continued to run his day-to-day operation from jail.

"Nonetheless, we look at Vega as a very dangerous man. This is a person who had no qualms about trying to gun down a Connecticut state trooper in the process of committing a felony."

They arrived at a secure, bolt-locked room with a tiny window on the door.

"You can record your conversation, if you like. But I ask you not to transfer anything to him physically or it will have to be confiscated."

Hauck looked in. A guard with a Taser was positioned behind Vega.

"You're about to meet ground zero of the human race, Lieutenant. Ready? I hope you didn't eat before coming . . ."

The warden nodded to open the door.

Vega was in an orange jumpsuit, seated at a metal table. He had a smooth, chiseled face, tattoos on his neck, a shaved head, a scar that ran from under his nose to his upper lip.

A uniformed guard who looked like he could bench-press most of South America stood in the corner with a stun gun tucked in his belt.

Hauck took a seat in one of the chairs across from him. "I'm Lieutenant Hauck. This is Detective Munoz."

Vega showed his wrists, making a show of the rattling of chains. "Sorry if I don't shake hands."

"I'm the head of detectives in the town of Greenwich, Connecticut, Mr. Vega. We're here to talk with you about a drive-by shooting that took place there last Saturday morning, at an Exxon station in town. A bystander was killed, who turned out to be a prosecutor out of the U.S. Justice Department in Hartford. Are you familiar with this incident, Mr. Vega?"

"Jeez, I heard the price of gasoline is sky-high out there," he said, shaking his head, "but *that's* a bit crazy, no?"

"The shooter was Hispanic," Hauck went on, ignoring the remark, "and wore a red bandana over his head. Are you getting where I'm coming from, Mr. Vega? As he drove away, he shouted the name of a local girl. Josephina Ruiz, who, it turns out, was a teenager from Bridgeport who was accidentally drowned last summer at a public pool. Is any of this starting to ring a bell?"

"Sorry to bring you all the way down here, Lieutenant." Vega jangled his chains. "But in case you hadn't noticed, my alibi's pretty tight."

"We know your alibi's tight, Mr. Vega. Later on that evening, another Hispanic male, also in a red bandana, was observed tossing a package into a Dumpster in Stamford. Inside the bag was a Tec-9 automatic that turned out to be the murder weapon."

"You making some kind of a fashion statement, Lieutenant, with all these bandanas? 'Cause if you are, I know I can fit you out in one just right."

Vega blew a kiss at Munoz. "What about you, *jefe*?"

Hauck went on, placing a hand on Freddy's forearm to hold him back. "The vehicle spotted at the Dumpster in Stamford was a tricked-out Jetta with a blue and red cross on the back. The car was traced to a Hector Morales in Hartford. Mr. M orales is from the same town in the Dominican Republic that you hail from, has a rap sheet that reads like a novel, and is a known member of the DR-17 gang."

"You come here with some kind of question to ask me?" Vega rocked back. "'Cause I don't mean to be rude or anything, but, you know, it's like almost time for *Ellen* and I was hoping to get in a little dancing. Got it? Talking to the police, without a warrant, ain't exactly a credo with me."

"*My question*, Nelson"—Hauck leaned forward, trying to cut through the prisoner's smirking glare—"is what connection was there between DR-17 and Josephina Ruiz? This thing won't be going away, Mr. Vega. I can put together a case right now against Morales that ties you in as an accessory after the fact. If it turns out Morales was in contact with you while you were in here, maybe more. The FBI's all over it. A federal prosecutor was gunned down, Mr. Vega. If he wasn't the intended target, then you don't need that kind of attention at all, do you? Not on top of all you're facing here."

"Lemme get this straight." The gang leader bunched his lips and nodded. "You come all the way down here like Homeland Security and try to scare me with some kind of TV *Law & Order* rap. You must've brought something with you, bro."

"Just some good sense, to get this off your back."

"*That's all?*"

Hauck shrugged. "How 'bout I toss in an Xbox 360? That do the trick?"

Vega's eyes sparkled. "That and an Escalade STS, maybe—to take me home. Shit, what show have you been watching, man? You think I need juice from any of you? Mr. big shot Greenwich detective? You think I'm gonna roll on my man because you come down here with your little badge and tell me you're gonna smooth out my way with the FBI?" Vega shifted around to the guard. "Hey, Leon, you better stun me now, bro, because I don't think I can sit and listen to this no longer. You know you ought to be on Leno, Lieutenant, because you are a fucking riot!"

When he turned back, Vega's laugh had quieted and his grin was gone. "Now you copy this, bro—I don't need your fucking juice. I don't need you to smooth anything out for me. You think you got it all sized up? Well, here's *my* juice: When I'm outta here, when I'm back home and you're still scratching your heads trying to put together two and two, you come to me and I'll smooth it all out for *you*. You copying *that,* bro?"

He laughed again, glancing back at the expressionless guard. When he turned back, Hauck grabbed the gang leader by the wrist.

"I leave, and the next time I see you it won't be *Ellen* that's on your mind."

"Oooh, you scare me, *niño*." Vega grinned.

Hauck got up. Something wasn't right here and he was starting to sense what it was. "One more thing. The woman at the restaurant. Who turned in the gun. Annie Fletcher."

"Who?"

"She's off-limits now. She's out of it. For good. You understand, Vega?"

"Not sure I know exactly what you're meaning." Vega looked back at Hauck with a smile.

"This is what I'm meaning." Hauck leaned forward and took the man's wrist. "One of your boys ever threatens her again . . . Demonstrates a sudden urge to try the crab cakes or maybe check out where she lives . . . I don't care if a goddamn water glass falls off the bar in the wrong way . . . I'll tear your head off. You understand? I'll rip your little network so wide open, the nickels and dimes will fall out on the floor. You hear what I'm telling you, Nelson? You copying *that,* bro?"

"Yeah." The gang leader pulled his wrist out of Hauck's grip. "I'm copying, Lieutenant. So let me get this straight . . ." He leaned in close and pretended to be interested in something. "This mean that Xbox is off the table?"

"You don't get it, do you, Nelson?" Hauck went to the door. "I'm gonna find out why that prosecutor had to die. Sooner or later, I'll be back on you for it. *That's my credo.*"

CHAPTER TWENTY-EIGHT

*O*utside, Freddy Munoz turned to Hauck as soon as they got to the parking lot. "What the hell was going on in there?"

It wasn't adding up to Hauck either.

"Why does a guy who's on the hook for fifteen to twenty in a federal jail laugh in our faces like we're a couple of high school bus monitors? What was it he said? 'When I'm out of here you can come to *me,* if you're still trying to put two and two together . . .'?"

Vega didn't need any help. From any of them.

"You know what I'm thinking, Freddy? I'm thinking we can look for a year for some kind of connection between Josephina Ruiz and DR-17 and we're never gonna find it. Because it's not there. Vega was doing a favor for someone. He knows he's never going to face those charges. The man's protected. That's what that act was about."

Someone had needed someone killed, and they used DR-17 to do the job.

That's why they shouted out "Josephina" at the scene. Why they left the newspaper article in the truck for them to find.

The whole thing was set up to only look like a retaliation.

"We're looking under the wrong manhole cover. Who the

hell wipes away a sheet like that? Who gets accorded that kind of protection?"

They stood there staring at each other from over the car.

"Jesus, Lieutenant, the guy's a CI!"

A *confidential informer.* Or people were in bed with Vega—the right people.

Hauck smiled. "Which one of us is supposed to be the high-priced honcho here, Freddy?"

Freddy slid behind the wheel. Hauck climbed in next to him, his mind racing with thoughts he didn't much like. They'd have to look at everything, he realized. *Everything.* Not just DR-17 or Josephina Ruiz, but who it was aimed at. Sunil. Sanger. *Two plus two . . .* Who the real target was that morning.

Munoz started up the engine. "Something else my mother always says, Lieutenant . . ."

"And that's what?"

"She says, 'I don't like it when people cover me up in shit and tell me that it's gonna make me grow.' "

Hauck looked at him. "That doesn't sound at all like your mother, Freddy."

"No," the detective said, pulling out. "You're right. That one's me."

CHAPTER TWENTY-NINE

The man in the flat tweed cap and Burberry raincoat, the political man from upstate, sat on a stool like any customer in the busy coffee section of Stew Leonard's in Norwalk.

He was short, a little paunchy, had a wrinkly, round face and wore narrow reading glasses, his graying hair starting to thin. He had on a Shetland sweater over corduroys and Top-Siders, glancing occasionally at *The Financial Times,* indifferent to the throng of shoppers and laughing kids passing by.

The person he was expecting, in a gray North Face jacket, wound his way through the crowd. "Let's make this quick," his friend said, pulling up a stool at the round table. "I don't like being here."

"Relax," the man in the tweed cap said. He pushed up his glasses. "Probably more people here right now than any place else in the state. I drive down every once in a while just for the chowder. The best around. Course, then I'm also loading up the car with the filets and lobster tails and chocolate chip cookies . . ."

"I don't really care about the fucking chowder, Ira," the man in the North Face jacket said, his handsome, athletic looks just beginning to dull into middle age. He leaned forward. "My kids are in the car . . ."

"That's right." The upstate man nodded. "You still have kids at home. Private school, isn't it? Then college . . ."

"Ira, what is it you want, please . . . ?"

The man in the cap took the reading glasses off his brow and folded the paper. He nodded in an obliging sort of way. "Okay, *champ* . . . " His expression stiffened. "Things are starting to move in a way no one's very happy with up there. There's a line of questioning I'm hearing, and if it leads anywhere . . . You're aware the local police have been down to visit your boy?"

"He's not my boy. I've never even met him. You didn't exactly ask me to handle a bond issue, Ira."

"Still, it was you who arranged things to be handled through them . . ."

"Through an intermediary. You wanted things done, I got them done for you. That's all."

"Why don't we just leave it that the revenge motive doesn't seem to be carrying a whole lot of weight any longer."

The younger man stared back. "What is it you want me to do, Ira?"

"What do I want you to do?" Ira grabbed his arm. "I want you to do what you always do, guy. I want you to fix things. Isn't that what that showy new house is all about? And how you pay for your kids to go to that school?" The man's face bore a smile, but it was a smile that cut right through him, an unwavering sternness in his eyes. "You didn't think it was that six handicap we've been paying for all these years."

"You don't understand."

"Oh, I understand. I understand why this is a problem for you . . . I'm just down here to make certain *you* understand.

Because what you don't want is for certain things to come out that don't need to. What you don't want is for a certain police detective to start honing in on the wrong line of inquiry. So finesse it, shortstop. Make it go away. That's your particular skill, right? You have a backup plan. Maybe it's time to get it rolling. That's why I'm down here—the chowder notwithstanding. Are we clear?"

The man in the North Face took a napkin off the table and tore off the edges. He nodded.

"I think I'm going to need something a little more definitive than that, champ. *Are we clear?*"

Their eyes met, the government man's gaze unmistakable.

The man in the North Face felt his stomach clench. "Clear as a golf ball on grass, Ira."

"Good." The government man stood up and folded the newspaper under his arm. "Now what you oughta do now is head back to those cute little kids of yours. Go out, take 'em to McDonald's, kick the ball around, whatever you had planned for the day." He opened a plastic bag and took out a box of Stew's chocolate chip cookies. "Here . . . rated best in the state." He pushed it over and the younger man took it. "On me . . ."

"There are other people involved, you know. There's other ways for this to get out."

"*Finesse.*" The man winked amiably. "I think that's the key word here. We'll handle our end; you just make sure you do yours. What you don't want is for this sort of investigation to fly back and take a dump in *your* lap. Know what I mean?"

"Or yours," the younger man said, angered.

"Or mine . . ." The government man nodded. "You're right." He balled his napkin into his cup, crumpled them into a ball, and tossed them into the trash. "But let's just say that in this state, I'll take my chances on that one. Agreed?"

CHAPTER THIRTY

Keith Kramer walked out of the Pequot Woods Resort and Casino in Uncasville into the predawn darkness, not from under the shimmering forty-story glass teepee that towered above the lobby, but with a nod to the waving guard at the rear door marked STAFF ONLY and into the anonymity of the employee parking lot.

He'd just finished up his midnight-to-six-A.M. shift as a pit boss for the casino. It was his job to watch the tables, make sure the payouts were okay, and stay alert for a sign of any known card counters or professionals. Keep an eye on the dealers too.

Basically, Keith watched hundreds of thousands of dollars each night changing hands with only the clink of a few chips, his share of the tip pool that night falling into his.

All that was about to change.

Keith found his car—he had the Voyager tonight. Their Beemer was in the shop. The payments were getting hard on that one too. He had taken the job as a dealer ten years ago, just to hold them over when Keith's job in the accounting department of Swiss Re fell prey to a merger, and Judy, riding the bubble, got her real estate license. Then Cameron came along, numero uno, and the casino dangled this promotion in front of him—the health plan, another twenty grand. Now, years later, he was still wearing the boxy navy jacket and black tie and going home wondering what had ever happened to his degree from Wesleyan and with the sour taste of a futureless career in his mouth.

He knew he was falling behind. His college friends were doing deals on Wall Street or had become partners in law practices—and he was living upstate in Madison, in a house Judy had found when the market was soaring, and utilizing math skills he had mastered in the seventh grade.

Now she hadn't sold a house in months. He still read the journals. Still devoured the chess column in the *Times*. He put aside dreams of going back to grad school or working in research for one of the medical companies nearby. Now they had three kids. Every night, he just stood there watching the tables, rolling around in his mind some foolproof way he could outsmart the house.

He started the car, removing a plastic soda cup belonging to one of the kids out of the divider.

He never noticed the headlights that pulled out after him.

Keith veered out of the casino onto the highway as he did every morning, straddling the point where opportunity collided with desperation, his mind a blurring roulette wheel of red and black. There were ways. Ways when no one was looking. When the cameras were off. So much money, it would never be noticed. The sky was just beginning to streak with light.

Cam had a peewee hockey game tonight and Ashleigh trumpet. He would catch them, help them with their homework, maybe catch the third period of the Bruins game on cable. Then it was a quick meal while Judy put them both to bed. Head back to work all over again.

He was running through his mind how at barely forty-one, you could feel this old.

It was all about probability. The probability of ever busting free from your life. Balanced against the risk. The risk of being caught.

Everything was always on the pass line. Until you rolled the dice.

As Keith merged onto 395 South, he felt a little drowsy. There was a Dunkin' Donuts franchise at the intersection. He stopped there every now and then for a wake-up coffee. He steered the Voyager onto the ramp and pulled in.

The Escalade pulled in behind.

He took the key out of the ignition and just sat there. His heavy head came to rest on the wheel. He was tired—tired of falling behind, tired of not doing something. But he knew he never would. *Right, Keith?* These were dreams, dreams he would never act on. Dreams he would roll around in his head every shift, watching the tables. While he waited for the housing market to click back in.

He went to open the door, but someone was standing there, blocking him.

He felt a constriction in his chest that something wasn't right.

But by then the passenger door had opened and a dark-skinned man in a hooded sweatshirt climbed onto the seat next to him. "*Yo, Keith . . .*"

The man removed a strange-looking weapon from under his top and sent fifty thousand volts streaming into Keith's chest, immobilizing him, all his dreams suddenly blurring like a spinning roulette wheel. Red-black-red-black.

Red.

Black.

Then just black.

PART TWO

CHAPTER THIRTY-ONE

*T*his was Hector Morales's kind of party.

All it had taken was the right kind of wink to the fox at the bar, a wink that held the promise of free-flowing lines of blow, a bottle of Patrón to go along with it, and the lure of whatever came to mind afterward.

Now they were back in his room, clothes littered on the floor, her thick blanket of black hair bobbing up and down between his thighs, her tongue in an adroit rhythm only a seasoned pro could devise.

Hector leaned back with his hands behind his head. "You sure know how to do that, mama."

She rose and crawled on top of him. Her breasts were everything he'd imagined when he'd pressed up to her at the bar, and her smooth ass slid easily over his muscular body, straddling him. "You just wait."

He had been back in the DR for over a week. He knew he had to keep a low profile, maybe for a month or two. Maybe all winter. But if this was any indication of what a connection to the right people and throwing around a little cash could bring, it wouldn't be torture. He was a big man back here, the prodigal son returned home stuffed with dollars, having carved out his mark in the States.

"Come on up here, mama."

He would show her how it was done. He pulled her up by the shoulders, hands rubbing hard and possessively across her small yet perfect breasts. *See what's available for just a couple of lines?* They would do anything. Anything for the power it held.

He had seen it in his own mother. In all his life, he had known nothing else.

"What does this mean?" the woman asked, running her tongue along the strong, hard lines of his chest and the colorful tattoos that ran onto his neck.

"This, this is for bravery," he said, pointing to the Komodo dragon. She kissed it. "This one's for secrecy," he said, pointing to the ornate red and blue serpent. She kissed that too. "And this one is for you," he said, drawing her hand to his taut erection.

She bent down and kissed that one too.

"I'll be back in a minute," she said, climbing off, skipping into the bathroom. "Don't you go away."

Hector grinned, conjuring up what was about to happen next. "Don't you worry about that, mama." He closed his eyes. He had done so many bad things, it scared him every once in a while when he shut them. The dark. It was why he had to drown himself in tequila just to go to sleep at night.

He conjured an image of when he was a boy. In Quisqueya, just thirty minutes from here. He lived in a shack with six others in his family. They had no power. Only a water basin outside. They used to kick around a tightly wrapped bundle of paper as a football on a rutted field. From the time he was ten he carried a knife and was known by the police. At fourteen, he learned to use a gun shooting at sparrows in the trees. Now he could buy any car he wanted, live like a king, dress in fancy clothes.

He heard her come out of the bathroom and felt her crawl on top of him again.

Have any girl.

He liked the feel of her warm body over his and kept his eyes closed. His hands traveled down her waist and found the curve of her smooth, hard ass. His prick sprang alive.

He felt her trace his lips. "So what is this one for, Hector?" He opened his eyes.

Pressed in his face was the barrel of a 9 mm gun.

Hector held back a laugh. Was this a turn-on? She must not know who he was. "You're kidding, right, mama?"

"Yeah." She smiled back. "I'm kidding, asshole."

She squeezed the trigger and Hector's head rocketed back against the wall, his mind hurtling back to times when he was not afraid of darkness, sparrows scattering.

CHAPTER THIRTY-TWO

Brenda buzzed in Hauck's office. "Lieutenant, call for you. Line one."

They'd been looking at everyone over the past days. The bank accounts, credit cards, phone records of everyone involved. Airlines and immigration for Hector Morales. Requesting a list from the warden at Otisville for anyone who had visited Vega over the past three months.

They were growing frustrated. Coming up empty. They'd found no link to the gangs, nothing to tie to Josephina Ruiz. Nothing in David Sanger's caseload or Sunil's past. The news reports were saying everything had stalled. And they were pretty much right. Hauck was even thinking about giving in and reaching out to the FBI.

"See if someone else can take it, Brenda . . ."

"It's a Captain Pecoric, from up in Madison . . ."

Madison was a small, picturesque town up the Connecticut coast, maybe twenty miles north of New Haven. Rustic inns, boat builders. The captain's name didn't ring a bell.

"He says it has something to do with the case."

Hauck picked up the flashing line. "Hauck here . . ."

"Thanks for taking the call. I'm Chief Pecoric, actually. I run the local PD up in Madison."

"How can I help you, Chief?"

"I think it's more like how I can help *you*. We found the remains of someone up here yesterday. In the Hammonasset State Park. A couple of mushroom pickers stumbled onto it deep in the woods. Looks as if it's been dumped there a couple of days . . ."

"Okay . . ."

"Homicides aren't exactly the norm up in Madison, Lieutenant. Especially ones who have been shot in the back of the head at close range. *Twice*."

Hauck arched up and removed the phone from the crook of his neck. "I'm listening . . ."

"The victim was a pit boss up at the Pequot Woods Casino. He and his family lived in town here. His name was Keith Kramer. The name mean anything to you?"

"No," Hauck said, jotting it on a pad and underlining it three times. "You were saying it had something to do with my case . . ."

"Yeah. That guy who was shot down there, in that drive-by. The prosecutor . . ."

"David Sanger?"

"*Sanger!*" the Madison chief exclaimed. "That's the one. Turns out my guy up here had a bit of a connection to him. We went to speak with the victim's wife. All upset, as you'd expect. Two kids. The guy had been missing for two days. Never came back from work. She muttered something about what a terrible coincidence this was. 'First that other guy from downstate, Sanger . . . Now Keith.' Seems they knew each other . . ."

Hauck wheeled around and snapped for Munoz's attention

in the squad room. He pushed on the speakerphone as the young detective rushed in.

"Knew each other exactly how, Chief?" Hauck asked, feeling the lift when something that heretofore had been hidden and opaque now began to come clear.

"They were actually at school together—back at Wesleyan, in the early nineties. Apparently they kept in touch. According to the guy's wife, the two of them were even roommates for a while."

It was Sanger. Hauck suddenly saw it. David Sanger had been the target all along. Josephina Ruiz was merely a diversion. The red truck had pulled up as soon as he stepped in line. Hauck looked at Munoz.

Now he had to find out why.

CHAPTER THIRTY-THREE

Wendy Sanger shuffled into the kitchen and stared at the three large boxes from David's office in Hartford that two of his colleagues had driven down last Wednesday. His files, mementos, and tchotchkes that he'd kept in his office. Personal mail. They'd been sitting in the corner of the family room since then. She hadn't had the heart to go through them. Not just yet. She knew she should move them out of sight and into the basement, but it felt like burying him all over again.

She poured herself a cup of coffee.

The two weeks since her husband had been killed were like a blur to Wendy. One day they were getting ready to drive to Vermont and David was prepping for an important case. A week later she was faced with confronting the rest of her life alone. Her sister had left the day before, having to return home to New Hampshire, where her husband taught at Dartmouth and she had two kids of her own. When all the attention died down, the house was eerily quiet. Now there was just the long, dimensionless expanse of time that loomed in front of her, somehow learning to think of David in the past. She didn't know how she was going to handle it. Not to mention Ethan, who didn't understand much of what was going on.

Or Haley.

Her daughter had been so angry since it happened. Wendy couldn't blame her. David had always been her "guy," a role Wendy could never fill. Imagine being jealous of your own daughter.

She had been hanging out with friends after school, not coming home until after dark, no matter how much Wendy scolded her. *Things don't change, Haley, just because of what's happened.* Not doing her homework, staying in her room by herself and playing music, saying she had eaten and not coming down to dinner.

It was just a phase, Wendy knew. Haley was always the closest to David. She had leaned on him a lot, in a way Wendy could not compete with. She knew her daughter always thought of her as weak, strict, always getting flustered over the littlest things. Always putting Ethan's well-being before hers.

Now who was going to be there for *her*?

Not to mention the financial situation. Wendy had always managed the bills. David was one of the smartest people she knew, but he didn't know an adjustable rate mortgage from the prime. They didn't have a lot of money. David was a government lawyer. He barely pulled in ninety grand. The house took most of it, living where they did, and now they were in contract on this new place. There was the insurance; her dad could chip in for a while. But it wasn't much.

If he'd just gone into private practice like so many of his friends, he'd have been worth ten times as much by now . . .

"Balloon!" She heard a shout from the TV room. Ethan. He had stayed home from school today. "Mommy, look, *balloon.*"

"Yes, Ethan . . . ," Wendy called wearily. He was watching a recording they had made of the Macy's Thanksgiving Day parade. He loved it. The colors, the floats. He was having a difficult time figuring out what was happening, why his father was gone. Death was a state his six-year-old, handicapped mind was having a hard time comprehending. "Daddy's on a trip," he said. "He's coming home soon?"

"No, honey, no he's not," she said.

She took another sip of coffee. *You're gonna get through this.* She sighed.

She felt so overwhelmed. She looked at the boxes.

Oh, David, how could you leave me alone . . . ?

Empty, needing to feel close, Wendy stepped over to the cartons against the wall and sat down, pulling open the top of the box closest to her. She took out a photo. The four of them kneeling around a giant sea turtle they had come upon in Hawaii. It almost made her cry. Wendy remembered how she had given it to David on their anniversary.

Wendy buried her face in her hands. Would she ever have moments like that again? She reached back inside.

She pulled out a large, stuffed envelope. From Michelle, David's secretary up there, marked RECENT MAIL. Wendy unfastened it and slid out the contents.

Letters. Bills. Bundled with rubber bands. Some legal documents, publications he received at the office.

David's things.

She dropped the bundle on her lap. It was too overwhelming. She bunched her lips, fighting back tears. She just wasn't ready to do this . . .

Ethan yelled, "Mommy, Mommy, look, *Kermit!*"

"Yes, Ethan, *Kermit!*" she heard herself yell. Crossly. She wiped her eyes, knowing that she shouldn't take it out on him. "I'm coming," she called back, stuffing the mail back in the envelope. "Mommy's coming."

Something caught her eye. She pulled it out of the pile.

An envelope from Bank of America. In Hartford.

The envelope read, STATEMENT ENCLOSED.

They didn't have an account with Bank of America.

All their banking was through Fieldpoint in Greenwich. She pretty much managed everything. David had never spoken to her about another account up there.

That didn't make sense.

She slit it open, thinking maybe he had something put aside for the kids through work. An IRA. That would be just like him, Wendy thought. Not ever mentioning it.

She took another sip of coffee and unfolded the statement. The account was made out to David Sanger. Not in trust. No Minors Act. Wendy put the coffee down. Her eye scrolled to the balance.

She froze.

There was $427,000 in it.

CHAPTER THIRTY-FOUR

*Y*ou believe in coincidence, Lieutenant?"

"No," Hauck said to Chief Pecoric, "not when it comes to murder."

The Madison chief nodded and the young tech from the local ME's office pulled out the body drawer; the pale, bloated body of Keith Kramer rolled into view. The victim was short, a little pudgy around the waist, with wiry, reddish hair. His face was youthful, affable, set in a calm that would have been in sharp contrast to his final moments.

Hauck kneeled, ran his hand along the railing next to Kramer's head. The sight of the corpse made him uneasy. Not just the stark, white body—never an easy sight—but that the two seemingly unrelated victims were now connected. Which didn't make this a random shooting any longer, but a double murder, and if he ran with that, it made David Sanger the target that day, not just an unfortunate bystander.

Which also implied that there was something these two had been hiding and made this a whole different case.

"You say his wife had no idea why anyone would want to do this?"

"Not a clue," Chief Pecoric said, standing behind him. "We went through the whole laundry list. Maybe they were a little hurting for money of late, she admitted. His wife had apparently been the breadwinner the past couple of years, sold real estate . . ."

"That game's over."

"Yeah," Marty Pecoric agreed, "it is. But they didn't seem to have any sizable debts. No threats she was aware of. No drugs, gambling. No history of cheating on his wife. You're welcome to talk to her if you want."

"Thanks." Hauck stood up, his knees cracking. "You got any gangs up here, by any chance?"

"*Gangs?*" The chief laughed. "Book clubs, maybe. Why?"

Hauck shook his head. "Just thought I'd ask. You say he worked for the Pequot Woods up in Uncasville?"

"Pit supervisor. Blackjack, roulette. I spoke to the guy in charge of security up there. Raines. He said Kramer was well liked, didn't miss his shifts, never attracted trouble. A model guy. He'd just ended his shift up there—midnight to six A.M.—never made it home. It's likely he was abducted somewhere en route home. You see that burn mark on the chest? It seems he was Tasered. I know they'd like to keep this under wraps as best they can."

"Did he happen to be carrying any amount of cash?"

"Still had his share of the night's tips in his pocket. Wallet in his pants."

"One thing I do know"—Hauck nodded to the tech, indicating he'd seen enough—"model guys don't generally get whacked in the head on the way home from work."

Kramer's stark torso disappeared.

"Tasered. No robbery. This was no random killing," Hauck

said. "You mind if I call that guy up in Uncasville, just to check it out? What did you say his name was?"

"Raines. Heads up security for the casino," Pecoric said. "Maybe you can get something out of him I couldn't. Be my guest."

CHAPTER THIRTY-FIVE

When Hauck got back to the station, Munoz jumped out from behind his desk. He and Steve Chrisafoulis followed him in.

"You had us checking into Sanger, LT . . ."

Steve dropped a thick folder on the round table next to Hauck's desk. Steve was short, barrel chested, with wiry, graying hair and a dark mustache. He was a ten-year veteran of the NYPD who did the crossword puzzle every day, had moved up here eight years ago for an easier life, and handled most of Hauck's fraud and bunko cases.

"What'd you find?"

Steve arranged a couple of piles. They seemed to be photocopies of bank and telephone records bound together with black clasps.

"First, I took a look at the guy's phone records, Lieutenant . . ." He picked up a stack and put the sheets in front of Hauck. "His cell. What you're seeing goes back to April . . . That's as far as I pulled."

There were dozens of handwritten annotations Steve had made in the margins, identifying most of Sanger's calls. Most of them seemed to be office related or to his home. Several had

been highlighted in green marker. Hauck noticed these all belonged to the same number.

203-253-7797.

"Guess whose?" Freddy Munoz rested his foot up against
the table.

Hauck shrugged.

"Kramer," Steve Chrisafoulis said. "Victim Number Two."

Hauck leafed through the calls. There seemed to be twenty
or thirty of them going back six months. Sometimes in
clusters—two or three in a matter of days.

They'd been speaking a couple of times a week up to the
day Sanger died.

"Then there's this . . ." Steve brought over a new stack, feeding Hauck individual sheets. "I looked through his bank records . . . You can see for yourself, they've got several accounts
in the Fieldpoint Bank, right here in town. Checking, savings, a
couple of CDs, fifteen, twenty thousand, one for each of the
kids. Under forty grand, the whole ball of wax. He and his wife
are the lone signatories on all accounts. There's also an investment IRA at Smith Barney in his and his wife's name. A shade
over a hundred and fifty grand in it . . ."

Hauck shrugged. "The guy's a government employee, not a
hedge fund manager."

"Yeah." Chrisafoulis nodded. "That's what I was thinking.
So then what do you make of this?"

He pulled out another couple of pages. He slid them to
Hauck. "He's got this other account . . . Not in Greenwich.
Not with his wife's name on it. But up in Hartford. Bank of
America. And just him on it—no one else."

Hauck leaned over the detective's shoulder and read.

"I mean, the guy's a federal attorney, right? So I figured, he's
just parking away a few bucks for the kids' college fund."

At the top, where the current balance was, it read $427,651. Hauck stopped on it.

Freddy Munoz was grinning. "Like you said, LT, the guy's just a government employee, right?"

"Check out the size of these deposits," Steve said, sliding a pencil down the page. "Forty-three K, thirty-one thousand. Twenty-eight . . . And the withdrawals . . . Generally the same— fifteen to twenty grand. Why does a government lawyer keep a private account with twice what they have jointly to their names stashed away there and totally separate from his wife?"

"And more to the point, where does a guy who pulls in ninety, maybe a hundred grand even get those kinds of funds?"

In itself, it didn't prove anything. It could all be family money he didn't want to commingle with his wife's. Or invest- ment income from something they hadn't found yet.

"I don't know," Hauck said, "but I think we're going to find out from Wendy."

"Before you do . . ." Chrisafoulis took a last sheet out of the folder. "There might be one last thing you want to ask her, sir."

CHAPTER THIRTY-SIX

Wendy Sanger was heading back up the walk to her house from the mailbox, leafing through envelopes, when Hauck pulled up, taking her by surprise.

He waved to her and smiled.

"You have a few moments to talk?" Hauck asked, stepping out of the car with a manila folder tucked under his arm.

"Sure . . ." Her reply was a little wary, sensing something. "Just watch out for the obstacle course." A tricycle and a plastic hockey net were strewn on the lawn.

Inside, Wendy offered some coffee, which he declined. But he followed her into the kitchen and asked how she was doing while she brewed herself a cup of tea.

"I can barely even get back to the basic things yet." She shrugged. "The wash, shopping . . . Haley's been taking it all pretty hard. She and David always had this bond. *Ethan* . . ." She stopped, pulled out a bottle of honey, stood with her back to the counter. "He still doesn't fully understand. How do I explain this to a six-year-old with Asperger's? It's his first day back at school today. It's like, you try to get everything back to normal, but then there's this huge, empty hole that just comes at you . . ."

"I know," Hauck said, "it's gonna take some time. Listen, I came out here because there are a few things I need to ask you, Ms. Sanger. A couple of things have come up."

Wendy poured her tea, motioned Hauck over to an old farm-house table in the breakfast nook overlooking the backyard. They sat down. "Okay . . ."

Hauck opened the envelope. "Did you know someone named Keith Kramer, Ms. Sanger? He may have been a friend of your husband's?"

"Keith. Yes. I know him. A little." She seemed surprised at the name. "He and David went to Wesleyan together. They kept up a bit, I suppose."

Hauck shifted. "Did you know that Mr. Kramer was killed, Ms. Sanger? Last week."

"*What?* Keith? *No* . . ." She put down her mug, clearly shocked. "Oh, my God, that's terrible. What a horrible coincidence. I don't think he and David had too much to do with each other lately. I think he worked for one of the casinos up-state. *How?*"

"He was shot. In the back of the head. Up where he lived in Madison. His body was found strewn in the woods."

"Oh, God, how horrible, Lieutenant." Wendy shot a hand to her mouth. "I think he had kids," she said after a few sec-onds, "a little younger than ours . . . I think his wife was in the real estate business or something. Joan, I think . . ." Then Wendy looked up at him, her face suddenly darkening. "You're not thinking this is a coincidence, are you, Lieutenant? *David. Keith* . . . That's why you're here."

Hauck asked her, "Do you mind telling me the last time you and your husband heard from Mr. Kramer, Ms. Sanger?"

"You mean David, not me. We hadn't socialized in years. I don't know. Keith was sort of an easygoing guy. He never seemed to have to have a lot of ambition. He was sort of a math whiz, if I recall, back in school. But most of their friends, they'd gone on to something. Wall Street. Med school. Teaching. The past couple of years, I'm not sure he and David had that much to do with each other. We went to dinner with them and a few friends in Stamford . . . I don't know, two or three years . . ."

Hauck took out the folders Steve had prepared. He opened one and removed the stack of bound pages marked up with yellow lines. "Don't be alarmed," he said, "but these are your husband's cell phone records, Ms. Sanger. This is all pretty routine stuff in a case involving an unsolved homicide."

Wendy wet her lips and took the pages onto her lap. She leafed through a few. "Okay . . ."

"The yellow highlighting you're seeing is all from the same cell phone number. Keith Kramer's cell. As you can see, the calls go back over a period of several months."

Wendy stared.

"You'd have to say they'd clearly been in touch a bit more than you suspected?"

She picked up the records, eyes wide, as seemingly in shock at the dates and the frequency of the calls. Her gaze came back to Hauck, unsure. "I don't understand."

"What can you tell me about Mr. Kramer, Ms. Sanger?"

She shrugged. "*Keith?* I don't know if I can tell you much of anything, Lieutenant. Like I said, he went to school with David—I think they were roommates at some point. But that was twenty years ago. He never really got going on the career track, was all I knew. He was one of those people who seemed to always go back to what it was like in college. You know, who never quite grew up. Still wanted to always get together. Watch the games, play cards. I mean, he was harmless, nice. He wouldn't get involved in anything. What does any of this have to do with David?"

"Did your husband ever talk about him?" Hauck asked. "Was there anything you can remember that would make them possibly be in touch?"

"No. I mean, once in a while, David would say he and a couple of his old friends were getting together or playing cards. Maybe David went down there once or twice when he stayed up in Hartford. It's possible once or twice he may have visited him at the casino. But that was all few and far between. We weren't even friends. I don't even know his kids' names." She shook her head and her eyes went back to the records. *"You're saying that what happened to David and Keith is somehow linked?"*

"I don't know. I don't want to alarm you right now. But you'd agree it's pretty unusual your husband was in such frequent contact with this person and then kept it all from you?"

"It is unusual," Wendy said. "David didn't hide things from me. But my husband's death was an accident, Lieutenant. You said so yourself. What ever happened to that girl who was drowned . . . ?"

"I want you to look at something else, Ms. Sanger," Hauck said, pulling out the copy of Sanger's Bank of America account in Hartford.

Wendy's face turned white. She looked back at Hauck. "Where did you get this?"

"Like I said, we're dealing with an unsolved homicide, Ms. Sanger."

She put a hand to her brow and nodded. "I just saw this . . . For the first time. Just the other day. A couple of David's colleagues from work brought down a bunch of stuff from his office." She looked up, confused. "I don't know what to make of it."

"You never knew about this account?"

"No." She shook her head. "No. I don't even know if I should be saying anything more to you, Lieutenant. I want to help, but I don't know what's going on here. My husband was a good man. He was a good husband and a caring dad, and he spent his life fighting for people, when other people he knew were just into making money or putting together deals. I don't know where you're going with this. I'm starting to feel like *I* should have some kind of lawyer . . . ?"

"Listen," Hauck said. He noticed her hands fidgeting and he couldn't help but reach out. "I'm not your enemy, Ms. Sanger. I want to find out what happened to your husband just as much as you, and the last thing I want to do is drag his name through anything untoward. I promise you that."

Wendy nodded.

"But your husband was depositing sizable amounts of cash in an account that he kept secret from you. An account you're not even a signee on. And that should worry you a bit. If this kind of thing got dug out by the press, or into the hands of someone else looking at this, such as the FBI, they're not going to be nearly as friendly, and you just don't know where that would lead. So I think you should talk to me, Ms. Sanger, if there's anything you know. Anything you might be holding back from me. Do you have any idea where these sorts of funds might've come from?"

"*No!*" Wendy's eyes grew fearful. "I only found out about this two days ago. I don't have a goddamn idea what it all means, Lieutenant. We didn't keep things from each other."

Hauck shrugged. "I'm sorry, but that's not the way it seems."

"*I can see that's not the way it seems, Lieutenant!* And you can see how it's making me feel."

Hauck nodded, shuffled the pages into a neat pile, and leaned forward, arms on knees. "I'm afraid there's more." He opened another folder and took out a fastened sheath of papers. "This is a MasterCard account your husband kept, Ms. Sanger. Have you ever seen it before?"

Wendy Sanger looked at it. She stared back glassily. "No."

"You see those charges? DealMeIn.com. Pokerbuff Online. Some of the charges run as high as five thousand dollars."

"I see that, Lieutenant!" Wendy Sanger nodded.

"Listen, I know how hard this is. I know exactly what you've been through. But your husband's friend, Kramer, he was executed, Ms. Sanger. He worked for the Pequot Woods Casino and your husband had been in touch with him several times over the weeks before they both died. I don't know what was going on. I don't know if he was advising him on some matter he wanted to keep quiet, in his capacity as an attorney—though these bank deposits and Internet charges don't lend a lot of credence to that. But there's something I've got to ask you and you've got to be truthful with me."

She nodded.

"Did your husband have some kind of gambling problem, Ms. Sanger?"

CHAPTER THIRTY-SEVEN

*A*s Hauck headed back to the office, his cell phone rang.

It was Munoz. "You're not gonna like this one, Lieutenant . . . You sitting down?"

"I'm driving, Freddy. What do you got?"

"*Vega,*" his detective said. "He's been released from jail."

Hauck almost rammed the car in front of him. *"What?"*

"You heard it. His case was thrown out. The evidence against him, a Glock 8 and a set of prints taken off the steering wheel, was ruled tampered with and corrupt. An FBI lab team out of the city seemed to lose sight of it for a day. A district judge in Bridgeport just came down with the decision."

Hauck pulled over to the side. He flashed back to Vega's laugh. *When I'm out, you come to me and I'll teach you about two and two . . .*

His blood was boiling. "You say an FBI lab flubbed it?"

"Starting to sound familiar, doesn't it? You remember what I said about being covered up in shit . . ."

"Yeah, Freddy, I remember. And I think I know just where to go to find the shovel."

. . .

Stan Taylor was at his desk grabbing a late sandwich when Hauck's call came through. "Glad you called, Lieutenant. Just having a bite of a late lunch. What gives?"

"The name Nelson Vega mean anything to you, Agent Taylor?"

"Vega?" The agent continued chewing. "Isn't he some gangbanger out of Bridgeport? Part of a drug search bust where he tried to shoot it out with a state cop?"

"That's the one. I just wanted to let you know, if you already didn't—the case against him just got bounced. Evidence tampering. He was given a free pass out of jail."

The FBI man snorted in disgust. "Can't say I like hearing that sort of thing any more than you, Lieutenant. The guy sounds like a total piece of shit. But what's it got to do with me?"

"Vega's the head of DR-17. They were the ones who pulled off the drive-by at the Exxon station."

"*Hmmph*. Now that doesn't help the home team, does it? You say he's already out. Out from where?"

"You ought to know, Special Agent. Your name was on the list of people who went to visit him in prison."

Taylor almost choked. He cleared his throat and it took a few seconds to recover. "Now before you let your little mind go crazy, Lieutenant, we were just pumping him for information, same as you."

"I can take being played, Agent Taylor. But not from you. The guy was looking at twenty years in federal lockup and he basically just laughed in our faces when we offered to help him out and told us to hit the road. You know what that tells me, Special Agent? It doesn't exactly sit well with me that he farmed out this job to one of his soldiers and ten days later an FBI lab team bungles the evidence and he's out free. *Is Vega your man?*"

"Maybe he knew what was in the works," the FBI man answered, tap dancing. "Lawyers have a funny way of sharing that kind of information with their clients, Lieutenant."

"*This was a hit*. He handled this job for someone, Taylor." Hauck couldn't conceal the anger in his voice. "All that stuff about Josephina Ruiz was just a cover. Sanger was the intended target all along."

For a moment, the FBI agent didn't respond, Hauck's accusation sinking in. "We're talking about a U.S. attorney, Lieutenant. I hope to hell you're not looking here."

"You didn't answer me. Is Nelson Vega a CI? *Is he your man?*" Hauck knew as soon as the words escaped he had overstepped his bounds. It was more of an accusation than a question.

No doubt he'd be hearing it from Fitzpatrick before the end of the day.

"I realize you didn't call up for advice, Lieutenant," the FBI man finally answered, "but let me give you a little anyway, just to keep things in a civil tone. You didn't want us looking over your shoulder, so don't swallow a brick if we work along parallel to you. I don't know what the deal on Vega is, but your tone is starting to ruin my lunch, so I'm gonna sign off now, before you get yourself in some real shit. I'll be sure to pass along your best to AC Sculley, Lieutenant."

CHAPTER THIRTY-EIGHT

A return call from Joe Raines of the Pequot Woods Resort was waiting for Hauck when he got back. He went into his office and shut the door.

"Mr. Raines. Thanks for calling me back."

"Just what is it I can do for you, Lieutenant?"

"I'm investigating the death of David Sanger." Hauck hurried behind his desk and scrambled for a pad of his notes. "You may have heard, he was a United States attorney who was killed down here in a drive-by a couple of weeks back."

"Hard to miss all that," Raines said. "How can I be of help?"

"Chief Pecoric, from up in Madison, gave me your name. I know you have your own situation going on up there. I had a photo and some credit card information on Sanger sent up to you . . ."

"Yes, I got them. And I'm familiar with the thing you're talking about. Just how does it relate to us?"

"Turns out," Hauck said, "Keith Kramer and Sanger were acquainted."

"Now that's a discouraging coincidence." The security chief let out a disgruntled sigh.

"If you take it as a coincidence at all. In fact, it turns out they were friends. The phone records indicate they'd both been in contact quite a bit over the past several months. I asked in my fax whether Sanger had been up to the casino recently."

"My impression was that you were dealing with a gang-connected killing down there, Lieutenant. Something about revenge . . ."

"Seemed that way. But it's starting to look as if there might be something else. That maybe some kind of gambling connection might have existed between the two of them, resulting in what's happened."

"You want to map that out a little clearer?" Raines said. "You can imagine how that makes me feel. Our employees are strictly forbidden from any gambling activity at the casino, Lieutenant Hauck. Or outside. That's a hard and fast rule. Unless you're implying something else was going on between them here, Lieutenant . . . ?"

"Two people are dead, Mr. Raines. Two people who were systematically in touch. One, we've uncovered, might have had a gambling habit that he kept secret. The other worked as a table supervisor in your casino. You connect the dots."

"I see."

"It's also possible Kramer might have been communicating with Sanger in Sanger's capacity as a U.S. attorney. Perhaps about something he'd been working on or uncovered."

Raines paused. "Just what are you implying, Lieutenant?"

"I'm not implying anything," Hauck said. "But that's why it's important to me to find out if Mr. Sanger had recently been up there, Mr. Raines. Or anything you can tell me about Keith Kramer that would be helpful in putting this together."

"Alright. I'll tell you just what I told Chief Pecoric, Lieutenant . . . Keith was a solid employee of the resort who never once drew any attention in the wrong way. Let's see . . . His friends here seemed to suggest he'd been acting a bit nervous lately. Financial pressures. Apparently his wife wasn't bringing in the bacon the way she had once been. Keith did always like to live a little big, Lieutenant, a bit more than others on a similar salary grade. He'd been pushing for an early review. Which was turned down. A month ago."

"Why?"

"We run a sizable operation here, Lieutenant. There are some sixty-eight pit supervisors at the Pequot Woods. Everything's handled at the scheduled time. I can pass you along to personnel if you like. But you mentioned a gambling connection?"

"Like I said, I'm just trying to connect the dots." There was something about Raines that seemed typically evasive. Standard-issue security. "Did they happen to connect on whether Sanger had ever been a guest at the resort?"

Raines said, "I ran the credit cards you sent me. And I showed his photo around the front desk and the casino staff. We have him in our records as up here *once*. Last August. Over a year ago. I can send you the details, if you like, but the gist is, he stayed one night, basic accommodations, picked up a tab at the bar, nothing from the dining rooms. No record of him charging up any playing cash against his account. No special courtesies . . ."

"*Just once?*" Hauck said, surprised.

"Sorry, Lieutenant, if that's not what you're looking to hear. He did order an in-room movie. We can check the kind of film it was, if that's where your investigation is going."

"No." Hauck let out a disappointed sigh.

"Look, Lieutenant," Raines said, easing up, "like you said, we *are* dealing with our own situation here. Truth is, I don't know why Keith Kramer was killed. I don't know whether he was robbed, if he owed someone money, if he was cheating on his wife, or if he had some kind of drug habit . . . I'm pretty satisfied that it had nothing to do with his work here.

"But what I am *keenly* interested in is that this isn't twisted or magnified in any way that—I think you know where I'm heading—affects the ongoing interests of the resort. We have our own way of handling things up here, with the tribal police, using whatever influence we have to keep this as quiet as possible. As you can imagine, stories and speculation of this kind do not serve our business at all. Especially ones backed up purely by supposition and innuendo. I figure you understand what I mean?"

Hauck tapped his foot on his desk. "I think I understand it perfectly, sir."

"So do we have an accord? Anything comes up you think would be a good thing for us to know, I'd appreciate hearing it from you. As, likewise, I promise you will from me. These tribal elders don't respond well to the long arm of the law, if you know what I mean . . ."

"I think I do."

"Nice talking to you, Lieutenant. I wish you best of luck in solving your case."

As soon as he hung up, Hauck called in Munoz and Chrisafoulis.

"You and Steve keep looking into Sanger. Find out if anyone confirms about his gambling. Check with his case files if Keith Kramer was mentioned in any way on anything he may have been looking into up there."

"You got it, boss."

"And look into the Pequot Woods. The two of them were connected. There's some record of it somewhere. You find out why."

CHAPTER THIRTY-NINE

Joe Raines put down the phone and stared out his office window at the brown November day.

He didn't like where this was heading.

All his life, in the army, on the force, in private life, he'd done people favors. The kind of favors no one wanted to do. That was how a guy like him rose. He got his boots dirty. He protected people and watched their backs.

Now, he wondered, who the hell was watching *his*?

He got up, buzzed his secretary to say he'd be back in a while, headed out of his office and down the corridor for a smoke. He went past what was known at the company as the Flight Room, behind two secure doors. The room contained sixty large monitors focusing on every gambling venue in the casino—every table, every machine, every restaurant. Every place money changed hands.

And in front of every cluster of screens a trained security specialist sat watching them.

Every action was observed. Every face in the betting room noted. Every known cheat or card counter checked against a profile. Every dealer too—to make sure he or she had not motioned to a player or made some unusual eye contact. That they shuffled the decks properly. Every supervisor was observed too, to make sure the table counts were handled correctly.

The finest security money could buy—tens of millions. To protect who? Raines shook his head. A bunch of fucking Indians . . .

It was from there, the Flight Room, that he had watched Keith Kramer leave the grounds the week before. From there that he had made the call, switching to an outside camera, watched him open his car.

Caught sight of the black Escalade that pulled out behind him.

Raines slipped through a door to the outside.

The doorway led to the third-floor balcony. It overlooked one of the lakes on the resort's property. He took out his cell and lit up a smoke. There was a chill in the air. Leaves had changed. He'd never get used to it up here, in New England. He was Southern to the roots. From Georgia. Hell, his great-grandparents fought fucking Indians. Now he was protecting them. He always felt out of place up here in the cold.

He punched in a number, took a deep drag, waited for the line to connect.

When it finally did, Raines knew the person would immediately recognize the number.

"Can you talk?"

"I'm in Hartford," the voice replied. "Heading into the capitol. Let me pull up on the steps." He came back on a few seconds later. "Go on."

"Just letting you know—I just had a call you might find interesting. I think you might know from whom."

"Hauck?"

"He was asking about Sanger," Raines said, looking over the new mansions lining the lake. *Indians,* he was thinking. *Billions. Who would have ever guessed?*

He flicked his cigarette butt over the edge and watched it disappear. "Seems he's put together the connection to the Kramer guy."

CHAPTER FORTY

*T*hat night, as Hauck was getting ready to leave, Vern Fitzpatrick knocked on the glass.

"Glad I was able to catch you, Ty . . ."

The chief had wavy white hair and a long, ruddy face. He had run the Greenwich force for twenty years because he'd always been a calming influence around town, a steady voice when tempers flared, and worked well with the local government. When he started, Greenwich was a sleepy commuter town with a single movie theater and an old-fashioned five-and-dime store on Main Street. He had seen the place go through its share of changes over the years.

He smiled. "Just got a holiday call from some of your favorite people, Ty."

Hauck looked at him and nodded. Sculley. Taylor. "You don't have to say it, Vern."

The chief came over and took a seat. "Maybe I *do*. Maybe I do have to say it, Ty. Maybe I have to remind you that you're not the only one who wants to see an outcome on this case. You're also not the only one feeling pressure here."

"I realize that, Vern, but you also understand, Morales may have squeezed the trigger, but Nelson Vega was behind it and someone's got his back. And if it wasn't Taylor and Sculley, who had access to him in jail, you tell me who? Josephina Ruiz was just a diversion. This whole thing had to do with David Sanger and that other guy up in Madison, something they knew about the Pequot Woods. I'm glad they called to say hello, but that doesn't change things."

"That wasn't why they called, Ty. They were only letting me know . . ."

"Letting you know what?"

The chief crossed his legs. "That APB we put out on Morales . . . ? He turned up."

Hauck looked at him, surprised.

"Down in the Dominican Republic—with a bullet between the eyes. Seems he'd picked up some hooker who either robbed him or was trying to tell him he'd gotten a bit too rough. I guess there was quite a stash of drugs and booze around. The locals down there are looking into it . . ."

"You know as well as I do Morales was only the triggerman, Vern."

"Yeah." The chief sighed. "I know that." He raised himself up. "You want to take it further, it's your call. Or you can just say we got the guy, Ty. You saw him yourself, plain as day. However it happened, the sonovabitch got what he deserved. I bet Wendy Sanger might feel about the same if you asked her, without tearing up the floorboards and potentially harming a good man's reputation to find out more." Fitz smoothed out his trousers. "Sanger and this other guy were friends; why don't we just leave it at that. No one's going to argue about a case of revenge gone wrong. You see what I'm saying, Ty?"

"Even if it's not?"

"Even if it's not, yeah." The chief stepped over to the door. "But you don't know that, Ty."

"It doesn't bother you, Vern, that a guy who tried to gun down a state trooper got the case against him dropped? Or that there's a Justice Department lawyer who had something going on with a pit boss up at the Pequot Woods and both of them are dead? And now the guy who pulled the trigger is dead too?"

"Just give it a little thought." Fitz opened the door but turned back. "You're asking if it bothers me that the person who came into our town and committed this horrible act is dead?" He rapped his knuckles against the glass. *"Yeah, it bothers me just fine!"*

CHAPTER FORTY-ONE

Morales's death put things on hold for a while.

The headlines ran that the triggerman in the Greenwich drive-by shooting had been killed. They still didn't have a connection to DR-17, but the newspaper article found in the truck and the connection to Sunil seemed to tie it up neatly enough.

Steve Chrisafoulis was waiting for Hauck as he came in the next day. "Are we shut down?" the detective asked.

"I don't know," Hauck said. "Why?"

Steve tapped together another set of papers. The smile sneaking through his thick mustache suggested he'd found something important. "Just thought I'd show you how I spent the weekend, Ty . . ."

He followed Hauck into the office and spread out a couple of piles on the conference table across from Hauck's desk. "This time I went after it a different way. I went back and cross-ran Sanger's social. I figured you can get credit under any name . . ." He paged through the first stack. "You see this Amex file . . ."

"Yeah."

"Took me all weekend to find it. The damn thing's made out to a D. Mark Sanger. The sonovabitch had it mailed to the god-damn U.S. attorney's office in Hartford."

Hauck paged through the statements. There wasn't a whole lot of activity on them.

It took maybe a second for Hauck to realize just why.

They were all gambling charges. Online poker sites. Casino cash advances. The whole credit card.

David Sanger had a life he kept secret from his wife and kids.

But that wasn't what had begun to make Hauck's temperature rise.

Steve drew his eye to a highlighted item. *October 17.* Just a few days before Sanger was killed.

A $327.61 charge from the Pequot Woods Resort and Casino.

"Turn the page," Chrisafoulis said with a slight smile, "there's more."

Hauck did, flipping back through statements from September, August, and prior. There were at least eight transactions highlighted. All visits to the Pequot Woods Resort. Some even had corresponding cash advances drawn against the card. Some ran as high as $10,000. Charges for lodging, meals.

It was clear Raines had been lying.

He would have known this. Sanger's name would have come up. His face would have been well known.

"And that's not all." The canny detective flipped a few pages. "I cross-checked the card against Sanger's bank account at Bank of America that we found up in Hartford. Check it out . . ." He drew the tip of his pen to a charge. "You see this Amex charge for eight hundred and forty-seven dollars on April fourth?"

Hauck nodded.

"Take a look what happened April *fifth*. In his bank account."

Hauck ran his eye down the column.

There was a deposit for $12,500 listed there.

"Here too," Steve said, pointing. June 10. Sanger had withdrawn $10,000 from his account that night he visited the resort. The next day he put $22,000 back in.

"It's a whole pattern," Steve said. "Withdrawals one day and the next day he hits the resort. Then deposits, sometimes spread out over the next few days. We're talking tens of thousands, Lieutenant. *Lucky* sonovabitch, wouldn't you say?"

"*Blessed.*" Hauck glanced again over the bank statements. It was showing over $400,000. Sanger's secret life. One he had gone to great lengths to conceal.

Sanger and Kramer clearly had something going on up there together. The two friends, who barely kept up with each other.

Both dead.

"So what's next, Lieutenant?" Steve Chrisafoulis shut the folder and looked at him. The papers had this thing as solved.

"Maybe it's time to try my own luck up there," Hauck replied.

CHAPTER FORTY-TWO

From the thousands of acres of rolling woods ceded to the Pequot tribe two hundred years ago as their tribal homeland, the Pequot Woods Resort rose like a towering glass teepee, reflecting the sun across the banks of the Thames River.

Back in 1996, the United States Supreme Court, having recognized that Native American tribes, as "sovereign entities," could open gaming facilities free of state regulation, the tribe, along with two large gaming and real estate conglomerates, TRV and Armbruster International, built the spectacular Pequot Woods, housing the largest gaming facility in the world. Not to be outdone, the Pequots' natural enemies, the Mohegans, on the other side of the river, did the same. Now, two hundred years later, the two warring tribes were battling all over again for the gambling dollars of New Yorkers and Bostonians with the two largest casinos east of Las Vegas.

The setting sun glinted amber as Hauck wound his Explorer around a bend and onto the casino's vast grounds.

He left the car at check-in in front of the lobby. A pretty, dark-haired receptionist in a well-tailored uniform came out from behind the reception desk.

"Mr. Raines is expecting you," she told him. "I'll have your bag taken up to your room and I'll escort you to see him now."

"Sounds fine," Hauck said, smiling back at her. He tucked his sunglasses into his jacket.

She informed him her name was Katie and led him up a wide, carpeted staircase rising from the lobby, a vast, glass-enclosed atrium with lava-colored rock formations rising spectacularly to the sky. They shared a little small talk on the way, about the casino, whether Hauck had been there before, the new celebrity-chef steak place that had just opened. Hauck couldn't help but admire her nice, long legs.

On the second floor, she took him down a long hallway to a door marked AUTHORIZED PERSONNEL ONLY. "We call it the Flight Room," Katie said. "Mr. Raines asked if you would meet him here."

She put an electronic key in the door and opened it. Hauck found himself in a massive, darkened room. The space was filled with hundreds of video monitors, many suspended high above, displaying wide angles of the entire gaming operation. Most were smaller-sized screens in workstations that seemed to be focused on individual betting tables, and observing them were security personnel in headsets.

Dozens and dozens of them.

It almost took Hauck's breath away.

The hush of low-key voices penetrated the air like an air-port flight tower.

"Everybody has the same reaction the first time." Katie smiled, observing him. "We have the largest security operation in the East."

A tall, lanky man in a dark sport jacket who had been talk-ing to one of the security personnel came over to Hauck. "Thank you, Katie."

She smiled and backed out of the room, saying, "Have a good stay."

"I'm Joe Raines," the man said. Raines was about fifty, with a pockmarked face, salt-and-pepper hair, sort of a military bearing, like a man who had worked himself up from the ranks.

"Ty Hauck," Hauck said. His shake was firm but cool.

"Impressive?" the security man remarked.

Hauck took in a wide scan. "Yes, it is."

"People always stare a bit their first time. Over four thousand slots, six hundred and eighty gaming tables. You know what the average daily take in an operation this size is?"

Hauck shrugged. "No idea."

Raines pursed his bloodless lips. "Thirty-one point six mil. Not counting food and beverage, of course. Weekends you could double that."

"I'll look for that one the next time I'm on *Jeopardy*." Hauck chuckled.

Raines gave him a smile. "And you know what the one thing is that holds the whole thing all together, Lieutenant?" He pointed to a large screen focused on a table of blackjack players. "Check out up there . . ."

On the screen, a man in a cowboy hat and aviators drummed his fingers while he studied his hand. The dealer showed a jack. The man in the hat had what seemed a troubled expression, deciding what to do.

"*That*," Joe Raines stated. "That it's the player who has to bust first—not the house. That the poor bastard has no idea in the world what to do because of that ten card showing there. That's our edge. Our *only* edge, Lieutenant. If he knows the dealer's holding a five, everything switches back against the house. But because he doesn't, we keep the advantage."

On the screen, Cowboy Hat tapped the table for a card and

the dealer flipped over a king. He busted. The dealer took in the man's chips. The next player in line stuck with a king and a seven, seventeen, and the dealer flipped over his hole card and revealed a six. Sixteen. He had to hit. He flipped over a ten and busted himself. Raines smiled knowingly. "You see . . ."

"You mind being a little clearer on what you're trying to tell me?" Hauck asked, drawing his gaze back from the screen.

"You care for something to drink?" Raines asked. "A beer? Soft drink? Something stronger, perhaps?"

Hauck shook his head. "Thanks. Still on duty."

"That's what I figured. In this job you have to size people up quickly and you look like a man who's serious about his work."

"I think we both know why I'm up here, Mr. Raines," Hauck said, growing impatient at all the dancing around.

"Yes, we do, Lieutenant. *Sanger* . . . " Raines nodded. His eyes were hooded and gunmetal gray. "Keith Kramer. Like I said, you upset that balance"—Raines looked at him—"it disrupts everything. You understand what I'm trying to tell you, Lieutenant?" He motioned around. "Everything you see here, all these fancy screens, these trained people, tens of millions of dollars—all of it's just here to protect that one thing. So that what that dealer has facing down on the table remains in doubt. All it takes is one bad egg on the inside, and this whole big show doesn't mean shit. Are you understanding?"

"I think I'm starting to see it," Hauck replied.

Raines had thick eyebrows and a serious conviction in his gaze. "And there are several different ways to upset that perfect balance, Lieutenant."

"You mean from the inside."

"Yes. A dealer can execute what in the trade we call a 'flash.' Flash a glimpse of his hole card to an accomplice at the table.

Doesn't take a whole lot of skill. That's what these operators are trained to look for. Or he can simply blink or just twitch his nose. A twitch to signal his accomplice to draw a card. Maybe only a moistening of the lips for him to hold. That's why we watch tapes of every one of our dealers in action, over and over, observing their mannerisms."

Hauck started to have a clearer sense of where this was going.

"Then there's what we call capping, Lieutenant. And pinching. Placing more chips over a winning bet than it deserves. Maybe substituting a black five-hundred-dollar chip for a green. Or taking chips off the table in a loss. We monitor the one-on-one tables most closely. Look to see if the same player shows up with the same dealer on a regular basis . . ."

"What were Kramer and Sanger up to, Mr. Raines?" Hauck asked, growing tired of dancing around.

"Almost there." Raines smiled. "There's one more technique I didn't mention. It's called a false shuffle. A dealer, say one motivated to participate in such a scam, slips a series of prerecorded, unshuffled cards on the top of his deck. It's called a slug."

Raines took out a handheld remote control. He flicked it toward the screen at the desk where he and Hauck were stationed. A video recording came on. It was of a man in an open shirt and blazer at a table with his back to the screen. Short hair, sunglasses. He was the single player at the table. Blackjack. The dealer was a middle-aged man with bushy graying hair and thick black glasses, in his uniform of a white shirt and red vest. The first hand, the player with his back to the camera lost. He took a sip of his drink. The next hand, he drew nineteen. Won. A light bettor. Only a couple of chips.

The next hand he upped his bet significantly.

To Hauck it appeared he pushed in several thousand dollars, though he wasn't familiar with all the denominations. This time, the player was dealt two face cards. *Bingo*. To Hauck's surprise, he left all his winnings on the table and the dealer dealt again. *Blackjack,* this time. The man in the blazer quietly raked in his winnings. *Thousands*. Then he stepped away from the table. All in all, it took less than one minute.

As he did, for the first time Hauck could see his face.

It was David Sanger.

It was like a jackhammer bludgeoned him. He'd been so focused on the dealer and what Raines was trying to show him, he hadn't seen.

The security chief stood up and flicked off the screen. A haughty smile on his face that at the same time was both condescending and all-knowing.

"Why don't you go up to your room for a bit and relax. I'll meet you down in the casino in the blackjack section at eight o'clock. I'll give you a glimpse of what you're after there, first-hand."

CHAPTER FORTY-THREE

*H*auck's room was large, on the thirty-second floor, with a huge Jacuzzi tub in the bathroom and a wide-screen TV. The view looked out over the river. It was dark and all Hauck could see were flickering lights. A pretty floor concierge escorted him down the hall and handed him his key.

Hauck stretched out on the bed and flipped on CNN on the TV. A cyclone was ravaging the Pacific, near the Philippines, killing thousands. A report from Baghdad showed a grown man crying that his family still did not have power. "How do you expect us to work?" he raged. "I ran a cement factory. Now I'm a ditch digger . . ."

He tried to absorb what he had just seen. Sanger and Kramer—friends from college; had they been hooked up in some kind of elaborate betting scheme? Had they gotten together to cheat the casino?

A United States attorney?

Hauck thought back to Sanger's hidden bank account. It pained him a little—from what he knew of him, from what his wife had told him and what he had seen at the funeral—that this seemingly "good" guy, a person of dedication and achievement, a devoted dad, could have been caught up in something like this. It was dangerous business, taking on a casino. Casinos have their own way of dealing with things.

Still, it didn't justify getting them killed.

Before eight, he put on a white shirt and corduroy jacket and made his way downstairs. At the entrance to the casino off the lobby, he was hit by the loud jangle of slot machines turning, the chime of bets paying off, the smell of cigarette smoke.

He wound through the crowded maze of tables and bettors and found the blackjack section. He spotted Raines in between tables, chatting with one of the staff.

The security chief saw him and came over. "Had a nice rest? How's the room? Okay?"

"Just fine." Hauck didn't much relish the idea of accepting any of the casino's courtesies. "You said you were going to show me firsthand?"

Raines grinned. "Always work, huh? C'mon, I've got a table waiting over here."

He took Hauck to a nearby blackjack table. There was a twenty-dollar minimum bet. The table was empty and there was an attractive female dealer who seemed to be waiting for them.

"You play?" Raines inquired, motioning for Hauck to take a seat.

"Nickels and dimes." Hauck shrugged, pulling out a chair across from the cute dealer, casting her a polite smile.

"This is Josie," Raines said, taking a seat next to Hauck. "She's actually working here while she gets her degree. This is Lieutenant Hauck, Josie. From Greenwich, right? The lieutenant here is looking to learn a little bit about certain dealing techniques we discussed."

The pretty dealer nodded. She had long brown hair braided back in an unassuming style. What seemed like a sexy figure hidden under her plain white blouse and vest. Liquid brown eyes.

"How're you doing today?" she said to Hauck, almost businesslike, and began to deftly shuffle together several decks.

"I'm doing fine, thanks, Josie."

Raines removed some chips from his jacket and pushed them in front of Hauck. He laid out two even stacks. "Nickels and dimes, you said. Here's a little stake from the hotel. For demonstration purposes only, of course . . ." He patted him on the back.

The nickels were six brown fifty-dollar chips, and the dimes were two black hundreds.

Hauck looked at Raines uncomfortably.

He kept his eye on Josie as she raked in the cards from the shoe and reshuffled them into the new, large deck. Hauck wasn't exactly a studied eye—he'd played a little poker in college—but he didn't spot anything irregular. Neatly, Josie merged the decks into the shoe.

"Cut, Lieutenant?"

"Sure." Hauck cut the deck in half in the middle.

Raines tapped the table. "Place your bet."

Hauck pushed forward a chip. A fifty. The lowest he had.

Josie dealt out a ten and then a seven. *Seventeen.* She showed an eight. Raines shifted around his chair to face him.

"*Good.*" Hauck held up his hand.

Raines said, "Our guest stays pat."

Josie turned over her hole card. A jack. *Eighteen.* She didn't react. Raines sighed and twitched his mustache. "Bad luck, Lieutenant. Try again."

"Your funds." Hauck shrugged resignedly.

He pushed across another fifty. This time Hauck was dealt a nine and a five. Josie showed a king. He looked at her as if he could spot some clue in her eyes. He brushed his fingers toward him, indicating another card. She turned over an eight.

He busted.

Josie's pink polished nails gathered in his chip. "Sorry, Lieutenant."

She shot a quick glance toward Raines. The security man said, "I'm not sure our guest has found his rhythm."

Hauck put forward another chip. This time, Raines took ahold of his arm. His gaze carried a steely importance to it. "Why not show a little confidence this time, Lieutenant?"

On the bet line, he stacked all of Hauck's remaining chips. *Four hundred dollars.*

Josie dealt Hauck a queen and a king. She showed a seven. Hauck stuck, of course, and she rolled over a ten. Seventeen.

"Lucky you!" Raines exclaimed, as if impressed. "What do you say, why not let it run again, Lieutenant?"

There was a manipulative sort of arrogance about the security chief Hauck didn't like. Not even a hint of uncertainty in his question. He smiled conspiratorially.

Hauck shrugged. "Your money."

Raines nodded and Josie dealt Hauck an eight and a three, turned over a six for herself.

Hauck paused. Eleven. The odds said he should double down.

"Have a little faith." Raines grinned. From his pocket he removed another large handful of chips. He stacked them next to Hauck's and began to count them out, matching the total for him to double down.

That meant sixteen hundred dollars on the table.

"Go ahead." Raines nodded to Josie. Her eyes met Hauck's and she turned over a nine. That made twenty. She flipped over an ace underneath. *Seventeen.*

Hauck was a winner. He made a move to pull in his chips.

"*Leave it!*" Raines said again. He had his hand on Hauck's wrist. Both sets of their eyes went to it. He nodded to Josie.

This time, she flipped Hauck an ace and then a queen. Blackjack. That paid one and a half to one. She met his eyes, no attempt at surprise in them, and stacked out two large piles of chips, this time mostly blacks and purple.

Thousands.

"A cinch, isn't it?" Raines said. "You see how fast it adds up when you're dealt with cards from a prearranged slug . . ."

Hauck looked at Josie. "You inserted it in at the top of the shuffle."

"Not at the top," Raines answered for her. "Anyone could've done that. Too easy for the cameras to detect. Besides, you cut. She inserted it several hands down. All it takes is a stare—a little eye contact between the dealer and the player when it's time . . ."

Josie stacked up Hauck's chips. Eight thousand dollars.

Raines lightly slapped Hauck on the back. "Quite a lucky night, Lieutenant. They're yours to spend, of course. For your amusement, around the casino."

Hauck turned to Raines. If disdain was an ocean, the entire room would be underwater now. He didn't like what the man was implying and didn't like the pile of chips in front of him now.

He stacked about half the chips, most of the purples and blacks, and slid them over to Josie.

"Tuition," he said with a wink.

Her brown eyes widened in surprise. She glanced at Raines, unsure; he seemed to nod begrudgingly, more of a dismissive twitch. "Thank you, Josie. Why don't you let the lieutenant and me have a few words now."

"Thank *you*." Josie smiled at Hauck, disbelieving her good fortune, sweeping the chips into her apron. She took her leave.

When they were alone, Hauck turned to Raines and stared in the security man's narrow eyes. "Why don't we skip the floor show and you tell me what happened to Kramer and David Sanger?"

"I have no idea what happened to them, Lieutenant. I could throw out a possibility or two—hypothetical, of course. A pit boss who's in dire need of money. An old friend from college with a bit of a gambling itch. Maybe more than that. Let's call it a compulsion. I've shown you the film. I think you understand where this little scenario is leading, Lieutenant."

"Who was the dealer?"

Raines shrugged and locked his hands. "That's a bit of a private matter, Lieutenant. In our little world here, we handle things our own way. All you have to know is we have the incidents on tape. Several, in fact. In themselves, they don't really prove anything. Like I said, all this is just a possibility . . .

"We run a very big business, Lieutenant, and it operates in the modern world. But at its heart, it still has an old-world way of handling things." Raines's mustache twitched. "You never know who you might upset, going up the chain. And you know how people of that ilk might possibly handle things. Remember what I said earlier, regarding balance?"

"You're saying you had them killed? For ripping the casino off."

"*Me?*" Raines screwed up his brow innocently. "This is the twenty-first century, Lieutenant. I'm only suggesting one scenario. You'll find, if you choose to dig around, there are a myriad of interests at play here. The consortiums who oversee the place. The Pequot tribe. Law enforcement. Even the state . . . It's hard to say *what* actually happens or who's truly affected"—Raines looked at him—"when certain people get in over their heads, you understand, Lieutenant?"

"You had them killed." Hauck wasn't sure who Raines's warning was directed at, Sanger and Kramer, or *him*. "You used that gang in Bridgeport as a cover. You're saying David Sanger risked whatever he had—his job, his family, his whole life's standing—" He looked around the floor and shook his head. "*For this* . . . ? This little *itch,* as you called it. What kind of person would do that, Raines?"

"I don't know, Lieutenant." Raines looked back at him. "What kind of person are you?"

Hauck's blood came to a stop.

The security man got up, his gaze never removing itself from Hauck's amid the noise and exultations all around. "You enjoy yourself here, Lieutenant. You let me know if you need anything." He raked in the rest of the chips, stacked them in two even piles. He pushed them over to Hauck. "Glad you came up. I hope it's been worthwhile. Be sure to call me if I can ever shed any further light on anything else."

Then he left, leaving the chips on the table, without putting out his hand.

CHAPTER FORTY-FOUR

*H*auck ate by himself in the trendy Italian café, then stopped at the bar situated underneath an enormous lava rock formation outside the entrance to the casino. At a nearby table, two young couples who had clearly been having a few were cheering on a Knicks game on the overhead TV.

Hauck ordered a Booker's bourbon before heading up to his room.

His blood was still heated from his meeting with Raines and the bourbon dulled his rancor. Raines's smirk and the implication that what had happened to Sanger and Kramer was simply the way the "myriad interests" here dealt with their dirty laundry didn't sit well with him. That Hauck was dealing with forces much larger than he could confront. The consortiums that ran the place. The tribe. The state.

Law enforcement . . . It would be difficult, he knew—more than difficult, maybe impossible—to tie Raines or the casino to Vega or DR-17. He could subpoena the tape Raines had shown him. *One of many,* he had said. He could look for Raines's number on Vega's cell phone.

But these people weren't exactly stupid.

He knew he would be pissing a lot of people off. Important

people. People in government. Not to mention Wendy Sanger. What he would do to her husband's reputation if he were to push this through.

What kind of man would risk all that? he'd asked Raines, and the security man had asked him back, *I don't know. What kind of man are you, Lieutenant?*

Hauck downed his bourbon, his attention shifting to the screen, where the Knicks were stumbling to another defeat in the final minutes.

He felt someone touch his arm.

He turned. It was Josie. The pretty dealer. No longer in uniform, but wearing a loose green halter top and a dangling chain around her neck, a pair of tight-fitting jeans. Which showed off the tantalizingly nice figure Hauck had suspected was there. Her hair was pulled up in a ponytail with bangs falling loosely over the sides of her face. Two gold hoops in her left ear.

"Heading to the library?" Hauck grinned.

"Not tonight," she said. "Semester break." Her round eyes shone with some amusement. "My shift's over. Four to ten. Kills me. Sometimes Steve here spots me a rum and coke before I head out. I saw you sitting here . . ."

Hauck shifted over. "Sit down."

"Sure . . ." Josie slipped in next to him. She nodded to the guy in the bolo tie behind the bar, who brought her her "usual." Hauck ordered one last nightcap as well. He noted a scent on her he found really appealing.

"To higher education," Hauck said, and tilted his drink.

"To financial aid." She laughed, clinking his glass. She took a sip. "I don't think I have to say how incredibly nice that was of you. It probably doesn't come as a surprise that I don't regularly get three-thousand-dollar tips on the job."

"It was his money," Hauck said. "Your charming boss."

"Not *my* boss," Josie was quick to say.

"Let's just leave it that I think you earned it a bit more than me. Pretty nifty hands . . . Somehow I think you didn't exactly learn that in college. What are you studying, anyway?"

"Sociology."

"Sociology!" Hauck laughed. "Well, you've got quite a good little laboratory going for yourself here."

"Six hours a day . . ." She shook her head and took a sip of her drink, her large brown eyes staying on him.

"So did you know him?" Hauck asked, taking a chance.

"Who?"

"The guy who worked here, who was killed. Keith Kramer?"

"Oh, that was horrible," Josie said. "Sure. Everyone knew Keith. He worked my tables from time to time. A good guy. Smart. Funny. I think he was educated. Not the normal kind of guy you find around here. Always backed up my counts, never hassled me or gave me any trouble."

"There's a story going around he might have been trying to cheat the house."

"*Keith?* If there is, it's gone around me . . . So that's what you're up here for? Keith? Mr. Raines called you 'lieutenant.' You're a cop, right?"

"I was a cop. I'm the head of detectives now. In Greenwich."

"I was thinking you might have been FBI or something. But Feds are always married. That's a rule, you know. And I don't see a ring."

Hauck reminded himself that he was on business up here, and a part of him was thinking maybe he should cut this conversation short and head back tonight, to avoid any complications.

Another part was enjoying hanging out with this pretty young thing.

"Divorced," he said. They were straying a bit from false shuffles and Keith Kramer. "And almost twice your age . . ."

"No chance," Josie said, sizing him up. "Anyway, you know what they say about age . . . Only matters when it comes to wine and cheese."

Hauck laughed. "And right now I'm feeling a little more like an old Barolo than a Beaujolais . . . I think I'm going to head upstairs." He signaled the bartender for the check.

Josie shrugged. "Your call." There was a gleam in her eye. He felt her brush next to his arm. A charge of energy ran through him. He couldn't help it. When she leaned closer, Hauck caught an intriguing view of what was underneath. And it was nice. *"Sure?"*

"Never sure." Hauck sighed with a smile. He stood up and tossed a few bills on the counter to cover both drinks. "Just *steady* . . . You make sure you put those funds to good use."

CHAPTER FORTY-FIVE

Upstairs, Hauck unbuttoned his shirt, sat on the couch in the large room, and turned on the flat-screen TV. He flicked to ESPN. There was a college basketball game on, and Hauck went over to the minibar and took out one last bourbon and some water and sat down to watch the game.

His blood coursed.

His mind drifted to Karen, to the gulf that lay between them now. He needed to put that all behind him. Whatever was happening was happening. He flashed to Josie again, pausing over the glimpse of her breasts underneath her halter and the thought that something between them might have been fun. *Your call* . . . Maybe she was still at the bar. Maybe he should go back down there. He brought his feet up on the table and rested his head on his knees.

There was a knock at the door. Housekeeping, maybe, to turn down the bed. Hauck got up and cracked it open. "*Yeah?*"

It was Josie.

Staring up at him, with a steady, not-at-all innocent look that communicated something she knew they both felt, which needed no words. She pushed the bangs on her face out of her eyes.

"I was just making sure there was nothing you might have forgotten down there."

"Like what?"

Josie shrugged. "Like second thoughts, maybe."

He looked in her smoky eyes. "Are you really just working here while you're going to school?"

She stared back at him. "Are you really up here just looking into false shuffles?"

Hauck didn't reply, just felt this undeniable urge rise up in him and the hair on his arms rise as she brushed by him into the room.

"This is bad, you know," Hauck said.

"Why?"

"I don't know." He shrugged. "Just bad."

"You know what they say about 'bad,' don't you . . ." She came up to him, so close they were almost touching, and curled a smile. "Only matters in wine and cheese."

Hauck looked at her, drew in the scent he found so intoxicating at the bar. He felt her arm go around his waist, the loose, breasts that she had been so willing to let him see pressed electrically against his bare chest. Everything he told to be quiet in himself sprang alive.

Josie's other hand draped across his cheek; she looked up at him and he kissed her. Her lips parted and her tongue gradually overcame the hesitancy of his indecision; his blood rose like a wave, surging against the feeling that he was doing something wrong to the person he loved . . .

Until he found his own hand sliding down the smooth curve of her back, inside the waist of her jeans. His breathing picking up and his foot shifting and the door to Room 3209 of the Pequot Woods Resort and Casino clicking shut.

CHAPTER FORTY-SIX

*H*auck opened his eyes the next morning. The light canted inside the shades, the slowly dawning sensation of what had taken place last night coming back to him like sun through a lifting fog.

Shit.

The clock read seven eighteen. He stirred. The covers were strewn haphazardly across the bed. *Oh, God, Ty, nice job*.

He shot up. Josie was gone. Her clothes picked off the floor where they had been scattered in the haste that had overtaken them last night. It had been delicious. He let himself fall back against the pillow, drift back to thoughts of the dreamy night they had shared. Once he had let her in there was no turning back. He had taken her right up against the wall, against the African animal print that was shifted sideways now. Once from behind at the sink in the fancy bathroom. Then they went at it on the bed until they both fell asleep. Hauck placed his hands behind his head.

Maybe not the single most professional thing he had ever done on an investigation.

But, jeez, they were both adults. Well, at least one of them was.

And it *was* fun . . . He felt his cheeks stretch into a sheepish grin. Karen had pushed herself out of his life. He waited for the admonishment.

None came.

He got out of bed, shaved, and showered. He took his bag downstairs by ten of eight. Even fighting the slow jam of traffic that was bound to be going south on I-95, he ought to be at his desk by nine.

What then . . . ? The decisions he had to make came back to him. *Where do you take this, Ty . . . ?*

In the lobby, Hauck called for his car and stopped at the front desk to check out. An attractive Asian desk clerk named Randi waved him forward. Hauck put a credit card onto the counter. "Checking out of 3209."

The desk clerk typed his room into the computer. She looked up and smiled. "Mr. Hauck, I see your room's been comped by the resort. You're all set."

"Thanks, but I'd like to pay," Hauck said. No way he was going to let the investigation be compromised or be indebted in any way to Raines. "It's okay, please . . . Just run me a bill."

"I'm afraid I can't do that, Mr. Hauck," the desk clerk said. "It's all been zeroed out."

"Randi . . ." Hauck leaned close and said nicely, "You do whatever you have to do, put it all on a minibar tab if you like, but I need to pay for my room. How much is the standard weekday price?"

The desk clerk grew a little flustered. "I'd have to look that up . . ." She punched it into her computer. "Two hundred and eighty-nine dollars, but—"

"Ring it up," Hauck said, pushing forward his card. "Charge me for whatever you like. Book it for tonight. It's inside the cancellation penalty window, isn't it?"

"Yes . . ."

"So that's fine."

Confused, Randi printed off a bill, which Hauck signed, and he thanked her for understanding. He folded the receipt into his pocket and was about to head out to his car when she called him back.

"I almost forgot, this was left here for you, Mr. Hauck."

She produced a large manila envelope, taped shut, his name on it, and handed it across the counter.

Hauck tucked it under his arm. "Thanks."

He walked away, wondering if this was some kind of good-bye from Josie. He put down his bag and slit the envelope open.

The blood left his face.

He was staring at a series of black-and-white photos. Photos of himself. Last night.

With Josie.

In his hotel room. In the throes of what they were doing. At the wall. On the bed. Josie over him.

A stomach-turning nausea rolled over in his gut.

There was a note clipped to one of the photos. Handwritten. On the hotel's stationery. As he read it, Hauck's fists tightened. Raines's contemptuous grin flashed through his mind.

"Fortunately, as the saying goes—what happens at the Pequot Woods stays at the Pequot Woods, Lieutenant . . ."

Hauck crumpled the note in his fist. His temperature escalated through the roof. He felt the veins in his neck bulge with anger.

He ran back to Randi. "Where is Mr. Raines's office?" he asked.

She was with a customer. "I beg your pardon, sir?"

"Where's Raines's office?" He knew his voice rang out too loudly, but he was barely able to control his rage.

"Up the stairs." Randi pointed. "Second floor. Security. All the way down the hall."

Hauck nodded, then bounded up the wide, red-carpeted stairway, leaving his bag sitting at the desk. His blood coursed with the torrent of just how stupid he'd been.

How could he have taken his eye off the ball so completely? Allowed himself to be played like some stupid rookie in heat? He flashed to Josie. The bit about what she was studying in school. A ripple of shame shot through him. She'd done her job well. He'd damn well let her. He should have seen it coming.

It had all been set up by Raines from the start.

On the second floor Hauck ran down the hall, passing the Flight Room, where he had met Raines yesterday afternoon. He didn't know how badly he had been compromised. Or whether Fitzpatrick would still support him. He was already on the fence.

But mostly, he wondered what it was these people had to hide to make them pressure him so strongly to back off the case.

At the end of the hall, Hauck came across a double door marked SECURITY. He pulled it open, and a secretary looked up at him from behind a desk. Hauck looked around the rooms for an office with Raines's name on it.

"Can I help you?" the secretary asked.

"Where's Raines?"

The middle-aged woman did a double take.

"Where's Joe Raines?" Hauck said again. He didn't identify himself. He could barely control himself. He didn't know what he would even do. Arrest him. That would blow everything.

Slug him. Hauck's pulse was racing so out of control, he knew she must be thinking he was crazy.

"Sir, Mr. Raines isn't here at the moment . . . ," she said, probably pressing a button for assistance underneath her desk.

Hauck dropped his badge in front of her.

"He won't be in today," the secretary said, surprised. "He's out of the office for the day. I don't know if there's anyone else who can help you, but—"

"You give him this," Hauck said. His eyes were fiery with rage. He took a pen from the top of her desk and scratched out a few words on the back of Raines's crumpled note.

"You make sure he gets this—today!"

The secretary looked at the card, startled, and nodded. "I will."

"Today."

Hauck left the suite and stood, decompressing, in the second-floor hallway. It was probably better Raines wasn't there. He knew he had behaved stupidly. But more than that, he knew he was opening up a current that could no longer be controlled.

You keep digging, Raines had said to him, *you have no idea the forces that are at work here . . .*

Someone had ordered those deaths. Someone clearly wanted him off the case. Hauck went back down the stairs. His blood calmed.

You wanted *to know what kind of man I am . . .* he had written on Raines's note.

I'm the kind who risks it all.

CHAPTER FORTY-SEVEN

By ten, Hauck made it back to the station. He went straight upstairs and knocked on the door of the chief's office. "Must be important, huh, Ty? You got that look in your eye . . ."

"Yeah, Vern, it is."

The chief waved him in with his mug of coffee; Hauck pulled up a seat across from him. "So what happened up there?" He laughed. "You get lucky or something, Ty?"

"You could say."

Hauck told him about Raines and the video he had shown Hauck of David Sanger at the table. The conspiracy Raines had mapped out about the prosecutor and his inside friend. And what might have befallen them.

"You're suggesting Vega and this DR-17 were merely acting out a hit for the Pequot Woods?" Fitzpatrick looked up at him and asked.

"I'm suggesting Sanger and Kramer may not have been as innocent as they appeared. Raines tossed out the possibility that people up there might've been handling things in their own way."

"A gambling scam? This 'false shuffle'? An up-and-coming federal prosecutor? With everything going for him?"

Hauck shrugged. "I know what you're saying, but there's the bank account he kept secret from his wife. Several of the deposits seemed to match up. Everyone's got their vices, Vern. I saw the guy walk away with a sizable pile of chips."

"Which proves he had a gambling bug, that's all. This Raines, he implied this was how the resort took care of it? How they 'balanced their books'?"

"He threw it out. Among many possibilities . . ."

"But I can see you're not exactly giddy about his explanation."

Hauck shrugged. "I'd like to shoot a fucking missile through it, if it's okay with you."

Fitzpatrick shifted back in thought. He tapped his fingers against his lips. "You're not taking on a bunch of Wall Street people here, Ty. You have any idea what type of interests you're stepping into?"

"Funny, Raines asked the same thing to me."

"Well, that's because you don't. You don't even have a goddamn clue. And I'm not even talking the general scum who are usually a part of this kind of business operation." Vern looked at him. "Those casinos up there are the principal reason we have a balanced budget in this state. That new thruway they're widening, between here and Fairfield? You think it's the declining real estate tax pool that's ponying up the funding for that? Or the new sports arena they're building up near Hartford? Trying to attract an NBA team? Half the goddamn high schools in this state—all those science labs and fancy new gyms and scoreboards . . . Who do you think's paying for all that, Ty? Or how we can support one hundred and twenty officers on our own force? Just what is it you think those billions in gambling revenue actually buy?"

"Three people are dead, Vern. Some piece of shit who empties his gun at a state trooper has his case mysteriously dropped. Makes you think they might be covering something up."

Fitzpatrick directed a stern look into Hauck's eyes. "You think there was pressure from Hartford when this drive-by initially took place, you don't even know the meaning of 'pressure' if we start looking into the Pequot Woods. Besides the obvious question of jurisdiction. Every politician in the state has their hands out to them."

Hauck stared in the chief's steady blue eyes, which, for the first time since Hauck had known him, looked haggard, even a bit afraid. Vern was going on seventy. He'd had the job as chief in Greenwich for almost twenty years, well past what anyone expected. Eighty percent of their job here was waving traffic down Greenwich Avenue, smoothing out spats at the high school or a fender bender between BMWs and Mercedes. Complaints between neighbors who could buy and sell them in a single trade.

"You asking me to back off, Vern?"

"I'm asking you to know what the hell you're doing, Ty!" Fitzpatrick pushed back in his chair, ran a hand through his wavy white hair. "Listen, son, what do I have—maybe two years left on my term? Then what? You'd be the logical choice to take over. You've got the experience. Everybody's behind you. You can build a good life here."

Hauck knew that was always the plan.

"But you step into this, Ty, you step into things you're better off just letting go. There's no telling where it takes you or who you may piss off. Ninety percent of what I do"—the chief winked with a modest grin—"is just not pissing the right people off."

"Too late for that," Hauck said with a halting smile of his own.

He opened the manila envelope he'd been keeping on his lap and laid out the series of photos of him and Josie.

Fitzpatrick groaned. The color in his cheeks waned. "Looks like you did get a little lucky up there . . ."

"I wanted you to see these, Vern. I should've known better. I just got careless."

Fitz put them back down on the desk. "So I would know the kind of headlines we're about to receive?"

Hauck winced. That had already crossed his mind. LOCAL COP INTERROGATING WITNESS ON CASINO LINK TO SHOOTINGS.

"To know what kind of people we're dealing with, Vern."

"*I damn well already know what kind of people we're dealing with, Ty.*"

"This was all just a threat, Vern. To get me to back off. They'd never dare use it. The whole thing would explode right back in their faces."

Fitzpatrick stood up. He came over to the edge of his desk and sat, leaning over Hauck. He looked at the photos one more time and began to rip them into tiny pieces. Then he tossed the piles into his trash. "You're a smart man, Ty—*generally* . . . It's just that sometimes you can be a bit naïve. Good people generally are. Seems to me you're still carrying a small reminder of what kind of people we're dealing with in your own right leg."

"Yeah." Hauck nodded. "I am."

"These types are far worse, Ty."

Hauck's eyes glanced to the torn-up photos in the can. "You want me to back off, Vern, I will. You want me to step aside on the case, I'll do that too."

"I'm not telling you to stop!" Fitzpatrick looked back at him, gritting his teeth. "I just want to make sure you know what the hell you're dragging us into here. I'm telling you to be careful, son." He placed his hand on Hauck's shoulder. "If they already killed a federal attorney, that badge won't protect you much. I'm telling you to watch your ass, Ty."

CHAPTER FORTY-EIGHT

*H*auck sat outside the gray shingled house on Pine Ridge Road. He ran through what he would try to say. What he was about to unleash.

Basically, destroying a good man's reputation. His family's memory of him. With only the most circumstantial and trumped-up evidence to back it up. If he decided to take this forward.

And over what?

Over a crime that hadn't been proven and could easily be swept away.

Maybe Fitz was right. Opening all this up would only unleash a torrent of misery and pressure. And what was he prepared to do? Indict Raines on a heresay comment? Subpoena the tapes? They'd be destroyed or misplaced before they ever saw the light of day. Pry open the questionable dealings of the largest tax generator in the state?

One day he could take over Fitz's job. He could build something here.

Be careful what you get yourself involved in, Ty . . .

Hauck stepped out of the car. Flurries had begun to fall. He rang the chime on the red front door.

"Haley, watch Ethan for me!"

The door opened. Wendy Sanger was dressed in a blue velour set, her short blond hair clipped up in back. "I saw you
waiting out there," she said. "In a way, I was hoping you'd drive
away."

"You said you wanted to know."

"What are you going to tell me, Lieutenant? That my husband was involved in something bad? That he wasn't the nice,
perfect person I knew? That all these noble things—"

"You said you wanted me to find out wherever it led. To find
out what happened."

Hauck looked in her wary eyes.

"Everyone has a side to them they don't want people to
know, Ms. Sanger. But not everyone is killed for it."

She opened the door. "Come on in," she said, "it's cold."

Hauck stepped inside, wiped his shoes on the mat. A large
pink orchid brightened a table in the foyer. "I asked you if your
husband had a gambling problem."

"And what if he did?" Wendy shook her head. "David didn't
hurt anyone . . ."

"And what if he did"—Hauck wasn't sure if he shouldn't
just turn around and walk away—*"hurt someone?* What if he'd
been going up to the Pequot Woods a lot more frequently than
you knew? What if he had something illegal going on? With his
friend, Kramer . . ."

"What kind of thing?" Wendy asked, growing frustrated,
anxious.

"He kept that account hidden from you."

"That money could've come from a lot of things," she said
with a hint of desperation.

"But it didn't." Hauck shrugged. "What if it wasn't entirely
legal?"

"You better have proof, Lieutenant! You want to come in here and make accusations about David—you better show me the goddamn proof, you hear. Not just a bunch of questions. Or innuendos. Not asking all these what-ifs . . . *Proof!*"

"We found an American Express card in your husband's name he was paying on a separate account. I can show you the receipts. It seems David had been up to the Pequot Woods several times over the past year and a half. Nine times, to be exact. I went up. They showed me some things. Video they had taken of him." Hauck shifted awkwardly. "They were suggesting they were involved in a card-cheating scam up there. His friend, Kramer, on the inside, trying to manipulate the system."

"*I don't believe it!*" Wendy's blue eyes flashed. "I don't believe it."

"I saw it," Hauck said. "They had this thing going on. It's called a false shuffle. You can look at the deposits back in his account after he went up there."

"I spoke with Judy Kramer," Wendy said. "Keith was on his way home to take his son to hockey practice. David was just filling up the car. These were just two people—good people, Lieutenant—who were murdered. Find out who did it. Don't turn this around on us."

There was a noise upstairs, her son crying. Ethan. Haley yelling, "*Mom!*"

Flustered, Wendy brushed back her hair.

"I'm saying that's exactly what I want to do, Ms. Sanger. I'm saying the people up there might have uncovered this thing and done something to them, maybe not fully knowing who he was. To right the affairs, in their view."

"*Right the affairs?*" Her eyes shone bright with tears. "You're saying David was cheating and these people had him killed? *To right affairs . . . ?*"

"We both know their deaths weren't a coincidence, Ms. Sanger. What I am saying is that if I go forward on this, things are bound to come out. The kind of things I'm telling you now. I can't stop that . . ."

"Did it occur to you that maybe he was investigating something? That maybe he and Keith were cooperating? And maybe that's why these people had him killed?"

"There's no open case file on this at his office. And we have his bank account, which is hard to explain."

"*No.*" Anger flashed on Wendy Sanger's face. "It's not hard to explain. What's hard to explain is you coming in here like this. David represented people's interests his whole life. He went after securities firms and drug companies. He exposed fraud, he didn't create it. He could've gone to any big law firm in the city but he chose to work for the government. He did this all because it was what he thought was right. That's who my husband was, Lieutenant. Not some cheat who stole money from a casino. You've got the wrong guy." She shook her head. "There's something else."

"The people who did this are already trying to pressure me off the case." Hauck lowered his voice. "The man who pulled the trigger on your husband is dead. He was murdered last week in the Dominican Republic. The person in charge of the gang he was a part of had an attempted murder case against him dropped—by the FBI. These things aren't happening because of some casino gambling scam. You want to know why your husband was killed, I want to help you, Ms. Sanger. I just don't know if I can stop what may come out . . ."

From the top of the stairs, Haley's voice rang out. "Mom, what's going on? *Who's here?* Is everything okay?"

Wendy looked up. "Yes, honey, everything's fine . . . Lieutenant Hauck is just here. He's giving me an update." She cleared her throat and ran a hand through her hair. "You have a daughter too, don't you, Lieutenant?"

Hauck nodded. "Thirteen."

"I bet she adores you. Daddys and their little girls . . ."

"When she's not trying to play me under the table." Hauck smiled.

"So then you know how it is . . . So what is it you want me to tell my daughter, Lieutenant? David's already been taken away from her once. Now you want to do it all over again. Not without proof." She shook her head. "Not even then."

A knot dug in deep into Hauck's chest. He pulled the door back open. "I'll leave you guys alone."

"You want my okay, Lieutenant? Well, I can't give it to you. You're saying these people killed my husband . . . ? I hope they fucking rot in hell. Do what the hell you have to do. But you better be right. You goddamn better be right in whatever you find. Because I choose to believe in David. And if you hurt my daughter all over again, if you drag my husband's memory through the mud and it turns out you're wrong, then goddamn you, Lieutenant, I'll never forgive you for that."

CHAPTER FORTY-NINE

*H*auck took the long route back to Stamford on the Post Road. It wasn't part of the plan to upset Wendy Sanger. He was thinking about what she had said. *I'll never forgive you, Lieutenant . . .* And what Fitz had warned him about. Not to mention Raines, the photos, and the sense that he was holding something back.

He made the right on Elm, past Annie's café. It reminded him he ought to get something to eat. The Stop & Shop on Cove was still open.

That's when he first noticed the glare of the headlights pulling up behind him.

A dark SUV. Looked like a Range Rover maybe. Bright halogen lights. He didn't know what it was that first made him suspicious. Instinct maybe.

It pulled in behind him and slowed, remaining a few car lengths behind.

He admonished himself. *A little jumpy, aren't you there, Ty . . .*

Hauck pulled into the Stop & Shop and ended up with a roasted chicken and a prepared Greek salad. At the register, he chatted a little with Melanie, the checkout girl. Her boy had been a point guard at Stamford West high and now he was over in Iraq. Usually he stopped in at nine, just before closing. Tonight he was early. Melanie laughed. "Half a day today, Lieutenant . . . ?"

Back in the car, he headed toward the sound. He stopped at the light. A Toyota pulled up next to him and made a turn. Two teenage girls. The driver was on her cell phone.

Hauck glanced in his rearview and noticed the same Range Rover pull away from the curb, falling in behind.

Okay, Ty, time to start paying attention . . .

As the light changed, he made a right onto Cove, keeping his eye on the mirror. A couple of other cars passed by; then Hauck was sure he saw the Range Rover make the same right, about fifty yards behind.

His blood tensed.

Something reared up in his mind, accompanied by a chill. About how Fitz had warned him about who he was dealing with. *You be careful, Ty . . .* That was when his heart began to accelerate. He was pushing his way into something no one wanted him to pursue. Three had already died. All were part of a cover-up. *That badge won't protect you, Ty . . .*

He glanced one more time in the mirror. The SUV seemed to slow. Connecticut plates. If he held a moment he could get a read. Call it in. He was almost near his street.

Take it slowly, Ty . . .

Finally, he turned onto Euclid. His house was just a hundred yards down on the right. He didn't see the lights of anyone following. He made the turn at his driveway and waited a moment with the motor on, his gaze fixed back down the street.

Then he saw the bright halogen lights. The Range Rover slowly turned down his street.

His heart started to go crazy.

He reached forward and opened his glove compartment.

With an eye on the mirror, he took his Sig out of the holster. He flipped the safety off.

Hauck begged his heart to quiet down.

The street was dark. It was after eight. Everyone was probably in their family room, doing homework, listening to their iPods, watching TV. He waited a few moments, considering what to do. He caught a glimpse of the SUV as it drove by.

But it didn't keep going.

It came to a stop further up the block.

Who the hell was in it? Someone sent by Raines or Vega? Or the FBI?

Hauck knew what he should do next. Go inside. Call the Stamford police. Tell them a suspicious car was lurking outside his residence. They would send someone. Let them come and intercede.

But he wanted to know who it was, and he didn't want the sight of cops to scare them away.

So Hauck crept out of the Explorer. He went up his stairs as if he was heading in, flicked on a light, spotting the brights from the Range Rover as it crawled past his house and down the block.

He shut his door and headed down the back stairway to the narrow walkway that led behind the fenced-in lots of the neighboring houses. His heart pounded. His nervous breaths were visible against the chill. It took Hauck maybe twenty seconds to wrap around the adjacent houses and come back out on the street. The Range Rover had driven past his house and pulled into a vacant spot about thirty yards away.

The driver dimmed his lights.

What worried Hauck was that Range Rovers weren't exactly standard FBI issue these days. But it was the sort of vehicle that might belong to a gang.

The driver's door opened and a man stepped out of the darkened car.

Only one. Which made everything easier. He was wearing a dark parka, a cap pulled over his face. Hauck couldn't make him out.

He saw the man check something in his palm and place it into his jacket pocket.

You have no idea the kind of people you're dealing with here, Ty . . .

Hauck crept his way behind a row of cars on the other side of the street.

The man crossed over. He stopped for a second on the curb. He took a glance up at Hauck's house. He looked about six feet, solid, cast in shadow. He reached into his pocket, grabbing something.

Hauck came up behind him. He eased off the safety from his gun.

The man caught a sense of it just a second late. He spun.

Hauck wrapped a hand around his neck and jerked him backward, at the same time kicked out the guy's legs. The guy rolled onto the pavement with a grunt. Hauck dug a knee sharply into his back.

"You wanted me, you got me, mister!" Hauck wrestled the man's arms behind him.

The guy let out a groan.

Hauck eased off his knee and spun him around. He pressed the barrel of his Sig into the man's face and a cell phone the guy had been carrying fell out of his hand.

"Now what do you want, asshole?"

He was staring into the face of his brother.

CHAPTER FIFTY

*J*esus, *Warren, what the hell are you doing here?"*

Hauck rose off his brother and helped him to a sitting position. Warren was fuzzy at first. He massaged the back of his neck. He had a cut on his lip where he had hit the pavement.

"Jesus, dude, a little jumpy or *what*?"

"Yeah, I'm jumpy. I always get jumpy when someone tails me, skulking around my place at night. You ever think of maybe *calling* or just letting me know? Or what any normal person might do—ring the goddamn bell!"

"I wasn't skulking." Warren brushed a knuckle against his lip and winced at the trace of blood. "I just didn't know I was stepping into a fucking Jet Li movie. Who the hell did you think I was?"

"It doesn't matter who I thought you were. Here . . ." Hauck offered his hand and helped him up.

In the filmy light he noticed his brother had aged since he'd seen him last. He looked heavier. Warren had always been trim and fit, and into his forties he could still toss a football fifty yards and take his nephews in a game of one-on-one.

Hauck hadn't seen him in over a year.

"You want to come up?"

Warren rubbed his jaw. "Yeah, well, that was the plan."

"Then c'mon . . . After that, it would be pretty damn rude to say no."

Upstairs, Hauck tossed Warren a damp cloth wrapped around a couple of ice cubes. Warren dabbed his lip and the scrape on the side of his face.

Hauck took out a couple of beers from the fridge and put one on the counter in front of Warren. "You're not going to sue or anything, are you?"

"Keeping my options open. You may, however, owe me a new pair of cords."

"Just feel lucky I didn't use deadly force."

Hauck sat on the stool next to him. Warren was three years older. He'd always been handsome. Always had an easy charm about him. The girls used to say he looked like Dennis Quaid. They hadn't talked much over the years. Actually, it had been like that as long as Hauck could remember. Since his brother had left for BC. Everything always seemed to come easy for Warren. Sports. Girls. Hauck had to bust his ass for everything he got. In college, Warren wasn't quite up to the level of a Division One team, so he morphed into Mr. Frat Boy. Took the LSATS. Didn't do so well. Somehow he talked his way into UConn law school, graduated middle of his class. But after a stint at an upstate firm in Hartford, he managed to get cozy with a bunch of the movers and shakers up there and went out on his own.

To Hauck, it always seemed like Warren lived a charmed life.

"So enough with all the yuks . . ." Hauck looked at him. "I know you just didn't find yourself in the neighborhood. What brought you by?"

"*Whatsamatter?*" Warren objected. "Can't a brother just check in on his younger sibling?"

"Cut the crap, Warren. You pass through Greenwich every other day and you've never dropped in before."

"Okay, okay . . ." He lit up a cigarette. His face took on a different cast. "Ginny call you?"

Hauck shook his head. "What's going on?"

Warren took a swig of beer, then drew a long drag on the cigarette and blew it out. "I don't know. I think I've gotten a little over my head on a few things lately . . ."

"What kind of things? Business?"

"Maybe." Warren shrugged, contrite. "Also at home . . . I partnered up on this housing deal near Waterbury. Low-income units, no money down, right in town. Need I say more? I helped secure the developer his permits with the state, so I figured, what the hell, why not buy in? I'd helped line enough pockets over the years . . ." Warren put the beer can against his swollen lip. "Picked a helluva time to go long in the housing market, huh?"

"C'mon, Warren," Hauck said, "you fall out of a roller coaster, you land on your feet." Their whole lives, Warren had never come to him for anything. He was never anything but 100 percent. "You need some cash?"

Warren chuckled. "How much you sitting on, bro?"

Hauck shrugged, feeling slightly foolish for asking. "I got a little saved up. Not your kind of money, Warren, but . . ."

His brother tapped him on the thigh with the closest thing to a look of affection Hauck could recall in years. "I didn't come here for a loan, Ty. But thanks . . ."

"Ginny know about this?" The two of them had been through a few rough patches before.

Warren nodded guiltily. "Which is not unrelated to the problem at hand, little bro."

Hauck regarded him suspiciously. "And that is . . . ?"

Warren drained the bottom of the can of beer. "Got another?" Hauck stepped over to the fridge and slid one across the counter. Warren popped the tab and took a swig. "I took some of the funds for this deal out of Sarah and Kyle's tuition fund."

Hauck stared. "Nice move, champ."

"Not so surprisingly, the wife and I haven't exactly been on the best of cuddling terms lately."

"Jesus, Warren, do you have a chronic aversion to sleeping through the night?"

"Coming completely clean," he exhaled, "there's been a few other things too. Truth is, I've been seeing the kids mostly weekends. The past couple of months, I haven't been living there much."

"What's the definition of *much*, Warren?"

"*Not at all*. Afraid that puts a little dent in our plans for Thanksgiving."

Hauck shook his head in disbelief. His brother had always lived on the edge. Now it seemed he'd completely gone over. "You need somewhere to stay?"

"Nice of you, bro, but . . ." He sucked in a breath. "I took an apartment up in town. That's sort of where I've been living out of lately . . ."

"That's good, Warren . . ." Hauck smiled philosophically and tapped his brother's thigh. "For a moment there, I thought you were about to ask me for a kidney."

CHAPTER FIFTY-ONE

*T*hey cracked another beer and stepped out on the deck. It was cold. Warren huddled in his fleece pullover and looked out at the sound, lights flickering miles away on the Long Island shore. He lit another cigarette. A few flurries stuck in his hair.

"This is nice, Ty. It really is . . . Million-dollar view."

"Not exactly like yours." Hauck shrugged. "But I make do."

"Never knew precisely how, on what they pay you." Warren grinned at him.

"This may come as a shock, guy, but some of us actually *like* what we do. You know, there's a certain niche out there who enjoy sleeping soundly at night."

"Heard about those people," Warren said. "Gotta learn more about that. How's Jess?"

"I actually haven't seen her much lately, since the shooting. I've been wrapped up in this case. Beth just thought it was better that way for a while."

Warren nodded and stared out at the sound. "She's probably right. And what about your gal you swept off her feet? Karen?"

"She's in Atlanta. Her father took ill. Parkinson's. She's down there taking care of him—sort of indefinitely. I'm not exactly sure where that stands right now."

"Too bad." Warren tilted his beer. "Nice gal. Not sure what she ever saw in you in the first place."

Hauck bent his leg on the wooden table. "Yeah, too bad. So . . ." He shifted gears. "Still flying?"

His brother nodded. "Still flying. That's what's keeping me together. Over a thousand hours now. I actually bought a new plane before all this happened. A Cessna 310 turbo. It can get me as far out as Colorado or down to Florida without stopping to refuel. You ought to come out on it some time . . ."

"*With you?* Up there?" Hauck chortled. "I'd rather give up that kidney."

"We could go visit Pop." Since their mom died, their father had been living in an assisted-living center in Myrtle Beach, South Carolina, the past three years.

"That would be something. The two of us just showing up. Like old times. If his heart's not bad enough, that would certainly kill it."

"You know, it's a beautiful thing," Warren said, eyes twinkling, "being up there. I wish I could describe it. It's somewhere between a feeling of power and of being completely at peace. You see the world down there and it's just this perfect grid and everything makes sense. And you've got the throttle. Would that it was all so easy . . ."

"You'll figure a way to get it back. You always do. Ginny also."

"We'll see." Warren reached inside a pocket in his pullover and pulled out something.

A hand-rolled joint.

Hauck's eyes went wide.

"You mind?"

"Why should I mind, Warren? I'm only the head of detectives in town."

"That's in Greenwich, dude. Here you've got no jurisdiction. I thought all you cops did this sort of thing anyway. To unwind." He took out a lighter and lit the tip. The smell of marijuana came alive. "Where I come from they all do."

"Is that how you grease the wheels of the local law enforcement up there? Make all those speeding tickets go away . . ."

"No, bro." Warren laughed. "That's *you!*" He drew in a drag off the joint, Hauck envisioning the strong smell wafting all over Euclid Avenue, praying no one was out walking the dog. Warren offered it to Hauck.

Hauck declined.

"Always the white knight, huh, Ty? Always living up to your obligations." Warren let out a plume of smoke. "Anyway, it works for me . . ."

They sat for a while in silence, Hauck studying the new lines on his brother's face. The youthful cockiness gone. Warren gazing out at the Long Island lights in the darkness.

"So what's the deal on that case? That gang killing?"

Hauck shrugged. "I'm not sure it was such a gang killing after all." He thought a second about how much he should say but gave in, going over the trail of evidence that led to the Pequot Woods, his meeting up there with Raines and his inference that Sanger and Kramer were ripping off the casino, leaving out Josie.

"Lawyers . . . can't trust them for shit." Warren grinned. He inhaled another hit. "You better watch yourself up there. I know those sharks. When they want to protect something, they don't stop. You say the dude who pulled the trigger is dead . . . ? Maybe you ought to take that as your lucky break. Call it a day.

You got a motive, a complicit dead guy . . . Everybody goes home happy. It's a win-win . . ."

"Maybe in my book we have different definitions of what's a win-win," Hauck said.

"Maybe." Warren took a swig of beer and shrugged. "Still, whatever this dude Sanger was doing—and let's assume you're right, that it's far, far deeper than some gambling scam—you really think you're ever going to get to the bottom of it? You don't know who you're dealing with up there. You think the waters are just gonna part, or the wigwam just open, or whatever the fuck it is up there . . ."

"I don't know . . ."

"What you *are* going to do is get yourself knee-deep in a bucketful of shit, señor. Maybe cost yourself a well-earned opportunity in life. Listen, this is my office up there. I know what you're facing. Every bloodsucker in the capitol's got a trail of pork that leads through them. This guy Raines was actually giving you good advice. Not that you would ever see that, stubborn bastard that we know you to be."

"Who's creeping around whose house here, Warren?" Hauck looked at him, irritated.

Warren took another hit and shrugged, blowing smoke over the rail. "You think I'm such a big honcho, don't you? You think I've done a pretty good job of fucking things up for myself."

"I think you've got a house that's worth about three times what I have to my name. I think you've got two terrific kids. Ginny and you have fifteen years . . . I think you have no idea what it is to give that up."

"The stuff I do, smooth over a little conflict with the state planning boards, reach out to some local commissioner who wants his golf pants lined, you have no idea the crap I've done."

"You don't have to go through this, Warren."

"Maybe I do. Maybe I do have to go through it, Ty." He stared a while and shook his head. "You remember when we went to the Poconos that summer? On that lake?"

"The Nightmare on Kelm Street?" Hauck said, relaxing. That was the place where their folks had rented a cottage. "Yeah."

It must have been twenty-five years ago. Pop's two-week vacation from the water department every August. They rented this cabin at a lodge with a bunch of their government-union friends. Warren must have been a junior then, which made Hauck fourteen. "I don't think Mom ever served fish again."

Warren laughed with a glaze of remembrance, drew in a drag. "I snuck along this bag of pot. In my sneaks. That's why I always was sneaking out at night. I'd go down to the lake. There was this girl from Jersey there, Camille or something . . ."

"You always bagged out at night and left me playing board games with Mom and Pop and listening to the Brothers Four and Joan Baez . . ."

Warren sang, " *'Farewell, Angelina . . . The sky is falling . . .'* Heard that till we were numb. Sorry, champ, you were goddamn fourteen. I was always afraid you'd rat me out."

"I wouldn't have ratted you out, Warren."

"Are you kidding? Look at you." Warren laughed. "You became a goddamn cop! Maybe *I'm* responsible! Hey, you remember those Jet Skis we would ride around on on the lake?"

"Coldest goddamn water I ever felt. Like taking a dip in Prudhoe Bay." Hauck shivered. "Still get a chill thinking about it."

"I remember you took that spill," Warren said. He blew out a ring. "All of us were watching you from the deck. Trying to prove you were the big shot trick artist, like you always did. One leg. Grabbing some air . . ."

"That's because you always made it so easy on me to feel good about myself," Hauck said with a humorless smile.

"Sorry, guy . . . I remember your ass hit the water like a stone. The Jet Ski went one way, up in the air—you the other . . ." Warren turned. "You probably don't even know this, but there was a minute there when you didn't come up and everyone was pretty goddamn afraid. Just this eerie quiet. The Jet Ski circled around and had come to a stop. *No Ty* . . ."

"I was under the water holding my breath," Hauck said. "Milking the moment."

"Trust me, your little moment was pretty much lost on everyone there. I remember how Mom got all freaked out and grabbed Dad. 'Frank, get the lifeguard, quick!' You remember who it was who dove in off the deck and went out to get you? Who swam out there like a fucking maniac, in his clothes, to make sure you were okay?"

Hauck looked back at him and nodded. He wondered where this was leading. "Yeah, it was you, Warren."

"Yeah"—Warren sucked in a drag—"it was me. You fought me off like I went out there to drown you or something. Like I was trying to embarrass you, not to save your pussy ass."

"I was fourteen, Warren . . ."

"Yeah, well, you came damn close to not making it to fifteen . . ."

The conversation had led somewhere Hauck wasn't completely sure of. Warren sat there with his feet up on the rail in some sort of shifting state—half brooding, half reminiscing.

"You know I'm sorry," he suddenly said.

Hauck turned. "Sorry for what?"

Warren shrugged. "I think you know what I'm talking about." He went quiet for a while, his voice softer. "I'm sorry for pushing you away, Ty. For what happened after that . . . You know, Peter Morrison." He looked at Hauck. "You may have put it away, but I haven't. It stays with me. I just wanted to remind you there was a time when I was there for you . . ."

There was something both fixed and very far-off in his brother's gaze.

"What the hell are we talking about here, Warren?"

"It's nothing. Nothing I should've brought up. Not anymore . . ."

Hauck went over and sat against the railing next to him. Warren seemed to be holding something back. Hauck wrapped his hand around his brother's neck and pulled him close.

"It's okay, Warren, whatever it is, it's okay." For a second, he thought Warren might be crying. Hauck leaned his brother's head against him.

What was going on?

After a few moments he pulled back. Warren's eyes were shiny. "Must be the weed talking . . . Not exactly how I thought I'd say hello."

"Don't worry about it," Hauck said. "Anyway, *you win*. You got the kidney, bro!"

His brother laughed, wiping his eyes, blowing out a breath as if relieved. "'*The sky is falling,*'" he sang, "'*and I must be gone* . . .' Course, we did have a few memorable times, like when the brothers Hauck almost single-handedly took down Stamford West in the states . . ."

"Yeah." Hauck grinned. "Two hundred and forty-one yards, three TDs. I remember I carved it into the trunk of that elm in back of the old house. Course you had to add your own personal touch to it . . ."

"*Two fumbles*. Just for historical accuracy." Warren winked back with an impish smile.

"Probably still there." Hauck grinned.

"Probably still is." Warren held out the joint to Hauck.

Hauck smiled, fixing on his brother's eyes. "Just this once. You tell anyone, and what I did down there will seem like a love tap next time."

"Just to remind you, bro—you did have the slight advantage of having snuck up on me from behind."

Hauck took the joint. "Just so you know."

"Not to worry, little brother." Warren put his feet up on the railing. "Your secret will be safe with me."

CHAPTER FIFTY-TWO

*I*t was later—after Warren had passed out and was snoring on the couch, after Hauck had cleaned up the beer cans and the cigarette butts and flicked off *Forrest Gump* on the TV.

When he was in bed, sleep slowly washing over his brain—then it came to him.

What Warren had been trying to say.

Hauck's eyes shot open. A name flashed into his head.

Peter Morrison.

It was the summer after the one at the lake. Warren was on his way to BC. He had this girlfriend—Dot. Dottie Sinclair. They lived in a big colonial with this huge lawn out on Lake Street. Her father was a bigwig at a financial company in town.

Hauck had a job at a yacht club in Darien that summer.

He crossed a leg over his knee in bed and remembered.

That was when everything changed.

Peter Morrison.

Peter was this tall, gangly kid with long blond hair. He wasn't into sports and had red, blotchy acne on his face. Warren always bullied him. Punched him in the back in the halls between classes as he was going by. *Tax,* he always called it, holding out his hand, and Peter would fork over a hard-earned buck or something. Hauck always told his brother to lay off. Warren always smirked back that the weirdo liked it and one day he'd give him back his cash. It was their game.

Twenty-five years later, it was like a punch caught Hauck in the stomach as he brought it all back.

He had gotten off early from the yacht club that day. Caught a ride home. When he barged in, the house seemed empty. Their father always came home from the department at 5:30, like clockwork, every day. Mom must have been out at the market. Hauck remembered he grabbed something out of the fridge—a wedge of Laughing Cow cheese, a Fanta—and went down to the basement, which his dad had redone, to shoot a little pool or throw himself in front of the TV. It was the only one worth watching in their row house in Byron.

He heard something as he lumbered down the stairs.

Coming from the guest room.

Pop had converted a back space into a room for his brother, Mike, who had died from cancer a few years before. No one ever used it unless there was family in town.

For a second, Hauck thought it was something running through the walls—a rodent or a squirrel. Then it occurred to him maybe it could be a burglar. The little room had a small window that led out onto an alley.

He listened.

He heard voices, muffled. He went over and put his ear against the door, about to shout *"Who's in there?"* when his footsteps creaked on the tile.

Everything went quiet.

Suddenly he knew. He knew who was in there. And why. He also knew he should've just turned around.

But he felt this sudden power—this giddy, adolescent urge to barge in and embarrass his brother. And maybe catch a glimpse of Dottie Sinclair in her bra or even better.

He yanked open the door.

Hauck's hand froze to the knob.

There was Warren, this look of horror and shame, his pants down at his knees, standing over Uncle Mike's bed.

But it wasn't Dot beneath him. And even now, years later, the recollection of it sent him reeling up in bed in a cold sweat, his stomach clenched as if gripped in a tightening vise, then crashing to the floor.

It was Peter Morrison.

Those bright blue eyes. Blond hair falling over his pimply face.

Years went by before his brother really talked to him again.

CHAPTER FIFTY-THREE

The next morning, Warren was just waking up as Hauck was getting ready to leave.

"There's coffee," Hauck said. "Milk's in the fridge."

"Jesus, what time is it?" Warren asked groggily. He picked up his Ebel watch. "Christ, I've got places to be." He sat up on the couch in his shorts, a bit disheveled, patting around for his cigarettes.

Hauck said, "You can grab a shower if you like. You can use the one in Jessie's room. I have to take off myself."

"Does this place come with an ashtray? Maybe a newspaper?" Warren said, pawing a hand through his unkempt hair.

Hauck went to the counter and tossed him *The Stamford Advocate*. Facing up, on the front page, there was an article about Richard Scayne, the local businessman who was embroiled in an Iraq corruption scandal.

"Christ," Warren said, "don't you get the *Journal* or the *Times*?"

"Next time, spring for the bigger room," Hauck said. "Listen . . ." He lowered himself on the arm of the couch. "Things'll work out here for you, bro. With Ginny. That financial thing. You always have a way of landing on your feet."

Warren nodded.

"I'll check in with you later. I realize that's a bit of a risk. Twice in two days . . ."

Warren smiled.

Hauck tapped his brother on the shoulder. "It was nice to see you, bro. It was good to go over some things . . ."

"Next time, maybe we can dispense with the cross-check onto the pavement."

"Next time, maybe you can call."

Hauck scooped up his wallet and his gun on the counter. He turned at the door. His brother was still massaging his face in his hands, elbows on knees.

"I always knew why you came in after me," Hauck said. "You know I would've done the same for you."

Warren looked up. His drawn face had a glimmer of understanding on it. He edged into a smile. "You stay outta trouble, Ty."

Outside, Hauck paused for a moment on the landing. He felt good, but through all the worry and joking last night, and the newly formed lines, there was something on his brother's face that gave him pause. The shadow of something else.

Hauck had seen it before.

It was the same look as when he had found him with Peter Morrison twenty years before.

CHAPTER FIFTY-FOUR

*T*hanksgiving finally came. Without providing the answer Hauck was looking for. The afternoon before, he shut down the office around two, the first break any of them had had in weeks.

Freddy Munoz knocked on Hauck's door.

"You have a good one, Freddy." Hauck stood up and shook his detective's hand.

His eyes flashed to Munoz's watch. "New one?"

"*Happy Days*, Lieutenant. Just found it on eBay. Collector's item." Freddy beamed. "You watch, one day it'll double."

Hauck shook his head. "Make sure you give my best to everyone at home. Everyone coming?"

"*The whole crew*. We got my brother and sister driving down from New Haven and my in-laws up from Maryland. Went out and got the turkey last night, nineteen pounds . . . Giants and Cowboys on high-def. Nothing better, Lieutenant. You gonna be with Jessie?"

"No. Jessie's with her mom this year . . ."

"That's too bad, LT. So what about your gal? I haven't heard you bring her up so much recently."

"Karen's away," Hauck said. He hadn't really told anybody.

"She's with her family down south. Her dad's sick. She's been down there about a month."

Munoz chirped a sympathetic whistle. "Jeez, that's too bad." As he made his way to the door he turned back. "So, listen, you got plans?"

Plans . . .

"I'm spending the morning at the Hope Street Mission in Stamford dishing out a little food," Hauck said.

"That's good, Lieutenant, *good*. What about after?"

"*After* . . . I may head up and visit my brother. I may just stick around and watch the game . . ."

Munoz stood there for a second, nodding. Then he shrugged. "You know, there may be some crazy departmental regulation against this . . . but if you wanted to come by, we got a boatload of food, LT. If you don't mind my relatives. We could open some beer. We got the plasma. You know Rosa would love to have you. Little Anthony never shuts up about you since you got him that David Wright baseball . . ."

Hauck smiled. He had gotten it at a community service golf outing and given it to Freddy's son, a die-hard Mets fan, for his confirmation. "I don't know, Freddy . . . There probably is a regulation about that somewhere. But it's nice of you to ask."

"You sure? I mean, it's Thanksgiving, man. Everyone's gotta have themselves some turkey on Thanksgiving."

"Say hi to the family for me. And don't you worry about the turkey, I'll work something out."

CHAPTER FIFTY-FIVE

*T*hanksgiving morning, Hauck woke around eight.

The day was crisp and bright. Hauck had a coffee on the deck overlooking the sound, for a day trying to push the case out of his mind.

He threw on an Under Armour top and went out for a jog along Hope Cove and the empty marina. When he got back there was a message waiting on the machine.

Karen.

"I'm calling to wish you a happy Thanksgiving, Ty . . . !"

She said how the kids were down there and that her dad wanted to say hello. "We're already at work here making a carrot soup and stuffing the turkey—my mom's acting like a crazy person as usual. And we're gonna watch a little football later. Hopefully, someone here will clue me in on who's even playing, right?

"Well, you're not answering and I hope you're out there doing something very un-*Ty-like*, like maybe going to visit your brother or even having a good time. LOL, babe . . . You give my best to Jessie. And, oh, I almost forgot—Tobey says hi too . . . He says he liked it a whole lot more when you were doing the cooking!" She paused. "I'm sorry not to be with you,

Ty . . . I do always think of you. I hope you're well and will have yourself a nice day. I'll try to call you later. *Bye, there . . .*"

Hauck thought just how sweet it felt to hear the sound of her voice, even considered calling her back. He got as far as picking up the phone before something held him back and he replaced it on the receiver and went in to take a shower.

He spent the morning dishing food at the Hope Street Mission in town with Reverend Alvin Bailey, who years back was his teammate at Greenwich High. In the afternoon he just sat around and watched the Giants and the Cowboys duke it out on TV, downed a beer or two, wondering whether he should have picked up the phone and gone up to his sister's in Massachusetts. His thoughts went to the case. To what Vern had said. *Bothers me just fine!* And how frustrated he was not to be able to make a connection between Sanger and Kramer.

He turned back to the game. *For Christ's sake, it's Thanksgiving, Ty.*

Around three, the phone rang again. This time, Jessie. She seemed sad to find him at home.

"I should be there with you, Daddy. I shouldn't have let you be alone."

"No, you're doing the right thing, hon. Your mom was right."

"You could come down here. Scott's parents are here. Everyone's in the family room playing Scrabble with the twins and looking through old albums. It's Grandparent Central here."

"Sounds about what Thanksgiving is supposed to be, Jess."

"So how come you didn't go up to Uncle Warren's?"

"We're all gonna be together Christmas. We'll go up and there and see your cousins. That's a promise, okay?"

"You're being a grouch, aren't you?"

"I'm not being a grouch," Hauck said. "It just didn't work out."

"You miss Karen, don't you, Dad?"

"Yeah. A little, baby doll."

"I love you, Daddy."

"I love you too, Jess. Thanks for calling. Chin up for the old folks. You be sure and say hi to everyone for me."

"Bye."

Hauck leaned back on the couch thinking just how much he loved her and how maybe she was right, just a little. He watched the game until close to seven and the Giants had pulled off a pretty good fourth-quarter comeback, and a restlessness started to rise in him. About Karen (how no matter how she tried to hide it in her tone, what they had was definitely gone between them, in the past); about how his case had stalled—not stalled, more like *vaporized*. Then to how all the people in the world he felt most connected to were so far away.

You gotta get outta here, Ty, before you explode . . .

He went into the bathroom and shaved. Threw on a nice shirt over cords and a tweed jacket. He didn't know where he was heading, just out. Maybe drive up to Warren's. Knock on the door. Imagining the look of total shock. *Hey, Ty, what are you doing here?*

Or up to Munoz's. *Everyone's gotta have themselves some turkey on Thanksgiving, right?*

As he went out the door and headed down the stairs, it occurred to him he had no idea where he was heading, feeling alternately foolish and frustrated, his own words coming back to haunt him.

I'll figure something out.

CHAPTER FIFTY-SIX

*T*he answer hit him as he drove along Elm, heading toward the thruway.

He passed the familiar sign and spun a U-ey into the parking lot. There were a couple of cars there. He turned off the engine and asked himself if he wanted to do this, giving himself a chance to back out. The little voice, the one that always got him in trouble, answered, *Why the hell not?*

Everyone's gotta have turkey on Thanksgiving!

Hauck hadn't heard from her since his last time here. He knew his warning to Vega had worked.

He pulled open the wood door and stepped inside Annie's restaurant.

A vase of hydrangeas in a vase brightened the entrance.

Hauck caught sight of her through the open kitchen. She was wearing a white chef's jacket, her hair tied up in a blue kerchief. She was dotting a plate of pie with a flourish. She looked up and did a double take as she saw him.

He waved.

A waiter in a white apron came up to him apologetically. "I'm sorry, but we just finished for the night."

"That's okay," Hauck said. He looked toward the kitchen. "I just came by to say hi."

Annie smiled back through the window, shrugging widely as if to say, *What's going on . . . ?*

The waiter, seeing they knew each other, said, "Sure."

There were only a couple of tables filled. Each looked like they were finishing up. Hauck took a seat at the bar.

A short while later Annie came around, removed her kerchief, and shook out her short black hair. "So you've finally come by to give me that protection, Lieutenant . . ."

"Happy Thanksgiving," Hauck said.

"Happy Thanksgiving to you. I don't have to be worried, do I?" She feigned a look of concern. "You're not expecting some kind of holiday attack here, are you?"

He shook his head and laughed. "No."

"Whew. You don't look like you're exactly dressed for duty, so okay, I'll bite. What does bring you in?"

Hauck shrugged. "How about some turkey?"

Annie screwed up her brow. "*Turkey?*"

"I don't have it wrong . . . It is Thanksgiving, isn't it?"

Annie laughed. "You may not believe this, Lieutenant, but you may have picked the one restaurant in America that doesn't actually serve turkey on Thanksgiving."

"You're joking." Hauck shifted around and glanced at the sparsely filled restaurant. "You, um, may want to rethink that plan next year."

Annie arched her brows. "And I see you've brought your stand-up routine too. Tell me, you think anyone really looking for a turkey dinner on Thanksgiving would end up coming here?"

"*I* did." Hauck shrugged foolishly.

Annie looked at him. "Don't you have a family to go to or

something? Didn't I see a couple of kids on the desk when I was in your office?"

"A daughter." Hauck nodded. "She's with her mom. In Brooklyn."

"My son, he's with my folks back in California." Annie sat next to him on a stool. "Two peas in a pod, huh? So you're looking for turkey? What a traditionalist." She said, "Gimme a minute to look around. I'll see what I can do."

A short while later, she came back with a neatly arranged plate that smelled sensational to Hauck.

"This is only because you did such a kick-ass job of getting those people off me," she said. "Turkey quesadilla, with peppers and a tomatillo coulis. A side of root vegetable ratatouille. We had some sitting around to use in salads for lunch. Maybe not exactly what the pilgrims had in mind . . ."

"It's great." Hauck smiled, digging in. "Thanks."

"Not so shabby, huh?" Annie took off her jacket and apron and had on jeans and a tight-fitting tee. She had a cute, pixie-like figure and a smile like a Caribbean sunset now that it was free of worry. "Mazel tov. So now I'll bite . . . What exactly *are* you doing here?"

"I told you, I live nearby. I wanted to come in and try the place."

"So you decided on Thanksgiving? At seven thirty?"

Hauck cut into his quesadilla. "It was an impulse. And this is great, by the way . . ."

"Tough order." Annie rolled her eyes. "Turkey on Thanksgiving . . ."

She pulled up a stool. Hauck ordered a Belgian Duvel beer and Annie took a sauvignon blanc. "I don't mean to talk shop," she asked, "but I heard on the news you still haven't caught those people."

"No." Hauck took a sip of beer and they clinked glasses. "Cheers."

"Cheers. Well, whatever magic you did worked. I haven't seen hide nor hair of any bad guys since."

"How's the Bridgeport clientele holding up?"

"A little soft." Annie smiled. "Ran out of red bandanas. But that's okay."

He coated a forkful of turkey in the sauce.

"Try the ratatouille." Annie nudged him. "It's a ten."

"Anyway, the good news is," he said, "I'm not sure you're gonna need to get involved any deeper. When we've got someone in custody, you can come in and take a look at a lineup. You won't have to testify. Just a deposition will do. You shouldn't have to worry about having to get up on a stand."

"I appreciate that, Lieutenant."

They talked for a few more minutes while Hauck finished. She asked about his family. Hauck told her that he was divorced. He didn't mention Norah. She said her son was nine. Jared. Back in California. Hauck didn't probe.

"It's a little complicated. I hope to have him here soon. Truth is, I haven't always made the best choices."

"No monopoly on that," Hauck said.

Annie nodded. "No. I know. I had a restaurant back in the wine country that fell apart. The guy I was married to, he did some things. Both to me *and* the business. I lost everything. I had to give up custody. I had to show them I was on my feet, which was why I was such a head case not to get involved. I'm hoping to bring Jared here in December."

"Good for you," Hauck said.

Behind them, the two occupied tables got up and went to the door. Annie wheeled around and thanked them both. "Happy

Thanksgiving." She waved. "See, satisfied customers all around."

Her staff had started breaking down the kitchen. Jason the waiter went around and collected the table settings.

"I think I'd better go," Annie said. "I promised I would break down the kitchen tonight. Only way I could get any of them to come in."

"I understand," Hauck said. "You were an angel. How much is all this?"

"Oh, come on." Annie waved. "How can I charge you? After coming to my rescue. You can bring your whole department in. Christmas, maybe?"

Hauck laughed. He drank up the last of his beer and got up. "Christmas."

"Question," Annie said.

"Shoot."

"What is it you go by when you're not called 'lieutenant,' Lieutenant?"

" 'Detective' generally works."

Annie stared back, not sure if he was teasing.

Hauck grinned from the door. "You can also try Ty, too!"

CHAPTER FIFTY-SEVEN

Monday, the first thing Hauck did was meet with Vern, inform him of the decision he'd come to.

Then he got his crew together.

Everyone had been in kind of a holding pattern since he'd come back from the Pequot Woods. He brought them up to date on Raines. The video he had shown him of Sanger, the false shuffle, along with the inference that Sanger and Kramer were involved in some kind of betting scam. He left out the part about Josie and the photographs.

"So what do you want to do?" Freddy Munoz asked.

Hauck sat on the edge of a desk and looked at him. "I want to get my hands on a copy of those tapes."

"You think they're gonna give them up like that? They're trying to scare you off the case, LT, not make it for you."

"Tell 'em if they don't, they'll be getting a subpoena from the state attorney general."

Steve Chrisafoulis snickered. "Assuming, of course, no one happens to get to him first."

There were a few laughs around the room.

Munoz said, "That *is* the sixty-four-thousand-dollar question, isn't it, LT?"

"No, the sixty-four-thousand-dollar question is why these people are trying to scare us off." Hauck turned to Steve. "I want you to pull up everything you can about TRV Gaming and Armbruster." The parent companies of the Pequot Woods. "I want to know who helped them get the deals and who ushered through their gaming licenses. The board of directors, overseers . . . I want to know if their paths crossed with anyone who ties in to this case. Sanger, Vega . . ."

"You got it, boss."

"And, Steve . . ." He took the detective aside. "That includes James Sculley and Stan Taylor too." The detective's eyes widened. "I want to know what these people are hiding," Hauck said.

"So, we're going after them?" Freddy Munoz said. "I mean, just to be clear, LT?"

"Yeah." Hauck pushed himself off the desk. "We're going after them, Freddy. To be clear."

When he got back to his office, the phone was ringing. He glanced out front. His secretary, Brenda, was away from her desk.

He picked it up and held it in the crook of his neck. "Hauck here . . ."

"Lieutenant, I'm glad I reached you," a voice said, surprised he had picked up his own phone. "My name is Tom Foley. I'm a managing partner in a company called the Talon Group. You may have heard of it? We're an international private security firm."

"I know the Talon Group." Hauck sat down. They were involved with providing security to the government staff in Iraq. As well as internal corporate security matters. "What can I do for you, Mr. Foley?"

"I have something that may be of interest to you. I was hoping I could buy you lunch."

"How urgent are we talking?" Talon was big. They advised a lot of companies on the scale of the Pequot Woods. Hauck was wondering how this fit in.

"How does one P.M. work? *Today.*"

CHAPTER FIFTY-EIGHT

*T*hey met at the Stanwich Country Club, out on North Street, which stayed open in the winter for lunches and maybe some paddle tennis. The club had a sprawling championship golf course.

Hauck had been there once, to help with security when Colin Powell had spoken there.

Foley was tall, thin lipped, light complexioned, with receding blond hair and an Ivy League air. He met Hauck at the entrance in a business suit and took him through the portrait-lined lobby up to the dining room. "Glad you were able to come on such short notice, Lieutenant."

Hauck shook his hand. "I was about to just catch a sandwich at my desk."

Only a handful of tables were filled in the large room overlooking the empty course. A couple of men in business discussions; two or three well-heeled members' wives doing lunch.

"Beautiful," Hauck said, looking over the closed course admiringly.

"You a golfer?" Foley asked.

"Some. I was hoping this lunch came with a rain check for eighteen holes attached to it." Hauck laughed.

"You never know." The security partner smiled. "It just might. Okay if I call you Ty?"

Hauck shrugged. "Sure."

At the table, Foley ordered a gin and tonic for himself, while Hauck took a Diet Coke.

"You're sure?"

"Workday," he said, trying to feel the man out. "You said you had something of interest to me pertaining to the case . . ."

"Many cases." The security executive smiled. "I've watched you on TV. The Grand Central bombing thing . . . You managed to make it above the radar. Cheers." Foley tilted his glass.

Hauck was trying to figure out what the hell was going on. The guy had something to divulge. Talon was the kind of firm the Pequot Woods might well be involved with. It also had the rehearsed, nuanced feel of another warning.

"So you've heard of us," Foley said, leaning back and crossing his legs. "Tell me what you know."

Hauck stumbled through the most obvious cases he had read in the papers or heard on TV. Corporate work, government contracts. Iraq.

"Yes, we have a side that does protective field work. But we leave that for the soldiers of fortune. The vast majority of what we do is perfectly benign. Forensic accounting, data mining for security purposes. Corporate espionage security. Some investigative work. You were a detective with the NYPD, I recall . . ."

Hauck nodded. "Six years."

"And why did you leave?"

The last thing Hauck wanted to do was to take him through his personal history, certainly that particular history, wrapped up in Norah's tragic death and 9/11. He tried to steer things back to the case. "I was transferred to the NYPD's Office of Information—"

"Under Marty Rouse, I think," Foley said.

Hauck looked at Foley. *So he knew.* Rouse had been police chief then. "Yes, under Chief Rouse."

A waiter handed out menus and took them through the specials. When he gave them a moment to think, Hauck put down the menu and leaned forward. "Look, Mr. Foley, I don't mean any disrespect. You said you were familiar with my case and had something urgent that would be of interest to me . . ."

"Very urgent." Foley leaned forward. "And quite worth your while. However, not directly related to the case."

"So why are we here?"

Foley smiled. He adjusted his wire-rim glasses on the bridge of his nose and clasped his hands. "Because the Talon Group has had its eye on you for some time, Lieutenant. And if you can find something you like here, I'm about to offer you a pretty lucrative job."

CHAPTER FIFTY-NINE

Maybe I'll have that beer after all . . ."

Hauck's head spun all the way back to the office later that afternoon. More like he'd downed a couple of killer martinis, not just the two beers he'd allowed himself.

The rest of that day, he did his best to focus on work. Munoz was having trouble contacting Raines, but what pissed off Hauck even more, the story of Sanger's gambling had somehow been picked up by the local press. He'd promised Wendy Sanger he'd try to keep a lid on that.

He'd failed.

Still, Hauck's mind kept finding its way back to the meeting he'd had with Foley. It had been a long time since Hauck had thought about changing his life. It had a seductive appeal. He felt distracted all day, both intrigued and agitated.

He thought about who he might possibly tell.

Only one person came to mind.

During a lull, he closed his door and punched in Warren's number.

"Twice in two days!" his brother answered, surprised. "People will start to talk! Listen, I'm fine, Ty, if that's why you're calling. Really, I am."

"Warren, something's come up." Hauck pivoted quickly. "It's important. I took a look around my life for who I could talk it over with. Yours was the only name that came up. Pretty pathetic, huh?"

"I'll have to find a way to see that as a compliment."

"I could drive up. I free up around six."

"Here? Not a chance. If you promise not to bounce me off of the pavement again, put a steak on, and grab the beers, I'll shoot by."

"Yeah. Shoot by."

Hauck had just gotten home when Warren knocked on the door.

"*Truce?*" he asked, putting up his palms in a defensive position.

"Truce," Hauck agreed, and they bumped elbows like when they were teenagers after playing one-on-one or tussling on the floor.

Warren stepped in and took a familiar look around. "Feels just like home . . ."

"Ought to." Hauck pointed. "Your ashes are still in the bottle cap over there."

"It *was* you, wasn't it, who said not to bother tidying up?"

Hauck tossed him a can of Heineken Light. "Beers first. The steak comes later."

Warren threw himself in the chair next to the fireplace and stretched his legs on the old wooden trunk Hauck used for a coffee table. He loosened his tie and popped the tab. "Shoot."

"I had a meeting today. Some honcho from a large security firm invited me to lunch. The Talon Group . . ."

"Everyone knows Talon." Warren nodded, impressed.

"I thought the guy had some information on my case, which

is the only reason I met with him. But that wasn't what he had in mind."

"And what was that?" his brother asked, taking a long swig of beer.

"He offered me a job."

Warren sat up, surprised, bringing his legs in from the table. "Go on . . ."

"They want to open an office up here in Greenwich. I guess a lot of their corporate clients are based in town. They're looking for someone local to handle the investigative side."

Warren nodded judiciously. "So just how much are they offering?"

Hauck met his gaze. "Two hundred and fifty grand."

"*Whoa!*"

"That's only half of it, Warren . . . A bonus plan based on performance. A car. They're even talking about the damn thing going public one day . . . I make a hundred and fifteen thousand dollars a year here. Even if I make chief one day—that's, what, one seventy-five, two at the most?"

"If I recall, you're the one who's always talking about sleeping through the night, Ty." He shot Hauck a cynical smile.

"*I know*, I know . . . But I'm forty-three years old. Maybe it's time for me to take a risk like this. It's like a new page."

Warren tilted his beer, focused on the gleam in Hauck's eye. "You'd have to wear a suit, you know."

Hauck grinned. "I could wear a suit. I could wear a Big Bird suit for that kind of money."

"So how'd you leave it with him?"

"I said I needed a little time. A week, ten days. It all came at me pretty quick. I said I was in the middle of a murder case."

"To which he replied . . . ?"

"To which he replied he understood, but that they had to get rolling on this pretty quickly."

Warren bunched his lips, assenting. He put down his beer. "Want an opinion on this?"

Hauck shrugged. "I figure there's got to be some reason I asked you here."

"Look, I don't know this guy Foley from Adam," Warren said, "but Talon's big. They're all over the globe. Opportunities like this don't come along every day. I guess what I'm thinking is, maybe someone else can tie up your murder case."

"I gave my word to people."

"This is the real world, Ty. People give their word all the time."

"I guess I just don't bag out on things so easily."

"It's not bagging out." Warren pulled his chair closer. "It's exactly the opposite, Ty. It's taking a chance to grab something for yourself. This is a chance to change your life. You're a capable guy. You deserve this. You've got people there, Ty. For once, why not let them see it through?"

Just for a second, Hauck let his mind drift to the thought of a fancy office, buying things he could not afford. A nicer boat. An upgrade on the Explorer. Helping out in a much bigger way with Jessie's college fund. Years back, he'd thought of himself as one of the luckiest men he knew. He had a rising job with the NYPD, was married to a gal he loved, had two young daughters. His belief in the arc of his life had been unshakable. Did he miss that feeling? That sensation of confidence?

The answer was yes, he realized. *He missed it to the core.*

"I don't know. I'll have to think about it. We'll see."

"Do it, bro." There was a gleam in Warren's blue eyes. "Look at your face. You're alive. Like years ago, Ty, *before* . . ." Warren didn't complete the thought but leaned forward and tapped Hauck's knee. "For once, you don't have to play the knight, Ty. I know a thirteen-year-old gal who you would make awfully proud of her dad if you did this."

"Listen," Hauck said, "this has to stay entirely between us, Warren. You understand that? Okay?"

"Course it stays between us, Ty." He laughed and went to take a swig of beer. "Now, can we celebrate with a meal?"

Hauck caught his arm, a warning in his stern gaze. "I mean it, Warren. Not to Ginny. Not to your golf buddies at the club. Not even to Jessie. *Understood?* I'll think it over, but I need to trust you on this, Warren. *Are we clear?*"

"*Clear?*" Warren leaned back and looked at Hauck, draining the last of his beer. "Clear as a golf ball on grass, little brother."

CHAPTER SIXTY

*T*hat same night, a black Lincoln pulled up to the stone-pillared gates of the large estate in Greenwich. The darkened window of the car rolled down and the man behind the wheel, who was actually the passenger's most trusted aide, leaned out and spoke into the security speaker. "Senator Casey."

"I was told to have you drive up to the office," the Filipino house servant said.

The "office" was a sleek stone and glass structure connected by an underground walkway to the large main house. The estate was situated on the point in Belle Haven, a promontory jutting into the sound where even the modest homes went for four to five million. And this was anything but. It had a helicopter pad, a dock that could moor a hundred-foot boat, a par-3 golf hole patterned after the famous sixteenth at Augusta. It even boasted a spectacular view of the Throgs Neck Bridge and the Manhattan skyline. It was the kind of place that anyone on the adjacent shore or passing by on the water might stare at in awe, wondering, *Who lives there?*

Senator Oren Casey had been here many times. For parties attended by some of the most influential people on Wall Street. Fund-raising galas at a thousand dollars a head. Or just for "business." The senator was one of the most influential people in the statehouse. When someone needed something done—bills brought up in committee, licenses granted—things generally ran through him. Over the years, he had been courted many times by Washington to run for higher office. "An honest man can feel no pleasure in the exercise of power over his fellow citizens," he always said, quoting Jefferson.

But privately, for thirty years, in his heart he laughed at the lie.

The Lincoln wound down the long drive leading to the house and came to a stop in the circular roundabout. The senator didn't wait for his door to be opened. He wasn't a fancy man and that wasn't his aide's job anyway. He bundled his overcoat against the breeze and waved through the glass to the old man who stood in the doorway.

Richard Scayne waved back.

They had known each other for decades; their fortunes had merged as their empires grew. The son of a Waterbury mill owner, Scayne had always been a bear of a man with round, thick shoulders and coarse laborer's hands. Piercing blue eyes that could read a man like an X-ray.

Over the years, the senator had smoothed the way for many lucrative arrangements for him, always, at first blush, to the benefit of the state. Securing the way for Datacorp, Scayne's "back office" data division, to buy their corporate headquarters in Stamford. Tax credits for relocating a large block of workers for their turbine factory up in Waterbury. Scayne even had a minority position in TRV, the consortium that ran the Pequot Woods, and retained a small but lucrative piece of the casino.

Casey thought it a shame to see what was happening to him now.

Not just the cancer, which had eaten away the man's once-powerful presence. But the fact that he was under indictment by the state's liberal attorney general. Caught up in this Iraq corruption mess. Under house arrest. A man who had brought more jobs to Connecticut than all the casinos strung together. His turbine plant in New London alone employed over fifteen hundred people.

The door opened and the two longtime friends embraced. Casey said to Scayne, "You know Ira."

"Of course." The billionaire nodded, extending his hand. "Ira."

Scayne's face was now gaunt, no longer robust and jowly. His formerly orange hair was white and sparse, his shoulders narrow. His usual machinist's grip was half its normal strength. He'd fought the cancer like he'd fought every battle in life, to win—not just to win, to mow it down. To stampede over interference. This time, it didn't seem as if God had gotten the memo.

The aide in the tweed golf cap nodded dutifully. "Mr. Scayne."

"We'll just be a minute, Ira," Casey said, indicating for him to remain outside.

The two men went into Scayne's office, a two-story glass and beam structure that looked out on the Long Island Sound. Casey couldn't help but notice the black tracking donut secured to the old man's ankle.

"Helluva risk coming here like this, Oren," Scayne acknowledged. He glanced down at the donut. For the past year, Scayne had been under house arrest. "Of course, there's not much chance anymore of me coming to you."

"Don't worry about it, Richard."

Casey plopped himself on the large leather couch, Scayne in

a chair across from him, exhaling as he lowered himself down. "Don't ever get ill, Oren. God's way of paying me back for all my sins."

"In that case, I can look forward to an equally uncomfortable demise." The senator smiled.

"Two peas in a pod?" He lifted his leg, the donut dangling. "Where the hell do they think I can go anyway? I can barely make it to the fucking toilet to take a pee."

He reached forward to the large Noguchi coffee table and picked up a couple of brochures. Casey saw that they were the annual reports of companies Scayne either owned or had interests in. Datacorp. Apex Turbine. The NHL's Nashville team. One by one, he tossed them back on the table.

The last was a product brochure from SRC Electric, which he made a point of tossing in front of Casey's eyes. "Suppliers of the Nova 91."

"Who would have thought a bunch of goddamn generators could bring the two of us down?"

"We're not down yet." Casey met the sick man's eyes. "I'm looking into the assignment of a new lawyer. They may appoint a new head of the office up in Hartford. Not such a rabble-rouser. One more sensitive to the good you've done for the state. I'm busting as many balls as I can. In the meantime, there is one pesky wrinkle that's come up."

"*Wrinkle . . .*"

"Not to worry, Richard. You've got more pressing things to occupy yourself with."

"Just as long as we understand each other, Oren . . . I won't be spending the last time God gives me on this earth in a courtroom watching a bunch of meddling legislators undo everything I've done. I'll use what I have, Oren, whoever I have to bring down. No reason for us not to be seeing things clearly between us now."

The senator smiled. "You make it very hard not to root for the cancer to get you first, Richard."

"I tend to think of it as motivation, Oren. I won't be participating in any trial."

Casey stood up. He took along the SRC brochure. "I think that's all I came to hear. From your lips. No reason to take up any more of your time."

"You mentioned a wrinkle . . ."

"I'm taking care of it. Some pesky local policeman. Sticking his nose where it doesn't belong." He waved it off. "Thinks it's all about some gambling issue. At the Pequot Woods. We've got it covered."

Scayne pushed himself out of the chair too. "You, if anyone, know how to handle that sort of thing."

The senator took a last view of the sound and moved toward the door. "I truly wish you the best, Richard. We've logged a lot of miles together over the years. It would be a shame to see it all undone at the end . . ."

Scayne took his arm. "Just remember—if I go, you go, Oren. I'm sorry to say that, but at this stage, that's the best guarantee I have. So go do what you do best—put the pressure on. Bust some balls. Just so you know that in the end, I won't be party to any trial."

They walked to the door and opened it; the man in the tweed cap stood up.

"Thanks for driving him down, Ira . . . I think we said all we had to say."

CHAPTER SIXTY-ONE

The next morning, Freddy Munoz leaned against the table across from Hauck's desk. He had finally made contact with Raines, pressed the security man for a copy of the video he had shown Hauck implicating Sanger.

"*And* . . . ?" Hauck pushed back skeptically in his chair.

"He actually said, '*What tapes*, Detective? I don't recall showing the lieutenant any specific tapes.' Smug piece of shit! He said, 'We have a virtual mountain of security footage here. You're welcome to come and look through . . .' I don't like that guy, Lieutenant."

"You've always been a pretty fair judge of character," Hauck said.

"He did mention something else," Munoz said. "He asked if you liked the postcards he sent you. He said that *those* he could get you copies of any time you liked. You have any idea what he's referring to, LT . . . ?"

Hauck's blood had already started to burn. Now it was bubbling over into a full-blown simmer. "*I know.* Listen, I want you to find someone for me, Freddy. There's a card dealer up there. Around fifty, maybe a little older. Thick glasses, salt-and-pepper hair. He was the one with Sanger. Start with Personnel . . ."

CHAPTER SIXTY-TWO

Annie Fletcher was at the computer. It was after eleven and she'd taken a shower to wash off the grime of the kitchen, applied a layer of lotion to her legs and hands, poured herself a glass of wine. This was the first moment she had had all day.

She was typing out an e-mail to her son.

> Listen, Jared, I have a surprise . . . I've made some plans to bring you here. For Xmas! I'll be able to take some time off and there's a bunch of cool things we can do, like hang out around NY, go to the Empire State Bldg and see the Lion King . . . And you'll be able to take a plane, all by yourself, cross-country . . .

She looked away from the computer, a tear of joy in her eye.

It had been so tough to be away from him so long. Nine months, and only a couple of visits. But she just couldn't have handled the responsibility right away. Now things had gotten settled. The restaurant was starting to do well. She'd been able to take out a little money. She'd found a center, and California had even agreed to transfer some of its care credits.

It's so tough not being with you, baby. I know everyone's doing a good job taking care of you there, and that you've been a real trooper, but I also know you're sad and I'm sad too . . .

There's this place I want you to see. It's like a school. Just like the Cunningham Center there. Except this place you can go to here, with me, if you like it. Because if you do, if you feel comfortable meeting new friends, maybe we can make it work to let you stay here. You and I . . .

It hit her how nervous she was feeling. Nervous that Jared might say no. That he'd made friends, gotten used to them being apart.

So what do you think? Don't keep me in suspense. I so look forward to hearing from you, honey . . .

After she signed off, she sat for a long time with her head in her hands and her eyes closed. Her ex-husband, Rick, had cost her so much. Every penny she had. Not to mention the feeling of being capable of taking care of the one person she loved. Of being human again . . .

He took it all away, but slowly she was starting to take it all back again.

The local Stamford paper was folded on her desk. She always tried to leaf through it, to know what was going on around town. Businesses that were opening, to try to figure out opportunities for the restaurant.

Annie opened it. There was a school budget story on the front page. Below it a headline about a teenage boy found stabbed in Upchurch Park in Bridgeport that grabbed her attention.

Ricardo Vidro. It seemed as if he had gotten involved in some local gangs there.

Such a waste. She opened the page and glanced at the photo of the victim.

Everything came to a stop.

Once again, she saw him staring back at her. His eyes holding a warning. A dare . . . That cocky smirk—*We know who you are. We know where to find you, lady* . . .

Annie's mouth went dry.

It was the boy she had seen outside the restaurant that night, tossing away the Tec-9.

"I'm sorry to bother you," she said. She caught Hauck on his cell at home.

"No bother at all," he said brightly. "I thought I might have to wait until Christmas to talk to you again."

"Sorry to ruin that. Do you have a local paper around?"

"I don't know, maybe." That's when Hauck noticed the wariness in her voice. "What's wrong?"

"There's an article on the front page. About some kid who was killed in Bridgeport."

"Hold on." Hauck searched around the kitchen, found the pile where he'd thrown it in the recycling bin. He straightened the front page.

BRIDGEPORT TEEN STABBED IN LIKELY GANG DISPUTE.

"That's him," Annie said worriedly. "That's the kid I saw throwing the gun in the Dumpster."

Hauck folded the page to the picture. He read the victim's name. "You're sure?"

"Course I'm sure. You think I could ever mistake something like this?"

Hauck took a long look at the young victim's face. First Morales in the DR. Now both of the shooters were dead. A squabble in a park. Someone pulled a knife. Everyone scattered. He knew this was anything but random.

This was a hell of a lot of "cleaning up" for a casino gambling scam.

"This doesn't go away, does it? I was just feeling safe. Now it's starting to worry me all over again."

Hauck asked, "Listen, what are you doing tomorrow night?"

"*What am I doing?* I don't know what I'm doing. Nothing, *working* . . . Like every night. Why?"

"Take a night off. I'll cook for you."

"Cook for *me?*" Annie hesitated. "You mean like on a date?"

"I don't know. We'll see. Whatever feels right."

She paused again. "I'm not a pro at this, Ty. You didn't answer me. Is this something that ought to make me afraid?"

"No," Hauck said, "you don't have to be afraid. Not any longer."

"And why is that?"

"Because now the two people you could tie anything to are dead."

"*Oh, great.*" Annie clucked in mock relief. "That's sure comforting!"

Hauck said, "So I guess that means you'll come?"

CHAPTER SIXTY-THREE

*F*reddy located the dealer. He came into Hauck's office carrying a faxed file.

His name was Paul Pacello. He had worked for the Pequot Woods since it first opened. Most of the staff was local—a key part of the casino's original agreement with the state. But Pacello was a career croupier. He'd had stints in Tahoe and on the Gulf Coast. Twenty-eight years behind the tables.

Just a month ago, he had put in his notice and retired.

How had Raines phrased it when Hauck had asked about the dealer? *We dealt with that situation privately.*

Freddy placed a grainy faxed likeness in front of Hauck, who nodded without hesitation. "That's him."

The man in the video dealing to Sanger, using the false shuffle. Kramer's supposed accomplice in the scam.

"Where do we find the guy, Freddy?"

Munoz had followed up with Personnel, but the gal there had gotten all nervous and told him they'd have to clear that through security before they gave out a forwarding address.

"I said, 'No problem,' Lieutenant. I saw his age."

Pacello was over sixty, and Munoz had been able to pick up

a social security number off the file. "I ran it by the local bureau in Connecticut where his checks were being cut."

"Twenty-two twenty-seven Capps Harbor Road," the detective read. "Brunswick, Maine."

Hauck was familiar with it. A picturesque town on the coast where Bowdoin College was located. Hauck had gone to Colby, only an hour away. Pacello had likely retired up there. It was about a four-hour drive away.

"And that's not all," Munoz said.

Steve Chrisafoulis had been delving into the Pequot Woods, scratching for some kind of link between the casino, DR-17, and Nelson Vega.

He'd found one.

He came in carrying the DR-17 gang leader's file. That same smug glint in his eye Hauck had seen before.

"Fire away."

"Vega did a short stint in the army. In 2001 to 2002. He was with the 223rd out of Fort Hood, in New Jersey. Munitions."

"I can't believe they even let an asshole like that in the service."

Chrisafoulis snorted. "Trust me, they caught on . . ." Steve opened the file on Hauck's desk. "He got in trouble right from the start. Sexually harassing a female enlistee. Insubordination to his senior officer. A drunkenness charge. Fighting. He eventually got bounced. Doesn't say exactly why, but it seems it involved some ordnance that went missing from the base's weapons stock. Dishonorably discharged. May 10, 2002. No charges ever filed."

Hauck picked up the paperwork.

"You see who his brigade captain is?"

Hauck scanned Vega's release, squinting at the signature on the last page.

One of the signatures was faint, but as Hauck made it out, he looked up, a surge of triumph running through his veins.

Captain Joseph W. Raines.

"Raines was a brigade commander in the 223rd himself," Steve said. "He left in 2002 and served as an instructor in the military police's antiterrorism school. From there he left the service and went to Iraq as a consultant in some security outfit there. But he knew him. He signed the fucker's release."

"Who the hell is he protecting, Steve?" Hauck knew Raines was just a pawn. "Who runs these companies?"

Chrisafoulis tossed him a glitzy annual report. "The Pequot Woods." Hauck flipped to the management page. A bunch of names and faces he'd never heard of. Professionals. Twenty members of the board. Plus a council of overseers.

A couple of names stood out. Senator Oren Casey. The guy who was caught in all that trouble—Richard Scayne.

"You know, if I were a good ol' boy, I'd toss this over to Sculley and Taylor and wash our hands of it right now," he said to Chrisafoulis.

"Or to Sanger's boss at the DOJ. Or the state attorney general . . ." The detective shrugged.

"Yeah." Hauck tossed the Pequot Woods report back. "Keep digging. If it's not a gambling scam, I want to know what the hell it is. Me, I'm taking a drive up to Maine."

"You know they know we know about him, Ty . . ." Steve looked concerned. "If I was looking to keep something quiet, that would be the place I'd start."

"Yeah," Hauck said, "me too."

CHAPTER SIXTY-FOUR

*A*nnie looked adorable.

When Hauck opened the door she stood on the landing in a short white parka and jeans, a knitted cap pulled over her ears against the chill. He wore an open plaid flannel shirt with the sleeves turned up over a T-shirt and Top-Siders. He knew he was staring just a bit. He couldn't help it.

"You don't look like someone who's so scared." He smiled.

He let her in.

"You told me to relax," Annie said. "Besides"—she grinned—"everyone who'd want to hurt me is dead, right?" She took off her hat and scarf, revealing a green cowl-neck sweater and a nice, toned figure. "Here." She handed him a Frank Family cabernet. "We serve it at the café. Anything I can do?"

Hauck asked, "You know how to do a fire?"

Annie shrugged. "Brownie troop 624, Oakland Hills, California. Merits for neatness and outdoor survival skills. I think I can manage."

"Good." Hauck handed her a log and a set of matches. "That gets you a glass of wine."

While Annie got the fire rolling, Hauck went back to the

kitchen and checked the oven, sprinkled the asparagus with some oil and garlic, and opened the cab.

"Nice view," she said, looking out at the sound through the sliding doors.

"Makes up for the décor." Hauck smiled. "Early frat house, I've been told."

"Early *single* looks more like it."

He came around with a glass of wine. "Thanks for being kind."

Annie had gotten a nice little fire going and brushed off her hands over the hearth. "All set for the next task."

"The next task is easy," Hauck said. "Just relax."

They clinked glasses and chatted for a bit, then Hauck took everything out of the stove. While he did, Annie took a look around, finding the stack of old watercolors Hauck had leaning against the wall. "I took this art class," he said. "The instructor somehow convinced me I had talent."

"They're not at all bad."

Hauck smiled. "Course, later he asked me if I could do anything about these parking tickets he had . . ."

Annie laughed. She picked up some photos on the console table. A shot of Hauck's family from years ago.

"*Yours . . . ?*"

"Jessie and Norah." Hauck nodded. He realized he was going to have to explain it to her at some point but didn't want to alter the mood.

"They're cute. Is this your wife?" She picked up a picture of Hauck and Karen, sailing.

"Just a friend."

"Sorry to be such a snoop," Annie said, placing it back down.

"I seem to recall I'm the one who asked you to look around."

He leaned across the counter. "Norah died about a year after that was taken. Car accident. Jessie's thirteen now. She lives with her mom in Brooklyn. Karen and I . . ." He shrugged. "We were together for a while, but now that's done. That's her and her family . . ."

"I'm sorry." Annie placed her hands on the back of a chair and stared at him. "About your daughter."

"So now you're up-to-date," Hauck said. He dug the spatula into the meatloaf. "C'mon, that's all old stuff now. Let's eat!"

CHAPTER SIXTY-FIVE

The meal came off beautifully. The meatloaf was flavorful and moist; the four-cheese macaroni Hauck made was a ten.

Cutting into it, Annie joked, "If this police gig ever falls apart, you can definitely come to me for a job!"

Hauck exhaled. "Whew, that takes a load of pressure off my mind."

He would have liked to have been able to tell her about Foley and the job offer he'd received, but he didn't feel it was right. They did talk a little about where he came from, in Byron, how he got to Colby and then went on to becoming a cop. Briefly, how things fell apart for Beth and him after Norah died and how he ended up moving back up here.

Annie told him about her. How she had grown up in the Bay Area and met the guy of her dreams in college. "U of Michigan," she said. "He had this dream of opening a restaurant out west and getting into the wine business. We went out to Healdsburg. I set the place up, planned the menus, did the kitchen . . . Even painted the goddamn walls. Once it proved to be a challenge, Richard just didn't like being tied down to it. Sort of a pattern, I soon discovered—that commitment thing. We put our life savings into it—actually, *my* life savings! All the money in the world I got from my dad, who died when I was fifteen."

"That's too bad."

"One day I woke up and found our accounts were down to zero. We owed every supplier three months in arrears. Richard cleaned us out. He had this little problem. You know, it involved a certain white powder and his nose. In the end he just bailed on me—with pretty much whatever we had left. Left me with a bunch of angry vendors and the place by myself—"

"And a son," Hauck said.

"*And a son*. Jared's nine now. He's got some handicaps he's got to deal with. *He's* . . ." She put down her wine and seemed to stop. "I've made some mistakes. I wasn't the perfect mother back then. I was broke. I wasn't *broke*—I was over my head in debt and my husband had just walked out on me and I was trying to manage this place and Jared, by myself. I just got overwhelmed . . ." Annie frowned. "Everything just seemed to spill over. I couldn't take care of him for a while. The state had to intervene. That's not easy for me to say. He's back in California with my mom. That's why when this whole thing crashed down on me I was such a basket case. I need this thing to work out. I need to bring my son here. You have your daughter . . ."

"Every other weekend . . ."

"Then you understand. The good news is, I think he's going to be able to finally come here with me. Before Christmas. I have a two-bedroom I'm renting. I'm trying to work it out that he can stay."

"I'd like to meet him one day." Hauck smiled.

"I'd like you to." Annie's eyes grew warm. "That would be nice. You know, you seem an okay guy, Lieutenant . . . And if I say so, not altogether terrible on the eyes . . . But that may be just the wine talking. Look at me, one night out of the shop and I turn into a total lush. I feel like I'm the one going through most of the wine."

"That's only because I have to be up at the crack of dawn in the morning."

"What time is that?" she asked. "I'm usually at the fish market by six thirty."

"Three A.M."

"*Three* A.M.*!* That's not the crack of dawn, Lieutenant. That's the frigging dead of night. You have a second job you're not telling me about?"

Hauck chuckled. "I'm actually heading up to Maine. It's part of the case . . ."

"I thought this thing was all about gangs. I didn't know they had gangs in Maine. I thought they just had lobsters."

"It seems retired blackjack dealers as well."

"Blackjack dealers?"

"I can't tell you, Annie, so don't even ask. I guess I *could* stop and pick you up a couple of four-pounders while I'm up there . . ."

"Sounds good. I'll be sure to tell my supplier that I'm covered. So, look, why don't I help you clean up a little then? I'm an even better dishwasher than a cook . . ."

Hauck grinned. "I've got chocolate chip cookies for dessert. Chunky Monkey ice cream."

"Oh, God, you pulled out all the stops, huh?" She rolled her eyes amorously. "We could eat them while we wash . . ."

"Not a chance. This is your night off." Hauck got up and picked up her plate.

"Jeez, why didn't I meet you ten years ago . . ."

They took in the plates and Hauck put out the cookies and ice cream, and they dug into them directly out of the container, leaning on the counter, talking about restaurants and movies they liked.

And after ten, when Annie said maybe she should go and

put on her parka and scarf and hat ("Still can't get used to all this cold . . ."), she turned at the door, all bundled up, looking irresistible to Hauck.

"I meant to tell you"—he stepped up to her—"you're not exactly bad on the eyes either."

Annie shrugged. Her eyes glistened. "So we can call it a date, right? I just want to know so when I get in the car on my way home and think, *That was really pretty nice,* I won't be wondering if this was some kind of lame excuse you came up with to get me to leave . . ."

"Yeah." Hauck smiled. "I worked on it all day. You can call me if you want to check. I'll be on the road by four."

She looked in his eyes. "You could kiss me, you know. That would be okay. I promise I won't tell anyone."

Hauck smiled. He looked into her mossy round eyes and leaned forward, pressing his lips softly to her mouth.

She placed her hand on his chest.

She was funny and vulnerable, he was thinking, and at the same time independent and strong. She had pulled her life together when it had fallen apart. And he liked that. He let his tongue peek through, and she did as well, meeting his. The kiss lingered. He was trying to decide if there were any sparks.

There were.

"Something to look forward to," Annie said, as he pulled away. "Don't worry. I won't stalk you tomorrow. But you be safe up there. And don't forget the lobsters . . ."

"Aye-aye."

He watched her cross the street, waving once, and climb into her Prius. He waved back too, feeling an undeniable lift in his heart as she drove away.

CHAPTER SIXTY-SIX

*I*n a darkened bar called the Alibi, off I-91, south of Hartford, Ira Wachman, Joe Raines, and Warren Hauck sat in a back booth.

"This is one of those little tête-à-têtes," Wachman said, "that no one is ever going to know existed, but where the fates of a handful of very important individuals swing in the balance."

"And then there's the rest of us," Warren said, draining the last of his scotch.

"Yes." Wachman nodded philosophically. "And then there's *us.*"

He looked at Raines. "I understand they know about this accomplice of yours? This dealer . . ."

"*Ex*-dealer. But that's nothing to worry about. I've got that under control."

Wachman chuckled gloomily. "Since my friend Warren here was kind enough to introduce us, you've said you had a number of things under control, and I haven't slept through the night since. This Pacello . . . This *ex*-employee of yours, he knows precisely what?"

"He knows this gambling thing between Sanger and Kramer

is just a sham. He knows that Kramer had nothing to do with it."

"No." Wachman shook his head. "It would not be good for that to come out at all." He sipped his Coke. "Is there some way we can, how to put it—step up the situation?"

Raines looked at him. *"Step it up?"*

"Ensure things don't go south any farther. Put a stamp of certainty on it."

"You mind telling me what that means?" Warren came to life, flicking an ash.

"You know precisely what it means, Warren. Shut this little line of inquiry down. We let this whole thing play out as a form of misdirection . . ." He looked at Raines. "All that shit you learned in Iraq, right? Problem is, it hasn't worked any better here than it did there. Now it's time to just get a little more direct. Up the tempo. What is it we don't understand?"

"Tell me precisely how you want it *upped*?" The casino security man shrugged, seemingly without concern.

"Hold it a minute." Warren didn't like where this was going. "You and I have an understanding, Ira. Personally, I don't give a flying fuck what happens to this guy up there, but you and I agreed from the start certain people were hands-off. And as far as I'm concerned that still goes. I've got stuff in the works. Give me a week, ten days, max. I'll get Ty off this. *My* way. It just needs a little finesse."

"I'm not sure if we have ten days," Wachman said to him. "I can't say I relish the idea of spending the rest of my life in federal prison, Warren. Do you?"

"Five days then. A week." Warren took hold of the government man's wrist as he went to pick up his drink. "Listen, you came to me, Ira, you asked me to play this out. I'm in this as deep as you. As deep as anyone." He turned to Raines. "You keep this Pacello dude under wraps, whatever you have to do. I'll handle my brother. I'm not the one who dropped this thing right in his fucking backyard." He shifted back to Wachman. "I said I would work it out. I still will."

His voice traveled across the darkened bar.

Wachman glared. "We're all in equally deep, Warren. It's just that some people have more to lose. Anyway, relax . . . Never leave it to a political hack to go back on an agreement, right? A week, ten days . . . Maybe you're right. I don't see how that makes a difference. But whatever you have had better work."

"It'll work." Warren nodded, exhaling a ring of smoke and leaning back. "Jesus, you're starting to make me jumpy, Ira . . ." He slid out of the booth. "I'll be right back. I'm going to take a pee."

Wachman watched the door to the men's room close, then said to Raines, "My group may not be as committed to our earlier understanding as my friend here. You understand?"

Raines nodded. "That'll get messy."

"*It's already messy, Mr. Raines.* A government prosecutor is dead. Several other people have been killed to protect that. But it'll end up the-fucking-Ninth Ward–messy if the rest of this shit hits the fan. My people met a couple of nights ago. We're all in agreement. Whatever has to be done, just get it done." His gaze was determined and unmistakable. "Don't worry about the mess, Mr. Raines. Just shut this investigation down."

The casino man downed the last of his drink. "Any need for me to hang around?"

"No." Wachman adjusted his tweed cap. "Sometimes a rising tide sweeps up everything in its path. I'll explain it to my friend as best I can."

CHAPTER SIXTY-SEVEN

*H*auck made it on the road before four, only the high beams of fast-moving truckers cutting the darkness on the thruway. He put on some Van Morrison.

By six, he had beaten the morning rush into Hartford, with Imus on the radio.

An hour later he was well into Massachusetts. Daylight brought the old mill towns of Auburn and Worcester passing by.

He wasn't sure what he would find up there. This had the choreographed feel of another cover-up. Josephina Ruiz, Raines's video, those pictures with Josie—all trying to ward him off. Both gang members who orchestrated the initial drive-by were dead. Vega was free. Someone was going to a lot of trouble and risk to tie up loose ends.

By eight, he had crossed into Maine, veering onto the 295 bypass around Portland. There was a trace of snow on the ground and the morning opened up into a clear blue winter day.

It brought back memories for Hauck. He'd gone to Colby, just an hour up the road from Brunswick. Bowdoin had been the scene of one his best college games. A hundred and twenty yards rushing; he'd bowled over from the two with the game-winning touchdown with thirty seconds remaining on the clock. He could still recall the elation of dancing all the way back to the bench, the groan of the packed stands deflating. Blood on his jersey—number 22. He'd returned a decade ago for his tenth reunion. With Beth and Jessie and Norah. A rising star with the NYPD, he remembered how proud he was showing them off.

Three years later, Norah was dead.

He'd never come back again.

The exit sign read BRUNSWICK. Hauck got off at the second exit. He stopped at a service station to hit the john. He plugged "2227 Capps Harbor Road" into the GPS.

The address was a few miles out of town. Past the college on Merepoint Bay.

It was eight thirty. Hauck drove past the college on 123, checking out the stands and the field house, everything looking different than he remembered.

He turned on Middle Inlet Road.

A layer of chunky snow was packed on the ground. The roads, this far from town, were not well plowed. He was heading toward the water. The houses here were upscale. Large, shingled capes and farms with renovated barns that backed onto the bay.

Not exactly the kind of neighborhood a career blackjack dealer could readily afford. Even here.

We dealt with that privately, Raines had said.

Hauck made a right onto Capps Harbor, the wheels of the Explorer crunching on the packed snow. A couple of homes were up ahead. The GPS announced he was approaching his destination. He went by a blue colonial with a mailbox reading 2210.

Hauck pulled to the side of the road. On the other side was a large white house with green shutters set back aways. Maybe once it would've been called stately, but now it was in need of repair. A wooden sign hung at the end of the driveway.

MEREPOINT BAY FARM. BED AND BREAKFAST. The sign said 2227.

CHAPTER SIXTY-EIGHT

*H*auck stared at the house a long time before pulling in. It was wear-worn, in need of several coats of paint. The driveway was all rutted. A three-bay closed garage was separate from the house.

Pacello had bought himself a little inn.

Hauck couldn't see any lights on or smoke from the chimney. No car in front. He drove down the driveway toward the house.

If we know, Raines knows, Steve's words rang in his head. He checked his gun. Four were already dead.

Hauck parked and stepped out, strapped the holster around his chest. He went up the chipped stone staircase leading to the front. Most of the shutters were closed. He peered in. He didn't see any sign of life.

He knocked on the front door. *"Anyone home?"*

No answer. A gull squawked, flapping its wings out over the inlet.

He tried a second time. No answer again. If the place was even open for business, there sure weren't any guests.

Hauck took out his cell and asked for the local directory assistance. He requested the number for the Merepoint Farm Bed and Breakfast on Capps Harbor Road. After a few rings a voice recording came on. "You've reached Paul and Katie Pacello of the Merepoint Farm B and B. If you'd like to make a reservation . . ."

Hauck flicked it off. The place looked abandoned. Shuttered up. It didn't seem as if the Pacellos had just gone out to the market.

He dialed the office back home, finding Munoz.

"How's the weather up there, Lieutenant? Find Pacello yet?"

"*Cold,*" he said, staring out at the gray inlet. "And no, no one's home."

He gave Munoz the address and told him to do his magic. "Call the local county clerk. Find me whatever you can. When it was purchased? Who from? I was expecting more like a trailer in a retirement home. I'm looking at an awfully nifty piece of real estate for a guy who likely never made more than sixty thou a year in his life. It's cold as shit. Don't keep me waiting too long. "

"I'll be in touch, LT . . ."

Pacello had just retired, around the same time Kramer had been killed. Now he was missing too.

The dealer was in this, Hauck knew.

He heard a noise and spotted an old black truck lumbering up the drive. He double-checked his gun.

The truck pulled to a stop in front of the garage. The side panel read NORTHLAND ELECTRIC. A man stepped out in a blue workman's uniform and cap. He looked up at Hauck and scratched his head. "It's off-season, mister. Hope you're not looking around here for a room."

"I'm looking for Paul Pacello," Hauck replied.

The man nodded, went around and threw open the back door of his truck. "You won't find him here. He called in early this morning and said he and the wife were gone for a few days. Told me to finish the job. Blown circuit casement in the basement."

Hauck removed his wallet, showing the man his badge. "Any idea where he went?"

The man grunted, "*Greenwich?* Connecticut, huh? I have a niece down there. Fairfield. I think it's close by. No, no idea in the world, I'm afraid. Just told me where the key would be left, that's all."

"When did you see him last?"

The man strapped on his tool case and yanked out a carton from the bay. "Yesterday. Helped me dig out that wiring. It's off-season now. Can't blame anyone for wanting to get up and leave."

"I need to talk to him. You know anyone who might know where they went?" Hauck put his badge away. "Anything you can tell me would be of help."

The man shrugged. "Mister, the only thing *I* can tell you is never cross a black wire with a white ground. You know what I mean? Anything else, you might check with the post office back in town. See if anything's being forwarded. But I mean, you must know that—you're a cop."

The electrician moved past him toward the house.

Hauck looked around the point, cold and dry with winter. Maybe the neighbors knew something.

"Thanks."

CHAPTER SIXTY-NINE

*T*he neighbors didn't help.

All Hauck was able to get from a tight-lipped woman in a parka backing her Volvo wagon out was that Pacello had some family who must live locally because she had seen a couple who seemed in their thirties with a young kid helping him fix up the place from time to time.

He drove back into town, stopped for coffee and a late breakfast at a place called the Green Horse on Pleasant Street. He checked through the local phone book and found no other Pacello. He asked around the café. No one seemed to know him there. A couple of people did know of the B and B.

An older woman nodded. "Yes, I heard that old place changed hands."

It was almost one when Freddy finally called back. "Enjoying your trip up there, Lieutenant?"

Hauck grumbled, "I've been up and down Main Street twice, bought Jessie some maple syrup and a pair of clogs, and now I'm standing here ogling a couple of hot-looking coeds. What took you so long?"

"The property was bought three years ago," Freddy said. "For $825,000."

Three years. That shot a hole in Hauck's theory, that the dealer's sudden "retirement" was connected to Kramer's murder.

"Seems Pacello put $275,000 down and took out a mortgage with Cumberland County Savings and Loan for the rest."

"*Five hundred and fifty thousand dollars.* That's an awful lot to carry for a guy who deals cards," Hauck said.

"That's why it took me a while to get back, LT. I had Steve check with the bank. Seems the Pacellos were three months in arrears. He had tried to refinance it twice over the past year. Lower the payments. Until last month . . ."

"Then what happened?"

"Then the mortgage was paid off, Lieutenant."

Hauck turned away from the street. "*Paid off?* You mean in full?"

"Yeah, one hundred percent, LT."

Over half a million dollars. Hauck's head started to spin. He thought of the surveillance video. "Maybe Pacello was in bed with Kramer and Sanger after all."

"I don't think so," Freddy replied. "That's why it took me so long. The mortgage payoff check was from the Washington Mutual in Wallingford, Connecticut. The funds for it came from a local real estate company, Saunders Properties."

Hauck shrugged. "Pacello probably sold his primary home."

"I don't know. We did a Dun and Bradstreet on it. Saunders is a local affiliate of a mortgage company called Heritage Financial, which is owned by a William Arthur Turner. When I ran it by Steve, he immediately recognized his name. William Turner is on the board of several large enterprises. One of them may not surprise you. You're probably already ahead of me on this . . ."

"The Pequot Woods."

Munoz chuckled. "That's why they pay you the big bucks, huh, LT."

It was all starting to fit together. That was Pacello's payoff. That was how they handled things *privately*. For his participation. Pacello *was* paid off, but not by Kramer and Sanger.

By the Pequot Woods.

For his silence.

That whole false shuffle thing was another diversion.

They had found the link between Raines and Vega. They'd found the payoff for Pacello. They'd killed Kramer and probably Morales and the kid in Bridgeport.

And David Sanger.

In itself, none of that proved anything. Nothing tied any of this to Sanger. Or to Kramer. Or implicated anyone in a murder. He still had to get one of them to come forward.

Pacello was the key.

"Anything else?" Hauck asked, a sense of elation mixing with uncertainty.

"Just this—the house isn't even in Pacello's name. It's in a trust. Steve figures probably for estate reasons."

"You have the name?"

"*Linda Ann Whyte,*" Munoz said. "The Linda Ann Whyte Irrevocable Trust."

"Stay with me, Freddy," Hauck said. He ran back inside the café where he'd had coffee, asked the woman at the counter for the phone book again. She bent down and handed it over. The Central Maine white pages.

Hauck flicked to the W's, scrolled down from "Wharton" at the top of the page.

Until he came upon it.

Calvin and Linda Whyte.

The address was 495 New Morris Road, in Auburn. There was a map on the front cover. Auburn was just outside of Lewiston. About thirty minutes away.

"We do okay?" Munoz asked when Hauck got back on the line.

"Aces, Freddy."

CHAPTER SEVENTY

*I*f Brunswick was idyllic, picturesque, Lewiston was its ugly older sister in shabby clothes. Run-down, boarded-up mills along the Androscoggin River. Motel 6s and Subways on the main drag instead of charming New England inns.

Across the river, Auburn was the sister's even plainer friend.

It was about a thirty-minute drive from the coast. Hauck crossed over the bridge and stopped at a 7-Eleven and punched "New Morris Road" into the GPS. The guidance system took him out to East Auburn, situated on a large, unfrozen lake, then continued, following the stark, wooded shoreline. Along the road, dingy farms with rusted old tractors and pickups in front mixed with more modern shingled capes, probably home to college students and professors from Bates, which was perched across the river.

Hauck continued on.

About halfway around the lake, the GPS alerted him to New Morris Road, a cluster of weather-beaten mailboxes marking the intersection. He headed toward the water. The road was paved but rutted. The harsh Maine winters had had their way.

Like to see Old *Morris Road*. Hauck chuckled to himself.

Ahead, a couple of run-down farmhouses came into view: 380, 440. Some even had covered boats dry-docked in the front yard.

At a curve, a rickety fence in front, was a white clapboard farmhouse.

Four ninety-five.

The house had black hanging shutters, a listing wooden porch, and backed onto the lake. There were a couple of vehicles pulled up in front, a Toyota SUV and a beaten-up Dodge minivan. Hauck saw the lights were on inside.

He climbed out of the car and checked his gun strapped against his chest. He caught sight of a curtain parting in a downstairs window.

They were here.

He went up the steps to the landing and knocked. He heard voices inside.

It took a few seconds before a heavyset woman in a white peasant top opened the door, carrying a baby in her arms.

Hauck removed his sunglasses. "Mrs. Whyte?"

The woman juggled the baby. "Yes."

"I'm Lieutenant Hauck. I'm from the town of Greenwich, in Connecticut. I'm sorry to bother you. I was hoping I might find Paul Pacello here."

"Pacello?" The woman seemed a bit nervous, acting as if she'd never heard the name.

"Yes, ma'am. He used to be an employee of the Pequot Woods Casino. You know him, don't you?"

"No, um . . ." The baby started to whimper. "Yes . . ." Her large eyes seemed ill at ease. *"Hush, Noah!"*

Hauck looked at her. "He's your father, isn't he?"

The woman shook her head, unsure what to do. She jiggled the squirming baby. "Yes, he's my father . . . But he's not here.

He lives about thirty minutes away. Down in Brunswick. He's probably there. I don't know what would have brought you up here."

"I've already been there," Hauck said. "I was told he and his wife left yesterday in kind of a rush. A workman at the house said he was gone for a few days."

"Oh. I wouldn't know anything about that . . . Listen, I've got to see to my child. You can see he's all in a mess. I can tell them you came by. What did you say your name was?"

"Hauck," he said again. "You're sure they're not here?"

"Of course I'm sure," the woman said, agitated. "Now I've got to go. I'm sorry . . ."

"One last thing." Hauck motioned toward the silver Toyota 4-Runner parked outside the garage. "That belong to you, Ms. Whyte? The one with Connecticut plates?"

Linda Whyte's face flushed red.

"Listen, Ms. Whyte, I know they're here." Hauck took a step up the landing. "They're probably inside there now and I only need a few words with your father, in connection with the murder of a Keith Kramer, whom I think he knew. And the fact that he's going to this much trouble to avoid talking only gives rise to the thought that maybe there's something to hide."

"I don't know." Her eyes flitted, nervously. "I—"

"*Linda* . . ." A voice sounded from inside. "It's okay, honey . . ."

Pacello came up behind her in the doorway. "I guess you're looking for me?"

He was dressed in a plaid flannel shirt and rumpled pants. The same salt-and-pepper crew cut and heavy oversized eyeglasses Hauck recalled from Raines's video.

"I don't have to talk with you," he said. "You don't have any jurisdiction here."

"May I come in?"

"No, you can't come in." Pacello eased his daughter out of the doorway. "What you can do is get back in your car there and drive on home. I don't know anything about any murder. I barely knew Keith. Sometimes we worked in the same section. I can't help you."

"How did you know I was headed up here? Did Raines warn you?"

"I don't know what you're talking about, mister. I came to visit my family. Is that a crime? And I don't have to continue this conversation if I don't want to, unless you've got a warrant. I'm retired. I don't work for the resort anymore. I don't know anything about what happened to Keith. That was all too bad. So if you don't mind, I'm sorry . . ."

He moved to shut the door.

Hauck caught it before it shut and met the man's eyes. "I can come back with a warrant if you like, Mr. Pacello. A federal one. I know about how you came to buy your inn. How you paid off the mortgage. I know precisely where the check came from. The Pequot Woods. Five hundred and seventy-five thousand dollars . . . That's a little more than a gold watch for your ten years. You wouldn't want to have to answer questions about that, would you? Sort of has the feel of someone who may have been bought off."

"*Bought off?*" Pacello opened the door wider. "I don't know what you're talking about, mister. Bought off for what?"

"For your silence." Hauck shrugged. "For your participation in a scheme to implicate a federal attorney in a phony gambling scam. For covering up what happened to Keith Kramer. That is how you got your little nest egg paid off, right? After falling three months behind in the payments. *Now* do you have an idea what I'm talking about, Mr. Pacello?"

Lines tightened on the dealer's face. For a second, he seemed about to lunge at Hauck.

"I also know your place is held in a trust. For your daughter here. Your grandkids . . ."

"That's enough, okay?"

"You don't want to risk that, do you? So far, I'm not sure you've done anything really wrong. Nothing that a few smart words from you wouldn't correct. But if you really want me to come back with that warrant, I'm not sure I can promise how someone else might look at that little transaction down the line."

"You don't understand." Pacello shook his head. His voice grew hushed. "I've seen what they would do."

"It's too late," Hauck said. "It's going to come out. Four people are dead. If it's not me, it'll be someone else."

From behind him, a woman stepped into the doorway. Graying hair, kind gray eyes. She put a hand on Pacello's shoulder. "Come on, Paul. We always knew this was going to happen."

"Get back, Katherine."

"No," she said, "I won't get back. I won't let this go on anymore. What's done is done." She stepped onto the landing and opened the door. "Let the lieutenant in."

CHAPTER SEVENTY-ONE

*T*hey went out to the back on a screened-in porch that faced the lake. Two green Adirondack chairs and a couch covered up for the winter in a canvas tarp. It was cold. Pacello sat with his elbows on his knees and a brooding expression. His wife and daughter stayed inside.

"You've got to protect them," he said, more of a plea than a demand. He ran a hand over his close-cropped hair. "Linda and Cal, they can't know."

"I'll do my best," Hauck promised.

"No, that's not good enough. You've got to give me assurances. What's anyone going to think? They know where we are. They know that place is all I got."

Hauck nodded.

Out on the water, a small boat chugged by, maybe a couple of hundred yards offshore. *Some kind of small fishing boat,* Hauck thought at first, *this deep into winter. Maybe checking traps.* An empathetic shiver rippled through him. *Cold as crap out there today.*

"I didn't do anything wrong," Pacello said. "They just told me they wanted to make this guy Sanger come out alright.

Sometimes you do a turn for the high rollers, certain friends of the house. It was part of my job."

"False shuffle." Hauck looked at him. "You stacked the deck so he would win." Hauck suddenly realized that was where all the money had come from in Sanger's account. That and whatever else Sanger had won online.

"You think I even knew who the hell this guy was? They told me to keep the table open for him. Let him win. I saw him there once or twice before and acted like I recognized him. He said I was his lucky dealer. I didn't do anything other than my job, Lieutenant. They came to me. I want that clear."

"'They'?" Hauck said. "Raines?"

"He wanted to point the finger at Keith." Pacello nodded. "Make it look like it was him. I knew it was wrong. I knew there was something else behind it. You ever have to make a choice, Lieutenant?"

Hauck nodded. "Every day."

"No." Pacello shook his head. "A real choice. Something that defines who you are. That won't go away. I worked thirty years across the felt and never took away shit. Maybe a hundred-dollar tip here and there when I tossed someone the right card or spun a lucky number. You sit across from all that money and you just have to look at it as if it's fucking oranges or cabbage. So I made a choice. They knew I wanted to retire and come up here. They knew I had this house, this stupid dream we had, and that I was falling behind. You can't let them take that from me, Lieutenant." Pacello stared at Hauck. "I've earned that. It's all I have. Thirty friggin' years . . . " He motioned inside. "For *them* . . . You understand what I'm saying. They deserve it. All I had to do was deal out some cards."

"Tell me what Raines asked you to do."

"Not till you get me a deal. I'll deny anything I said. You don't know what they'll do."

"Raines warned you I was coming, didn't he? He told you to get out."

Pacello took off his glasses. He massaged his brow. "Yeah, he called me." Pacello sat back. "He told me to get out. He said if you asked anything about Kramer . . ."

His eyes drifted from Hauck toward the water. Hauck noticed that the fishing boat had come in closer. It was just sitting there. Its engines appeared to have been cut.

Something didn't seem right.

No reason for anyone to be out here this time of year . . .

Hauck stood up, stared out at the water. "Mr. Pacello, I want you to get down now—"

The first shot whined in, catching Pacello in the throat, a burst of crimson spraying all over the deck.

The shocked dealer coughed, his eyes stretched wide.

The second shot caught him in the chest, before Hauck could even react. He turned, confused, spewing a spittle of blood and tendril all over his chest.

Hauck screamed into the house. *"Everyone get down!"*

Another shot zinged in, barely missing Hauck's head, crashing into the siding. *"Stay inside!"*

Then another. Hauck felt the heat from it against his shoulder as he leaped and pushed the wounded dealer to the floor. The screen door opened. Pacello's wife rushed out. *"Paul?"*

"Get back in!" Hauck shouted. *"Get down!"*

She stared down at her husband in horror. *"Oh, my God, Paul!"*

Hauck pulled her down from the line of fire and took out his own gun, leaping up and running to the railing. The trawler had started up. It was moving away. He aimed and squeezed off six shots from the Sig. The boat was over a couple of hundred yards out. *"God damn it!"* he yelled, helpless, at the retreating hull.

He ran after it down the steps and continued squeezing off eight more rounds, emptying his clip.

Out of range.

Hauck looked back at Pacello. *"Sonovafuckingbitch!"*

He ran back onto the deck and found Pacello's wife lying over him, talking to him. *"Paul! Paul!"* She was covered in her husband's blood.

The dealer's eyes were beginning to glaze.

Hauck kneeled. The man was fading. He didn't have much time.

"Kramer wasn't guilty, wasn't he?" Hauck lifted Pacello's head. "There was never any scam. They just told you to frame a case around him—*isn't that right?* That they'd pay off the mortgage?"

Pacello coughed out a bubble of blood, nodded. *"Keith . . . ,"* he wheezed, almost smiling. "He was a good guy . . ."

"What was it all about?" Hauck demanded.

Pacello's wife screamed, "Please, God, can't you see what's happening? Just leave him alone!"

The man's gaze started to dim.

"Why did they kill them?" Hauck pressed. "Kramer knew something, didn't he? He brought in Sanger. What the hell did they know, Mr. Pacello? They tried to make it seem like it was all a gambling scam. What was it all about?"

Pacello gripped Hauck's arm. The desperate grasp of someone's last glimmer of strength. He raised himself up, lips quivering. "Ask Raines . . ." His eyes locked onto Hauck, his smile hapless. "Bad choice, huh?"

Hauck saw his pupils were no longer moving.

"*Paul. Paul . . .*" Pacello's wife latched onto him.

Hauck leaned back against the deck and slammed his fist against the boards. He gazed out over the lake, his chest bursting with rage. Pacello's blood was still warm and sticky on his palms.

The boat had disappeared. Only an evaporating and widening wake where it had once been.

CHAPTER SEVENTY-TWO

The twin-engine Cessna 310 lifted off the ground from the small Connecticut airfield. It found that magical cushion of air, rose gently into the sky.

Warren banked away from the airport.

That's what it was for him. *Magic.* Something he couldn't explain. The science of flight contained in one exhilarating rush. Out the cockpit window the trees grew small.

He trimmed his flaps for cruise and checked his engine indicators. He dialed in a southeasterly course. Up here, he always felt at ease. Everything made sense. In control. He headed toward the coast, angling the small plane up to three thousand feet.

Why was it never as simple as it was up here?

He knew he had made a mess of so many things. His life with Ginny and the kids was history now. He had cheated. Destroyed what trust they still had. He had been on so many sides of so many business deals he no longer knew which side was up. Now he had placed his own brother in grave danger.

How?

He had started out, like everyone, with the right goals. To do well, make a little money. Live in a way that his father, who had worked for the Town of Greenwich's water department for thirty years, never could. To give his family things he had never had. Private schools. Fancy trips.

No, Warren knew, watching the countryside below and the interstate leading to New Haven, those were never his goals.

They had never been his goals.

He had used his charm, his easy smile and natural good looks, his instinct for survival—even his fucking six handicap in golf—to guide him past the boundary where his lackluster law degree left off. He flattered the right people. Offered his services. Took risks for them. Curried favor with people in power.

It was easy. He simply let them in. Everything else just seemed to grow. When did he become someone he didn't even know?

He banked the Cessna south along the coast.

Maybe he never was that person. Someone who stood up. Who saw clearly the distinction between right and wrong. Maybe Ty was that person. But now he had the chance to do something about it, Warren knew.

The first thing was to get his brother clear of danger. The second was to patch up things with Ginny and the kids. Become a family again. Maybe that's why he was feeling so empty.

The *third*, Wachman, Casey, Raines . . . The third would be harder. The third required something he wasn't sure he was capable of. Something deeper.

He'd see how it all played out.

Warren vectored the plane northerly, back toward the air-field, away from the coast. The suburban grid of towns and homes formed a perfect patchwork below him. He'd thought it out. It all made sense now. What he had to do . . .

How had he fucked it all up so royally? How had he let it get so far over his head?

Anyway, that part was ending. This new part, this new Warren . . .

The airstrip came into view. Warren announced his approach to the tower.

Why was it always so clear and simple up here?

CHAPTER SEVENTY-THREE

*T*o Hauck, the drive back felt like days. He felt an urge building inside him, like he was going to explode.

From the realization he had cost a man his life—watched
him die in his arms. From the silent, stewing rage he could not
contain, his fingers gripping the wheel like a gun handle, to get
his hands around Raines's neck. Turn him upside down. Until
the truth came out.

Wipers flashing, he crossed back into Massachusetts.

The boat had turned up. It had been stolen from a local marina and ditched at a dock at someone's summerhouse that had
been closed up for the season. No bullet casings or prints were
found on it. A team from Portland was coming in to check it
out the next day.

The local head of detectives in Maine showed up at the
scene, an easygoing white-haired guy named Hazens—who
hadn't handled a murder case since he'd moved up to Lewiston.
Together they went through Pacello's cell phone. Calls from his
kids, a son in Tucson, but the recent numbers that might lead
somewhere were untraceable. Disposable cell phones.

Hauck had told Hazens as much as he could. Why he was
up there—part of a murder case connected to a gambling scam

back home. That Pacello was a potential witness. He even mentioned the Pequot Woods and Raines. Pacello's grieving wife
certainly would. *But what could the guy do?* Hauck asked him
for a few days to let him take the lead. They struck a deal. Hazens would go over the boat and the marina, look for anything
up there.

Hauck would go after Raines.

He hadn't learned much more than when he'd driven up that
very morning, which now seemed like days ago. Only that
Sanger and Kramer hadn't been killed as part of any gambling
scam. That had been another smoke screen. Just like Josephina
Ruiz had been a smoke screen. What was the Pequot Woods
hiding? Who else was involved?

What had Fitz said? *Every politician in the state has his
hands in the Pequot Woods pockets.*

How high did that go?

He had called Fitz from the scene, informed him what had
taken place. This thing would have to be expanded, the chief
said glumly. It had crossed states. The FBI would *have to be
more deeply involved.*

"Come on home," he told Hauck. "We'll start to put it all
together tomorrow."

*All those new state roads, Ty, those fancy stadiums, you
have any idea where the money for those comes from?*

Hauck had asked Raines, referring to Sanger, what kind of
man would risk it all like that—his job, his family, his reputation, everything—over some kind of compulsion. A few hundred thousand dollars.

What kind of man are you, Lieutenant . . . ? Raines had just
smiled back.

Now he knew.

One day you could be chief, Vern had said. *You could build a nice life here, Ty . . .*

His cell phone rang, cutting his thoughts. Hauck picked up and it was Warren. He didn't want to go into things now.

"Hey, guy, just checking in," his brother said. "You give any more thought to that job?"

"The job's off for a while, Warren," Hauck replied.

"Off?"

"I can't go into it. It's just off."

"Ty," Warren objected, "that's not making sense . . ."

"Who does the Pequot Woods have in its pocket, Warren?"

That seemed to take him by surprise. *"Huh?"*

"C'mon, Warren, you know about these things. Who do they own? Who's on their payroll?"

"Ty, I really think you're making a huge mistake here . . ."

"You remember that game we used to play when we were kids? Goal-line Stand?"

Warren hesitated. "Yeah, I remember, Ty, but—"

"I was always John Riggins. You were LT. I'd barrel into you and try to move the pile. You'd try to force me back."

"What the hell does that have to do with anything, Ty?"

"Who always won?"

"God damn it, Ty, I'm trying to talk a little sense into you . . ."

Hauck pressed. *"Who always won?* In the end. What was it you always said about me? You remember . . ."

His brother let out a frustrated breath, giving in. "We used to say God gave you a whole lot more balls than he did sense, because you'd never stop until your face was bloody. You realize it wasn't exactly meant as a compliment, Ty . . ."

"Maybe, but as to why the job's on hold . . . *that's why.*"

They hung up. Warren seemed disappointed, even a little pissed. Hauck was coming up on Hartford now. The skyline came into view. It was almost nine. He grabbed his phone again and called Munoz.

The detective's eight-year-old, Anthony, picked up. The one Hauck had gotten the signed David Wright baseball for. *"Uncle Ty . . . !"*

"Hey, bruiser, what are you still doing up? Your dad at home?"

"He's at home." Hauck heard the sound of the TV in the background. "We're watching *24.* He's right here."

"Caught me," Munoz said guiltily as he took the line. "I'll let him stay up and we watch *24* together. Our Tuesday-night ritual. I heard what happened, LT. I'm sorry about that. It's bad."

"How's your DVR working?" Hauck asked.

"It's working fine, Lieutenant," Munoz said. "Tell me what you need."

"I'm just passing Hartford. I want you to meet me at my house—in an hour. That okay? I'm sorry to interrupt things, Freddy, but the shit's going to hit the fan tomorrow, and I want to map out some things before we get in."

"Key in the same place?" Munoz asked unhesitatingly. He had once had to pick up some files Hauck had there. Hauck kept a key in a fake rock along the side.

"Same place," Hauck said. "And, Freddy . . . thanks."

"I'll see you there, Lieutenant."

What kind of person are you? Raines had asked.

He didn't fully know until that moment.

I'm the guy who's gonna bring you down.

CHAPTER SEVENTY-FOUR

*I*ra Wachman had put on his Burberry raincoat and cap and was about to turn off the light in his statehouse office in Hartford. He often worked this late. His was the kind of job you couldn't just put away at night. That gnawed at him when he lay awake in the dark going over every detail and point to be covered, anticipating every objection.

He had devoted twenty years to watching the back of his boss. Dealing with every problem, resolving every dispute. Taking care of the senator's "dirty laundry." Some would say Wachman had made the senator the man he was today.

Wachman would say he'd just done what needed to be done. Politics was a shifting line. The A axis of opportunity met the B of survival. Long as he'd been around, those lines had intersected many times. He sat holding his briefcase, full of briefs and position papers to be gone over that night.

Wachman's cell phone rang.

He checked the number. It wasn't familiar. One he would never see again. "Wachman here," he said when he picked up. He looked out the window at the lights of the capitol dome, glistening brightly.

"That detail we spoke of," the caller said. "You can mark it down as done. It was taken care of today. We 'upped the tempo,' as you called it. You won't have to deal with it again."

"Good to hear." Ira Wachman sighed. He crossed that issue off his mental list. He was about to ask the man just how; then it occurred to him that the less he knew, the better.

"And that other thing . . . ?" he inquired.

"The *other* thing . . ." Joe Raines paused. Hopefully, this would be the last time they would have to speak. "The night's still young, Mr. Wachman."

CHAPTER SEVENTY-FIVE

*H*auck exited the thruway at Atlantic Avenue, finally home. He was drained. He had washed off the blood, but the image of Pacello, pinned back in his seat, the hole in his throat gushing, still remained.

He drove past the antique warehouses, past Annie's restaurant, heading toward the sound. He made the right onto Euclid. The street was dark. It was after ten o'clock. Munoz was waiting for him. He drove down the street toward his house.

He saw Freddy's Acura SUV parked along the street and figured he'd gone inside.

"Thataboy . . ." Hauck smiled. He punched in the number to his house, then realized he should've called Freddy's cell. Still, he decided to let it ring. Munoz would see it and pick up. Hauck saw a light on in the living room through the second-floor front deck's sliding doors. He just wanted to tell him he was here.

The line rang. He was about to pull into the driveway.

Freddy came into view, standing before the glass.

Hauck waved. The detective gave him a wave in return. He had Hauck's house phone in his hand and went to slide open the doors.

Hauck heard him pick up. *"Yo, Lieutenant . . . ,"* Munoz said, flashing his familiar smile.

Then there was a second click.

He looked up to the deck in panic, realizing what it was.

"Freddy . . . !"

A second later the glass doors exploded, followed by a fireball of orange flame. In horror, Hauck turned away from the shower of splintered glass and the gust of searing heat.

"Freddy!"

It took a moment for the heat to fade before he could even look back.

By then it was too late. Everything was quiet. Upstairs, the curtains were incinerated, the glass doors gone. He smashed his fist against the dash. Debris and burning embers settled around him like a cloud. Hauck shielded his face with his arm, smoke stinging in his eyes.

"Oh, Jesus Christ, Freddy, no . . ."

Hauck leaped out of the Explorer, heading for the stairs.

Then he just stopped.

Powerless, disbelieving, he stood there watching the flames. The heat baking his cheeks. Hearing only the haunting flap of the wind.

"Oh, God, *Freddy . . ."*

Something yellow and shiny came to rest at his feet. Hauck bent down and picked it up. A small disc, still hot from the blast. Almost melted. The image on it was barely recognizable. Hauck turned it over in his palm.

It was a yellow plastic image of the Fonz.

PART THREE

CHAPTER SEVENTY-SIX

*T*he same dream left him sweating and awake for days.

He is running up a flight of stairs. The rooftop of an apartment building, back when he was a detective with the NYPD. Somehow Beth is part of it. Waiting for him at home. With the girls. He and his partner climb the last set of stairs, in pursuit of someone. "You behind me, dude?"

"Right behind you."

It's Warren.

They open a latched metal door and step onto the darkened rooftop. They hear the guy they're chasing stumbling around, crashing into metal trash cans and storage bins.

"I'll go this way." He points. Warren understands. He'll go the other.

"Roger." They split up. The structure housing the stairwell blocks their view.

Nervously, he flicks the safety off his gun. He hopes he's handling this right. Warren isn't a cop. What's he doing there?

He hears a scuffle. A shout. "Ty!"

Gun drawn, he rushes to the other side, but it's obstructed. blocked. All kinds of containers and rusted old machinery in his way. "I'm coming!" he yells. When he finally makes it around, there's no sign of the guy they're chasing. "Warren!"

He hears a shout. He goes to the ledge and looks over the side. It's Warren, hanging ten stories above the ground.

Terrified, he wraps his hand around his brother's wrist. "I've got you!" He sees the look of fear on Warren's face.

He starts to pull him up.

But it's as if Warren's somehow fighting. "Pull," he says, straining with everything he has.

At first his brother begins to rise. Then he slips. Dangling by a hand over the edge. "I'm not going to let you go."

"Ty, it's okay," Warren says.

But there's nothing he can do. His weight is just too heavy. His grip begins to slip. Every muscle in his body is straining to the edge.

"Ty . . ." His voice is calm, resigned.

"Why aren't you pulling, Warren?" He looks into his brother's face.

"I'm sorry," he says, feeling his grip begin to slip.

But suddenly the face has changed. It's no longer Warren's. It's Freddy's. "Yo, Lieutenant!"

Hauck pulls back in horror. He loses his grasp.

Freddy slips into the night.

For days, Hauck couldn't bring himself to be part of the investigation. He kept reliving the same scene: driving down the street, spotting Freddy's car, punching in his number.

Freddy coming out onto the deck. With a familiar wave. *"Yo, Lieutenant!"*

Then everything blew up.

A pall was cast over the department. It was hard to define the feeling that took him over in the days after. Anger. Depression. Guilt. Anger so deep rooted, it was like all the rage he had ever felt boiled down to a hardened, dense dot that couldn't be reduced any more.

Gripped by the same type of numbing guilt as when Norah was killed. That what happened had been his fault. It had all been set up for *him*. Freddy had simply wandered in.

Hauck had pushed him in.

He went to visit Freddy's widow, Rosa, almost silently pleaded for her to beat her fists against his chest and scream *You did this. You killed my husband.* Instead, she just looked at him with those dark, forgiving eyes. "No one blames you, Ty . . . Freddy worshipped you. You know he would have done anything for you."

And he did.

At the crowded wake, he sat down on a bench with Freddy's two boys, silently placed his hands on their knees, and if it wasn't for the rage he felt for Raines hardening in his heart, he would have surely broken down and cried. He stared at the casket and imagined what people must be thinking.

What *he* was thinking.

That should be him in there.

Many times, he wished it were.

For days, the department operated basically at half speed. Steve Chrisafoulis took charge of the investigation. They combed for prints or suspicious fibers all over Hauck's house. Didn't find a thing. These people were pros. They canvassed the neighborhood for anyone who might have been spotted going in. A neighbor down the street did recall seeing a white van. "ABC Plumbing or something?"

The very first thing anyone checked into was Raines's whereabouts.

The casino security chief had been in Baltimore all day, at an industry trade show. He'd been hosting a large group out to dinner when the explosion occurred. He had the contacts to prove it.

Hauck wasn't surprised.

He had Steve drop off the files on the casino. He kept going over them as a distraction to keep from driving himself crazy. He just about gave in to the urge that he should give up. Turn it all over, whatever he had. Let the FBI handle it from here. Pacello was dead. Raines was clean. No one wanted to take on the Pequot Woods. They didn't have any leads.

He looked over the faces of the Pequot Woods management team. Names he didn't know. The board of directors. William Turner. Senator Oren Casey. Richard Scaynes. Not people he could take on. They knew Turner had paid off Pacello. That was a place he could start. He looked at it from every possible angle. Look once, it's one thing to you.

Look twice, it shifts. It's something else.

Everything is always something else.

Vern called two days after Freddy's wake. "I need you back, Ty."

The next day he finally came back in. He stopped in to see Vern. He said that Sculley and Taylor were heading down that afternoon and wanted to share notes on the case.

This time Hauck didn't object.

He pulled his team together and told them business had to go on. There were other cases to work on. People were counting on them. Freddy would want no less.

"C'mon." Steve Chrisafoulis stood up. "The lieutenant's right. Let's get moving."

Gradually they all did.

A short while later, Steve came in.

"Appreciate the support," Hauck said to him. "Any chance you got anything for me?"

"I don't know," the mustached detective said. "I'm not sure if this is the right time . . ."

"Time for what?" Hauck asked.

Steve seemed a little nervous. He unwrapped a couple of large bound folders. "You had me digging into whoever was tied into the Pequot Woods . . . I was tracing that payment to Pacello, through Bill Turner, and I started perusing some of the affidavits on file. Public record . . ." He opened the folder in front of Hauck. "This was when the tribe first applied for sovereign nation status . . ."

Petition A23. Before the Department of the Interior on behalf of the Pequot Indian tribe for Sovereign Nation Status.

"Yeah . . . ?"

"See here . . . One of the legal firms on behalf of the tribe was an outfit out of Hartford called Parker, Kegg."

Hauck looked. He knew the name. The firm was familiar to him.

"And here . . . This is to the state gaming board. This is to renew their tax-exempt status. The casino's in-house attorneys handle it, but they need an outside counsel to sign off on it as well. They have to file a Ten-B every year."

Hauck looked at the long tax form replete with appendices of charts and graphs. Steve flipped to the signature page.

"And here . . ."

The detective pointed and Hauck stared at the line.

He felt like he'd been hit by a truck.

All of a sudden a lot of things became clear.

In familiar script. On several documents. Some as part of a firm, others, later on, on his own.

Warren C. Hauck.

CHAPTER SEVENTY-SEVEN

*I*t was after six that day when Hauck pulled up across from the two-story white colonial just off the green in Southington, twenty miles out of Hartford. It was a quiet small-town street, a stone's throw from the town square, a bank and a dry cleaner around the corner.

A white sign that read WARREN C. HAUCK, ATTORNEY AT LAW hung from a post on the gate.

Warren's white Range Rover was parked next to the house in the small lot. Hauck went up the front stairs and opened the wood-paneled door. There was a small reception area inside. Framed color portraits of well-known golf holes from around the world hung on the walls. The par-3 over the ocean at Pebble Beach. The fifteenth green at Augusta. The road hole at St. Andrews. A LeRoy Neiman watercolor of Jack Nicklaus.

Worth a pretty penny.

The front desk was unoccupied. It was after six. Everyone had gone home.

He knocked.

A hallway led past a staircase to a row of offices in back. A man who seemed to be in his early thirties, in a collared shirt with a satchel slung over his shoulder, stuck out his head. *"Help you?"*

"I'm looking for Warren Hauck," Hauck said.

"He expecting you?" the man asked.

"I wanted to surprise him. I'm his brother."

"Hey!" The young man lit up. "I can see it. I'm Ken Wolfe. I work with Warren." He pointed down the hall. "He's straight down there. End of the hall. I was just heading out."

"Thanks." Hauck waved, following a voice. "I think I hear him now."

He went down the hall. He could hear Warren plainly now, on the phone. His office door was open. It didn't seem as if anyone else was around.

Hauck stuck his head in. The office looked like it might have once been the living room in the house. Large, airy, paneled. French doors led out to a rear yard. His brother had his back toward him in a swivel chair, in a pink knit shirt and one of those headsets on. Cole Haans elevated onto the credenza, facing out the window.

"So listen, I'm gonna have Tom call you about that filing in the A.M. . . . We'll button it up with the planning board, then go forward with the petition . . ."

Hauck knocked on the door.

Warren spun, his eyes arching in complete surprise. He didn't smile at first. He didn't wave Hauck in. What he seemed to be doing was ratcheting through his startled brain just why his brother was here.

"Okay, guy, talk soon . . ." Warren switched off the line. He took off the headset and stood up. *"Ty . . ."* His face registered bewilderment. "Jesus, bro, what the hell are you doing here?"

"Can't a guy just visit his older brother when he's passing through town?"

"Yeah, right." Warren grinned, trying to decipher just what Hauck meant. "C'mon in, take a seat. I'm just trying to think if you've ever been here before."

"Long overdue," Hauck said. He sat down across from him and put his satchel on the floor. Warren's desk looked like a train wreck—papers, briefs, piled high in towers; an ashtray and a beer bottle. The place smelled like smoke.

"Want something? Bottle of water? Beer? Something stronger?"

Hauck shook his head. "No, thanks."

"Well, *I* do. So what have you got in there?" His eyes darted to Hauck's bag. "Looks like you're going to trial!" He went over to a small fridge and took out a longneck bottle of Bud Light. "I tried to call you," he said, throwing himself back in his chair. "When I heard about what happened up there. *Jesus, Ty* . . ." He shook his head grimly. "That must've been fucking awful. I can't tell you how sorry I am about what happened to your guy . . ."

"*My guy* . . . ?"

"You know, your detective. *Munoz*, right? Here's to staying safe . . ." Warren downed a gulp of beer; with his free hand he tapped a pen against the desk.

"Let me tell you about him, Warren. He worked for me for six years. He almost went to law school himself. He had two young kids. His wife is a wreck. But I guess you know about that kind of thing, don't you, big brother . . ." He met his eyes. "He picked up the fucking phone at my house . . ."

Warren stopped tapping. He stared back at Hauck, put down his beer, leaned back, and put his hands behind his head. "Just why are you here, Ty?"

"I'm *here* because for weeks I've been trying to find some connection between the Pequot Woods and the murders of David Sanger and Keith Kramer—other than the horseshit I've been stepping around that they were party to some gambling scam up there. So I've been going through Joe Raines"—Hauck shrugged—"and some of the people on the board up there, Bill Turner of Heritage Financial, Senator Oren Casey, that dealer who was killed, Pacello . . . Trying to figure out what they would all have to hide that would be worth this kind of killing for. Looking for the thread that knitted it all together . . ."

"Oh, yeah," Warren said, jiggling his pen again. "And what'd you find?"

"*You*, Warren." Hauck stared back at him. "I found you."

Warren grinned and made the kind of defensive, deep-in-the-throat chuckle that comes when someone's brain is desperately groping for what to say. He rocked back in his chair, crossing his legs. "You found me?"

"I've had my people scouring over the Pequot Woods's records. The board of directors, the council of overseers. DR-17 was just doing the dirty work for Raines. They tried to make the Sanger shooting look like a payback of some kind. So if it wasn't about gambling, what was it about? There had to be something he found out. Something worth killing for. So *what* . . . ?"

"Is that a question, Ty, or are you just trying to piss me the fuck off?"

"I'm afraid it is a question, Warren." Hauck's blood started to heat. He leaned over and opened the flap of his case. He pulled out the large sheath of papers Steve Chrisafoulis had arranged for him—two dozen documents and affadavits filed on behalf of the casino, going all the way back twelve years to the original sovereign nations filing to the federal government by the Pequot tribe. He dropped the stack on the desk. "You've been there every step of the way, Warren. When you worked for Parker, Kegg, up in Hartford, they represented the tribe. You became one of the lawyers of record. Your name's right there on the filing. You handled several of their motions. Tax-exempt requests, land swaps . . ."

Warren didn't reply.

"And then when you went on your own . . . ," Hauck went on, "you continued doing work for them. Senator Casey is on the board of overseers there, and guess what turns up? You've done work for him too. Bill Turner of Heritage. He's a member of the board. It was his company that paid Paul Pacello off when he left the casino. And lo and behold, he happens to be on your client list too. Seems you handled a real estate trust for him." Hauck's gaze bore into him deeply. "See where we're going now?"

"Yeah, and it all proves *what,* I'm trying to figure out. I'm a lawyer. I get paid to represent people. Where you're going—"

"Where I'm *going*"—Hauck leaned forward, his tone hardening—"is someone tried to kill me the other day in my own home. *Me, Warren!* And then it sort of hits me, I've been looking for this common thread linking everything together, coming up blank . . . And here it's been right under my nose all the time. In plain sight. I looked at everything I had, every which way I could find, and didn't see it.

"And then I looked *twice.*"

Warren's fists tightened and he rocked back in the chair. "And what is it you see, little brother?"

"*You.* Suddenly you just drop back in my life. With some tale of woe about how your life is falling apart. So I call Ginny. And you know what? She didn't know shit about some real estate investment that got in between you . . ."

"I wish you hadn't done that, Ty . . ."

"I think you have a pretty fair idea what the fuck's going on, Warren. Just what these well-heeled clients of yours have to hide. And I think it has something to do with Senator Casey, not gambling at all, and that you're up to your dick in the middle of it and that that's why you showed up again out of the blue. And you know what? I'm not going to stop . . . I'm not going to get out of your face until I know what the hell is going on."

Warren laughed. "This is all a little crazy, Ty. I'm thinking you kept some of that shit we were smoking at your house, 'cause this is all nuts . . ."

"You better hope it's nuts." Hauck felt the heat of anger on his face. "You better hope I'm fucking crazy . . ."

Warren just stared, trying to form a response, until Hauck could see it plainly in his eyes.

All of it.

He was totally involved.

Whatever was holding Hauck together snapped. He lunged across the desk, taking his brother by the collar, pulling him out of his chair and back across the desk.

"Five people are dead, Warren! Do you understand? *Someone tried to kill me in my own home!* I lost a friend. A cop. And now I want to hear it from you. No bullshit. No pretending you don't know what the hell I'm talking about, Warren. You're my goddamn brother! So tell me! Who's behind it? I'm going to find out. *What the hell is going on?*"

"What is it you're going to do, Ty?" He looked back unrepentantly. "You going to take me in because I happen to have a few influential friends?"

Hauck threw a punch to the side of Warren's face. His head rocked back and Hauck hit him again, his knuckles finding

bone, splitting open Warren's cheek. Papers and affadavits flying off the desk. The phone clanged to the floor.

"*I'm your goddamn brother, Warren!* Don't you understand
that? That man was my friend. *I* told him to meet me there. *I*
called him from the street. I set off that bomb. What happened
there was meant for *me. Me, Warren . . .* Don't you see what
you've done?"

"I told you to get out," Warren said, glaring back.

Hauck threw him with everything he had against the wall.
Warren fell. Framed mementos and diplomas crashed to the
floor.

"I told you to take the job!" Warren glared back at him. "I
tried to warn you, Ty. I know these people. Why didn't you just
listen to me? I told you to take the fucking job!"

Hauck lunged again and lifted him against the wall. He
punched him again, this time in the hollow of the stomach.
Warren let out a gasp, bent over.

"I'm bringing you in," Hauck said, pulling him back up.
"Your life is fucking done, Warren. You're going to tell us. One
way or another, it's coming out. What was going on?"

"Ty, *please . . .*" His brother's eyes stiffened between denial
and tears. "Can't you see. *Can't you fucking see?* I tried to
warn you. I know these people. I know what they're capable of.
I know who you're pushing up against, Ty."

Hauck grabbed him by the face and reared back his fist
again. He held—fingers clenched, twitching, eyes welling with
burning tears. Of rage. "Who, Warren, *who . . . ? Who am I
pushing against?*"

"Ty, I can't." Warren helplessly shook his head.

Hauck raised back to punch him one more time. Warren
didn't make a move to resist. Hauck just stood there, the tide of
anger and grief and powerlessness heating to a boil. He wanted

to smash his brother's face. His breaths churned like turbines. Then finally he just dropped his fist and shouted, *"God damn it!"* Let Warren sink to the floor.

Hauck looked down at his brother, seeing him in a different way than he had ever seen him before. Not the strong, familiar lines of his father, the seductive charm, the chummy brown eyes. Something different. Something weak and unfastened and way over his head.

Scared.

For the first time in his life Hauck felt stronger than him. His legs grew heavy and limp. He sank to the floor himself, across from him. "God damn you, Warren."

"I never meant to hurt you, Ty. You have to believe that. I'm so sorry. I truly am. I wish I could undo what's gone on. But I can't. I tried to protect you."

Hauck sat there looking across at his brother. A welt had come out on his eye. "What the hell's happened, Warren?"

Warren closed his eyes and rested his head on his hand. "I don't know."

Suddenly the trill of a cell phone rang. A Bach melody—"A Lover's Concerto." *Warren's.*

Both sets of their eyes went to it. It was on the floor near Hauck's feet. When he had pulled Warren over the desk it must've fallen out.

He didn't know what made him look.

Maybe the glimpse of fear in Warren's face, eyes darting toward it. Maybe just the frustration of everything else. Not knowing if he was judging his brother unfairly. If he had gone insane.

Whatever it was, Hauck reached, and as he was about to kick it across the floor, his eyes locked on the caller ID.

"Oh, Jesus, Warren . . ."

A sinking sensation fell in Hauck's gut. His gaze froze directly on his brother. Suddenly, Hauck's mind raced back to images of when they were kids: sharing the same room, brushing their teeth in their pajamas, trading secrets in their bunk beds before they fell asleep. A perfect spiral Hauck had once flung that landed in his brother's arms. Warren, dancing a celebratory jig, spiking the ball on the street. *Oh yeah! Oh yeah!*

That all seemed so distant now.

The name on the caller ID was Tom Foley.

CHAPTER SEVENTY-EIGHT

The phone continued to ring.

Hauck just sat there staring at Warren.

His brother just shook his head. "I told you to take the job. I tried to get you away from it, Ty. *God damn it!* I did everything I could." His gaze was hollow and, maybe for the first time in his whole life, completely guileless. Sincere. "I tried to warn you. Everyone tried to warn you, Ty. *Why couldn't you just take the fucking job?*"

"What have you gotten yourself into, Warren?"

His brother slammed his fist against the floor. "You stubborn, stupid, pigheaded shit!"

The ringing stopped. Hauck just continued to look at him. The anger was now gone. His gaze grew glassy with tears.

"I'm your brother." Hauck shook his head. "What the hell have you become?"

"*What have I become?*" Warren rubbed his swollen lip and glared at him. "I am what I've always been, Ty. You think I'm so different from every other fucking guy in this world. Just 'cause it doesn't fit into your neat little view of the world.

"You know what I wanted. I wanted to be in that room with the big boys. In the same boardrooms, in their clubs. You think we're a part of that world, coming where we came from? So I did what I always wanted, Ty. I found my way in the room. *My way.* I rubbed my hands a little bit in the dirt."

"*In the dirt?* You got filth all over you, Warren. I'm your brother."

"*And I tried to protect you, goddamn it!* I did! Just like at the lake. Don't look at me like I'm some kind of monster. So what are you going to do, arrest me?" He put out his wrists. "You going to arrest me for that, Ty?"

"You think you won't be next?" Hauck looked at him. "You think they won't kill you just like they killed Pacello? Just like they tried to do to me? You think I can just let you walk out of here? That things are going to somehow find their way back to normal?"

"*No . . .*" Warren sank his head back against the wall and shook it from side to side. "I know things will never go back to normal, Ty. You just have to believe me. Foley, that job, all I was trying to do was just protect you. To give you a way out. I wish I could turn back the clock. I wish I could've been a better brother. I wish I could've been a better husband to Ginny, a dad to my kids. I wish I could be a lot of things, Ty . . .

"But I am who I am. There's no big white line you cross, Ty. I've always been the same person who you came upon when you opened that door in the basement room. I do favors for people. I smooth things out. I get things done. And sometimes, these things . . ." He shrugged sullenly. "Sometimes they just get larger, Ty. That's all. All I tried to do was get you out."

"They're gonna kill you, Warren. Casey, Raines . . . Your friends. For whatever they're hiding. Just like Pacello. They're gonna tie you to all their dirty work and not let you walk away."

"You know me, guy. I always find a way . . ."

"Not anymore," Hauck said. "And there's Ginny. Kyle and Sarah."

"You just don't understand, Ty . . ." Warren stared at him. "There's no way I'm going to spend the rest of my life in jail."

Hauck shook his head. "You think I can just walk out of here now, Warren? And things are just going to pick up where they left off?"

"So what are you going to do? Slap the cuffs on me? Take me in? On what grounds? Because I have ties to some influential friends? Because Tom Foley is on my speed dial? None of it ties me to shit. I'm a lawyer, Ty, remember? Go ahead, tell me the charge."

Hauck knew there *was* no charge. "They'll kill you too, Warren."

"Go on, get out of here," Warren said, "leave me alone . . ." His eyes regained a measure of composure. "I wasn't lying, you know . . . when I said those things at your house. I did try to protect you. I want you to believe me on that. I just couldn't get it done. You're a good man, Ty. Just let me be who I am. Just know, nothing was ever supposed to happen to you. That was always a part of the deal. That was the basis for everything. I swear."

"What's this all about, Warren?"

"What is it ever about?" He sniffed. "It's all about power, Ty."

Politics. Casey. "Everything's always about power, Warren."

"No." His brother smiled. "Not that kind of power . . ." There was a look in his eye, both fraternal and resigned. "Read the papers. It's everywhere. It's right in front of you. Now get out. Please. I'm sorry. I'm sorry to have dragged you into this, Ty. I'm sorry to disappoint you."

"If I leave here, I can't help you, Warren."

Warren smiled at him. "Since when have you ever been able to help me, Ty?"

Hauck got up. His brother wiped the blood and mucus off his face. Hauck left him leaning against the wall.

CHAPTER SEVENTY-NINE

Warren remained there, blood on his shirt, his eye throbbing, long after Ty had left. He knew he had made a mess of everything. A mess of whatever hope had once guided the arc of his life. He had crossed the lines of every oath he had ever taken. As a lawyer. As a husband.

A dad.

Over the years, that line had blurred so many times he no longer recognized it.

He had an urge to just fly. He had to figure a way out, and up there, the world always seemed clearer to him. He knew Ty wouldn't let up. He needed a way out. To get Ginny and the kids clear. And not to end up in the Witness Protection Program somewhere. He doubted if his family would even go along with him.

Yeah, that needs a whole lot of work too.

Okay, think . . . You've always landed on your feet. You hit a drive into the woods, you find the angle to the green. You fly without instruments, you find the path through the clouds.

So where's the path now?

Ty was right. He suddenly realized *he* was the weak link now. *He* was the exposure. Even though Casey's man had come to him first and explained in the vaguest way how he needed something done.

All those deals, Warren. The fancy house, the clubs . . . It's payback time now. The senator needs a little favor in return, Wachman had said.

At first it horrified him. What they were asking. He laughed. He thought it was a joke.

A fucking federal attorney . . .

But no, it wasn't a joke. It was serious. Serious as cancer. *You set it up, Warren. You find someone to do the job. Just this once,* he said. He thought where he could go. He didn't know those types of people. Then he got the idea. First, he broached it to Turner, on the casino's board, who was deeper into Casey than he.

That led to Raines.

It was just one time, he kept telling himself. One more little line to cross. Then it would be over. Ty was never supposed to be involved. That had just been a freak. He had told Raines to take care of it. The fewer details the better.

How did he know they would choose to do it right in the middle of his brother's goddamn town?

His eyes filled up with hot, shameful tears. *Where, Warren, where is the angle through the clouds?*

Where are the lines now?

Warren heard a noise. From outside, the front door opening. He figured it was Ty again. He couldn't just leave him like that! What would he say to him now? How could he explain? How could he make things right?

Warren mashed the tears against his cheeks. "You back?"

"Yeah, Warren, we're back."

Two people stared at him in the doorway. One had a long

scar running down the side of his face. The other, in a baggy sweatshirt and Mets cap, pointed a gun.

"Jesus, hombre," the guy said, shaking his head. "You don't fuckin' look so good, Mr. Hauck!"

Warren was surprised. He always thought if this would come he would be taken with fear.

And now he didn't feel any. In fact, he felt lighter. *Free,* finally.

Almost like he was flying.

CHAPTER EIGHTY

*H*auck drove out of town, heading back toward I-84 and Greenwich.

He had no idea what to do. He knew his brother was deeply involved. That was clear. Warren knew where the pieces led. But what could Hauck do? Arrest him? Throw him in a cell? Hand his own brother over to the FBI? *With what?* Warren was right, Vern would laugh in his face.

He had nothing on him.

Seeing Foley's name on that phone tore a hole in Hauck's heart. He thought of the slick, polished manner in which the executive had made his offer to him. His familiarity with Hauck's cases and personal history. Dropping in how his old boss at the NYPD had recommended him.

You've been on our radar for a while, Ty . . .

All the way up here, since finding Warren's name on those Pequot Woods documents, Hauck prayed it was all just some big coincidence. Something he was reaching for in the vacuum of no other answers.

Now he knew. Warren had set it up.

Set *him* up.

Now he had to figure out what his brother knew.

It all came back to Raines. He could arrest him. Put him and Warren in a room. Let the chips fall where they may.

Hauck flicked on the radio. Desperate to clear his thoughts. The news. There had been an avalanche somewhere in the Rockies. Two off-trail skiers killed. Another suicide bomber had blown up a market outside of Baghdad.

But his mind wouldn't clear.

Instead, he was brought back to how the road growing up had made them so entirely different. The reckless, self-destructive choices Warren had made.

The sight of leaving him there. Broken. In tears. *Why couldn't you just take the lucking job? Ty . . .*

His entire life had always been on a collision course with ruin.

It's all about power, Ty . . .

Hauck was about to switch stations when another story came on.

"In local news, Richard Scayne, the Greenwich industrialist accused of making improper payments to secure no-bid contracts for Iraq, is set to go on trial in federal court in Hartford in February. Scayne's power generator unit, SRC, has been implicated in payments to Republican figures to obtain a two-billion-dollar contract for Nova 91 power generators in Iraq. The September suicide of Lieutenant Colonel Mark Shafton, a member of the U.S. Army's General Purchasing Office, has been linked to the scandal. Scayne, in deteriorating health, has maintained he cannot stand up to the rigors of a protracted trial . . ."

Hauck went to turn it off when a thought suddenly wormed into his mind.

Power, Warren had said. *Not that kind of power, Ty . . .*
Generators.

He almost swerved off the road.

Scayne. Richard Scayne was going on trial for illicit payoffs related to his generator unit.

Nova 91s.

Hauck's head throbbed.

Scayne and Casey were tied at the hip. Scayne had an interest in the Pequot Woods. Casey was on the board there as well.

Hauck's pulse began to race with the beat of something he did not fully understand but was slowly fitting together.

Generators.

Warren had done work for each of them. Scayne's trial was set to proceed out of the federal offices in Hartford. Where Sanger had worked out of. Hauck had never fully followed that through. *Why would he?* Josephina Ruiz had diverted his attention. Then the trail to the casino. The motives all seemed so clear at first.

Look twice.

Scayne had made payments to Republican coffers to gain a two-billion-dollar contract with the Coalition Provisional Authority. Everything was for sale over there. The purchasing officer in the Pentagon had taken his own life. All connected to Scayne's case. He was doing whatever he could not to go to trial. Hauck's brain ached—who would handle such a thing for him? And Casey? Someone who owed them. For licenses granted, maybe. Favorable tax arrangements. Someone who could handle that sort of thing.

The Pequot Woods.

You have no idea what kind of forces are at work here.

The casino owed them. Raines was just the guy who was paying them back.

And who would someone like Scayne have come to? So as

not to get his own hands dirty? Someone to act as the intermediary. Someone who owed him. The person to put it all together.

You don't know how many ways I've sold myself, Ty . . .

The entrance to the highway was just ahead.

Hauck stopped at a light, his whole body pulsating.

He spun the Explorer around.

CHAPTER EIGHTY-ONE

*H*e threw a top hat on the roof of the Explorer and sped back to Warren's office.

Weaving through traffic, Hauck suddenly felt something different toward him—no longer the swell of anger or disgust, but pity. Pity at how his brother's own misdirected actions had overtaken him. He'd lost his footing, his family. The shame on his face was clear.

Still, Hauck couldn't help but think about how he had known this person every day of his life.

Honking his way through the lights, Hauck made it back into the center of town, cut the sharp right onto High Street. Warren's Range Rover was still in the lot. He was about to pull up behind it when his eyes fixed on the black Jeep parked on the street.

It sent a jolt of caution running through him.

Not just because of the darkened windows and jacked-up wheelbase, or that it hadn't been there minutes before.

It was what he saw on the rear bumper—the cross of red and dark blue. He had seen it before.

On the rust-colored Jetta Annie had spotted next to her Dumpster.

Dominican colors. *DR-17.*

God damn you, Warren, I told you they wouldn't let you walk away . . .

Hauck drove past Warren's office. He pulled up down the street, in front of a sleepy colonial, two houses away. He reached inside the glove compartment and took out his gun. The ammo clip on the Sig was full. He jammed it back in. No time to call for backup.

If they were in there for what Hauck thought they were there for, he might already be too late.

There was no sign of anyone still inside the Jeep. Hauck jumped out of the Explorer and hurried over to the side of Warren's office. No chance he could go through the front door. Anyone inside would hear. He had no idea how many there were. But he knew he had to move.

Hunched over, Hauck ran behind the Range Rover to the rear of the blacktopped driveway. A picket fence and gate led to the backyard. Hauck stepped over it, drawing alongside the house. He blamed himself for not taking Warren with him the first time. Holding the gun to his chest, he looked in through a window.

It was someone's office. Empty. Probably one of Warren's associates. The office door was closed. Hauck couldn't see past it to what was inside.

No way they're going to let him just walk away . . .

He crept around to the back of the house. There was a small yard back there, fenced in by tall hedges. A wrought iron table was set up with five chairs. Warren's office was on the far end off a slate-tiled patio. Hauck spotted the French doors.

Clinging to the side of the house, he moved down the patio toward it.

There were voices through the glass now, coming from

inside. Sweat began to stream down Hauck's temples. His heart rate started to climb. Hauck peered in.

He saw Vega.

He recognized the gang leader instantly. His head was shaved. He had on a midlength denim jacket and black jeans. He was swiveling back and forth in Warren's desk chair like a kid in his father's office, gesturing, enjoying himself, orchestrating whatever was going on. Hauck saw a gun tucked between his legs.

Vega's accomplice had Warren pressed up against the wall. Hauck watched as the man teasingly dragged the muzzle of his gun along his brother's face. They were making him pay, punishing him, not just carrying out what they were here to do. Warren just stared back, glassy, without emotion, seemingly resigned to whatever fate was about to take place.

Vega began to chuckle. "Too bad you just couldn't take it, man. Took it out on yourself. 'Cause that's the way it's gonna look." He nodded to his accomplice. Hauck saw him cock his gun and finally jam it against Warren's temple.

His brother shut his eyes.

Now. Hauck kicked in the doors.

Glass shattered over the floor. He picked out the guy on Warren first, who spun, aiming wildly, as Hauck squeezed on the Sig—four times—blotches of red exploding against the folds of sweatshirt gray.

The man toppled back against a bookshelf, leather volumes and mementos crashing down on him.

Hauck shifted toward Vega, who spun the chair across the floor and leaped out, fumbling for his gun, which had fallen to the floor.

"Don't!"

He was trapped, frozen in midmotion, his desperate eyes

locking on Hauck, who stood with his gun trained on him with both hands.

"Don't move a muscle," Hauck said. "Don't even breathe, Vega. You must know how little I would care if I had to blow you away."

The gang leader held himself there, crouched, his gun to the side. His finger tensed around the trigger guard. He looked at Hauck, a smile creasing his lips, and straightened up. "Surprised to see you again, bro."

"*Why?* You said to come see you. You said you'd give me a lesson, how one and one didn't add up to two." The guy had murdered Sanger. Probably been responsible for the hit on Kramer too. Not to mention the charge he had beaten for shooting it out with a state trooper.

Hauck fixed, steadfast, on him. "*So, I'm here . . .*"

Vega glanced narrowly at him, then at Warren. Then he nodded with the resigned state of someone who was about to end it here. He blew Hauck a kiss. "So we are, *maricón*." He nodded. "So we are."

There was a gleam in Vega's eye. His finger curled around the trigger.

Hauck shook his head. "*Don't.*"

Vega righted his arm, the gun darting at Hauck sideways. Hauck squeezed and the Sig recoiled in three sharp retorts. The rounds ripped into the gang leader's chest. He fell back against the couch, his gun turning toward Warren. Hauck squeezed off three more rounds until Vega landed upright against the wall, a glassy defiance in his eyes, and slid down slowly, a dark smear of crimson against the cream-colored wall.

A weight seemed to free itself off Hauck and he slumped wearily against the desk.

"*Ty . . .*"

He turned to Warren. "You alright?"

"You shouldn't have stopped him, Ty." Warren shook his head and fell, head in hands, to the floor. "You just should've let it happen."

"There's a part of me that wishes I had . . ." Hauck went over and collapsed against the wall next to his brother. He put his hand on his knee. "The other part said Pop would wipe the floor with me."

Warren laughed, his face riddled more with shame than joy. "You were never supposed to be involved, Ty. You have to believe that. It was supposed to be just one time. One fucking time . . . I told myself I could just look away. In a million years I never guessed they would carry it out right there in town."

"Raines?"

Warren hung his head and nodded.

"And what about above him? Scayne? Casey had arranged this big Iraq reconstruction contract for his generator division, right? That's what you meant when you said, 'Not that kind of power'? It was Sanger who was assigned to handle the case. That's what this was all about, the killings—*payoffs*? Two corrupt fat cats who scratched each other's back protecting themselves."

Warren put his head back against the wall and nodded. "They came to me to get the casino to carry out the hit. Casey had been running interference for them for years. It was all a game." He shut his eyes. "You have no idea how much I owed these people, Ty."

"And Kramer? That was just another smoke screen, wasn't it? To back up the appearance that it was all a gambling scam?"

Warren flattened his lips. "Plan B."

Hauck shook his head disgustedly. "Plan B . . ."

They sat there for a while. The weight of everything sinking in. Tears made their way down Warren's cheeks.

Hauck pulled his brother's face to his shoulder. He had no idea what to do. Arrest him? Send his own brother away for the rest of his life? Destroy whatever was left of their family?

Warren took in a deep breath. "So, partner, what happens now?"

"*Now* . . ." Hauck pulled himself up. He looked at Warren slumped there and held out his hand. Hesitantly, Warren reached for it.

"Now we get Raines."

"That won't be that easy," Warren said. "Vega's dead. I was never privy to much of the details. It's his word against mine. You understand I don't exactly make the most compelling witness, Ty."

He was right. The people who had carried out the acts were all dead. None of the murder weapons could be tied to Raines. Whatever he and Warren had discussed, it was now just Warren's word against his. Any lawyer worth a lick would cut it to shreds.

Hauck pulled his brother up. "I know how."

CHAPTER EIGHTY-TWO

*I*t took a few calls to set up. Vern was able to arrange some interference before the word leaked out. The final call went to Raines. Hauck caught him just as the security man was about to leave for the day.

"*Lieutenant* . . ." He was probably trying to reach Vega. Hearing Hauck, he sounded a little surprised and wary.

Hauck said, "I'd like another shot at blackjack with you, if that's okay."

"You seem to like the odds here, Lieutenant. You're welcome here any time as a guest. When would you like to come?"

"How about an hour?"

"*An hour?*" Raines seemed startled. "You need a refresher course on what you saw before?"

"I thought we might also have a chat about generators," Hauck said. "How does that sound?"

"*Generators* . . . ?" Hauck knew that would get his wheels turning. "I'll make sure we have your special table reserved."

When Hauck arrived, alone, Raines and two of his security men were waiting in the hotel lobby. This time there was no phony glad-handing. No playacting back and forth. The security chief's handshake was cold and perfunctory.

"You mind?" Raines eyed him suspiciously, nodded to one of his crew. A black guy in a slick brown suit with a linebacker's build stepped forward and made a move to pat Hauck down.

"It's in the car," Hauck said, raising his arms freely to comply.

"I'm not interested in whether you're armed," Raines said. His associate passed an electronic wand over him, searching for recording devices. Hauck didn't resist. The sensor didn't emit a sound. The man nodded back to Raines, satisfied.

"Just to make sure the conversation is entirely between ourselves, Lieutenant," the security chief said.

Hauck shrugged. "Wouldn't have it any other way."

"C'mon, then." Raines grinned. "I have a surprise waiting for you."

The security team stayed behind as Raines led Hauck into the large casino. It was a Thursday night and the giant room was jammed. The cacophony of a thousand slots, the clanging of bells, and bettors shouting hit him as they walked through the entrance.

"Busy night," Hauck said.

"Carrie Underwood is here. You should stay for the show, Lieutenant."

"You know me." Hauck winked. "All work, no play."

Raines's eyes gleamed with amusement. "And no bags this time, I see. Shame." Weaving through the throng, he guided Hauck up to an empty table. Hauck recognized the dealer who seemed to be awaiting them.

"You remember Josie, don't you?" Raines grinned, his mustache parting in a smile.

Hauck smiled, trying to put her at ease. "Course I remember Josie." The cute blackjack dealer was behind the table, in her starched shirt and vest, her auburn hair in a braided ponytail again. Looking a little humiliated.

The bastard had pulled out all the stops.

"How's school?" Hauck said to her.

Josie blushed, trying to remain professional.

"Oh, *please*." Raines laughed. "The two of you don't have to be so formal. You probably wouldn't know, but Josie's changed her major since you were here last . . . She's suddenly been taken with a passion for photography, isn't that right, dear?"

Josie gritted her teeth and didn't reply, but her gaze said it all. It was like daggers back to him, her face finally settling into a compliant smile. She removed several decks of cards and began to shuffle them into a large stack.

"It's good to see you again, Lieutenant . . ."

"So what is it tonight?" Raines asked. "A refresher course in how things are done here? Oh, that's right, you said something about generators . . . You'll have to explain what that means. Sounds a bit out of my expertise." He reached inside his pocket. "Usual stakes? I've brought along some chips . . ."

Hauck put up his hand and took out five twenties. He slid them across to Josie, who stacked four green chips. "How about tonight I just play mine."

"As you wish . . ." Raines shrugged and pulled up a chair across from him. "So what is it you wanted to talk about?"

"*Power*," Hauck said to him as Josie continued to shuffle, cutting the deck several times. "In Iraq. You know how some of those sweetheart deals got set up at the beginning of the war . . . ?"

"I'm afraid I'm not much interested in politics, Lieutenant.

You've come a long way and I'm afraid I can't be of much help to you."

Josie merged the decks together and slid them across the table to Hauck for a cut. Hauck pushed one of his blue chips into the box.

"I trust you." He grinned, tapping the top card.

Josie smiled demurely and slid the merged deck into the shoe. She began to deal, sliding Hauck a ten and then a queen across the green felt table.

Twenty. She showed a seven.

Hauck said, "Pat."

Josie flipped over her hole card, revealing a king. Seventeen. Hauck was a winner.

"Nice start," Raines said.

Hauck kept the same bet on the table.

"I see you're a little more cautious tonight."

"This time it's my money."

Josie dealt out another hand. She started Hauck with a queen. Followed it up with an ace. Blackjack.

Raines said, "Seems like you don't need our help at all tonight, Lieutenant. So no more baiting around; what was it you came to talk about . . . ?"

"I wanted to tell you Vega's dead," Hauck said to him.

Raines's jaw twitched. His granite-colored pupils barely moved. He feigned ignorance. "Vega?"

"He's dead," Hauck said. "And I know about Warren. So we're back to generators, Raines. And Richard Scayne . . . Is it all starting to come clearer now?"

This time, the defenses in Raines's gaze seemed to waver and Hauck noticed his fists curl into tight balls. "Josie, do you mind leaving us for a while?" he said. "I don't believe the lieutenant came all this way to play Twenty-one after all . . ."

"No problem at all," Josie said. She righted the decks in the shoe. "Good to see you again, Lieutenant."

She left, right on cue.

"Now, I'm not sure I'm understanding just where you're going with all of this, Lieutenant . . . ," Raines said, a cutting edge to his tone.

Hauck said, "Oh, I think you do. It's all coming down now, Raines. I know why David Sanger and Keith Kramer were killed. Paul Pacello too. I know who came to you to set it up. I know you enlisted your old army buddy, Vega, along with DR-17, to carry it out." He looked at him. "So we're back to generators, Raines . . . Which is the one part I don't yet have figured out. Or maybe it never got there for you. Maybe your higher-ups just asked you to do a favor and that's what you do."

The veneer on Raines's hard face began to crack.

"Warren talked," Hauck said. "The party's over. You're the first to go."

Raines spun a chip on the green felt, staring, as he sorted through the possibilities. The man was no fool and one thing went to the top of the list pretty quickly. He shrugged. "So why haven't you arrested me yet, Lieutenant?"

"Because there are bigger fish to fry . . ."

Raines nodded. All around, the festive din of the casino seemed to be drowned out. "I don't think so, Lieutenant. Want to know what I think? You say Vega's dead? I don't think you have as much as you're trying to bluff me you do to build a case on. You don't have a weapon. You can't put me at any of the scenes . . . No lines of communication. You don't even have a witness who ties me to whoever you say did these things."

"I have Warren."

"*Warren?*" Raines's face lightened into a grin. "What *I* think you have is a very suspect witness, Lieutenant. Despite the fact that he's your own brother, he probably couldn't even procure a fishing license for himself these days, not to mention a license to practice law. And whose fingers, when it all comes out, are deep in a lot of shady deals." He nodded sympathetically. "I can see why this is such a pickle for you, Lieutenant. You have your own brother, trying to save his own skin. Whatever we might have talked about, it's just his word against mine. And I have a lot of people backing me up on this. Important people. Just who does your brother have these days? *My* advice . . . You'd better be careful whose house you try to bring down. It just might fall on you." He flung out his fingers. "*Boom!* You know what I mean, Lieutenant?"

Hauck forced back the urge to go for the man's throat right there. He held it in check. "I'm giving you a chance to save your skin, Raines, much as that makes me gag. You didn't set this in motion. You were just carrying it out. Like I said, whoever you're protecting, there are bigger fish to fry . . ."

Raines seemed to be thinking it over, suddenly noticing the resolve shrink just a bit in Hauck's eyes. The tide turn in his favor. "I don't think so, Lieutenant. Don't much like the odds." He leaned closer, lowering his voice, his tone chummy. "Just between us girls, Lieutenant, maybe your brother and I did talk over a few things. Maybe a certain U.S. attorney's name did come up once or twice. Maybe we did toss around how things might be different if he wasn't so much on the scene. And maybe we did have to cover our tracks just a little . . ."

"Plan B," Hauck said.

Raines chuckled. "Everyone's got to have a backup plan, Lieutenant. Poor Keith . . . how he stumbled in this mess I'll never know. But seems to me your problem is, just how are you ever going to prove all that, Lieutenant? You have any illusions that your brother's testimony would stand up at trial? With the kind of people he's bedded down with in his career? With all he's got to hide?" Raines laughed loudly and nudged Hauck, clearly enjoying the shifting tide. "Seems to me, you've got nothing that ties me to shit—*nothing,* except a corrupt local lawyer out to save his own skin who might say anything. And his policeman brother, who, in my view, ought to give some serious thought to standing aside as the lead in this investigation." He grinned. "Maybe take a good look at how to fill some of those new personnel holes in his department . . ."

It took everything Hauck had not to lunge across the table and mash Raines's face into pulp, the well of anger building up inside him so strong.

Just let the man talk, Ty . . .

"And let's say you did, Lieutenant, bring me in on this trumped-up testimony. What do you have, beyond some kind of watered-down conspiracy charge? You think any of it would stick? *Generators . . . Iraq war contracts . . .* You know who pulls the arm of justice around here, Lieutenant. You're bumping against it right now. Me, I'm just a simple employee of the resort. Paid to protect their interests. And their interests are everywhere. Make no mistake.

"So what do you think?" Raines smiled haughtily. "You got a case against me?" He flicked the black hundred-dollar chip he'd been playing with across the table. "I think not. First rule of gambling, Lieutenant, know who brought the deck before you sit down at the game."

CHAPTER EIGHTY-THREE

*H*auck gazed past Raines's shoulder at the crowd of milling bettors, the flashing lights, the musical chime of slots going off.

Steve Chrisafoulis stepped out of the crowd.

Raines's back was toward him, so he didn't see him. Steve came up and placed a small recording device next to the unsuspecting security chief's ear.

"Maybe your brother and I did talk over a few things. Maybe a certain U.S. attorney's name did come up once or twice. Maybe we did toss around how things would be different if he wasn't so much on the scene . . ."

The color drained from Raines's face. He spun, panic rising up in him, saw the recorder and heard his own damning words.

"What the hell is going on?"

Hauck reached over and lifted the stack of cards out of the dealer's shoe. He sorted through them until he came to a place in the deck where a tiny silver disc was attached to one of the cards. "What was it you called that trick . . . ?" Hauck screwed up his brow. *"The false shuffle . . ."*

Raines's eyes burned through him. "I don't understand."

Hauck led his gaze across the room to Josie, a couple of tables away, who gave a contempt-filled one-handed wave to Raines.

"Like you said"—Hauck stood up from the chair—"you ought to know who brought the deck before you sit down at the game."

Raines glared toward Josie. "You're dead. Fucking bitch whore . . ."

Chrisafoulis twisted Raines's arms behind his back. "Joseph Raines, you're under arrest for plotting the deaths of David Sanger and Keith Kramer. You're also under arrest for conspiring to commit the murders of Paul Pacello and Detective Frederico Munoz."

He slapped a set of cuffs roughly over the security man's wrists.

"You're making a mistake." Raines spun around. "You don't want to open this up. You don't have any idea where it leads. It won't go anywhere, except to get your own fucking pension revoked, Lieutenant, along with a little brown speck going around in the bottom of the bowl that'll be what's left of your career."

"Too bad . . ." Hauck reared and slugged him in the jaw, Raines's feet sliding out from under him, held up only by the two cops who clasped him by the arms.

"Freddy Munoz says hello." Hauck glared into the cuffed man's eyes.

"I'll be out before morning. You'll see." Raines tried to jerk out of his grip. "This won't go anywhere. You don't have a fucking clue who this will piss off!"

They turned, the local police running interference as they took Raines through the maze of tables and out of the casino.

Hauck felt jubilant. They had one more stop to make. Up in Hartford.

Who this would piss off? Hauck had a perfect idea.

They took Raines through the posh glass-atrium lobby.

Suddenly Hauck ran face-first into the last two people he expected to see.

Sculley and Taylor. Flanked by three other tan suits. "Just one minute, Lieutenant . . ."

What were they doing here?

Agent in Charge Sculley removed a document from his jacket. "We have a warrant to take Mr. Raines into custody for the deaths of David Sanger and Paul Pacello, executed by James Puig, chief prosecutor for the U.S. Department of Justice in Hartford."

"*What?*" Hauck felt like a sucker punch took the air out of him. He blocked Sculley's path. "You don't have jurisdiction here."

"I'm afraid we do, Lieutenant. U.S. Attorney Sanger was in the employ of the federal government at the time of his death and the shooting of Mr. Pacello in Maine occurred across state lines. Not to mention that this very building is on property granted by the United States government, making this very much our jurisdiction, Lieutenant. Feel free to petition the Justice Department for the right to transfer Mr. Raines out of our custody. I'm sure they'll be awaiting your state attorney's brief."

He stared helplessly at the warrant as two of the junior agents took hold of Raines.

Stan Taylor smirked. "Sorry about this, Lieutenant . . ."

Ire flashed up in Hauck. It was like with Vega all over again. Hauck had put his life on the line. Freddy Munoz had given his life.

They were stealing his case.

"You can have your attorneys file a petition of subrogation," Sculley said, "but I wouldn't be overly confident. Mr. Raines is a pivotal cog in an ongoing corruption investigation of ours . . ."

"Corruption investigation?"

"I told you." Raines cackled as they whisked him away through the lobby. "I told you you had no idea where this went or what was involved. Have fun, Lieutenant! It was awfully nice playing with you. Have fun proving your case."

CHAPTER EIGHTY-FOUR

Stan Taylor drove the Crown Vic away from the Pequot Woods. Sculley sat in back next to Raines.

Raines had his cuffs fastened to a bar on the seat in front of them.

How he had enjoyed that! Being whisked out of Hauck's grasp. Wachman had always said they would come through for him. And so they did! He had always done the hard jobs, the jobs no one else was willing to do.

Now he was being paid back.

He had no idea where he was being taken, other than he was with people who knew how to handle things and make things go away. Wachman. Casey. They'd said they had people in their pockets. They'd work out some kind of safe haven. They knew that if Raines ever had to face those damaging charges, he could take a lot of very important people down.

A pivotal cog in an ongoing corruption investigation . . .
That was priceless!

They rode for a while in silence. The car banked onto the highway south, in the direction of New Haven. The headlights of the second FBI car shone brightly behind them, hovering a few lengths behind. This time of night, the traffic was light.

Raines allowed himself a moment to feel relieved. *Ecstatic.* He had performed his duties capably and without question. He had done what he was paid to do. Protect his employer's interests.

"So where are you taking me?" He turned to the agent in charge seated next to him.

The man was balding, a little reddish fuzz around the sides. He merely shrugged. "The less you know, the better."

Probably right. Raines sat back. "Tell Mr. Wachman I appreciate this."

Sculley nodded obligingly. "I'll be sure to pass that along."

The road was dark. The highway was basically a link between the casino and I-95, the main north-south artery along the coast. Pretty much nothing in between. Raines settled in, then glanced behind him.

The headlights from the car behind them had disappeared.

The black agent driving slowed the car.

The slightest tremor of anticipation shot through Raines. *"What's going on?"*

Taylor pulled off onto the embankment on the side of the road.

"Making a transfer," Sculley said. The agent in charge reached across and undid his cuffs.

"Transfer?" There wasn't a light on the highway. He didn't see anyone else around.

Taylor climbed out of the front on the passenger side.

"Here," Sculley said, "this may come in handy." The FBI man reached under his jacket and, to Raines's shock, handed him his own gun. A Smith & Wesson .40 caliber. Raines was familiar. Standard agency issue.

Raines's heart picked up. This wasn't like any transfer. *"What the hell's happening?"*

"Take it," said the agent in charge.

Warily, Raines wrapped his hand around the gun. The weight seemed a little light. He was about to check the clip when Taylor opened the door.

"C'mon, get out."

"*Out?*" Raines looked back, not quite understanding. The anticipation he was feeling had now crossed into uneasiness. With a bit of hesitation, he climbed out the open door. He rubbed his wrists and fingered the proffered gun. He noticed the safety was off. It still felt light. He looked around for some kind of activity on the road.

There was none.

"This is some kind of joke, right?"

"Yeah, Raines," Sculley said, "a real knee slapper. Now get the fuck going."

"*Going?*" He looked around. *They were in the middle of nowhere . . .*

Taylor, the driver, opened his sport jacket. His own gun was holstered at his waist. "Get moving, Raines. Call it your lucky day. Must be all those people watching over you. This is the end of the line. *Run.*"

Run? Raines looked back and forth between Sculley and Taylor, trying to figure out what was going on. All he saw was a ditch on the side of the highway. *Where the hell could he go?*

The uneasiness had deepened into worry, worry into freaking out.

"*Where's Wachman?* You let Senator Casey know that I'm here. *Call him!* I've done favors for him. He'll want to know."

"Good-bye, Mr. Raines," Agent in Charge Sculley said.

In front of him, Taylor removed his gun.

His eyes widened. *He was being set up.* He lifted Sculley's Smith & Wesson. Raines took a step back, dread kicking up in his blood. The black FBI guy stood there unconcerned.

You sons of bitches . . . Raines panicked. He fired.

Nothing happened. All he heard was a click.

In fear, he pointed and kept on firing. Several shots, in rapid succession. Aimed at Taylor's chest.

Just clicks.

Raines's jaw dropped. He put the gun down. He started to back away.

"Senator Casey sends his regards," Agent Taylor said.

Anyone within half a mile would've heard the two rapid retorts.

CHAPTER EIGHTY-FIVE

*H*auck's phone sounded as he headed north to Hartford.

Raines was gone—but there was still one more link in the chain, and he had to get there before the FBI, or whoever else was involved, closed that one too.

Vern's voice came on.

"They took him, Vern. Sculley and Taylor. They stole him right from under us. Arrested him on a RICO charge."

"It doesn't matter anymore." The chief sounded tired and a little disappointed. "You can turn yourself around and come on home, Ty."

"Come on home?"

Vern paused. "Raines is dead, Ty."

"Dead?" Hauck felt slammed. He slowed to the side of the road. "How?"

"Taylor shot him. Attempting to escape. On their way down to New Haven. Raines forced them to pull over. Somehow he managed to take Sculley's gun."

Escape. Another door was shut. Another link back to Scayne and Casey. A troubled thought knifed into his mind. "You see what's going on, don't you? It's happening all over again. Just like with Vega. Evidence is lost, the case against a killer gets dropped. Except now they're not taking any chances. *The leak just died.*"

"You have to be careful about just where you take this, Ty . . ."

"These people killed Sanger and Kramer, Vern. And Freddy. They tried to kill *me.*"

Oncoming headlights glared sharply in the windshield. Innocent people had been caught up in this, this cover-up, and died. He'd made promises. This doesn't just get shut down. Swept under the rug. It didn't end with Raines. People ordered this. And it didn't end with Warren either.

"I can't, Vern."

"Turn back around. I mean that, Ty. You had a shooting today. Don't make me give you an order."

"I don't know if I can, Vern."

CHAPTER EIGHTY-SIX

*T*he gated community was named Arapahoe Farms, about twenty minutes outside of the capital. The homes were modern colonials, nice, midsized. It was after ten o'clock. Most of the houses were dark. Minivans and Beemers were parked in front of their garages.

Hauck stopped at 3377 Albion Circle.

This one was not dark. Hauck had the feeling they were expecting him.

He parked the car, walked up the flagstone landing, and rang the bell.

"Just a minute!" He heard footsteps. An attractive middle-aged woman in a robe cracked open the door. Looked as if she was getting ready for bed. "Yes?"

"I'm sorry to bother you," Hauck said. "I'm looking for Ira Wachman . . ."

"Ira . . . ?" She turned back into the house. "He's . . ."

A short, stout man with receding, wiry gray hair in a cardigan sweater came to the door. "I'll take it, Alice . . ."

He looked at Hauck, unsurprised. "I'm Ira Wachman, Lieutenant."

He peered outside, past Hauck, for the sight of other police cars and flashing lights. There were none, and he gave Hauck a sagacious smile. Wachman's eyes seemed tired and heavy, but there was something in them, wisdom, experience. He opened the door. "Why don't you come in, Lieutenant."

Hauck stepped into the white-tiled foyer.

"Alice, why don't you go on up to bed. I'll be up in a while. Lieutenant, I'm sure we'll be more comfortable in here."

He led Hauck through the formal living room with skylights and an atrium into a paneled, book-filled den. The shelves were painted red, the furniture English, maybe antique. It had a built-in TV and some hunting paintings and lots of photographs and mementos out on the shelves. "You take scotch, Lieutenant?"

"No."

"Hope you don't mind if I do." Wachman opened a cabinet and poured himself a glass from the bar, while Hauck's eyes found the silver-framed photos on the polished wood desk. Wachman with many familiar faces. Senator Casey. The governor. The former secretary of defense, who a year ago had been forced to resign.

A portrait of his wife and two grown boys.

"One of my sons graduated from Georgetown, Lieutenant. He's in the Marines now—on assignment. You know where. The other is a senior at Penn, wants to go to Wall Street . . ."

Wachman motioned for Hauck to take a seat on the tufted leather couch and pulled up an ottoman across from him. He raised his glass. "Cheers."

"I came here to arrest you, Mr. Wachman," Hauck said. "For your involvement in the murders of David Sanger and Keith Kramer."

"And . . ."

"And . . ." Hauck shrugged. "I wish I could."

"I used to wish for a lot of things, Lieutenant." Wachman took a sip of scotch. "Politics has cured me of that."

"I don't have such reservations. Raines is dead. But somehow I suspect that's something you already know."

"I heard." The government man nodded, making no attempt to conceal it.

"Word travels fast among friends."

The government man smiled, looked Hauck in the eyes. "Are you miked, Lieutenant?"

Hauck said, "No."

"I don't think I'm making a mistake to take you as a man of your word. I won't make any attempt to deceive you, Lieutenant. Too bad about Raines, but what happened to him was not, shall we say, inconvenient. Of course that all sounds a bit clichéd. The man had gotten himself in a lot of shaky shit. Nor will I make any attempt to hide my connection to your brother."

"Warren talked. He gave you up. Sanger. Cascy. Scayne. The generators to Iraq. *Plan B* . . . I think I know what it was about—and what I don't know, I'll figure out."

"That so?" Wachman put down his glass. "I've known him for a long time, your brother. Warren's always proved himself to be a friend. A willing one. Why shouldn't he be? He's built a nice life around it. Isn't that what we all want? A nice life. Free and clear of worry? What is it you want, Lieutenant?"

"Just the truth."

"That's all? Even if it brings down the people closest to you? Even if it comes so close, you can feel it on your skin?"

"What else can you possibly give me, Mr. Wachman?"

Wachman leaned back against the desk. "Only one thing. I can give you back your brother."

That took him by surprise, a blunt force against Hauck's chest.

"I can make this all go away. *His* role. His part in it. Everyone's part. I can shroud this thing in such a hole, ten reporters from the *New York Times,* all vying for fucking Pulitzers, couldn't figure it out. Richard Scayne will be gone soon. Senator Casey will be making an announcement that this will be his last term. A year from now, those generators will be forgotten. Politics is politics, Lieutenant. It will just go on."

"To me it's just a little too late for all that now."

Ira Wachman nodded resignedly, then shrugged. "I can also make your life a living hell, Lieutenant." He said it so evenly and matter-of-factly it almost didn't come across as a threat. "You say you know? *You don't know*. It was 'open for business' over there. Everyone wanted a piece of the action. Everyone got it. Bechtel. Halliburton. Blackwater. KPMG. You think any of them did anything any differently? Some well-placed money changing hands. That was the ticket in, Lieutenant. The price." Wachman chortled. "This sonovabitch in the Pentagon goes and blows his brains out . . . Why do we suddenly give a shit about a handful of generators?"

"It has nothing to do with generators," Hauck said.

"It has *everything* to do with generators, Lieutenant! Everything. That fucking country was nothing more than blood and sand. We stuck the needle into its heart and then we had to find the way to resuscitate it. The government couldn't handle it. *It was too big for the fucking government!* It had to be built back up by private hands. That's what we do, Lieutenant. We, Americans. That's the way history is built."

Hauck didn't answer, just let him go on.

"So what did they need there?" The veins on Wachman's neck began to swell. "What did they goddamn need, before all the schools, the police academies, the air-conditioned shopping malls? Before the Starwoods and the McDonald's? They needed to get the machinery back up again. The cement mixers turning. The lights back on. *They needed hope!* That's what the people were begging for. *Power. Generators. Hope.* And what was so wrong about giving people a little hope, Lieutenant? Ultimately, when history is written, who gives a piece of lint however we got them there?"

"Hope? Is that what you think you bought with their lives? Sanger. Kramer. Freddy Munoz . . . *Hope?*"

"It doesn't matter what we bought with their lives, Lieutenant. My job is to make sure a good man doesn't go down in the dust for it. A man who devoted his career to this state. Who built roads, schools, businesses. Hired police, put people to work. Raised their lives. *That's* what I care about, Lieutenant. You come after me on this—that's all you're going to get. We arranged a contract. They needed people who could get the job done, not rules. Not bidding processes, transparency . . . Halliburton got sixty billion, for God's sakes! Richard Scayne got two. You come after us, Lieutenant, that's all you're going to get. A tale of how wars are run in the world today. You're looking for *scandals?* It's one of many. A pebble on a white sand beach."

"So is it all worth it, Wachman? Sanger. Kramer. Pacello. Munoz. You think they had any idea what they were dying for?"

"Sometimes it is, Lieutenant." Wachman clinked his ice against the glass. "Sometimes it just depends on what it is you're trying to protect."

Hauck stood up. "You seem to like clichés. Here's another. Don't leave town."

"Not high on my list." The government man smiled. "The senator's got a transportation bill before the legislature this week . . ."

"And here's one more. Anything happens to my brother—he

trips while jogging, cuts himself shaving . . . Or happens to have an accident in his cell. You know it'll be personal then, Wachman. You'll wish I took you in . . ."

The government man smiled, sat against the credenza. "No worries, Lieutenant. Among your brother's virtues—and there are a few—being an effective witness against a U.S. senator is not chief. I think I'll take my chances there."

"Finish your drink," Hauck said. He headed toward the door. "I'll show myself out."

"Remember what I said, Lieutenant. About getting your brother back."

Hauck stopped at the door and turned. "You're wrong, you know. All this talk about how wars are run and people standing up. That's just a lie. We both know what it was, don't we? It was just greed. Greed and self-preservation. Not some noble idea, Mr. Wachman. Pretty much the basest motive known to man."

"It's been fun hashing things out with you, Lieutenant," Wachman said, taking a last gulp from his glass. "I look forward to seeing you again. Maybe in court."

CHAPTER EIGHTY-SEVEN

*I*t was going on midnight when Hauck got back to Greenwich. Instead of heading home, he drove to the station.

The avenue was dark and quiet. All the restaurants had already shut for the night. He parked his car in the back lot and waved hello to Steve Palazzo, the duty officer, doing the graveyard shift at the front desk. Only a handful of people around this time of night. For a second Hauck gave some thought to heading upstairs. He felt like a thousand-pound weight hung on his shoulders. Was it days ago he had burst into Warren's office and rescued his brother? *No, hours* . . . The sweat was still on his hands.

I can give you back your brother.

He went downstairs to the basement.

A dim fluorescent light burned near the row of holding cells.

"How's it going?" Hauck waved to the young duty officer who was on the overnight down there. Guardino. Ralph. Been on the force for just a couple of years. Most nights they had maybe a domestic dispute or some drunk driver in lockup down here. The Yankee game was on the TV. Guardino was sitting with his feet up on the desk and jumped, straightening his uniform, when Hauck appeared.

"Lieutenant!"

"Relax," Hauck said. "What's the score?"

"Yanks by two. Bottom of the ninth. Mariano's in."

"Chalk it up!" Hauck said with a nod. "What do you say I take over for a few minutes? Go grab yourself a coffee."

"No, sir, I'm okay," the young officer said. Seemed eager to prove it.

Hauck patted him on the shoulder and this time didn't phrase it as a question. "Go get yourself a coffee, son."

"Yes, sir," the young officer muttered, and headed out.

Hauck opened the key box. He searched for the right one and went down the row of six cells. He stopped at the end and stared at the curled-up shape on the cot with his back to him, still in his clothes.

What is it you want, Lieutenant? Wachman had asked.

I want the truth.

"Warren . . . ?"

His brother stirred. He turned over and fuzzily opened his eyes. *"Ty . . ."* He looked for his watch. "What the fuck time is it?"

"Almost midnight."

"Midnight? Damn . . ." Warren sat up and rubbed his face. "How did it go?"

"Raines is dead," Hauck told him.

"Huh?"

"Shot trying to escape. By the FBI. They trumped our collar and took him in custody on their own RICO charge."

Warren looked surprised. *"The FBI?"*

"Seems he managed to steal someone's firearm on the ride down. Even while in cuffs . . ." Hauck cocked his finger and squeezed an imaginary trigger. *"Pow . . ."*

His brother blinked, his brain kicking. He drew a hand

through his tussled hair. "You're not believing any of that for a second, are you, Ty?"

"Not for a second, Warren." Hauck shook his head.

He opened the cell.

Warren stood up. He located his glasses on the stool and slipped his feet into his Cole Haans. "Thanks . . ." He rubbed his back a little stiffly. "Nice décor. A little minimalist for me, and I have to say the mattress sucks . . ."

Hauck stared. "I'm sorry, Warren."

"Sorry for what, little bro?"

I can give you back your brother.

"Warren Hauck, I'm arresting you for the murders of David Sanger and Keith Kramer . . ."

"*What!*" Warren looked at him, confused. "Ty, please. Don't . . ."

"You have the right to remain silent. Anything you say now can be used against you . . ."

Warren shook his head. "*Ty* . . ."

The rest of it Hauck said but never remembered. He pressed his brother against the cell wall, realizing he was fighting back tears.

PART FOUR

CHAPTER EIGHTY-EIGHT

*H*e thought it was over.

After he drove back up to Hartford the following day and took Ira Wachman in for the murders of David Sanger, Keith Kramer, and Paul Pacello. After the press had gotten hold of it and everything started to tumble out.

Cascade was more like it.

Scayne's half-million-dollar contribution to the Republican Senate Election Fund, much of it finding its way back to funds controlled by Senator Oren Casey. The awarding of the lucrative contract for two hundred and fifty thousand Nova 91s.

The dying tycoon, riven by illness, desperate to avoid a trial. The six-term Connecticut senator citing "the changing times" for his sudden decision to end his career in public service.

Casey's closest aide, Wachman, disavowing any link that tied him to Raines or any of these "terrible murders," other than to a corrupt local lawyer "who would do anything to save his own skin." The senator's lawyer claiming on the capitol steps that the senator had never even met Joe Raines and recalling only the most distant lawyer-client relationship with Warren Hauck.

All over.

Warren, released from jail, putting up his home to collater-
alize his two-million-dollar bail. Spilling everything out to the
Fairfield County DA. Business deals the two had worked together, committees they had served on, golf outings.

And Sanger, innocent of any wrongdoing. Just a guy with a
gambling urge he kept secret and the wrong friend. Dealt the
right cards by his "lucky" dealer and whatever else he had won
online.

Like Wendy Sanger had said, you'll find out. A good man.

It all came out.

The military procurement officer's suicide. William Turner,
on the board of the Pequot Woods, who facilitated an illegal
transfer of funds. An investigation into the suspicious death
of Joseph Raines. Sculley and Taylor.

Like Wachman said, if you were looking for stories, it was
only one of many.

Ten reporters vying for a Pulitzer wouldn't be able to put it
together. A pebble on a white sand beach.

But it wasn't over. Everything had managed to come out
but one.

The truth.

The truth why Sanger was killed. The truth, like Wachman
said, that was truly worth protecting.

*Even if it brings down the people closest to you? Even if it
comes so close, you can feel it on your own skin?*

CHAPTER EIGHTY-NINE

A week later, Hauck had begun the task of finding Freddy Munoz's replacement, meeting with a detective from Philadelphia whose TV weatherperson wife was being transferred up here.

While they were talking Hauck's cell phone rang.

He saw it was Warren. "You think I could excuse myself for just a couple of minutes?"

The guy answered, "Sure." Hauck stepped outside.

"Warren?" They hadn't spoken since his brother had gotten out on bail. He didn't think it was appropriate. Any interaction between the two of them could jeopardize both their impending cases.

"How's it going, bro?" Warren sounded sheepish.

Hauck said, "You know this isn't really such a good idea . . ."

"I know that, Ty. Who's the lawyer here, anyway? But I laid it all out for them. It's a slam-dunk from here. I was just wondering . . ." His tone shifted. "You remember that kid Paul McDonald?"

Paul McDonald was the son of a golf pro at a public course where they used to play who developed Hodgkin's. Warren had set up a local tournament to help raise money for his care. Hauck always thought it was about the nicest thing his brother ever did.

"Yeah, I remember, Warren. *Why* . . . ?"

"I don't know. I was just sort of wishing that kid hadn't died."

Hauck shifted the phone. There was a vagueness in his brother's voice. This was all something that had been decided long ago. He hadn't heard Paul McDonald's name in years. "You okay?"

"Yeah, Ty, I'm okay. I am."

"You talk to Ginny yet?"

"I think that one's gonna be a bit of a project, bro."

"What about the kids?"

"Yeah, *um* . . . " Warren started to answer, inhaled, then stopped.

"Where are you?" Hauck asked, hearing some background noise that sounded like engines running.

"At the office. Just putting a few things together. While I still have a license."

"You want me to come up?" *The hell with how it might seem,* he decided. "We could talk. Brother to brother. A lot's gone down. Have a couple of beers."

"No, I don't want you to come up, Ty. Like you said, bad precedent, anyway . . ."

A few seconds passed. Neither of them spoke. Suddenly Hauck asked the only thing he could think to say. "Warren, *why* . . . ?"

"I don't know." It took a while for him to answer. "You think I don't ask myself that a million times? We were just different. I didn't see the line." Then out of the blue, he went, "You ever tell anyone?"

"Tell anyone *what*?" Hauck asked.

"You know what I'm talking about, Ty. Peter Morrison. Who ever knew?"

Hauck waited a time before answering. "No one, Warren. I never told a soul."

Warren chuckled as if impressed. "Yeah, I guess I always knew that, Ty. You know it was always you, don't you?"

"*Me?*"

"*You* I was afraid of letting down. Not Pop or Mom." He stayed silent for a while. "*You.*"

Hauck nodded as if his brother was in front of him. "Yeah, I think I know that now . . ."

"So, listen," Warren said, "I've got to scoot. Lemme get back to those files . . ."

"You know you can call me anytime, Warren, right? Fuck the precedents. Whenever you need to. Okay?"

"I know that," his brother said. "You stay outta trouble, Ty."

CHAPTER NINETY

Warren put down his phone. He put the Range Rover in gear and drove it through the gates of the small airfield.

Somehow it just felt right to come here.

He went right up to the hangar where his small Cessna was kept. Pete, who maintained it, waved hi. "Taking her up, Mr. H?" This time of year, there wasn't a whole lot of traffic.

"Just to stretch out the blades." Warrren laughed.

"An Italian tune-up, as they say, huh?" The mechanic grinned.

"I'll have her back in no time."

Pete wheeled her out, and Warren admired how beautiful the lines on the plane were. Nothing else seemed to give him so much joy.

"Want me to fuel her up? She's a bit low," the mechanic asked.

"No." Warren shook his head. "Just gonna take her up and back for a quick spin."

He climbed into the cockpit and checked the wind reading and the instrument panel. The fuel gauge read less than a third. He shut the door and waved.

The mechanic slapped the side. "All yours, boss."

Warren strapped himself in, contacted the tower. There was no one else on the tarmac in line. He started the engine, watched the blur of the propellers. He heard the hum of the engine as he pushed forward. In seconds, he was holding at the head of the runway.

Sam, in the tower, called out, "Cessna 3K986, you're free to go."

Warren gave a thumbs-up and pushed the throttle forward, felt the satisfying rush of acceleration as the small plane gained speed. He pulled up the nose. It lifted. He felt the heavy air cushioning him as he rose, the bare trees growing smaller, the runway becoming just a thin matchstick against the receding ground.

Warren's heart soared.

He checked his flaps, enjoying the energizing rush of takeoff.

Everything started to fall in place.

It was a cloudless day. He immediately climbed to four thousand feet. The skyline of Hartford shone thirty miles away, the sun glinting off the capitol dome. He vectored twenty degrees to the east and pulled around.

Ahead, he could make out the outline of the coast.

Warren headed there.

He checked his fuel. It was less than a third. About an hour's ride. The afternoon was beautiful, the sun shining brightly against the cockpit shield. He angled his way toward the coastline. The outline of Fishers Island in the distance. The ground was a patchwork of farmland and roads. He felt relaxed. Everything just seemed natural up here.

He thought of his life. Ginny and Kyle and Sarah—they were lost to him now. How would he ever patch that up? How could he ever look any of them in the eyes again?

He'd told Ty—no way he could spend the rest of his life in jail.

Just no way . . .

He banked the Cessna east, over the ocean. Away from the coastline.

There was a bump or two and Warren rode them. Like riding a roller coaster. Or skiing moguls. No more exhilarating place he could be than up here.

It had always been you, Ty.

He realized that now. Always Ty with whom he tried to compete. Whom he couldn't disappoint. From the moment Ty had come on him in that basement room. It was funny—it gave him a feeling of peace now. Finally.

It had always been you.

Warren continued east. The coastline merged with the ocean and faded farther away. The fuel gauge now showed a quarter tank.

The strangest memory came back to him. When he was nine. At his first communion. He was an altar boy at St. Roch's. In his white robe. The pews filled. Father Murray, his rector, holding the communion cup. Pop and Mom were kneeling down to receive it. Ty, all of six, standing next to him, in his first Sunday suit.

Warren jabbed at him under the robe. Ty jabbed him back.

With a Cheshire grin, Warren elbowed him, making sure no one could see. "Gotcha last."

"Missed."

His mother pulled him away. *"Ssshhh!"*

"Warren," the old priest said, noticing their game, "it's God who gets you last."

Damn. Warren grinned now. *The old codger was right . . .*

Warren looked at the vast expanse of blue spreading on

both sides, the uninterrupted sea. Ten thousand feet. A beep sounded. A fuel warning. Eighth of a tank. He'd been up for close to forty minutes. He wondered if Pete would start to be worried now.

Warren's attention was drawn to the window. A layer of frost built up, making a kind of random design.

A white robe. Wings. And a forgiving smile. Warren traced his finger on the condensation.

Sonovabitch, an angel. Warren smiled.

An angel, guiding him home.

He pulled back the throttle and lifted the nose. Above the drone of the propellers, the Cessna's engine purred.

He turned the radio off.

A tear burned in his eye. He suddenly realized how intensely he missed his kids. *An angel . . .* He pointed the nose upward.

The fuel light blinked.

And he continued, setting an even course over the ocean, guiding the plane's nose to a destination it seemed to know by heart, the bright and forgiving circle of the sun.

CHAPTER NINETY-ONE

A Coast Guard helicopter spotted the wreckage about a hundred miles offshore. The tail of the small craft continued to bob on the surface.

They never found Warren's body.

The following week, they held a private service at St. Roch's. Their sister, Angela, drove down from Boston with the cousins. Beth and Jessie were there. Vern. A few members of his staff. His father flew up from the nursing home in Charleston. He was seventy-eight and not walking so well. He kept muttering to anyone who would listen about what a happy kid Warren had always been, unable to comprehend. "You remember that, Ty, don't you? Always had so many friends. So much promise . . ."

Hauck straightened his father's tie. "Yeah, Pop. I remember."

Afterward, Ginny's sister held a reception for everyone up in New Canaan, where Hauck saw his father step into the bathroom, put his hand over his face, and sob.

Two days later, Hauck received a call he didn't expect.

From a woman who identified herself as the personal assistant to Richard Scayne.

"I know you're mourning the death of your brother,

Lieutenant—but Mr. Scayne is hoping you might be able to come by the house. *Today.*"

The *house,* as she called it, was situated on a promontory jutting into the sound off Glenhaven Point. Hauck gave his name at a security gate and was told to drive up an expansive circular driveway to the main house. It was glass and brick, modern. Sort of in the style of Frank Lloyd Wright.

Probably was Frank Lloyd Wright.

A similarly designed structure was connected to it off the circle. A middle-aged woman wrapped in her coat met him on the front steps.

"I'm Helen Dryer, Lieutenant." She held out her hand. "Thank you for coming. Mr. Scayne asked me to bring you into the main house."

Hauck followed her up the stairs. "As you may know," she said, "Mr. Scayne has been in ill health. He may no longer resemble any of the public images you have seen of him."

Hauck nodded. "I understand."

"It's very unusual that he asked to see you. He's not met with anyone other than his closest advisers in several weeks. I'm sorry, but I'm going to have to have one of the staff do a security check. Mr. Scayne is quite particular about that . . ."

A man in a suit politely ran an electronic wand over him. He passed the test. Then she walked him into an expansive glass-walled living room with sleek modern chairs and what Hauck thought was a Brancusi bronze. A tall picture window ran the length of the room, overlooking the sound like a giant movie screen, maybe fifty feet long.

"Please bring the lieutenant over here," called a raspy voice.

Richard Scayne sat in one of the square white leather chairs. Scayne—or a fraction of what Hauck recalled of him, like his assistant had said. His hair was thinned and white; the round, ruddy face sunken. The once-imposing frame looked almost frail in his blue hospital gown.

An IV was connected to his arm.

He waved for Hauck to take a seat, his limbs blue, twiglike. Hauck sat down in a matching leather chair across from him.

"Sorry about the security check, Lieutenant." He chuckled. "You're probably wondering what a man in my condition has to careful about . . ." The laugh broke into a hacking cough, his assistant making a move toward him. Scayne waved her off. "*Habit*," he said, regaining his voice. "Just plain old habit. Nonetheless, I wouldn't want anything we might discuss here to find its way beyond these walls. Helen, you can leave us now."

"Let me know if there's anything you need, sir," the assistant said on her way out.

Scayne turned to Hauck. "Loyal woman. Funny, in life, Lieutenant, who ends up taking care of you. If this were a social call, I would ease into our conversation slowly to let you admire the view."

"Million dollars." Hauck nodded, impressed. The water, the towers of the Throgs Neck Bridge. The outline of the Manhattan skyline towering behind it.

"*Fifty* million." Scayne snorted. "But I'm afraid it's not a social call. I've no doubt you're wondering just why I asked you here. I know my name may have come up in recent times . . ."

"Yes, it has."

"It's because I know something about dying, Lieutenant Hauck—dying for all the wrong reasons . . ."

He might have been talking about a variety of people: Sanger, Kramer, Freddy.

But Hauck sensed he was referring to Warren.

"My condolences, regarding your brother. I've had to bury one myself. A son too. It can make a man hard."

Hauck nodded.

"Funny thing about violence . . . ," the old man said. "It has a way of misdirecting you from the interests it actually serves . . ."

"I'm not sure I know what you mean."

"You think you know what happened, don't you? You think it was *me*. That I somehow ordered these events. Had these people killed. Because I was unwilling to put myself before a trial."

Hauck didn't respond.

"You think I pressured my friend, the senator, who had engineered some favorable business terms for me, to enlist your brother—who owed him a few favors too—to take care of things . . . And that he brought in his client the Pequot Woods. Things that claimed the life of that attorney and then his friend in order to cover it up. Then your colleague, Munoz—I think that was his name—which I soundly regret. And ultimately, your brother . . ."

"If I could prove it"—Hauck stared at him—"we'd be having this conversation from a room with a decidedly different view."

"*Well, you'd be wrong, Lieutenant,*" Scayne said. "Dead wrong."

The bluntness of the old man's statement took Hauck by surprise. Scayne drew his IV stand closer. "What I'm going to tell you, Lieutenant, I'll say just once. Do you understand? If you repeat it, I'll deny it. If you try to prove it—be my guest. It'll suck you up like a cat in a cyclone—and like your friends, it will not spit you out."

"You're the one who asked *me* here, Mr. Scayne." Hauck nodded, agreeing.

CHAPTER NINETY-TWO

Y ou think you know how the world works, don't you, Lieutenant?" Scayne looked him over, sizing him up. "Because of what you do. But I assure you, in many areas—the areas that count—you have no idea.

"It was like an IPO over there, those first years of the reconstruction in Iraq. Everything was plated with gold for people like me. Every deal was on a cost-plus basis. You know what that means? The higher the cost, the higher the profit. No fixed price. No termination to the contract. Who wouldn't want a piece of that, Lieutenant? You just had to get it done . . ."

"And that just took a little money under the table," Hauck said. "Some may have found its way to the military procuring staff who approved those kinds of decisions. Some to the re-election fund of your friend, the senator."

"My job was to please my shareholders. And this was the most profitable piece of business we could find."

"You mean more like *pillage* . . ." Hauck shook his head. "They were auctioning off the country. All it took to play was some well-concealed payoffs to the right people."

"Yes. I won't deny it. They *were* auctioning off the country," Scayne said. "So we raised our hand.

"Don't look at me so judgingly. Those people needed things. Without them there would be no country. And we could give it to them. Sewers, schools, plants. So yes, I put half a million dollars into the pot and got two and a half billion in return. Most profitable thing I've ever done. Businesses *need* power, Lieutenant. Houses and schools need light. Two hundred and fifty thousand Nova 91s. Quite a production line. Where the hell else were they going to go?"

"Maybe our government?" Hauck said, angry.

"This was too fucking big to be left to the government!" Scayne's blue eyes came alive. "Government isn't able to get this done."

"Why did you ask me here, Mr. Scayne? You bought yourself a cushy deal. Business went up. Until things fell apart. Some military procurer went out and bought himself a Lamborghini, got the Government Accountability Office on his back. Blew his brains out. And you didn't want to spend the rest of your life in jail . . ."

"That's not what it was . . ." Scayne shook his head. "Maybe that's what it *seems* like. If they had left it up to us, the lights would've gone on. The water would have flowed. Maybe everything would have been different. But they didn't want those things . . ."

"*Who?*" Hauck asked. This was all making him angry. What was the man trying to get off his chest?

"Who do you think I'm talking about? The people who make the policy of this fair land. In this case, the Coalition Provisional Authority. All this rhetoric about wanting the Iraqis to stand up . . . They wanted to strip the country down to dust first. A nation of millions, Lieutenant, and only fifteen thousand of them were ever put to work. All the work went to the '*consultants,*' Bechtel, KBR, Carlyle . . ."

Hauck noticed a new glimmer in the man's eyes.

"Why did you ask me here, Mr. Scayne? I'm a policeman. Five people are dead. You want to atone for past sins, call the *New York Times.*"

"I asked you here to tell you why David Sanger died," Scayne said. "Why your brother died." He shook his head. "They never wanted the Iraqis to take control. They had the whole thing planned out. *We* would take control. JP Morgan. Bechtel construction. Starwood Hotels." Scayne grinned at Hauck. "Why do you think they called it the fucking *Green Zone?* They even had fucking McDonald's coming in . . . *That* was our big vision. Straight from the head of the CPA."

Scayne leaned forward. His bony fingers picked up a glossy booklet from the coffee table. He pushed it across the table to Hauck.

It was some kind of promotional brochure. SRC Electric. Nova 91s. "*The leader in portable power today.*"

"One of my firms," Scayne said.

Hauck randomly flipped through. Floods. Hurricanes. Blackouts. Pictures of satisfied families and companies.

He came across something slipped inside.

It was an 8½ × 11-inch black-and-white photograph. The inside of some kind of large warehouse. Massive shelves stocked with crates. Hundreds of them.

Maybe thousands.

Hauck was able to make out the name emblazoned on the crates.

Nova 91.

"That photograph was taken about a month ago," Scayne

said, "in a warehouse located in Amman, Jordan. There are five others in similar facilities in Cypress, Kuwait City . . ."

Hauck shook his head, confused.

"Bought and paid for by the U.S. government," Scayne explained, revealing a cynical smile. "By our own taxes. *Triple* the list price. Paid for"—he shrugged—"just never *delivered*. Three years later, the Iraqi government is just getting the first shipments now . . ."

"I don't understand."

"You're not supposed to understand, Lieutenant. You're not supposed to *know*. I'm showing you why David Sanger died.

"No one really wanted them to have power. What they wanted was their society stripped down to the core. It wasn't about business, it was policy. They wanted the whole goddamn country nothing more than a shell, a shell for our own interests to fill . . ."

Hauck stared at Scayne, the anger in his chest starting to coil. "You knew this all along, didn't you? You told this to Sanger. You used it as your leverage not to go to trial."

"Yes, I told him," Scayne acknowledged. "I told them all—right from the start. There was no way I was ever going to trial. Not at my age. Not with what I've built in my life. *Not for this*. I'd use what I had to. Whatever leverage I had. And I did. The rest . . . whoever they felt they had to protect, how they chose to go about it, that wasn't on *my* shoulders."

"Sanger knew." Hauck stared at him. "He knew these stupid generators were in some warehouse somewhere. He could expose it."

"They wanted to put me on trial . . . ," Scayne said, a stone-like hardness in his voice, his blue eyes piercing. "Let 'em do it at their own risk."

"Who?" Hauck threw the photo back across the table. "Who

are we talking about here? Five people are dead, Mr. Scayne. Who's behind this?"

"Oh, that's one you'll have to figure out for yourself, Lieutenant." Scayne's face edged into a gaunt smile. "I think you may know where you might start, but I doubt, with your brother out of the picture, you'll have much leverage against him now."

"Casey?"

Hauck recalled what Wachman had told him. When Hauck had pressed him about whether it was worth it, this killing. *Sometimes it just depends*—the government man had smiled—*on what it is you're trying to protect.*

This was it. This was what they had to protect. *Ten reporters from* The New York Times *couldn't find it.*

A pebble on a white sand beach.

Scayne shrugged. "So there it is. Now you know why that poor sonovabitch was killed. Why all of them were. Like I said, I know something about having to die for the wrong reasons . . ."

Scayne bent over and began to cough, lightly at first, then deepening into a raspy, gravelly attack. He grabbed for the IV. Helen Dryer rushed in. She eased him back upright in his chair.

He recovered and held up his hand.

"You bring this up to anyone, I'll deny it. And I'd be careful, if I were you. You've seen firsthand what comes with having this kind of information."

Hauck stood up.

"I'm going to sleep well, Lieutenant. When it finally comes. Contrary to what you might think. But you know what I do wonder?"

"What's that?" Hauck looked back, the dying man's features blanched against the chair.

"I wonder whether six months in, if it all had gone well . . . If drinking water ran from those Bechtel pipes and DynCorp-trained policemen patrolled the streets; if our Novas actually lit those factories and schools—questionable payments or not—if you'd even be standing in front of me now."

CHAPTER NINETY-THREE

A few days later

As Hauck approached them, Annie waved to him from along the harbor. The two of them were leaning against the railing, feeding a few gulls.

He waved back.

She was in the same short white parka as when she had come to dinner, a knit cap tucked over her ears. She took her son's hand and pointed.

The boy turned.

Hauck saw the same dark, happy features in his face. The bright, wide-eyed smile. It was a smile that suddenly made many things clear.

Her son had Down syndrome.

Hauck looked in Annie's eyes and smiled.

"Hey," she said, putting her arm out and giving him a tight hug. He kissed her warmly on the cheek and hugged her back.

"Hey, you."

She looked at him, and no matter how Hauck tried to mask it, he knew she could see the strain of the past weeks in his eyes.

"So I wanted you to meet Jared. Jared, this is Lieutenant Hauck."

"*Ty . . .*" Hauck said to him. He extended his hand. Jared squeezed it. "*Whoa!*" Hauck said, massaging his knuckles. "That's a major-league grip."

"My mom said when you meet someone you should give them a good handshake and look them in the eyes."

"Well, your mom is right." Hauck winked at her. "And I thought all she knew about was making a quesadilla."

"Full of surprises." Annie smiled.

"So what have you two been up to?" Hauck asked.

"We've been up at the Bruce Museum. They had a great kids' exhibit there—on what, honey?"

"*Robotics,*" Jared said. "They had Roomba from iRobot and you got to operate this one and put a puzzle together."

"Pretty cool." Hauck widened his eyes, impressed.

"Uh-huh." Jared gazed up at him with a curious stare. "Mom said you were a policeman. Where's your gun?"

Hauck grinned. "Don't need it when I'm hanging out with the good guys," he replied.

"*Jared!*" Annie said reprovingly with a shake of her head.

"Did I say something wrong?"

"Not at all." Hauck grinned conspiratorially. "How 'bout I bring it next time . . ."

"Why don't you go feed the gulls some more, honey?" Annie handed her son the remaining crusts of bread. "I'll come get you in a bit."

"Okay, but you said we were going to take a drive and you were gonna show me snow . . ."

"We will. I promise. Go on."

"He's adorable," Hauck said as the boy went over to the railing.

"Thanks. That's means a lot, Ty."

"He's just like you. He's got your same smile."

Annie touched his arm. "Are you okay?"

Hauck shrugged. "I guess."

"I wanted so much to come, Ty . . . I really did. I wish I could have shared some of this with you. It was just the day Jared was coming in . . ."

"Probably better you didn't. It was mostly family. My ex and my daughter were there. Only a couple of people from the office . . ."

Annie nodded.

"You know, he wasn't a bad guy . . ." Hauck rested his arms on the railing and stared out. "I know it's easy to think that, with all that's come out. But I just think of him when we were growing up . . . How he was like a hero to me . . . Somehow he just crossed the lines on what became important. And never crossed back."

"All of us have crossed those lines at some point, Ty."

Hauck nodded and glanced toward Jared. "And come back."

"And so have you . . ." Annie looked at him. "Look, I don't want to push and you can shut me up if this sounds totally corny . . . But I'm hoping we might have something here. I know it's early, and I don't want to get ahead of things. But if you're up for it, Jared and I . . . We'd like to be near you, if you're okay with that. And if you're not . . ."

"*If I'm not . . . ?*"

"I don't know. I didn't think that all the way out. I guess if you're not, well, that's just tough . . ."

"*Tough?*"

"Yeah." Annie nodded defiantly. "Tough."

"So you want me to eliminate the suspense or let you twist around a bit . . ."

"Twisting works. I feel like I've been twisting for years."

Hauck met her gaze with a smile. "I'd like that too. And the first step is . . ." He looked down the railing and called out to her son. *"Hey, Jared!"*

Jared tossed a last piece of bread at a couple of gulls and ran over.

Hauck asked, "Anyone ever teach you how to skate?"

He shrugged. "We've gone Rollerblading, right, Mom? But I'm not so good."

"Rollerblading? I'm talking *ice-skating,* dude. This is New England."

Jared scratched his head and looked at Annie. "I could try."

Hauck kneeled and pulled up the boy's jacket collar. "By the end of the day, I'll have you knocking people into the boards. What do you say we go lace 'em up, bud?"

Jared's face lit up. "What do you say, Mom?"

Annie's eyes grew bright. She looked at Hauck. "I say we go lace 'em up."

Hauck placed his hand on Jared's shoulder and they headed away from the harbor. Annie looped her arm through Hauck's. "You know, I probably never told the lieutenant this, but when I was at Michigan I had a boyfriend who played on the hockey team there and he used to take me skating all the time. I bet I skate even better than I cook . . ."

"Why am I not surprised?" Hauck looked at her with a smile.

CHAPTER NINETY-FOUR

The week before Christmas, Hauck sat in the Explorer and gazed up the old, familiar street.

A million memories rushed back to him.

His first elementary school was still on the corner. Mostly Hispanic these days. On Delevan, shops still looked like they did twenty years ago. Pepe's Market. Al's Guitars. Sophia's Fabric and Trim. Though he hadn't been up here in years, he would never forget the way.

Ms. Powers had been the last of their neighbors. She had passed away three years back. Hauck had gone to the funeral. He cruised up the short, hilly street until he stopped at the small white clapboard near the end of the block.

Three twenty-two.

It wasn't quite so small anymore.

To his surprise, it had been completely redone and expanded. Now it had a raised ceiling on the second floor, skylights, a large bay window. Pretty landscaping adorned the patch of lawn in front. Fancy wooden garage doors. A BMW X5 sat in the driveway. He laughed. "Upwardly mobile" had found its way even to Byram.

Hauck climbed out of the Explorer and stared up at the remodeled facade.

Why hadn't they ever thought to come here? So much of it went all the way back . . .

Above him, the front door suddenly opened. A woman with a baby stepped out onto the landing. Pretty. Latino. Maybe a little wary. Wondering who the stranger was staring up at their house.

"Can I help you?" she asked.

"I didn't mean to bother you. I'm Lieutenant Hauck. From Greenwich. I used to live in this house."

"*This* house?" the woman exclaimed. With surprise.

Hauck nodded. "Grew up here. Shared the upstairs bedroom on the right with my brother. Course, we only had three of them then. Now it looks like there are more . . ."

"Oh, we expanded that old room up there," the woman said. "We've changed a lot around. You're welcome to come in and see if you like."

"No." Hauck smiled and shook his head. "Looks nice though. But maybe if you wouldn't mind, there is something I'd like to check out in back."

"Be my guest," the woman said. She jiggled the baby. "Hear that, Carmelo? This nice man grew up *here*."

Hauck waved and went up the short, steep driveway along the side of the house. There was a wire gate on top that led to the back. Hauck popped it open. They had a smart-looking in-ground pool. Covered up for the winter. Hauck thought back to when Pop first got theirs. It was tiny and round and aboveground. Still, he and Warren used to have some wars to the death splashing around in there.

He stood and looked back at the elevated redwood deck,

remembering the hundreds of times they had all had meals and barbecues out there. He heard the thuds of footsteps bounding up the stairs, glass breaking from an errant pitch that crashed through Mom's kitchen window. How they used to sneak in on their sister in the shower.

Hauck's eyes grew moist.

He stepped out to the edge of the property, the line of bushes and pines they shared with the Fraleys, whose yard backed up against theirs. The trees had grown. Hauck could barely even see into their backyard. Or that of whoever lived there now.

Hauck went up to the tall elm in the corner, its branches bare. He kneeled down.

And there it was.

Just above the root base, where he had carved it—Hauck thought back—twenty-five years ago.

To commemorate his greatest high school game.

12/8/83. 241 yds. 3 TDs. State Champions.

Hauck placed his palm against the bark. It all rushed back to him. Like he was touching a part of his past, his family's past. Feelings that hadn't been opened in a long while.

Tears began to flow.

He never got to say it.

I did love you, Warren. I know you wanted the best for me. You saved me that time, and I never forgot it. I swear . . .

Hauck bowed his head, the tears refusing to stop. *You stupid sonovabitch, why didn't you come to me? How could you let yourself get that far?*

Then he noticed something, something that turned the tears into a smile. Then the smile into a laugh, seeing the two words carved underneath.

2 Fumbles, his brother had added.

*V*ern?"

Hauck knocked on the door. The chief looked up from his desk, surprised. "Jeez, I didn't expect to see you in here today, Ty . . . Thought I told you to get a little Christmas shopping done. Take some time off." He clasped his hands behind his head. "You just buried your brother, for Christ's sake. Shame we couldn't nail that government guy . . . But we got Raines. And Vega . . ."

"Funny, I feel like I've taken enough time off, Vern," Hauck said, looking at him.

The chief rocked back in his chair. "Is there something to how you mean that, Ty . . . ?"

"I'm not sure." Hauck stepped in, placed his hands on the back of one of the chairs facing Fitzpatrick's desk. "I guess I've been wondering . . . How'd Sculley and Taylor know I was bringing Raines in, Vern?"

The chief crossed his legs. "I don't know. They had their own investigation going. Maybe Raines called them. Told them you were coming up. What are you asking there, Ty?"

"They knew I went to see Vega. In prison. From the very beginning you've been pushing me to back off. When the guy in the Dominican Republic was killed. When Vega was freed. When we were able to trace things to the casino. How did you phrase it, Vern? 'You better know what you're getting into, Ty . . . That casino has its paws on every politician in the state.' Was that out of concern for me?"

The humor drained from the chief's expression. "Just what are you saying, Lieutenant?"

"I'm saying that this thing didn't end with Wachman, Vern. Or even with Scayne. It was set up. By Casey. Through Warren. Through the casino. For people higher up. I guess what I'm asking, Vern, is—did you get a call too?"

Fitzpatrick's gaze narrowed. "A call?"

"Cut it, Vern, you know exactly what I mean. Did they get to you too? The FBI. The Pequot Woods. Casey. All those new bleachers and highway bills, a hundred and twenty people on the force . . ."

"Get to me . . . ?" The chief clenched his teeth and grew red in the face. But he didn't answer.

"Jesus . . ." Hauck felt like a weight toppled off a cliff inside him. He shook his head. "We lost Freddy, Vern."

"You listen to me . . ." Fitzpatrick stood up. He looked at Hauck, a stonelike fixedness in his gaze. "You've got it mapped out for you here, Ty, if you want it. Everybody respects you. You're a goddamn hero, for Christ's sakes. You can have a nice life here. You just have to know not to push where it don't need pushing, Ty. You understand? That's a hard lesson for you, Lieutenant. Sometimes there's forces that you just don't buck. Whether it's your own state government, Ty, or the goddamn FBI. Sometimes you just have to know how it's done."

"You're right," Hauck said, nodding. "It is a tough lesson for me." He backed away from the chair and let out a long breath, then smiled. "But I'm learning . . . I'm slowly learning, Vern, just how it's done."

Outside, Hauck stepped onto Greenwich Avenue. The streets were busy, shoppers crowding the stores. Christmas decorations shone brightly.

At the corner, he waved to a patrolman he recognized on traffic detail. The officer stopped the flow a moment and motioned Hauck across the street with a good-natured flourish. "The street is yours, Lieutenant . . ."

Hauck jogged across and waved back.

He went onto the small green at the top of the hill where Arch Street intersected, up from the fancy boutiques: Polo. Saks. Ferragamo. In that moment, Hauck saw what he loved about it here. The town had rescued him when he had been lost. Brought him back to life.

He also saw what he was prepared to walk away from too.

You've got it mapped out for you here, Ty . . .

He leaned against the ledge of the stone wall and took out his phone.

The number was still there on his call log. He had looked at it from time to time. Part of him urged him to call and another part warned him, *You could be making the biggest mistake of your life . . .*

He'd been a policeman for eighteen years.

He punched in the number and drew his arms together against the wintry chill. The call connected after two rings.

"Tom Foley here."

"Mr. Foley . . ." Hauck drew in a breath. "It's Ty Hauck."

"*Ty!*" The Talon partner seemed startled to hear his voice. "I heard about your brother . . . I'm very sorry."

Hauck said, "I hadn't realized that the two of you knew each other when we met."

"We didn't, actually. We only met once or twice. Somehow he must've heard we were looking for someone up here and he called to give me your name. I guess I always thought it better you never knew our interest came from him."

"*So it's legit . . . ?*" Hauck asked. "The offer you made to me?"

"Completely legit, I assure you." Foley seemed surprised.

"Then I was wondering," Hauck moistened his lips, "with everything that's happened, if it still stood?"

The Talon partner remained silent for a long while. Hauck steadied himself for the worst.

"Yes, Lieutenant, it very much still stands. In fact, I was just waiting for the proper time to give you a call . . ."

Hauck gazed down the bustling street. The Christmas music coming out of Saks. Kids tugging at their parents. His mind drifted to Freddy. Gone. Then to Vern—the life that could still be his here. All he might be throwing away.

He thought of Warren and a smile crept onto his face. *You deserve this, Ty . . .*

"Then I accept," Hauck said.

ACKNOWLEDGMENTS

My whole life, I dreamed of writing one novel. *Don't Look Twice* is now my tenth! (That includes a handful with James Patterson and one still in the back of the drawer.)

The more I do, yes, the easier it becomes. But the more it also becomes clear what a collaborative process it all truly is.

It starts with the people and resources that help you convince readers you actually know something about what you're writing on. In this case, that's my friend Vito Collucci, of Collucci Investigations, who has worked a whole lot of high-profile cases and whose face can be seen on news channels a lot more than my own. Then there's Stephen Karoul, of Euro-Asian Casino Consulting, who led me through the murky world of casino gambling scams. And not to forget Dr. Greg Zorman, my brother-in-law and longtime medical authority, whose place in this book is due to a sudden expertise on flying. I still won't go up with you, but I will call you every time!

I also want to credit an important book for me, *The Shock Doctrine,* by Naomi Klein, whose research and vision on politics and economics became part of the plot.

Then there's my team at William Morrow and Harper-Collins, and that runs all the way to the top. Not only my editor, David Highfill, for his acumen and guidance, but Pam Jaffee, Lynn Grady, Michael Barrs, Juliette Shapland, Gabe Robinson, Buzzy Porter, and Julia Wisdom and Amanda Ridout in the UK, for putting up with my prickly disposition and stubborn ways. Also, my thanks to Lisa Gallagher, Michael Morrison, Jane Friedman, and Brian Murray for their deep belief in me and strongly felt commitment. I always wondered at what stage I'd be able to look in the mirror and not imagine a famous, top-selling author behind me and say, "You can actually do this thing."

I guess that's now.

Thanks as well to Simon Lipskar of Writers House for his counsel, and to Josh Getzler as well. Also to Roy Grossman, Liz Scoponich, and Brooke Martinez, early readers of the draft, who helped shape this book into the best it could be. And David Mickleson at Greenwich Research, who didn't have a hand in this book, but whom I forgot to mention last time.

And as always, to the team at home—my narrowing team, with two kids moving away. This is the first book my wife, Lynn, didn't read as I wrote it. Hopefully there won't be a hue and cry to get her back on the job!